Above All Earthly Powers

BOOKS BY JACK CAVANAUGH

An American Family Portrait series

The Puritans
The Colonists
The Patriots
The Adversaries
The Pioneers
The Allies
The Victors
The Peacemakers

African Covenant series

The Pride and The Passion
Quest for the Promised Land

Book of Books series

Glimpses of Truth
Beyond the Sacred Page

Songs in the Night series

While Mortals Sleep
His Watchful Eye
Above All Earthly Powers

Postmarked Heaven

Above All Earthly Powers

Jack Cavanaugh

Above All Earthly Powers
Copyright © 2004
Jack Cavanaugh

Cover design by Dan Thornberg

Published by Bethany House Publishers
11400 Hampshire Avenue South
Bloomington, Minnesota 55438
www.bethanyhouse.com

Bethany House Publishers is a Division of
Baker Book House Company, Grand Rapids, Michigan.

Printed in the United States of America

Library of Congress Cataloging-in-Publication Data

Cavanaugh, Jack.
Above all earthly powers / by Jack Cavanaugh.
p. cm. — (Songs in the night ; 3)
ISBN 0-7642-2309-7 (pbk.)
1. Berlin Wall, Berlin, Germany, 1961–1989—Fiction. 2. Germany—History—1933–1945—Fiction. 3. Youth with disabilities—Fiction. 4. Berlin (Germany)—Fiction. 5. Germany (East)—Fiction. 6. Escapes—Fiction. 7. Widows—Fiction. I. Title. II. Series.
PS3553.A965A64 2004
813'.54—dc22 2003028169

Dedication

To pastors and their wives who,

by their example,

inspire others to acts of heroic faith,

both great and small.

JACK CAVANAUGH is the author of fifteen novels, including the award-winning AN AMERICAN FAMILY PORTRAIT series of which *The Puritans* won a Silver Medallion Award. His novel *While Mortals Sleep* has earned multiple honors, among them the Christy Award for excellence in Christian fiction. Jack and his wife, Marni, live in Southern California.

Prologue

Monday, November 30, 1989

The higher the sun rose, the darker became Elyse Scott's world. Never before had there been a day like this one.

Her woolen coat hung heavy on her shoulders. She stared at coil upon coil of barbed wire that had been shoved aside at the border crossing called Checkpoint Charlie. Twenty-eight years ago she stood in this same spot. Then, the barbed wire was newly in place. New. Shiny silver. That was the day the borders closed; the day the Communists imprisoned over a million Berlin residents.

Looking back on it, she couldn't believe how foolish she'd been. Despite all the warnings, she'd crossed over. And look what it cost her.

"Elyse?"

Someone touched her shoulder. She flinched.

"I'm sorry," Lisette said, "I didn't mean to . . ."

Elyse grabbed her friend's hand and hugged it. "No, dear, *I'm* sorry. My mind was . . ."

"I know."

She did know. Dear, sweet Lisette. Of all the people in the world, Lisette knew, and Elyse loved her for it.

"How much longer do we wait?" Elyse asked.

"That's up to you, dear. After all these years, I'm content just to stand here with you."

Tears edged Elyse's eyes. She hugged this woman who was

family—not by blood, but by years of dedication, sacrifice, and love.

"Was it '60 or '61 when Park joined us at Café Lorenz?" Lisette asked.

"I was twenty-one at the time, so that would make it 1961."

Lisette smiled. "I could go for a cinnamon streusel right about now," she said.

"Yeah. Me too."

A loud shout caught Lisette's attention, the kind the Indians made in the old black-and-white Westerns. A bare-chested young man stood atop the Wall with arms raised. Elyse looked at Lisette instead. Her second mother, now in her mid-sixties, had aged well. And she, just shy of fifty. So many of those years Elyse would like to forget. Others, she'd treasure to her grave.

Then Elyse's attention was drawn back to the border crossing just as it had been all night. The thousands of celebrants, the television lights and cameras, the horns honking, the singing, dancing, tears—all these things were temporary distractions at best.

"It's been six hours since they crossed," Elyse said.

Lisette put an arm around Elyse's shoulder and pulled her close.

Two weeks earlier Elyse Schumacher Scott had flown from the United States to West Berlin with Park. At that time the Berlin Wall was still the Berlin Wall, covered with graffiti on the west side, stained with blood on the east side. Imposing. Grim. A monument to world tension and animosity between communist and democratic nations.

They'd flown in after receiving word that Elyse's mother would finally be coming out. Illegally, of course. Through a tunnel under the Wall. With three babies. Brothers. Last name, Dittmer. Over the years Mady Schumacher had helped dozens of people escape from Communist East Germany. Now she was coming out too.

Only the time of her escape had come and gone, and there was no sign of her, no word of her fate. That was two weeks ago. Two unbelievably torturous weeks.

Had she only waited! Elyse moaned. *But who could have known this would happen? Who could have known?*

The border between East and West Berlin opened as suddenly and unexpectedly as it had closed. And people from every nation gathered to celebrate with the biggest spontaneous party the world had ever seen. Not only Germans, but French, Italian, English,

Dutch, and Americans. Like Elyse, they were in shock, a good shock, not like the day the border closed. No one could believe what they were seeing: people passing freely through the checkpoints, the same ones that for nearly three decades had been associated with suspicion, fear, and death.

Reporters broadcast the news in every language. Pictures were beamed into the living rooms of a disbelieving world. Images of men and women dancing and embracing and singing, some standing on top of the beast like David on Goliath's chest while the Israelites gathered in exultation around him.

Elyse felt happy for them, but she couldn't join them. Not yet. Not until she knew her mother's fate. Like so many other East Berliners, the Wall had dealt death to her once already. It may appear to be an impotent giant now, but who's to say it couldn't stir to life again?

Had Mother only waited!

Thousands had attempted to breach the Wall. More than two hundred of them were killed, most recently Chris Gueffroy, who was shot by guards, and Winfried Freudenberg, whose homemade balloon crashed at Zehlendorf. Elyse knew of them because their deaths had been publicized as a warning to others. Most remained anonymous, however. While some were seriously injured in failed attempts, others were either caught and sentenced to prison or, though not lucky enough to make it over the Wall, were lucky enough to escape detection so that they could try another day.

And her mother?

Elyse had to know. Her desire to know surged until it was stronger than her fear of reentering Communist East Berlin. She took a tentative step toward the border. There were more people coming out than going in. That said something, didn't it? She took another step, smaller than the first.

"Are you sure?" Lisette said. "I'll go with you."

"Am I the only person who remembers how quickly things can change?" Elyse said. "The border's open, but there's no guarantee it'll stay that way. Remember how quickly it closed?"

"You stay here, dear," Lisette said. "I'll go in. Wait for me here."

Elyse grabbed on to Lisette's arm. She gripped it with a ferocity that frightened them both.

"It's been six hours," Elyse said.

Ernst had turned and waved just before he and Park melted into the throng. They went to get Mady. Six hours ago.

Retired from NASA, Ernst Ehrenberg had flown in from Huntsville, Alabama, when he heard the news about the Wall coming down.

"Tell me what you want me to do," Lisette said.

Elyse took a deep breath. "I have to know."

She began making her way toward Checkpoint Charlie. It was slow going. They had to weave their way through a tide of humanity moving the opposite direction. Twenty-eight years ago, it was slow going too. They stood in line to enter captivity. How foolish. Elyse couldn't shake the feeling that this time was just as foolish. She had to will her feet forward.

Beneath the shingled overhang of the guard post, armed American soldiers watched the procession. Judging from the perplexed expressions on their faces, they weren't sure what to make of it either. In the last forty-eight hours reality had changed dramatically. It was at this very spot, when tensions were at their highest, that Soviet and American tanks had faced off against each other and the world held its breath.

Elyse kept moving with Lisette at her side. Now they were in no-man's-land. The East German guards came into view. And more barbed wire. Piles and piles of it. Elyse tried not to look at it. She knew if she did, it would be her undoing. Too many images of the past were tangled up in the stuff. One in particular.

A body. Snared. Limp and hanging like a rag doll.

She stopped.

"What's wrong, dear?" Lisette said.

She saw what Elyse was staring at.

"Don't look at it."

She tugged gently, urging Elyse forward. Elyse didn't move. Nor could she disentangle her eyes away from the coils of silver-spiked wire.

"Elyse, look at me! Look at me!"

Lisette cradled the younger woman's jaw and physically forced her head away from the barbed wire.

Elyse began to weep.

"Do you want to go back?" Lisette asked.

"I can do this."

"Take your time, dear. Just keep looking forward. Keep your eyes on the road. Try not to think about it."

They were moving again. Past the first row of barbed wire. Almost to the border.

Elyse gasped.

She froze.

Lisette glanced in the direction of Elyse's gaze, expecting to see more barbed wire. But that wasn't what Elyse was looking at.

"Oh, God. Oh, God . . ." Elyse whimpered.

"Oh dear," Lisette said. "Elyse, honey, I'm so sorry you had to find out this way. I wanted to tell you."

Elyse sank to her knees. Eyes wide. Shaking.

"Dear God in heaven, what are you doing to me?" she cried.

"Mr. Gorbachev, open this gate.
Mr. Gorbachev, tear down this wall."

—President Ronald Reagan, June 12, 1987

Chapter 1

Sunday, August 13, 1961

The sun dawned on a changed world. People went to bed living in one world and woke up in another. The first thing most of them heard was special news bulletins. Waking Americans switched on their television sets to hear newscaster Walter Cronkite, tired and disheveled, go to live feeds from France, Great Britain, and Germany. In every nation the story was the same. Military forces were on high alert.

Twenty-one-year-old Elyse Schumacher had problems of her own. She couldn't decide which pastry to order.

She sat at a table in the late morning shade of a sidewalk café. Talk of world events buzzed around her. She brushed it away like so many flies. It wasn't that she didn't understand the implications of the news; she did. No one could grow up in Communist East Germany and not be aware of the tension between communism and capitalism. She just wasn't going to let it ruin her holiday.

All year long she listened to Communist harangues, attended mandatory workers' meetings, walked among a gallery of street banners and posters boasting of the superiority of the communist way. All year long she endured the eternal tedium of factory work, dwelt in their colorless flat with its stained wallpaper, and stood in endless queues for hour after foot-aching hour for sickly vegetables, discolored meat, and morbid-looking soupbones. All year long she scrimped and saved and sacrificed just so she could have two days of shopping and fun and indulgence in the Western sector. And she wasn't about to let the crisis *du jour* spoil the pastry *du jour*. She didn't let her mother spoil it, and she wasn't going to let the Communists spoil it.

It had always been the three of them—Lisette, Elyse, and her mother. Then, two days before holiday, her mother announced she wasn't going.

"Park will be in Berlin this weekend. He wants to meet us!" Her fist clenched a crumpled letter. "I'd sooner spend a holiday with Nikita Khrushchev."

Elyse said she thought Khrushchev looked like Alfred Hitchcock. Her mother didn't think that was funny. Lisette said that if Mady didn't go, none of them would go. They could go another weekend.

Even though it made no sense to Elyse, her mother insisted she and Lisette go by themselves. She became quite animated about it, telling Lisette exactly what she should say to Park. It was clear that he'd hurt her mother. What Elyse didn't understand was her mother's continued fascination with the man. Lisette said she didn't feel right about seeing Park without Mady being there. In the end, her mother won the argument. She always did.

The good news was that their holiday excursion was still on. Lisette had reservations about going without Mady. Elyse thought it would be great fun. The idea of going to the Western sector without her mother had a delightfully risqué appeal to it.

As it turned out, there was little that was delightful about the trip and it didn't even come close to being risqué. The crossing was a nightmare. The East German guards behaved nastier than usual. They harassed everyone, shouting at them for no reason. At the S-Bahn station one guard, with a bloodhound face and whose jaws flapped when he talked, pulled Lisette out of line. He was accompanied by two other guards with rifles.

"Identity card!" he barked.

Lisette handed it to him.

"Where did you get this?" he shouted. "It's a forgery!"

"I assure you it's valid."

The guard took insult. He leaned within centimeters of Lisette's face and shouted at her, calling her a liar, a traitor, a decadent materialistic fascist. He grabbed one of the other guards' rifles and pointed it at her, threatening her with jail, telling her she'd never see her family again.

She began to cry.

He kept shouting.

Then he let her go. Just like that. He grabbed her by the arm, shoved her back into line, and looked around for his next victim. Lisette was still shaking when she and Elyse boarded the train that took them across the border to the Western sector.

The crossing set the tone for the holiday. Lisette was moody and withdrawn. Who could blame her?

Café Lorenz was going to be Elyse's last chance to salvage the weekend. So what happened? In the middle of the night some nameless, faceless Communist muckety-muck issued an order that set the entire city, the entire world, on edge.

It had something to do with the borders. Elyse didn't listen to the details; she didn't want to know. She wanted to think about pastries, not politics.

She glanced at Lisette. No help there. The woman who had been her mother's companion for more than two decades sat moodily watching the pedestrians pass by in front of the sidewalk café. This was to be Elyse's introduction to the American. Lisette told her that she'd met him before when she was little, but Elyse didn't remember him. She was nervous about meeting this fellow named Park. If there was going to be any holiday in this weekend, Elyse would have to create it all by herself.

Squaring her shoulders, she smiled, as though a smile, no matter how manufactured, would lure a spirit of levity and good times to the table. With a carefree toss of her head, she drank in the colors and the aromas of the grand avenue Kurfürstendamm. Only she called it *Ku'damm*. All the locals called it that.

They had a perfect table location. It was situated in the shade under the red-and-white striped awning that had become for her a holiday landmark. Magical trees lined the avenue, trees that were greener and leafier and grander than anything in the Soviet sector where they lived. Dappled shadows danced on the bright summer shirts and dresses that swished in front of her on the sidewalk. Large concrete planters overflowed with flowers, splashing the avenue with an impressionist's palette—brilliant yellows and whites, blazing violets, bold reds.

"I carry a flag, and that flag is red."

Like a brash intruder the school song popped into her head. Every time it did she wondered why the Communist Party was so fascinated with the color red. They displayed it everywhere with their flags and banners. Yet let a student wear a red shirt to school and he'd be hauled down to the principal's office and reprimanded for his decadence.

Elyse wrinkled her nose in disgust. She was thinking about politics again. She came to Café Lorenz to get away from all that nonsense. Just then, a waiter came to her aid.

He emerged from the swinging door of the café carrying a tray of sizzling sausage. One tangy whiff of spiced meat and all thoughts of politics vanished. Elyse watched in fascination as he set the plate in front of a big man in a business suit. When the plate touched the table, the man's eyes—just for a second—sparkled with little-boy delight.

That's why we come to Café Lorenz! she thought. She wanted to order that same sparkle. Maybe she'd find it this year in the sausage instead of the pastry.

Over the years they'd collected holiday experiences the way a numismatist collects coins. On dreary nights she and her mother and Lisette could escape the grayness of their existence by pulling out their collection and reliving the memories. This would be good to add to the collection.

Remember the sizzling sausage at Café Lorenz?

She turned to Lisette, hoping to find that she too had fallen under the sausage's spell. Lisette's face looked tired and older than her forty years. There was no sausage glint in her eyes. Her attention was divided between rearranging the tableware and staring anxiously at the parade of passersby.

Elyse wasn't going to give up on the sausage memory so easily. "Doesn't that smell heavenly?" she said.

Lisette shushed her, raising an index finger to her lips. In her excitement Elyse had forgotten to use her quiet voice. Born deaf in one ear and partially deaf in the other, she tended to be loud. She tried again, this time quieter but no less emphatic.

"The sausage. Don't you smell it?"

"Yes, dear. Order anything you like." Lisette turned her head back toward the street.

Elyse sighed. The battle to make a holiday of this weekend would not be easily won. She checked her watch. "It's still early," she said. "He's not supposed to be here for another ten minutes."

Lisette forced a smile. Even forced, it was a nice smile. Elyse grew up with that smile. She had loved it for as far back as she could remember.

"It's just been so long," Lisette said. "I'm not sure he'll recognize us. My goodness, certainly not you. You were five years old the last time he saw you."

"Will you recognize him?"

"People change." Lisette resumed her watch.

Elyse opened a menu. It was a waste of time for her to join the search. "What are you going to order?" she asked.

"You order, dear. I'm not hungry."

Elyse sighed. It was a conspiracy. The whole world was against her. First Mother. Then the government. Now Lisette. She turned to the pastries section.

She smiled. She'd found paradise.

The list of pastries was an orgy of taste sensations. Cinnamon streusel, plum cake with crumb topping, raspberry cream roulade, lemon strudel, and Sacher torte, a chocolate torte with apricot jam filling that was world-renowned for its light, buttery flavor. And for a little extra charge they would add the most exquisite chestnut whipped cream. Just as she had hoped, Elyse found an entire page of holiday experiences just waiting to be discovered, courtesy of the brothers Lorenz.

A paragraph at the top of the menu described the origins of Café Lorenz. It began as a family-owned restaurant on the Unter den Linden, dating back to the 1830s when two Viennese brothers, Karl and Emil, immigrated to Berlin and opened a restaurant. They were an immediate success. During the war the restaurant was destroyed by bombs, prompting the move to their current location. Yet in good times and bad, for over a hundred years the Lorenz family had been bringing the taste of Viennese pastry to appreciative Berliners.

"I heard they're ripping up entire sections of street and forming blockades."

Two fashionably dressed women burdened with packages settled into the table beside them, rudely bringing politics with them. They looked like sisters.

"The railway lines too!" said the younger-looking one. "Not just shut down, but ripped up! Both the S-Bahn and the underground. Heinrich said that no trains are going in or coming out. None."

"But what about all the people who work in this sector?"

"All I know is that the radio said they're not letting anybody out."

Elyse buried her head deeper in the menu. She focused on the descriptions of pastries, urging them to transport her to the sugary paradise that knew nothing of politics.

"But what about the East Berliners who are caught over here? Are they going to keep them from returning to their homes?"

Elyse's head popped up. *Not be allowed to return home?*

"Who in their right mind would want to go back?" the older sister said. "Oh, dear, you have to try the raspberry cream roulade. It's heavenly!"

Scratchy voices droned on incessantly through the radio's speaker. Mady Schumacher needed the sound of voices right now, not the information. She'd already heard enough to scare her. She just didn't want to be alone, and the radio was all she had.

Sitting on her heels, Mady rummaged in the back of her closet. She ignored the ache in her knees and back and instead kept digging. She could work quickly because she wasn't looking for anything. She just needed a distraction. Something meaningless and mind-numbing. Activity for its own sake. Anything to keep the black dog of depression at bay.

The growing pile at the closet doorway was a time capsule of their lives—*her* life now, for Elyse and Lisette would no longer need its contents. Old clothes. Worn-out shoes with a generous coating of dust. Various colored belts; some that still fit and others that made her laugh. A Benny Goodman record. Random table-game pieces and cards. A picture book of Grimm's fairy tales. A pencil sharpener. A framed black-and-white photo of their old church in Pankow with Josef and herself standing on the front steps. Loose pages of Elyse's *Oberschule* school drawings. One gaudy green earring.

Mady laughed. If Lisette were to walk through the door right now and see this ungodly pile in the middle of her clean living room, she'd come unglued.

Her hand flew to her mouth, catching a sob before it could escape. It was always the little things that hit the hardest.

On the radio the voice of politburo member Erich Honecker feverishly defended the merits of the "anti-fascist protection barrier." The one that was now separating Mady from her daughter and best friend. His monotonous harangue was nauseating to her, but if she switched from Berlin Radio International to a Western station, Herr Puttkamer might hear it and turn her in.

Mady fought back a fresh attack of tears. She told herself it was for the best. The closing of the borders hadn't taken God by surprise. It was providential that Lisette and Elyse were in the Western sector when the borders closed. And if she hadn't let her feelings for Park get in the way, she would be too. If someone was at fault, she was.

She told herself she should be happy. At least Elyse and Lisette were safe. They were free. Free from the constant barrage of Communist propaganda. Free from having to watch everything they said, every day, for fear someone would report them. Free from the weariness of dingy colors, and the long lines, and the endless hours at the factory.

But she would miss them. That was what hurt most. She knew it was selfish, but she couldn't help it. If she stopped and thought about it, even for a moment, the reality of what her life was going to be like without them—alone—it drove her here, on her knees in the closet, digging mindlessly, doing everything to keep her hands busy and her mind from thinking about it.

But then something would get her started again. A hairbrush. A shoe. A broken crayon.

That's the way it had been for her since first hearing the news. Flip-flop, flip-flop. Back and forth. Glad for them. Sad for herself.

"You can get used to anything," she muttered to herself. Wasn't that the East Berlin mantra? People repeated it every time the Communists introduced one more hardship, one more horror. If she said it often enough, maybe she'd come to believe it.

"You can get used to anything," she repeated.

It's what she told herself every time a new production quota was announced at the factory.

You can get used to anything.

It's what she told herself every time a queue closed a few people shy of her being able to buy a few tomatoes or a soupbone.

You can get used to anything.

It's what she told herself now when she realized she might live the rest of her life alone.

You can get used to anything.

She continued digging, tossing aside old boxes of who knew what. Digging and crying.

You can get used to anything.

But could she? Could she get used to life without hope of ever seeing her daughter again?

"You can get used to anything."

Her sobs made the words unintelligible.

"You're not going to try to go back, are you?"

The Café Lorenz waiter stood with a white pad in one hand and a pencil poised in the other. Like everyone else—everyone except Elyse, that is—his mind was on the day's news.

"I have a brother in the Soviet sector," the waiter said. "I may never see him again. Still, you couldn't drag me across that border. It's not worth the risk."

He shifted nervously from foot to foot. Lisette guessed him to be about seventeen. He was painfully thin, with a protruding Adam's apple and black hair to his collar. He could get away with long hair on this side of the border. If he was on the Soviet side, the Vopos would manhandle him down to the station and give him a haircut, compliments of the Communist Party.

"Are you close to your brother?" Lisette asked.

"Sure, we're close. He's the one who told me to get out of there. He's supposed to join me in a month or so. Now . . ."

"Where does your brother live?"

"On Singerstrasse. In Friedrichshain."

"Write him a note," Lisette said, "and I'll see that he gets it."

"Really? You'd do that?" His smile showed gums; it was almost comical. "Friedrichshain. You know the area?"

"I've lived in Berlin all my life."

He tore off a sheet from his pad, wrote a word, paused to think about what he wanted to say, then began scribbling. He folded the note twice and wrote again.

"I put the address . . ."

Lisette reached for the note. Suddenly the strangest look came over him and he withdrew it. His eyes narrowed suspiciously.

"You'd have to be insane to go back there after today. Insane or . . ."

Working with the government. Possibly Stasi.

His eyes said it clearly enough, the words unnecessary.

Lisette smiled and held out her hand. "We live there. That's why we're going back. You can trust us."

"My mother's still there," Elyse added. "We have to go back."

But the waiter looked unconvinced. He looked up, acknowledging a presence across the table. Lisette hadn't heard any footsteps. She turned to see who the waiter was looking at.

"Park!"

Before she knew what she was doing, she was out of her seat and hugging the American. And if her reaction surprised her, it shocked Elyse.

Lisette had always liked Park, even though Mady had spoken ill of him. And while she'd felt anxious about meeting him again after all these years, to see him like this—so suddenly—well, it was almost miraculous.

He spoke her name in a warm, familiar way. "How do you do it?" he said. "How do you stay so sweet after all this time?"

Looking up at him through a blur of tears, Lisette said, "My goodness, Park, you look as handsome as ever."

The way they embraced was unseemly for a public setting, but Lisette didn't care. Besides, it was worth it, if for nothing else than to see the expression on Elyse's face.

They parted. Everyone was staring at them and smiling. Lisette felt the public gaze.

"Herr Parker," she said, "this is Elyse."

"This is little Elyse? You've got to be kidding! This stunning vision is little Elyse?"

Elyse loved the attention. She drank it in. For the first time since they crossed the border Lisette was glad Mady wasn't with them. It would hurt Mady to see Elyse basking in the compliment of a man she despised.

"You have your father's eyes," Park said. "Don't you think so, Lisette?"

"And her mother's wit."

Park's eyebrows rose, as though he'd been duly warned. "You don't remember me, do you?"

"No, sir." Elyse blushed.

"You're old enough to call me Park. What do you remember of your father?"

"I remember a sofa in a room with large windows, and him pulling me onto his lap."

Park grinned. He pulled out a chair and sat down. Lisette sat too.

"Let me tell you something about your father," Park began. "I never met him, but I talked to him on the radio and got to know him well enough that I can say this with confidence. If he could see you now, the way you've grown up, he'd be busting his buttons."

Elyse didn't just smile, she radiated. Lisette had never seen her take to a man as quickly as she was taking to Park. Already there was a connection between them. And despite what Mady would think, Lisette approved. She liked Park. There was a genuineness about him. He was a man without guile. Wasn't that in the Bible somewhere?

Lisette never agreed with Mady that Park was to blame for what had happened to them. Sometimes we just need someone to blame, she guessed, and Mady blamed Park, which was fine back then because they didn't think they'd ever see him again. But now here he was. She wondered if Park knew how much Mady hated him.

He was what? Forty-two, forty-three years old now? And still handsome. While many Germans thought of John Wayne as the typical American male, Lisette cast Park in that role. John Wayne was too quick with his fists for her. Park was gentler, more intelligent, and definitely more romantic. He was tall, at least six feet, with broad shoulders and a trim waist. His haircut reflected his military background. His clothes were neutral in color—charcoal pants and a tan shirt. For some reason, Lisette expected more color for an American. And although his German was at times flawed—he sounded like an American speaking German—it was fluent, and only occasionally did he have to stop and think of the word he wanted to use.

"Before I forget it," Park said, pulling at a strap around his shoulders. The strap was attached to a camera. A Leica. He removed the lens cap. "Do you mind?" he asked.

He snapped a couple of pictures of Lisette, more than enough to put color in her cheeks. Then even more of Elyse, enough to give the appearance she was a movie star.

"I didn't think to bring my camera," Lisette said.

"Maybe we can press this young man into service," Park said, extending the camera to the waiter who had left and had just now returned. "Would you please?"

The waiter obliged. He still had the note he'd written in his hand. He shoved it into his pocket and took a couple of pictures of Park sitting between the two women.

"I'll send you copies," Park said to Lisette.

The waiter handed the camera back to Park. Lisette tried to make eye contact with the boy. She wanted to assure him that it was safe to entrust her with his note to his brother. But he didn't, or wouldn't, look at her. He turned and left hurriedly.

"What is that heavenly smell?" Park cried, unaware of Lisette's concern for the waiter.

"The luncheon special," Elyse said with obvious pleasure.

"German sausage," Park said. "Worth the trip here."

Elyse turned giddy. She'd finally found a kindred spirit!

"Have you ladies had lunch yet? I hope you don't mind, but I've flown hundreds of miles with Café Lorenz on my mind."

"You've been here before?" Lisette asked.

"You can't come to Berlin and not eat at Café Lorenz!" he said.

"Have you tried their pastries?" Elyse said.

"Tried them?" Park said. "I dream about them."

Elyse laughed. It was a welcome sound, the first laughter Lisette had heard all day.

"And the chestnut whipped cream?" Elyse said. "Have you tried, I mean, dreamed about it?"

Park's eyes closed. His shoulders slumped with pleasure.

Elyse was all smiles. For nearly ten minutes Elyse and Park swapped stories of their culinary experiences at Café Lorenz. Then the waiter arrived to take their order, only it was a different waiter. This waiter was portly, pimple-faced, and a little oafish. His skin glistened with perspiration.

"We had another waiter," Lisette said. "A thin young man. Long black hair."

"He left. Are you ready to order?"

The portly waiter showed no concern over his co-worker's departure. Maybe it was nothing, though Lisette had her doubts.

Park ordered the luncheon sausage, which came as no surprise to anyone, to be followed by a cinnamon streusel with the chestnut whipped cream. Elyse ordered a Sacher torte, while Lisette set her eye on the plum cake with crumb topping.

When the sausage arrived, both Park and Elyse made a fuss over it. Elyse took Park up on his offer to let her sample it. Afterward he finished it off with appetite. The pastries came just as he took the last bite.

As they ate, they continued to talk. Lisette made the appropriate excuses for Mady's absence. Park was obviously disappointed.

"And the Ramah Cabin children?" Park asked. "Of course, they're not children anymore."

"No, I'm twenty-one," Elyse said.

"We've lost track of them," Lisette answered. "After the war Mady was allowed to keep only her blood relation."

This news cast a shadow over Park, and he lost his jubilant glow.

Lisette filled in some of the details. "After we left you, we managed to get the children back to Berlin. However, the Soviets took them from us. For years Mady went to every agency imaginable trying to get them back, but no one would even acknowledge they existed. Then a couple of no-nonsense government officials showed up at our flat. They told Mady to drop the matter or they would declare her mentally unstable and take Elyse away from her too."

"You think they had a special interest in the children?" Park asked.

"I think they were just tired of having to deal with Mady," Lisette said. She looked away, toward the street but at nothing in particular. "We can't stop thinking about them, can't stop wondering how they're doing. If they are well, still together . . ." She chuckled. "If Tomcat and Annie have learned to get along together."

"I miss Tomcat," Elyse said with a touch of melancholy. She didn't wear it well. Melancholy and Elyse didn't belong together.

Park set his fork down, his streusel half finished.

"And what of Ernst and Rachelle?" Lisette said, trying to lighten the mood. "Do you hear from them?"

Park grinned at the telling. "They live in Alabama. Ernst works for a company called NASA, a space agency. He helps them build rockets. They have two children, both boys. Both look like Ernst. Skinny as rails. Unruly straw hair. Eyeglasses."

Lisette smiled broadly. "Ernst. A father. That's hard to picture! How does Rachelle like the States?"

"Her French accent has taken on a Southern twang," Park said.

Lisette laughed.

"And what of Konrad?" Park asked.

His tone was hopeful but cautious. The last Park knew, Konrad had been shot helping the children of Ramah Cabin escape.

Before replying, Lisette exchanged glances with Elyse, who gave her a nod of sympathetic support.

"We are certain he's dead," Lisette said, deciding the direct method was best. "We don't know where or when, even if he survived his wounds at Ramah Cabin. But if he did, he ended up in a prison camp. The Russians were especially hard on the SS. We heard of unspeakable abuses. Thousands of deaths."

"You made inquiries?" Park asked.

"We checked the lists. You have to understand that in the days after the fall of Berlin, everything was chaos. Often there were too many dead to keep records; it was enough just to bury them all. For years I kept hoping that someday we'd find someone who had seen him or knew what had happened to him. We'd hear reports that German soldiers were being released from one prison or another, and I'd allow myself to hope again. Every time I heard the sound of a door, I'd imagine looking up and seeing him standing there." She managed a weak smile before continuing. "Then, in 1953 . . ."

"Stalin's death," Park said. "The general amnesty."

Lisette nodded. "The last soldiers returned home around January 1956."

"Five years ago," Park mused.

The table fell silent, a memorial moment to Konrad.

"You know," Park said, "all this time, whenever I think of Konrad, I can't help but think of the injustice. Here was a guy who went after Hitler. Had him in his gunsights. And in a moment of Christian compassion, didn't shoot. Then, at the end of the war, Hitler took the coward's way out and left good men like Konrad to take his punishment."

Lisette said, "Konrad believed he deserved to be punished for allowing himself to be duped by Hitler in the first place."

"Possibly," Park said. "But there were many Germans who never bent a knee to Hitler, who now bear his punishment."

Again the table went silent. But not for long.

"Lisette's getting married!" Elyse announced in her loud voice.

Lisette shushed her while blushing.

Park grinned. "Really? Who's the lucky fella?"

"His name's Herr Gellert," Elyse answered for her. "He's the shift supervisor at our factory. And he's rich!"

"Elyse!" Lisette cried.

Park reached across the table and took Lisette's hand. "I hope he realizes what a prize he's getting. And I hope he makes you happy. You deserve it."

"Thank you, Park."

Lisette hoped her response sounded enthusiastic enough. Yet she was unable to look at Park directly when she said it, and he seemed to notice her uncertainty but was too much the gentleman to say anything.

Park sat back and sighed, pushed his plate away. "Happy news indeed. Only it complicates what I'm going to say next."

"Oh?" Lisette said.

Elyse leaned forward so she wouldn't miss a word.

Park leaned forward too, looking around to see if anyone nearby was listening. Using a low voice, he said, "It's not by accident that I found you after all these years." He leaned closer still and spoke even lower. Lisette could see that Elyse was having trouble hearing. She was staring intently at Park's lips. "I'm here to help you defect."

"What?" Elyse said loudly.

Lisette shushed her, aware that the ladies at the next table were staring at them.

Chapter 2

This wasn't how Park had imagined it. But then, reality and daydreams are rarely twins.

Park always imagined Mady being here. The details of their rendezvous varied, but never her presence. He'd imagined her sitting here at Café Lorenz. He imagined walking down a Berlin street and catching sight of the back of a brown-haired beauty walking a no-nonsense walk. He'd call to her. She'd turn and it would be Mady. Every time. Whether he dreamed it on a sleepless summer night or while dozing off in the library over a philosophy book—Plato or Hegel or Kierkegaard, or any number of philosophers whom he hated—it would always be Mady. She was always there.

When it became obvious she wasn't with Lisette and Elyse, his disappointment was crushing. He tried not to show it, but it was like trying to hide a knife stuck in the chest.

Mady never promised she'd be there. He'd given her such short notice, not even enough time to reply, and it wouldn't have been unreasonable if no one had showed up. It's just that in his dream, she always did. Sometimes with Lisette and Elyse. But in the best dreams, she was alone.

Seeing Lisette again helped to salve the sting of his disappointment. Slightly. He'd forgotten how sweet she was. She looked older. Who didn't? But on Lisette it was comely, as though her body had finally caught up with her maturity. Park knew no one else like her.

She was so unassuming, yet there was a toughness about her, as there was about most German women of her generation. How else could they survive the hardships life had dealt them? Somehow, Lisette not only survived, she never let her smile become a casualty of war. It was sweeter than anything on the Café Lorenz menu.

And then there was Elyse. The girl sparkled without effort. Park fell in love with her instantly. The fact that she was Josef and Mady Schumacher's daughter was chestnut whipped cream topping.

Like her father she had light brown hair, a full-toothed easy smile, and eyes that glistened like sunlight off a lake in the summertime. She had a zest for life that was contagious. In the hour that he'd gotten to know her, she coaxed out of him protective, fatherly feelings he never knew he had, which made what he was saying to them all the more urgent.

"You've heard the news of course," he said to both of them.

Elyse frowned.

"Actually, the timing couldn't be better," he whispered. "You're on the freedom side. Don't go back. I have connections to keep you here."

"You're still in the military?" Lisette asked. The three of them were now leaning so far across the table their heads were nearly touching in the middle.

"My military service ended with the war."

"What kind of connections do you have?"

"I can't tell you."

Lisette absorbed this, then said, "Can you tell us what you do for a living?"

"I'm a professor of philosophy at UCLA, in California."

Lisette sat back. "A professor of philosophy?"

Park winced. "Afraid so."

She smiled. She started to say something, stopped, and tried again. "Park! I never knew. I mean . . . well, that's certainly unexpected. You just don't seem . . . I don't know why, really, since we haven't spent a lot of time together . . . It's just that, I mean, I never thought of you as the philosopher type."

Park shrugged sheepishly.

Lisette leaned forward. "A cover, right?"

"No, I really am a professor of philosophy."

Elyse said, "But you seem so normal."

Park let out a laugh that caused too much attention, but he couldn't help himself. The three of them pecked at the remains of their pastries with their forks until the attention died down.

"Now is the time to get out," Park whispered, leaning forward again. "I thought so before I made contact with Mady, even more so now with the closing of the border."

"You didn't know this was going to happen?" Lisette asked.

"No one did. It took the whole world by surprise."

"I heard someone say it was temporary," Lisette said.

"Don't count on it. Listen. I can get you to a refugee camp at Marienfeld, and after that to America."

"America?" Elyse squealed loud enough to cause more stares.

The forks got busy again.

"If you go back, you may never get out," Park whispered after a while.

"What about Mady?" Lisette said.

"I was hoping she'd be here. But let's concentrate on what we have right now. Let's get you and Elyse safe, and then we'll work on getting Mady out."

"What about Herr Gellert?" Elyse said.

Park suppressed a sigh. He'd expected that Lisette might be married, but he'd thought it would be to Konrad. Gellert was a complication.

"What kind of man is he?" Park asked.

"A Communist," Lisette replied.

"A Communist!"

Elyse had no trouble hearing this. She smiled at Park's embarrassment and overreaction.

"How did that happen?" he asked quietly.

"Long story."

Park sighed. "Would he consider—"

"No," Lisette said. "Regardless, I'd never leave Mady."

"Mady," Park said, still stuck on Herr Gellert's party affiliation. "I'm sure she's heard the news by now. Don't you think she might be hoping that you and Elyse will stay on this side of the border? Maybe we could phone her."

"We don't have a phone in our flat," Lisette said.

"We're not rich," Elyse added. "Herr Gellert has a phone."

"Mady and I have stuck together since the war," Lisette said.

"We've always been there for each other. A closed border is not going to change that."

"At least let me take Elyse, then. She'll be safe with me."

A curious dance of emotions played on Elyse Schumacher's expressive face. Excitement and fear were the principals.

Lisette reached over and took the girl by the hand. "I know you mean well, Park. Believe me, I do. Pastor Schumacher trusted you; I trust you. But I couldn't return home to tell Mady that I left her daughter in the Western sector."

"I suppose not," Park said.

His sixteen-year-old dream was on life support. Nagging moments of doubt had warned him he couldn't just swoop in and save Mady, Lisette, and the Ramah Cabin kids.

"When do you return?" he asked.

"Now."

Park stared at the table. "I was hoping I'd have the rest of the day to convince you."

"You've always been a dear friend, Park."

"Can I walk you to the border?"

They had return train tickets, tickets that were useless to a train with no track. Streets were blocked as well. Mounds of rubble appeared from nowhere, piled high to prevent passage. If that weren't enough, antitank obstacles had been dragged into place. Spiraling coils of barbed wire stretched across every thoroughfare linking East and West. For added measure, armed guards stood five meters apart. Behind them, Soviet tanks.

Communists knew nothing of subtlety.

The pesky news reports Elyse had so casually shrugged off now had threatening faces. She thought of her mother and fought back tears.

They heard people were crossing at Friedrichstrasse, so that's where they went.

While the Eastern side of the border was rubble and tanks and guns, the Western side was chaos. The closer they got, the thicker the number of protestors pumping fists and angry, hastily made signs. Shouting at the guards. Throwing rocks. Grabbing and heckling the East Germans who were trying to cross the border and get home.

Lisette, Elyse, and their American escort skirted the crowd until they reached the border crossing at Friedrichstrasse. The mood was riotous. Park mentioned something about them being one insult away from a massacre.

At Friedrichstrasse a familiar queue had formed, only this time it wasn't for fruit or vegetables or soupbones. The line at the border had a single direction. In. There was no exit. Not today.

"Thank you, Park," Lisette said, turning to him. "For the visit and for your generous offer. I know you're thinking of our best."

"I'll walk you to the line," Park said.

"There's no need."

"I'll feel better if I do," he said.

Both Lisette and Elyse were glad he did. No sooner had they penetrated the outer perimeter of protestors than a woman grabbed Elyse.

"Stop!" she shouted. "You're not going back in there!"

Elyse struggled to break free, but the woman was bigger and stronger. She had clamped onto Elyse with an angry mother's grip, acting with all the fervor of a woman trying to keep one of her own children from slipping into hell.

"You're hurting me," Elyse cried.

Park stepped between them, towering over them both. He grabbed the woman's wrist. "Let her go," he said.

She didn't. If anything, she gripped harder.

"American?" the woman shouted. "You're American, aren't you? Of all people you should know better! What kind of friend are you?" Her eyes narrowed to slits. "American, but Communist. Right? Do you get paid for rounding them up, or do you just do it for fun?"

Park twisted the woman's wrist until she let go, then so did he. She spit at him. He turned his back on her. She pelted him with curse words. Several other protestors joined her but, having seen a sample of his strength, did so at a distance. Two bare-chested teens blocked their way, yelling and jeering, but stepped aside when Park made a move toward them.

He led Lisette and Elyse to the queue and stood with them.

"Thank you, Park," Lisette said.

"Yes, thank you," Elyse added.

"My sentiments are with them," Park said.

Lisette smiled warmly, touching his arm. "Which only makes

what you did for us that much more heroic."

For the next half hour they shuffled their way toward the barbed-wire border.

"Get your pass and identity card out," Lisette said to Elyse.

The queue was as quiet as the crowd was noisy. With the guards, the dogs, the shiny coils of barbed wire, and the rifles and tanks, the Soviet sector of Berlin resembled a concentration camp.

"I guess this is where I leave you," Park said when they were half a dozen people away from the border. "Sure you won't reconsider?"

Lisette stood on her toes and kissed his cheek. "Thank you again, Park. I only pray it won't be another sixteen years before I see you again."

Elyse followed Lisette's example. She kissed Park on the cheek. "Thank you, Herr Parker," she said. "I've added you to my Café Lorenz memories."

"If you don't think it will upset her too much," Park said, "give your mother my best."

He stepped out of line.

Lisette handed her papers to a uniformed guard. He studied them, then asked her something. Park couldn't hear what the guard said because of all the shouting around him. The guard handed Lisette her papers and waved her through. She stood on the Soviet side while the guard inspected Elyse's papers. Lisette glanced up and gave Park a parting smile. Elyse was waved through. She saw Lisette's smile, looked over her shoulder, and waved good-bye to Park.

A tremendous feeling of powerlessness swept over Park as he stood there and watched the Soviet sector swallow up Mady's only child and her best friend.

Two days later, like the slamming of a great iron door, the closing of the border became permanent. With frightening speed, concrete blocks replaced the rubble and barbed wire. The Berlin Wall was now an indelible mark in world history.

Chapter 3

Tuesday, August 15, 1961

Tomcat crouched in the shadows, his back pressed against a chain link fence. He was very much aware of the sound of his own labored breathing, more from a sense of excitement than from exertion. His right foot found a pebble, which he clenched and unclenched with his bare toes the way a sighted person would play with it using the hands. He heard no sounds that alarmed him but only the droning of the compound's electric floodlights and the distant cough of a car on the main road that wasn't hitting on all cylinders.

Confident he'd made it this far undetected, he did a slow, deep knee bend and waited. He was early. Early because the orderly was early, and the orderly was early because he didn't like tonight's episode of *Lassie* and so had started his rounds earlier than normal. So Tomcat had time to kill while waiting for the heavy clunk of the automatic switch that turned off the floodlights. Night's cloak was a friend worth waiting for. His blindness gave him an advantage in the dark. That, and new information.

"Third time's a charm," he muttered.

He grinned. This time was different. This time he wouldn't have to play detective. He knew exactly where he was going.

Tomcat credited God for his good fortune. Good had come out of misfortune. Wasn't that what God did best? In this case, misfortune was his frequent insomnia. Good was an overheard telephone conversation.

It wasn't uncommon for Tomcat to roam the halls late at night while all the others slept. He'd never needed as much sleep as the others, possibly because he took catnaps in the afternoon. All he knew was that there were nights when he couldn't lie in bed any longer and the need to roam came upon him like an itch. Therefore, he'd prowl the hallways until he was caught and forcibly led back to his bed.

Most nights he wandered undetected until dawn. It was easy. He knew the orderlies' routine better than they did, and Tomcat was practiced at being where they weren't. The nights he was caught were usually the nights when Herr Witzell, the K7 administrator, stayed late. On those nights Tomcat fell victim to his weakness for Frank Sinatra. It was a weakness he shared with the man.

Tomcat liked Herr Witzell. He was a decent man, one with a good heart and a kindly voice. He protected Tomcat and the others from the orderlies who all, sooner or later, felt it their privilege to shove and hit and grab and choke and slap the inmates. Sometimes they did it out of frustration. Some of them were just plain mean. Like Fricke, who wasn't skilled at much, though he was skilled at being mean. One time Viktor dropped his food tray and splattered pig's head goulash on Fricke's shoes. It was an accident; Viktor would never do anything like that intentionally. He was scared to death of Fricke.

Fricke forced poor Viktor to lick the goulash off his shoes. He grabbed Viktor by the back of the neck and shoved his face against his shoes, shouting obscenities the whole time. Viktor turned scared and started crying. Then he licked every bit of goulash off Fricke's shoes. Fricke would have made Viktor lick the goulash off the floor as well, had Witzell not showed up to see what all the fuss was about.

Tomcat never knew how Witzell did it, but somehow he got Fricke out of there. Most likely, favors were traded or something because more than once Tomcat heard Witzell say to one of the orderlies, "If I had control over staffing, you'd be history." With Fricke, somehow he managed to gain control over staffing just long enough to get rid of him. There were no tears shed for Fricke when news of his departure reached the ward.

That's why Tomcat liked Herr Witzell. He was always looking out for them—Viktor, Annie, Hermann, Marlene, and him. Annie called Witzell their guardian angel. It was one of the few times Tomcat agreed with her.

Then there was Sinatra. In his office Witzell had a complete collection of Sinatra albums going back to the days when Old Blue Eyes sang with the Harry James band. Witzell played the albums when he stayed late at night. Tomcat would hear them and, like a moth to a bare bulb, be drawn to Witzell's closed office door. He'd lean against the door and listen and forget all about where he was and that he wasn't supposed to be out of bed. He'd also forget to listen for the orderlies, and inevitably one would see him and he'd be given the iron-hand escort back to bed.

Of course the others made fun of his obsession for all things Sinatra. Annie said that only old men listened to Sinatra. She herself was an Elvis fan, as were the others. Tomcat couldn't stand the hound dog, nor did he care for rock and roll in general. It was too pushy. He didn't like music that forced itself on the listener. Good music was a seduction. It was suave. Smooth. And when it came to smooth, Sinatra was king. Not even Annie could argue that.

It was one of those insomniac nights when Tomcat overheard the telephone conversation that prompted another escape attempt.

Sinatra was crooning a promise that there would be no more tears and no more fears, that they'd always have tomorrow. As always, his voice and the music combined to cast a spell over Tomcat. He sat on the floor, his ear pressed against Witzell's door.

"You found them? Excellent."

Tomcat tried hard to separate Witzell's words from Sinatra's. "Your kiss, your smile . . ."

"Wait . . . I'm reaching for a pen. All right, go ahead."

Sinatra would treasure them forever.

"Say that again? Twenty-three Kellerstrasse. Yes, I'm writing it down. Great. How did you find them?"

Tomcat frowned. As much as he liked Witzell, at the moment the man's voice was an irritant. Tomcat pressed harder against the door. Again Sinatra was promising they'd be together again.

Herr Witzell then said something that cut Sinatra completely out of the picture.

"Frau Schumacher. Uh-huh. You're certain it's her? Mady Schumacher? Uh-huh."

Tomcat sat up. His heart pounded with an excitement not even Sinatra could inspire.

"Does she have a husband?" Witzell asked. "Okay. Does anyone else live with her?"

Sinatra warned against temptations and letting the blues make you sad.

"Good. Let's have that name too," Witzell said. There was a pause. "Last name. One *s* or two? All right . . . got it . . . Lisette Janssen. Anyone else?"

Frank continued singing.

"Elyse," Witzell said.

Tomcat's chest constricted at the sound of her name. His head grew light, dizzy.

"Got it . . . all right . . . I understand." A pause. "Send it to my office. I'll messenger the money to you . . . no. No, that won't be necessary. I'll take it from here."

That was when Tomcat felt himself being lifted to his feet. Orderlies. Two of them. They half dragged, half carried him back to his room.

Now, leaning against the chain link fence in the compound, Tomcat didn't have to repeat the address he'd overheard to remember it. It was as much a part of him as his own name.

23 Kellerstrasse.

Even now, nearly a week later, just thinking about it made his skin tingle. After all these years, he'd find them. He knew someday he would. Annie was the one who kept saying he'd never find them. Well, this would shut her up, wouldn't it?

The metallic clunk of an electrical switch sounded. The compound lights went out. Not wasting any time, Tomcat began searching the fence for an opening.

"That's him? Are you certain?" Spuhler whispered. He was tracking Tomcat with field glasses. "He doesn't move like he's blind."

Otto Witzell mopped his forehead with a handkerchief and squinted into the darkness. His eyes had yet to adjust to the dark. When they did, on the far side of the compound, he spied Tomcat gliding along the perimeter of the fence, feeling it with the flat of his hands.

"If he moved like a blind person," Witzell snapped, "I would have no need of you, would I?"

Spuhler lowered the field glasses. He obviously didn't like Witzell's tone.

"My apologies," Witzell said. "It's the heat talking."

The day had been a Berlin pressure cooker. The night wasn't much better, especially inside the institution, where the air hung still and close and everything felt sticky. Outside, Witzell had hoped to find a pleasant breeze to ease his suffering. As it turned out, the breeze proved to be more elusive than Tomcat.

The heat appeared to have no effect on Spuhler. He stood stiff-backed with that insufferable Prussian military bearing of his, his skin pasty white and dry. The absence of sweat irked Witzell. He guessed the man was about his age—late sixties, early seventies perhaps. Both men were short in stature, although Witzell was a good twenty to twenty-five pounds heavier. He'd lost his personal battle of the bulge in his fifties. Spuhler had won his; the man's belt size was half that of Witzell's. While Witzell attempted to dam the rivers of perspiration running down his forehead and neck, Spuhler stood beside him powder dry. *Maybe they train Stasi agents not to sweat,* Witzell mused, *and Spuhler has carried his training into retirement.*

"He's not wearing any shoes," said Spuhler, his gaze once again magnified by the field glasses.

"We can't keep shoes on him."

"Then you haven't tried hard enough."

Witzell pursed his lips and swallowed a retort, something to the effect that not everything could be solved by force. Maybe recruiting Spuhler was a mistake.

"You have to understand," Witzell explained, "putting shoes on Tomcat is like putting a blindfold on a sighted boy. He reads the ground with his feet."

The field glasses came down. "Tomcat? You told me his name was Scott."

"Tomcat's a street name, hardly a suitable name for his official record. He answers to Tomcat."

"Now what was that about reading the ground?"

"It's like Braille. Only instead of his hands, Scott . . . Tomcat uses his feet. So instead of a series of bumps on a page, he reads the features of the ground. He also has a keen sense of hearing and smell. He puts them all together and forms a map in his mind that he never forgets. Once he's been to a place, he can move about almost as well as any sighted person. In the dark, even better."

"And I once owned a dog who could talk and knit scarves," Spuhler scoffed.

"Don't underestimate the boy, Spuhler. If you do, you'll lose him."

Spuhler took exception to this. "I've tracked agents and double agents for over a decade. I think I can handle a blind boy. Realistically, how far can he go?"

"The last time he escaped, he made it to Alexanderplatz before we caught up with him."

Spuhler made his disgusted sound. Witzell was getting tired of it.

"Alexanderplatz? Someone's feeding you a line, Witzell." The field glasses were up again. "He's testing the fence at that post."

"That's where he escaped last time."

"You had it repaired? Why?"

"He'd suspect something if it wasn't."

"Strapping young man, I'll give him that," Spuhler said.

Elyse was a Sinatra fan too. Tomcat was sure of it. It was part of his fantasy about finding her. He'd mention Sinatra and her face would light up. She'd say whenever she listened to a Sinatra song, she thought of him. They'd discover that Sinatra music was the unbreakable tether that linked them over all these years.

Like the song. They had each other under their skin and deep in their hearts.

Tomcat sang the words softly as he searched for the opening in the fence he used to escape last time. It was a section near the bottom of a post where a metal tie had broken. If it was still broken, all he would have to do was pull the chain link up like a corner of a piece of paper and crawl under. He found the spot. He pulled. It held fast.

Tomcat wasn't surprised. A good administrator knew every inch of K7, both building and grounds, and Witzell was a good administrator. Tomcat continued his search—testing, pulling, pushing—looking for any sign of weakness in the fence, all the while singing about how he'd sacrifice anything, come what may, just for the sake of having Elyse near, because he had her under his skin.

He couldn't remember a time when she wasn't under his skin. The fact that he hadn't seen her for fifteen years didn't matter. The two of them were meant to be together. They both knew it. They knew it when they were kids, and some things just don't change over time.

That's why he'd escaped two times already. Not to get away from K7, but to search for Elyse. The problem wasn't so much getting around as it was getting information. Once people saw the white shields over his eyes, all they could think about was handing him over to the Vopos, the People's Police. He'd mention K7 and get a free ride home.

Where he'd then hear it from Annie. She was his sharpest critic. Annie with the shriveled left hand. She reveled in his failures and spent way too much time thinking of ways to irritate him.

Tomcat paused in his fence inspection. A thought stopped him. A thought that made him chuckle. He may have Elyse Schumacher under his skin, but Annie was the dirt under his fingernails.

He liked that. He couldn't wait to tell it to Annie.

Just then his feet noticed something. An earthy odor confirmed the finding. He pawed the ground with his toes, then dropped to his knees. The dirt here had been freshly turned. It was still soft. He began digging.

"He found something," Spuhler said.

Witzell dabbed his neck with a handkerchief. "We don't have much time."

Spuhler turned to Witzell. "You softened the dirt for him."

"I had some old fence posts replaced."

"What kind of game are you playing, Witzell?"

The administrator shushed him. "Not so loud. He has superior hearing. Your job is to follow him and report back to me. That's all you need to know."

"I'll not be part of anything illegal."

"Don't be absurd. We're not breaking any laws."

Spuhler's face scrunched up. He wasn't convinced.

"He's almost under," Witzell said. "Follow him. If he makes contact with anyone, report back to me. If he gets into danger, or if anyone detains him, step in and bring him back here. It's as simple as that."

"Then my debt to you is paid."

"In full."

Witzell glanced over Spuhler's shoulder.

"He's out."

Spuhler cast one last suspicious glare at the K7 administrator and then turned to follow after the blind boy.

"Spuhler."

"Yeah?"

"You understand your assignment?"

"Follow. Don't intercept."

"If he enters a house, I want the address."

Spuhler cocked his head. "You know where he's going, don't you?"

"If I knew where he was going, why would I have you following him?"

The former Stasi agent turned to go.

"Spuhler! Don't underestimate him."

Tomcat emerged on the freedom side of the fence and dusted himself off. He lifted his head and sniffed.

Witzell.

Witzell was outside. Nearby. The man loved his cigars. Tomcat could smell them on him even when he wasn't smoking one. That in itself was odd. Witzell smoked in two places. His office and on the cement steps just outside the back door. It was unheard of for him to be in either place without puffing a cigar.

Tomcat heard footsteps at a half run. Not Witzell. Witzell was too heavy to move that quickly. They stopped.

If they knew he was out of the building, why weren't they calling his name? Why hadn't they turned the compound lights on? What was going on here?

Tomcat grinned. Until he felt their hands on him, he'd keep going as planned.

The Sinatra tune that he'd been singing continued to play in his mind. It was about a fool who could never win, who needed to use his mentality and wake up to reality.

He followed the fence to the gate and the dirt road that would take him to the main road. He listened as he walked.

Witzell stepped from his hiding place next to the K7 building, a stark cinderblock structure with wire mesh over the windows. It was an old converted military training barracks. Witzell watched as Tomcat reached the front gate and headed toward the main road. Within seconds darkness swallowed up the boy.

Spuhler was in pursuit. He cast a quick glance at Witzell before following Tomcat.

"You'll have to stay closer to him than that," Witzell muttered. "You arrogant fool. You're going to lose him."

He wiped at his forehead and neck, then pocketed his handkerchief and produced a cigar, which he lit with an unsteady hand. A sense of dread gripped him, the kind desperate men feel just after committing to a risky course of action.

The staged phone call. Letting a blind inmate wander the streets of Berlin at night. Involving a former Stasi agent.

For what?

Selfish reasons.

The last time Witzell had this feeling, it was he who was attempting to escape. Unsuccessfully, as it turned out.

"Lord, he's in your hands now."

For nearly an hour Witzell sat on the concrete steps and stared into the night. Then he stood and moved inside, a Sinatra tune playing in his head about a fool who could never win, who needed to use his mentality and wake up to reality.

Spuhler muttered to himself, "He walks at a steady pace for a blind lad, I'll give him that."

He'd been tracking Tomcat for over an hour, down a country road that was lined with mature trees. A strip of stars twinkled overhead, which would disappear in another ten years or so when the arching limbs touched to complete the canopy. The road they traveled was a long trough with gently sloping grassy sides. Tomcat walked with one foot on the grass, using it as a guide. Spuhler trailed at a discreet distance. He focused on the dappled moonlight on the boy's broad shoulders to keep him in sight.

After five kilometers, Tomcat stepped into the direct moonlight just as the dirt road intersected the paved main road.

The boy stood in the middle of the main road. He seemed indecisive as to which way to go. Instinctively, Spuhler hid behind the last tree. He chided himself. What was he doing? The boy couldn't see him. He was blind. And from the looks of it, confused.

Spuhler leaned against the tree. He was glad for the rest. Though he walked daily and did exercises to keep fit, still, he was feeling his age.

"Alexanderplatz," Spuhler scoffed, shaking his head. "Look at him."

Tomcat toed the pavement, turning in circles, flailing his arms.

It was going to be a short night, which was perfectly fine with Spuhler. His debt would be paid to Witzell, and that would be the end of it.

Tomcat had come to a decision. He began walking toward Berlin.

Lucky guess, Spuhler thought.

Tomcat looked every bit the blind boy now. His arms were extended like feelers. His feet inched forward hesitantly, zigzagging at a turtle's pace down the center of the road.

Spuhler took off after him. He'd give the boy a few more minutes. Maybe if he got scared enough this time, he'd realize there were reasons he was kept locked up.

A car appeared. Spuhler first heard it, then saw the headlight beams sweep across the trees as it rounded a bend on the main road. It was heading straight toward Tomcat.

Spuhler shouted a warning.

He was too far away. Tomcat didn't hear him. The boy was still feeling his way down the middle of the road.

Luckily the driver saw him just in time, leaving rubber on the road to keep from hitting Tomcat. The screeching sound frightened the blind boy. He swung around, stumbled, and fell to the pavement, bathed in the car's headlights. The driver jumped out of the car and ran to him. A woman climbed out of the passenger side and stood by the car and watched.

Spuhler shouted again, but he couldn't be heard over the sound of the car's engine. The shortest distance between him and Tomcat cut the corner where the roads met. It was a ravine, not too deep. Spuhler ventured into it, shouting. The moon lit his way. He was careful not to trip. The road disappeared from view.

Actually Spuhler considered himself fortunate. The boy got the fright he needed, and now Spuhler could perhaps talk the driver into giving them a ride back to K7.

He began his ascent up the slope, his legs churning, his lungs complaining. The slope was rutted. Spuhler slipped, tore his pants, and scraped a knee. Regaining his footing, he crested the roadside just in time to see the driver shut the car's back door.

Tomcat sat in the backseat.

Spuhler tried shouting again. He slipped, started losing ground.

A second door slammed shut, followed by a grinding of gears.

Spuhler emerged from the ravine in time to see the woman turn and say something to Tomcat. Her manner was consoling. The engine revved. The car picked up speed.

Spuhler lumbered into the center of road, screaming now, waving his hands, jumping up and down.

The car continued down the road but not before Spuhler got a good look at Tomcat. The boy turned his face Spuhler's way. Sure, the boy was blind, yet Spuhler could think of no other way to describe it. Tomcat's face filled the small oval back window, illuminated by the moon, and Spuhler could swear he was grinning.

Chapter 4

Wednesday, August 16, 1961

One afternoon," Mady said. "You spend one afternoon with a man and you think you know him?"

"He was nice," Elyse said.

"You don't know him like I know him."

"I know he's a respected professor at an American university. He's kind and caring. And he likes cinnamon streusel."

"The perfect man," Mady said.

"Well, he's certainly not the monster you make him out to be."

Lisette, who had been sitting in the corner chair darning, looked up. "Elyse, don't use that tone with your mother."

Mady pulled a blouse from the basket of laundry that she and Elyse had been working on. She shook the blouse, folded it, and set it aside for ironing. The late afternoon sun streamed in through the living area window.

"A man doesn't have to be a monster to hurt you, Elyse," Mady said. "At least with a monster you know what you're up against. Park . . . Herr Parker is worse than a monster. He's a worm."

"Mother!"

"He lures you into deep water with his smile and promises, then he abandons you to swim on your own."

"Mady, that's not fair," Lisette said.

"You make him out to be a coward," Elyse said.

"Call it what you will. I speak from experience. The man can't be trusted."

Elyse disappeared into the bedroom.

Lisette and Mady worked on in silence. The last two days had been tense. The relief Mady felt when the girls had walked through the door was short-lived. It lasted from the time the door opened to the time Elyse began talking about Park.

Elyse didn't care what her mother thought of Herr Parker. She liked him.

After brushing her hair, she switched off the light and climbed into bed. She could hear voices on the other side of the wall. While she couldn't make out the words, her mother's insistent, unreasonable tone was clear enough. Lisette was reassuring, like she always was.

Elyse turned her back to the wall. She thought of Café Lorenz. And Herr Parker.

A thought struck her. A happy one.

Ericka. She couldn't wait to tell Ericka about Herr Parker. Oh, this was good. This was delicious! Ericka was always making a fuss over her rich uncle in America. What was his name? Uncle Abner? Uncle Albert? Once, after receiving a package from Uncle Albert—American shirts, American books, and American chocolate—Ericka proudly showed her two photographs.

The first black-and-white photo was of a distinguished-looking gray-bearded man in his home study. There was a big leather armchair and a big desk with a leather blotter, a marble inkwell, and two pens. A painting of an American president hung on the wall, and there was a grand oval rug on the floor. The man, the mythical Uncle Albert, stood proudly to one side of the ornate desk.

The second photograph was of Frau Uncle Albert. She was a round woman. Really round. She looked like a snowman with clothes. Friendly looking, with happy eyes and thick cheeks. She stood next to a bird feeder in front of a large house with an enormous window that stretched from one side of the house to the other. The garden in front of the house was not only large but landscaped. A great many beautiful flowers bloomed there. Surrounding the garden were trees and shrubs and a birdbath.

Elyse couldn't wait to show Ericka pictures of Herr Parker, the ones he'd promised to send them. She grinned with satisfaction at the thought. Not only did she have an American uncle to rival Ericka's Uncle Albert, but one who made the vaunted Uncle Albert look like a schnauzer! Elyse giggled. Yes, compared to Albert, her new uncle Park looked like a movie star.

The door to the bedroom opened. Her mother stepped inside, bringing her anger with her. Elyse could feel it. While her mother got ready for bed, Elyse pretended to be asleep.

Mady climbed into bed. Rolling to her side, she stared at the silent silhouette in the bed across the room.

Elyse didn't know any better. The girl was taken in by Park's good looks and his lopsided smile, just as she had been at one time. Elyse was too young to remember the danger, the daily fear.

"They're German nationals, for pete's sake, Parker! What were you thinking? Get them outta here."

That was the greeting they'd received upon arriving at the American camp. Her, Lisette, and six children. With that, they were escorted out of the American Third Army camp, by armed men. What were they afraid of? That two German women and a handful of children would suddenly attack them?

Just like that, all of Park's promises to protect them dissipated, and Mady and Lisette and the kids were left to fend for themselves while the Soviets and Allies tore Germany apart like dogs snapping at each other over a scrap of meat.

And what did Park do to help them? Nothing. Why should he? He got what he wanted. He'd gotten his German rocket scientist and probably got a medal for his effort. What did he care that Mady and the children had been tossed out like so much trash?

There was a moment while standing outside the American camp, under the gaze of the armed perimeter guard, that chilled Mady to her bone marrow. It chilled her even now just remembering it.

Hermann and Marlene were crying. Lisette held Elyse in her arms. Tomcat was clutching her skirt with muddy hands. And Mady realized the hopelessness of their situation. They had no shelter; the children were hungry and she had no food to give them, nor any prospect of food. It would be dark in a couple of hours and they had no means for making a fire. They had nothing except the clothes they were wearing. She had no idea how far they were from Berlin, only that they'd driven all night in the back of a truck. All she knew was that she and Lisette and six children were standing between three armies that were intent on killing one another. That was when the American guard had said, *"Move along now."*

Apparently all of them standing there was some kind of threat.

The guard took a couple of steps toward them, motioned with his rifle, and repeated, *"Move along! You can't stay here."*

Couldn't he see she was too scared to move?

Somehow she found the strength. She grabbed the hands of two of the children, turned her back on the Americans, and they all began walking on their way back to Ramah Cabin. Had she known what separated them or what they'd find once they arrived there, she probably would have just sat down in the middle of the road and sobbed.

It was her anger that kept her going. Anger was her daily bread. She fed on it at night while the children were asleep, enough to get them through the next day.

One of the first lessons she learned was that they weren't in Germany anymore. Not the Germany she knew. There was no civilization. No laws and little food. The land had become like a jungle with every man for himself. The same went with women and children.

The Russian armies were marauders, exacting revenge on the German nation for all the destruction that had been visited on their cities and villages. But they were not the worst. Bands of scavengers—Wehrmacht soldiers and battered remnants of Waffen SS troops—roamed the countryside looting, plundering, and terrorizing villages and farms in search of food. Fueled by rumors that Hitler was still alive and organizing a counterstrike in Spain, these leftover soldiers saw themselves as Germany's last line of defense. They sabotaged roads and bridges and set booby traps in houses, never knowing if their weapons would be set off by a Russian soldier, a German farmer, or one of Mady's children.

It was through this jungle that Mady led her ragtag group of children. They slept in forests, barns, and ditches, eating roots and red currants, drinking rainwater and brackish water from ditches.

Mady and Lisette took turns begging farmers for vegetables, fruit, berries, and eggs. Most of the farmers they approached turned their backs on them and shut their doors in their faces. But somehow

Mady and Lisette managed to scrounge enough food to keep them all from starving.

Most of those they encountered along the road were traveling the opposite direction. They were fleeing the Russians, attempting to reach American-occupied villages. They shook their heads and wagged their tongues at Mady. She was leading the children to their deaths, they told her. But Mady was insistent on going home. She thought that if they could reach Ramah Cabin, they would survive.

In one village Mady begged a length of rope from a sympathetic old Prussian farmer who smoked a hand-rolled cigarette made from a scrap of newspaper. Gunfire popped in the woods on the edge of his property. Mady connected the children by tying the rope around the waist of each child. This made it easier to keep track of them. Most days this worked fine. There were other days, however, when one of the children became tired, or ill, or obstinate. Then it was like a ship dragging its anchor.

Mady and Lisette divided responsibilities according to their strengths. Mady charted and navigated their course. Lisette kept the children's spirits up. She did this by telling them stories, drawing mostly from the Old Testament wilderness wanderings of the Israelites.

Lisette had the children role-play the stories. Mady was Moses, the leader under God. The children took turns playing Aaron, rotating each day. Aaron would be at the head of the rope line and would relay necessary information to the sojourners, with Mady whispering the words to them.

Looking back on it, it was a miracle they made it to Ramah Cabin. When the structure came into sight, Mady knew what Moses must have felt like standing on the east bank of the Jordan River and gazing into the Promised Land. Only, instead of Canaanites, she saw Russians. They were using Ramah Cabin as some sort of area administration center.

Mady never had time to think about where they would go from there. German soldiers surrounded them. She and the children were caught. The children were taken from her. Their journey—the dirt, the hunger, the begging, the weariness, the fear, the running and hiding—all of it had been for nothing.

To some degree she blamed herself for trusting Park in the first place. But mostly she blamed him for making promises he couldn't keep and then for doing nothing to help them after leaving them stranded.

"So you see, dear," Mady said softly to the darkness, "I, too, was once deceived by the charms of Herr Parker. Only now I know better. Never again will I trust a word that man says. And never will I forgive him for what he did to us."

Chapter 5

Hans Spuhler was sweating, and it wasn't from the heat. The proud little Prussian came to confess that he'd failed in his mission.

Seated behind his desk, Witzell lit a cigar.

"I lost him," Spuhler said.

"What?" Witzell was now on his feet, his teeth clamped onto his cigar. "You lost him?"

"One minute he was helpless, standing in the middle of the road, flapping his arms . . . the next—"

"He played you. That was just a show for your sake."

"I don't think so."

Witzell looked at the end of his cigar. It hadn't yet caught fire, which angered him more. He slammed it down on his desk. "Didn't I warn you not to underestimate him?" he shouted.

Spuhler stood ramrod straight, his eyes fixed on a point on Witzell's wall, insufferable as always, refusing to shed his cloak of Prussian superiority.

"I followed him to the road. Then—" Spuhler swallowed—"then he acted like he was blind."

"He *is* blind, you arrogant nitwit!"

Spuhler's face reddened considerably; his eyes bulged as he attempted to restrain himself. "You know full well he doesn't move about like a blind boy." He then went on to describe how Tomcat was nearly hit by a car.

"He heard a car coming," Witzell said. "He flagged it down."

Spuhler shook his head. "I don't think so."

"He knew you were following him," Witzell said.

"Impossible! He couldn't have known. I'm a trained Stasi agent. I've tracked international spies halfway across Europe without once ever—"

"Can it, Spuhler! He spotted you. Whether he smelled you or heard you or sensed you or an owl whispered it in his ear is irrelevant. The fact is, your assignment was to keep him under surveillance and you let a blind boy give you the slip."

"But I caught up with him," Spuhler said.

Witzell raised an eyebrow. "Where?"

"Alexanderplatz. You mentioned it earlier. I spotted him walking into a movie house."

"Movie house?" Witzell chomped his cigar. What was Tomcat doing at a movie house? For that matter, why Alexanderplatz? It was nowhere near . . .

"I followed him in and took up a position three rows behind him."

Witzell eased himself back into his chair, hoping to hear a happy ending to Spuhler's little escapade.

"You didn't tell me the boy was retarded," Spuhler said.

"Retarded? What are you talking about? He's blind, not retarded."

Spuhler thought about this a moment. As he did, his mouth twitched. A drop of sweat ran down his cheek.

"Well, he acted retarded," Spuhler concluded. "It was like he was working himself up to a seizure or something." Spuhler's eyes slid side to side as he reviewed the events in his mind. "At first, everything was fine. He sat there like all the others, staring at the screen like he was watching the movie. I remember thinking, What's he doing? He can't see a thing. Then I thought, Even if he's just listening to the movie, he'd sit facing the screen, wouldn't he?"

"What happened to Tomcat?" Witzell prodded.

But Spuhler ignored the question and instead continued at the same reminiscing pace, analyzing the experience as he relived it.

"He started bobbing up and down in his seat, doubled over like he was having a first-rate bellyache, then popping back up. I was cautious not to overreact. Bellyaches aren't fatal. Messy, but that's the cleaning crew's problem, not mine. He kept doing it—down, up, down, up—for a good fifteen minutes. It annoyed the man sitting two rows behind him. He got up and left."

"You lost him again, didn't you?" Witzell said.

Again Spuhler didn't answer him. His eyes were unfocused. "The thing is, the intervals were inconsistent," he said.

"Spuhler, tell me you didn't lose him again."

"He started staying down longer. Out of sight. But he'd always pop back up. So when he didn't—"

"Spuhler!"

The former Stasi agent inhaled deeply, and his eyes sharpened. He returned to the present moment. "When I went to check on the boy, he was gone."

"How long ago was this?"

Spuhler hesitated, which irritated Witzell even more.

"How long?" Witzell shouted.

"Twenty-four hours."

Witzell went nuclear. "And you're just telling me now?"

"I thought I could pick up his trail again."

"You were protecting your blasted Prussian pride! You didn't want to admit that you couldn't track a blind boy. That you lost him—not once, but twice!"

"Listen here, Witzell. You're not my superior. I don't have to stand here and listen to this."

"You're right, you don't. Get out of my office!"

Witzell came from behind his desk, passed by Spuhler, and yanked open the door.

"Listen, Witzell . . ."

"Get out."

Spuhler moved toward the door. "I want it understood that I consider my debt to you paid in full."

"I said, get out!" Witzell shouted.

Night shift orderlies began appearing at both ends of the hallway, drawn by the commotion, glad for a break in their monotonous routine.

"I want your word on that, Witzell."

"I'll give you my foot!"

Spuhler stepped into the hallway and then turned back around. "I'm not leaving until you—"

Witzell slammed shut the office door.

Kellerstrasse.

Otto Witzell did not need directions to find it. He eased his little yellow Wartburg sedan against the curb and turned off the motor. Though it was dark and he couldn't see the numbers on the buildings, he knew exactly which one was number 23, just as he knew exactly where to park to have a good view of the building without being conspicuous.

He checked his watch, angling it this way and that so as to catch enough light to see the hands. The sky was beginning to show streaks of the approaching dawn.

The passenger side window was down and yet he was perspiring. It was going to be another scorcher of a day. Even so, a shiver went through him, the kind that every child who plays hide-and-seek is acquainted with.

Witzell reached absentmindedly for a cigar. When he realized what his hand was doing, he pulled it back.

A line of ten-story residential buildings ran the length of the street for one and a half kilometers. The one Witzell had in view had a sign on it: Schönner Industries. Schönner was a brand name for shoes. Factory workers lived here.

Though the complexes were less than a decade old, already they showed signs of aging and disrepair. The street-side lawn lay filled with weeds. Garbage littered the entryway, the lawn, and also the street, despite a sign that warned of penalties for throwing garbage out the windows. The complex had three entrances, two of which were padlocked.

Witzell craned his neck to check the street behind him. He was looking for two things: Tomcat and any indication that he was being spied on by another, even while he himself spied on the apartment building. He'd tried to be careful about coming here too often. Today he had no choice in the matter.

Though he could never be sure—someone could be lurking behind any one of the hundreds of curtained windows—as far as he could tell, no one was watching him. So he turned his attention to his reason for being here.

Tomcat could be curled up in a doorstep. Under a bush. Or

possibly in the shadows between the buildings. Even if the boy had made it to the right street, how would he know which of the buildings was the correct one?

He'd know.

Don't underestimate him, Witzell reminded himself. He wasn't sure how Tomcat would know the correct building, but somehow he'd figure it out.

The sky grew lighter. Witzell didn't have much time. To be sitting in a parked car in the light of day begged too many questions for which he had no good answers.

He began regretting his plan. Spuhler's part had been to safeguard Tomcat. Witzell had never intended to endanger Tomcat. Had he thought it would come to this, he never would have undertaken this whole thing.

There was no sign of the boy.

Witzell placed a hand on the door handle. His position had been adequate for general observation, but there were areas that remained hidden to him, areas large enough to conceal a man. And although, because of their age difference, Witzell would always think of Tomcat as a boy, by the world's standards he was a man. Witzell had a choice. He could start the motor and cruise the street, or he could search on foot. Using the car kept him mobile, yet it limited his search, and the sound of the motor might attract others' attention. Walking was quieter, more efficient, even if at the price of exposure and mobility.

Just as he was about to pull up on the door handle and climb out, a movement caught his eye. Low. Emerging from between buildings. A man crouched down, his fingertips brushing the side of the building.

That's my boy!

Tomcat moved slowly as his feet read the ground. He made his way to the front of the building. The correct building.

How does he do it? Witzell wondered.

Tomcat found the side entrance, felt the chain and lock, then he stepped around a bush that needed trimming to the front of the building and found the unlocked entrance. He stopped.

"Go on," Witzell urged from across the street. "Go on. Up the stairs now."

Tomcat moved into the entryway.

"Good boy!" Witzell said.

He waited for several minutes to see if Tomcat would reappear. When he didn't, Witzell reached for the ignition switch.

A hand stretched through the driver side window and grabbed his arm.

"What game are you playing, Witzell?"

"Spuhler . . ."

The little Prussian glared at him. "You knew the boy was coming here all along, didn't you? Why did you have me follow him?"

"To insure no harm would come to him," Witzell said.

Spuhler glanced at the apartment complex. "What is this place to you?"

"That's none of your concern."

"It is my concern, Herr Witzell. When someone makes a fool of me, it is my concern."

"You made a fool of yourself, Spuhler. You didn't need any help." As soon as he'd said it, Witzell regretted it. Not that it wasn't true. There was just something about Spuhler that brought the worst out of him.

Spuhler bristled. "I would remind you that I still have Stasi contacts."

"And I'm sure they would love to hear how a blind boy gave you the slip last night—twice."

The two men eyed each other. Witzell was the first to back off. "Walk away and we're even," he said.

"My debt's cancelled?"

"If you walk away now. No questions asked."

This was what Spuhler wanted. Witzell could see it in his eyes.

"I would need one thing more," Spuhler said.

"What?"

The former Stasi agent looked again at the building. "Your word that there's nothing illegal going on here."

"It's a personal matter, Spuhler."

"No foreign espionage?"

Witzell laughed. "If there was, would I admit that to you?"

Spuhler glared at him.

"You have my word," said Witzell, hoping to tip the scales back to the side of reason.

This seemed to satisfy the Prussian. With a final glance at the building, he turned and walked away.

Witzell slumped in his seat. After a moment he started the car and drove by the complex slowly, checking one final time for Tomcat.

The entryway was empty.

Satisfied, Witzell pressed down on the accelerator and headed home.

As the sound of the car died away, Tomcat emerged from the entryway of the apartment complex. He felt a sense of satisfaction knowing that Witzell was concerned enough for him that he'd drive all this way to make sure he'd arrived safely.

Chapter 6

Thursday, August 17, 1961

Lisette and Elyse sat next to each other surrounded by the hum of fifty sewing machines. The needles of the machines were a blur as experienced hands pushed and pulled precut leather pieces, though not as quickly as usual. Like everyone else in the factory, the two women were victims of the heat. As a result, production on the floor was down and it was Mady's unenviable job to report the low count to shift supervisor Herr Gellert.

There were eight steps to the process of making Schönner shoes: cutting and stitching the precut upper portion; stock fitting, which prepared the sole; lasting, which attached the upper to a wooden foot; bottoming, which attached the sole to the upper; heeling, which attached the heel to the sole; finishing, including polishing and stamping the Schönner name to the sole; treeing, which included attaching laces, bows, and buckles; and final cleaning and inspection.

Lisette and Elyse were bottom stitchers; they worked the heavy industrial sewing machines to attach the soles to the upper portions. The work required strong fingers. By the end of the workday, their fingers were so sore and stiff that it was difficult for them to do simple tasks such as write with a pencil or grip a doorknob.

It could be worse. And it would be had they been bottom stitchers in a quality factory. But Schönner shoes were cheap shoes. Imitation leather was used for the tops, and while a good sole required two or three plies, the Schönner factory made their soles with but a single ply.

"Shoes are made to wear out," Herr Gellert had explained to Lisette one day. "We could make shoes that last twenty years, but why would we? It would put us out of business. As it is, people who buy our shoes need a new pair every year. For some, more often than that. We sell them shoes at an inexpensive price, a price they can afford. So everyone benefits. They have shoes, workers have jobs, and the factory stays in business."

Elyse glanced in the direction of Herr Gellert's office, located on the far side of the factory, just as her mother knocked on the door. Mady waited for permission to enter before stepping inside.

Elyse's fingers ached, only she hardly noticed. It was the heat that was unbearable. All the windows of the factory were open, but there was no breeze. With all the machines and bodies generating heat, the place was like an oven. She didn't want to touch anything. Even her own arm against her side was hot and uncomfortable. So she sewed with her elbows away from her body.

She guessed that there was at least an hour before quitting time. It was a guess because Herr Gellert didn't allow clocks or watches on the factory floor. He said it only encouraged clock-watching, which in turn slowed production. A good worker is not concerned about the time; a worker's time belongs to the Party. A good worker is concerned with only one thing—production.

"Is it just me or are the machines melting?" Elyse said.

Lisette smiled. "I know. I could use a cool drink about now."

"It's like everything's moving in slow motion. Will this shift ever end?"

Her machine jammed. Elyse threw her head back and let loose a frustrated grunt. She raised the needle, yanked the leather from beneath it, and proceeded to unjam the machine. She groused about the antiquated equipment.

"You'll not get any sympathy from me," Lisette said. "Your mother and I started on machines much older than these. These machines are a dream compared to them."

Elyse tossed an offending clump of thread to the floor. She rethreaded the needle and reassembled the machine. "Let's talk about something else," she said. "Anything that will distract me and keep me from going mad."

"We're not supposed to talk at all," Lisette said.

"And if you get caught, what will Herr Gellert do? Send you packing? Not likely." She grinned playfully. "Instead, he'll take you into his private office, and he'll—"

"Stop right there. Not another word," Lisette said. "What Herr Gellert and I do behind closed doors is none of your business."

Elyse raised her eyebrows suggestively. "All I was going to say was—"

"None of your business!" Lisette repeated.

Elyse returned to her sewing, a half smile playing on her lips.

"You're just full of mischief lately, aren't you?" Lisette said.

"It helps pass the time."

"Maybe you should pass the time by thinking about how you've been disrespectful to your mother."

Elyse scowled. But she said nothing.

The two of them had a unique relationship. Lisette was her friend and second mother. Elyse could confide in Lisette intimate things, things she never would tell her mother. Then there were times when Lisette admonished her. Like now.

"I don't like the way Mother speaks about Herr Parker," Elyse said. "She makes him out to be a coward and a cad. I don't think he's either. You don't think Herr Parker is a bad man, do you?"

It took a moment before Lisette responded. "Herr Parker is a good man," she said. "However, your mother has her reasons for feeling the way she does."

"Well, I can't think of anything Herr Parker could have done that deserves the kind of anger she carries for him."

Lisette's machine slowed to a stop. "Are you just spouting steam, or do you really want to know?" she asked.

Elyse's machine stopped. There was an ominous tone to Lisette's voice. Elyse wasn't sure if she wanted to hear this or not. "Is it bad?"

"It's life."

"Will it help pass the time?" Elyse quipped, trying to lighten the mood.

"You're old enough now to hear these things. Do you want to know or not?"

Lisette set to sewing again. Likewise, Elyse coaxed the needle on her machine back into action. "Yes. I want to know," she said.

Lisette checked the supervisor's office. Mady was still inside. "We were losing the war," she began. "Soviet troops were just a few kilometers outside of Berlin. It was Park who suggested we might find protection among the Americans."

"How did you first meet Park? I mean, he's American. . . ."

"Through your father. Ramah Cabin was a safe house for downed American fliers who were trying to get back to their units."

"But why would you help them? They were the enemy."

Lisette smiled. "The lines of alliance are never as sharply defined in war as they are in the history books. Your father provided humanitarian aid in exchange for food and supplies to keep you children alive. Anyway, Colonel Parker was the team leader for the Americans and your father's radio contact. So, with the Soviets closing in, he offered to get us to an American base."

"And Park thought they'd help a couple of German women with children?"

"We had a bargaining chip. A genuine rocket scientist."

"Uncle Ernst."

"Only as it turned out, they took Ernst and turned us away."

"Herr Parker lied to you?"

"He gave us no guarantees. We knew it was a risk from the start. It wasn't Park's decision to make."

"What does my mother blame him for, then?"

"She blames him for what happened to us afterward. She thinks he could have done more to help us after we were turned away."

"Do you blame him too?"

"No."

"Then Mother is just being unreasonable."

"You haven't heard the story yet."

Lisette checked the floor supervisor's office. The door was closed, with Mady still inside.

"We call them our Three-Suitcase Years," she said, resuming her story. "When we talk of them, that is, which isn't often."

Elyse listened intently.

Lisette continued, "I'm convinced that if it weren't for your mother, none of us would be alive today." She looked at Elyse with tears forming in her eyes. "Your mother never gave up; she had a fire within her that kept us all going. This was after the war. It was just the three of us then. The other children had been taken from us. We drifted from farmhouse to farmhouse, village to village, looking for a place to live. Everything we owned was packed in three suitcases. It's hard to describe how scared we were. We lived in occupied territory." She swallowed hard. "The Soviet soldiers thought no more of using us to meet their needs than they would using a road or a house. Everywhere we went they shouted 'Uhry! Uhry!' That meant they wanted something from us. I remember one soldier yelling at a woman who was clutching the handlebars of a bicycle. This Ivan—"

"Ivan?" Elyse said.

"A nickname we used for the Russians. The woman wouldn't let go of the bike. Ivan pulled on the rear wheel, yelling 'Uhry! Uhry! Uhry!' "

"Did he get the bicycle?"

"Probably. I don't remember. I just remember the expression on the woman's face. That battered bike meant more to her than it meant to Ivan."

Lisette finished a shoe and set it aside, mechanically reaching for a new sole.

"A couple of times we had to steal into the woods to keep from being raped. The only German some of the Soviet soldiers knew was *'Frau, komm'* ('Woman, let's go.'). That's what they'd say as they dragged you into a room or an alley or a field."

Lisette's machine came to a stop. She reached for a tissue.

"If this is too painful for you . . ." Elyse said.

Lisette shook her head. "If you're to understand your mother, you need to hear this." Composing herself, she said, "In one village—I can't remember the name; I'm not sure I ever knew it—we lodged with a woman who had three daughters, fourteen to sixteen years old. The woman was hysterical. She kept saying that the Russian soldiers were going to rape her and her daughters. Mady tried to get her to think about other things. She asked the woman about food and water and other necessities. But all the woman could think about was that the soldiers were going to rape them.

"She began talking about suicide. Cutting their wrists. She said it would be rather painless but that her younger daughters were afraid. Your mother said she was being foolish. She told the woman how God watched over us like He watched over the Israelites in the wilderness. But the woman didn't respond."

Lisette dabbed her nose with a tissue.

"The next morning we found her and her daughters in a room

on the floor. Every one of them, dead."

"Oh my!" Elyse gasped.

"Tragedy was a daily part of life in postwar Berlin. Nearly half the city was rubble, the result of over three hundred and fifty air raids. Living space was scarce. Most of the apartment buildings had been destroyed. Mitte, Tiergarten, Freidrichshain, and Kreuzberg districts were the worst hit. Have you ever heard of the *Trummerfrauen*?"

Elyse shook her head.

"Rubble Ladies. That was what they called us. It was cheaper to demolish and rebuild structures than it was to repair them. That's where we came in. There were sixty thousand of us. We dug through the rubble and cleared entire blocks with our bare hands, brick by brick. Of course, we found a fair number of corpses buried in the rubble.

"I remember one day, three French soldiers saw us working. They started cursing and throwing stones at us."

"Why would they do that?"

"They called us Nazis. So the next day our supervisor put up a poster at the site, written in French. It said, *Here there are no Nazis.* I tell you that because it was the prevailing mood in those days. No one bothered to ask us how we felt about the Nazis and Hitler. In their minds all Germans were Nazis. They thought Hitler spoke for all of us.

"Many nights we slept in alleys and huddled against a building. You were small enough so that your mother would open up one of the suitcases and it became your bed. You were just the right size to curl up inside on top of the clothes."

That brought a smile to Elyse.

"As for food, most days it was rutabagas or sour bread or, if we were lucky, a potato. If we were really lucky, we got our hands on some meat and butter, but those were mostly black market items.

"I remember we once got word that a farmer's horse had died. That meant meat would be available the next day. Word spread through our ranks that a local butcher had secured the horse and would be processing the carcass.

"Well, it was my turn to stand in line, so the next morning I got up early and went to the butcher shop. By seven o'clock I was standing in line. The shop was scheduled to open at one o'clock that afternoon. By the time I got there the line stretched nearly a block long. We all wore black or gray coats in those days—most of them didn't fit us—and shawls. It was bitter cold and we were all hunched over to keep warm."

Elyse wiped perspiration from her forehead with the back of her hand. "I'm having a hard time imagining it," she said.

"Two women stepped into the line behind me. They must have been friends because they chattered nonstop like a couple of magpies. This went on for an hour or so. Then, just as I noticed that the women had stopped talking for a while, one of them said to the other, 'Do you see them? There. On her coat. Look, one is crawling across her back.'

"Do you know how it is when you just know someone's talking about you? Well, that's how I felt. I knew they were talking about me and that they thought they saw lice. But I also knew I didn't have lice. You know how I am about cleanliness."

"Obsessive, fanatical," Elyse said.

Lisette looked at her. "I wouldn't have chosen those exact words," she said.

"The women behind you—they thought you had lice."

Lisette nodded. "I ignored them. So they got louder. 'Why do we have to stand behind a louse-infested woman?' they said. 'We'll probably get lice ourselves, just because we want to put meat on the table for our hungry families.'

"I'd always been taught that there can't be a fight if one side doesn't show up, so I kept to my original plan and ignored them. This went on for an hour. Then two. Then three. The other women in line were now irritated. Not at the two women, but at me. They scowled at me, cursed me, told me I should leave, that I had no right to be there spreading my lice all over them, possibly infecting their children and babies."

"What did you do?"

"I pulled my coat and shawl around me and tried to ignore them. When that didn't do any good, I tried telling them I didn't have lice. But they wouldn't listen. Another hour passed without them letting up. Finally it got to be too much for me. I just couldn't take it any longer. I left the line and ran back to the room where we were staying.

"Of course I was in tears. Your mother asked what had happened.

I told her. As I was telling her, I took off my coat and a dead louse fell to the floor."

Elyse shuddered.

"Exactly," Lisette said.

"So you *did* have lice."

Lisette shook her head. "Your mother said she'd seen that kind of thing happen before. She told me one of the women put it on my back just to get me out of line."

"They did that to get one person ahead in line?"

"One person could mean the difference between getting meat for your family and going home empty-handed."

"Was Mother angry with you?"

"She went with me back to the butcher shop. The line was gone and so was all the meat. I felt awful. I'd let her and you down. All I wanted to do was to go home and cry, but then your mother took me by the hand and marched me into the butcher shop. She told the butcher my story and asked if there was anything at all he could give us. The butcher was a kind man, and he truly seemed moved by the story. He gave us a bone for stew, and he didn't charge us for it."

On the opposite side of the factory, the floor supervisor's door swung open and Mady stepped out. She made her way through the maze of sewing machines with a yellow paper clutched in her hand. Her face was a mask; she showed no emotion.

Lisette said quickly, "As bad as it was during those Three-Suitcase Years, your mother never gave up, neither did she stop trying to locate the other children to get them back."

Mady was halfway across the factory floor, coming toward them.

"But she can't blame Herr Parker for all the things that happened during those years," Elyse whispered.

"She doesn't. But she does blame him for placing us in a situation where the children were taken away. The other things, if you're going to understand your mother, you need to know what she's been through. There's a lot of resentment and anger. Herr Parker is her lightning rod."

"You're not like that," Elyse said, "and you lived through all those things too."

Lisette looked up. Mady had reached the end of their row of machines.

"Your mother's the strong one. Had it been left to me, none of us would be alive today."

Lisette and Elyse gave their sewing their full attention just as Mady arrived. She took her place behind the sewing machine next to Lisette. Without a word, she went straight to work. The needle on her machine sprang to life.

After several minutes, when the rest of the workers stopped checking on her with curious glances, she said, "He's going to call a meeting."

The last bit of energy that Elyse had now melted inside her. She slumped. This shift was never going to end.

"He's disappointed with the production numbers," Mady explained, "and thinks we don't appreciate how much the Party has done for us. So he's calling a meeting to rally the workers."

No sooner had she said this when the door to the floor supervisor's office opened again. The floor supervisor walked out first—a short man with a Stalin-like mustache and a belly that strained the lower buttons of his shirt. Behind him came his boss, Herr Gellert.

They moved to a raised wooden platform that had a table with a sound system. Switches were flipped. The microphone was tested with five finger taps. Not three. Not six. It was always five. Next came the supervisor's voice, breathy and muddied by the system because he always pressed the microphone against his lips.

"Your attention," he said. "In ten minutes, at the end of the shift, there will be a worker's rally. Attendance is required. Roll will be taken. That is all."

There was no audible response. Such things would indicate a lack of Party spirit, which could lead to dismissal or other more severe reprisals. But spouses and children would certainly hear about it tonight in the flats.

Ten minutes later the drone of sewing machines died out. The women remained seated behind their machines while one Party speaker after another took the microphone.

It was the longest and hottest day of Elyse Schumacher's life.

Chapter 7

Little was said during the walk home from the factory. The heat combined with the workers' rally to sap the three women of their energy, but that wasn't the only reason. They'd learned to be careful about what they said in public.

It was common knowledge that East Berliners led two lives—a unit of the state by day, an individual in the privacy of their flats by night. Personal opinions were guarded and for good reason. The wrong opinion shared with the wrong person, sometimes even family, was seen as criminal.

Therefore, in public the women never dropped their guard. The Party had ears everywhere. The slip of a tongue could, at best, result in the loss of a position and privileges. At worst, it could earn them a visit from the authorities or get one of them arrested. It seemed everyone had a story about an uncle or co-worker who said something in confidence to the wrong person or who spoke too loudly in a restaurant.

"I'm going to take Elyse to Kirsch's Department Store," Mady said. "She needs a blouse. Do you want to come?"

"Thanks, no. I'll go home and start supper."

"We won't be long."

"Wave to Herr Puttkamer for me," Elyse said.

Herr Puttkamer was the resident apartment complex spy. Nothing went on in the hallway without him knowing it. A retired floor supervisor at the shoe factory and faithful Party member, he lived in the flat at the end of the hall, where he spent his time monitoring the hallway through a peephole. He had turned people into the authorities for having a late-night visitor or for keeping irregular hours. At times he'd roam the halls and listen at doorways and report anyone he heard watching a Western television broadcast.

Years ago, when Elyse learned that Herr Puttkamer was always watching them, she took to waving to him. Sometimes Mady would find her sitting in the hall outside his door, talking to him. When she inquired what she was doing, Elyse told her that Herr Puttkamer would tell her stories. At first Mady thought nothing of it, until she learned the kind of stories Puttkamer was telling her.

His stories were about voyages to lands where muscular women carried out raids on the male population, or of the Mariposa Islands where the natives had transparent skin, so a person could watch their digestive process in operation, or of how in America the women's legs were so weak they couldn't walk half a kilometer due to their excessive use of automobiles. That was when the story sessions stopped.

Alone, Lisette turned up Kellerstrasse. At the entryway to building 23, she dug in her purse for the keys to the flat.

"Meow."

The sound startled her. Mostly because it was a man's voice. He stepped out from the shadows. Although she hadn't seen him for sixteen years, Lisette recognized him instantly.

"Tomcat!"

"Where are you living?" Lisette asked. "How did you find us? And how did you know it was me in the entryway?"

She and Tomcat sat facing each other on the sofa. She held his hands. Ordinarily she'd never allow such familiarity from a young man, but this was Tomcat. When sighted people are reunited, a single glance can reestablish years of shared memories. With Tomcat the exchange was hand to hand.

Naturally she'd invited him into the flat and thought nothing of it until she heard a distinct "tut-tut-tut" from behind the door at the end of the hall. Herr Puttkamer. She knew how it looked but she didn't care. She'd deal with him later.

Tomcat seemed in no hurry to answer her questions. His eyes

were closed and he wore a contented smile as his thumb stroked the back of her hand.

"One of my earliest memories is your scent," he said. "Actually, I remember two scents from that night."

"That's amazing!" Lisette said.

"The other scent was a perfume. I don't know the name of it, and I haven't smelled it often since then, but every time I do, I get a cold, frightened feeling."

"The night I found you," Lisette said. "There was another woman. Really, it was she who first found you."

"But it was you who rescued me."

"You frightened her."

"She didn't like me. I could tell."

"That was so long ago. How do you remember something you smelled that long ago?"

Tomcat chuckled. "I remember you like it was yesterday."

"But I don't wear perfume."

His smile grew wider. "You held me tight against you. I felt safe."

"I had to walk all the way back to the cabin that night."

"Your breathing was labored."

"I was running."

"I wanted to stay in your arms forever."

The front door rattled. A key was being inserted into the lock. Mady's voice came from the other side. "We'll try again tomorrow," she said.

The door opened. Mady's head was lowered as she twisted the key to extract it. Behind her, Elyse's attention was directed to the end of the hallway. She waved. "Hello, Herr Puttkamer!" she said in a loud voice.

Mady looked up and was startled to see that Lisette wasn't alone. Then, "Tomcat?"

The reunion began with that exquisite moment of disbelief. Tomcat stood, grinning ear to ear. Mady rushed across the room and threw her arms around him. Elyse, hearing his name, followed close behind, all smiles. It was clear she wanted to hug him, was almost desperate to hug him, yet was held back by a shyness that came from the years of being separated from each other.

So when it was her turn to greet Tomcat, Elyse settled for a verbal greeting and a rubbing of his shoulder. Tomcat's reply was equally repressed. He blushed and waved awkwardly.

"Hermann is the Parcheesi king," Tomcat said. "He needs a five—boom!—he rolls a five. Annie gets so mad at him when he does that."

It was late. The three women and Tomcat sat around the kitchen table. There were only three chairs, so Tomcat sat on a footstool, lower than the others. He looked and, at times, talked like a little boy, the way they remembered him, only his voice was much deeper. That took some getting used to.

One by one, Tomcat told them about the others, whom he had dubbed the Hadamar Six. While there were only five of them at K7, when choosing the name he'd included Elyse in the hope that she'd be one of them again someday.

According to Tomcat, not only was Hermann the Parcheesi king but he was the intellectual among them. While his clubfoot may have slowed his body down, his mind seemed to have no limit. He spent his days reading and practicing speaking different languages. He spoke five languages and was working on his sixth.

Annie claimed Hermann was making them up. How would they know if he could actually speak French, Russian, English, Swedish, and Italian? There wasn't anybody at K7 who could speak any of those languages. And certainly not Latin, his sixth language. How did they know he wasn't just fooling them? Hermann didn't let Annie get to him. He just let her rant.

"We spend a good part of the day just ignoring her," Tomcat said.

Viktor liked television. A lot. The orderlies picked on him because of his Down's syndrome.

Marlene was as quiet and sweet as ever, still quite self-conscious due to her harelip, covering her mouth when talking.

"Does she still draw?" Mady asked. She hadn't stopped smiling since entering the flat. She was relishing every word of Tomcat's stories.

"Marlene still draws. And paints too. Watercolors mostly, because they don't cost as much. She says she wants to paint with oil paints and so Herr Witzell is trying to get her some. I think he has to put it in the budget or something like that."

"How about Annie?" Lisette asked.

Tomcat let out an exasperated sigh. "Annie is still Annie," he said.

"You have to tell us more than that," said Mady.

Tomcat screwed up his face. "Well . . . she sits around all day brushing her hair—as though it would do her any good. And when she's not doing that, she's irritating the life out of the rest of us."

The three women exchanged amused glances.

"Herr Witzell, he's a good man?" Mady asked. At first, all three of them had pelted Tomcat with questions faster than he could answer them. Mady had assumed the role of interviewer to keep him from being overwhelmed.

"Herr Witzell's the best," Tomcat said. "He looks out for us. Only, he's old. Some of the orderlies say he's too old, that he should have retired years ago."

"Why doesn't he?"

"I think it's because of us," Tomcat said. "I think he's afraid if someone else takes over, they'll split us up. Marlene says he's our guardian angel."

"He sounds like a good man," Mady said.

"One time an orderly—a guy by the name of Fricke—was picking on Viktor, calling him all sorts of names and making him mop up the floor with his own shirt because Viktor got sick and threw up. Viktor isn't very strong so I stood up for him. The next thing I knew, Fricke and two other orderlies wrestled me to the ground, then locked me in a closet. They were going to let me out before Herr Witzell showed up, only they got to watching *Gunsmoke* and forgot about me. When Herr Witzell found out, he really lit into all three of them, Fricke especially. I've never seen him that mad before. Like I said, he looks out for us."

"I'd like to meet Herr Witzell someday," Mady said.

"Can I ask a question now?"

The three women laughed. They'd been bombarding Tomcat with questions for nearly two hours.

"Go ahead," Mady said.

"What happened to Konrad?"

An awkward silence settled in the room as the three women looked at one another. First Park, then Tomcat. This was the second time in a week that someone had asked about Konrad.

It was Lisette who told him. Tomcat took the news hard.

"I always thought Konrad was like Superman, you know? Invincible," he said. "What about his evil brother?"

"Tomcat!" Mady said. "Willi isn't evil. What made you say that?"

Tomcat shrugged. "I sense things," he said.

"We don't know what happened to Willi," Lisette said.

Elyse changed the subject. "So how long can you stay?"

"As long as I want."

"When is Herr Witzell expecting you back?" Mady asked.

"He's not. I ran away."

"Ran away! Tomcat! We need to call Herr Witzell and let him know you're all right," Mady said.

"Can't," Elyse said. "Fräulein Lotz is visiting her sister in Mecklenburg."

Having no phone of their own, on occasion they used Fräulein Lotz's phone, who lived above them on the sixth floor.

"Herr Gellert has a phone," Mady said to Lisette.

Lisette cringed. "He really doesn't like other people using it," she said. "And I'd hate to have to ask him."

The only other telephone in the building belonged to Herr Puttkamer. Mady had asked to use his phone once when Elyse was running a temperature of 104. Puttkamer had breathed on her during the brief call, holding out a wrinkled hand and demanding payment the second she hung up. Mady swore she'd never use his phone again.

"There's no need to call," Tomcat said.

"It's the least we can do," said Lisette. "Herr Witzell must be beside himself with worry."

"He's knows where I'm at."

"He knows?" Mady said.

"He followed me. Only, he doesn't know I know he knows."

Mady looked at Lisette. "Did you follow that?"

Tomcat grinned. "Who do you think gave me your address?"

"Wait, I'm confused," Mady said. "You said you ran away."

"Correct."

"But Herr Witzell gave you our address."

"I overheard it. I think he let me."

The three women fell strangely silent, and not until that moment did Tomcat think that the circumstances which led him to 23 Kellerstrasse might not have been a good thing.

Chapter 8

"How come you never came for us?"

This was the second question Tomcat asked. This one was even harder to explain than the first.

"We always thought you would," he said, "everyone except Annie. But I kept telling them you'd come for us someday. Konrad for sure. Of course, I didn't know he was dead."

Mady winced.

"Annie keeps saying I'm crazy." He laughed. "Won't she be surprised!"

Mady reached across the table and took Tomcat by the hand. "We tried to find you," she said. "We tried every agency, every official we could think of. After a while, there just wasn't anyone else to ask."

"Well, now you know where we are!"

"Just what is it you expect us to do, Tomcat?" Mady said. Her tone was soft, sympathetic, but lacking in promise.

Tomcat looked hurt that she had to ask.

"Take us home," he said.

Mady squeezed his hand. "They won't let us do that. You're wards of the state. That's why they took you from us in the first place."

"Then rescue us," Tomcat said. "Rescue us like Pastor Schumacher rescued us when we were little."

"Hadamar," Lisette said. "That was so long ago, like it was a different life."

"And take you where?" Mady said, her voice rising, her tone increasingly defensive. "We don't have room for you here."

"You did it before," said Tomcat.

"No," Mady said, standing. "No, we didn't do it before. Josef did it before. Josef and Sturmbannführer Wolff and . . . and that other one."

"Herr Adolf," Lisette said.

Mady began pacing. "The situation was different then," she said. "The children would have been put to death. You're in no danger now. You are fed. You have clothes, a roof over your head, with Herr Witzell to watch over you."

"But you're our family," Tomcat said.

Lisette, who was sitting somberly, bowed her head. Elyse sat with folded arms, her mouth pressed into a thin line.

"We'll come visit," Mady offered. "Go on outings. Spend holidays together."

"Konrad would have come for us."

Had Tomcat slapped her, Mady's reaction would have been no different. It took her a moment to recover. "You can stay the night," she said. "In the morning we'll arrange for your return."

"But we don't have a phone," Elyse objected.

"I'll use Herr Puttkamer's phone."

Mady left the kitchen without saying good-night.

Tomcat stood by the sofa while Elyse made it into a bed with a sheet and a blanket.

"You probably won't need this," she said, referring to the blanket. "It's been pretty hot lately."

Lisette had said her good-nights and followed Mady into the bedroom. Muffled voices could be heard through the wall.

"Maybe I shouldn't have come," Tomcat said.

"I'm glad you came," she said, maybe a little too eagerly.

She stood and faced him. She wanted to kiss him good-night. Just a peck on the cheek. And she almost did it, but then at the last second she chickened out.

Tomcat sat on the sofa. "I remember Konrad used to sleep on the sofa at the cabin."

"I set out a cup for you in the kitchen," said Elyse, "in case you need a drink of water during the night."

"Thanks, but I'm a pretty sound sleeper."

He was waiting for her to leave. She wondered, *Will he take off his shirt? Will he take off his pants too? Here in the living room?*

Her face flushed when she realized what she was thinking. It's not as though she wanted to think it. The thoughts just popped into her head before she hardly knew it.

"Good night, Tomcat."

She had planned on saying more, but at the moment that was all she could manage without fear of betraying herself.

Tomcat stretched out on the sofa. "Elyse?"

"Yeah?"

"Do you like Frank Sinatra?"

"Eeeewww. No! He sings old people's songs. Why?"

"Just asking."

Chapter 9

Friday, August 18, 1961

Lisette had learned that it was useless to talk when Herr Gellert was lighting his pipe. This was a private matter. The first time she witnessed one of his ritual pipe lightings, she was embarrassed, as if she were intruding on something intimate. Over time, she became more comfortable with it.

The man lighting the pipe was smug and fastidious. When he found the way something worked, he performed the task the same way every time. Lisette could only guess how many years Herr Gellert had been practicing his lighting ritual.

The pipe securely in hand, with his free hand he opened a tin of tobacco. He smoked only one brand and gave the housekeeper strict instructions to keep his supply fresh. Then he stuffed the bowl full of tobacco, first with his fingers, then tamping it down with a silver tobacco packing tool. Lisette was certain there was a name for this special tool, but she couldn't remember it and wasn't interested enough to ask.

The lighting of the match came next—a grand, sweeping gesture. Herr Gellert always closed his eyes at this point, when touching the flame to the tobacco.

Then came the sucking noise. A horrible hissing sound. If the tobacco didn't ignite immediately, the hissing sound got louder, accompanied by a frown. The final phase in the ritual was the *aaaahhhhh* phase. Herr Gellert leaned back in his chair, eyes still closed, and in a blissful state produced the first puffs of smoke. Half a dozen puffs were made before he was ready to entertain the idea that a world outside of his pipe existed.

With an open book on her lap—one Herr Gellert chose for her to read—Lisette gazed at the man she would marry. She had come to the decision gradually.

Did she love him?

Not yet, but she thought she could grow to love him in time. And it wasn't as though she had a lot of prospects. In fact, he was the only prospect who had presented himself. Men her age were scarce in the days following the war. Those who were available were either very young, very old, or suffering with war wounds.

One day at the factory, not long after the death of his wife, Herr Gellert approached her. It was sort of cute. He had no reason for standing there as long as he did. He didn't talk about work. He just stood and made small talk, which he wasn't very good at.

"He's courting you," Mady had said. A grinning Elyse agreed with her.

They were right, of course, yet at the time Lisette didn't want to admit the fact. Soon it became obvious he was fabricating reasons to be near her sewing station. He was kind to her, gave her little gifts, invited her to dinner, and Lisette was introduced to a world that knew nothing of long lines and shortages and doing without. She had never known such comforts. She found it addicting.

It was like coming upon a store that had a ready supply of meat and other goods, with her the only customer. Not only was there plenty for her, but for Mady and Elyse too.

Herr Gellert settled into his chair, content with his pipe.

He'd kissed her only once and that was on the cheek. Afterward he had apologized for it.

They'd gone to the opera following dinner at a ritzy restaurant on Unter den Linden, the kind where the waiter never leaves the tableside but sends others to get what he needs to serve you, the kind of restaurant that had individual place settings and salt and pepper shakers on every table. All the other restaurants Lisette had visited piled the utensils in the center of the table, and a pair of salt and pepper shakers was shared by everyone in the restaurant.

Herr Gellert and Lisette dined alone.

Maybe it was the wine at dinner or maybe Waldemar—Herr

Gellert's given name—was just feeling mischievous, but as they exited the cab in front of the opera house, he impetuously leaned over and pecked her on the cheek. It shocked them both. For the remainder of the evening Waldemar brooded. Later, he apologized.

"I lost my head!" he confessed. "What was I thinking? What if someone had seen it? Such an unseemly public display. I could lose my position in the Party. It was a foolish thing to do. Foolish!"

As it turned out, he didn't lose his position, nor his standing in the Party. Yet, from that night on, whenever they were in public, he was aloof, always on his guard, lest his emotions run away with him again.

For a Communist, he was a good man. He treated her well. Having grown up with an abusive father, this was important to Lisette.

He was a loyal Party member. But who wasn't these days? Although she had to admit that sometimes his ranting about the Party could be annoying.

"Heaven is a Communist state," he often told her. "Good is what comes from hard work. Evil is what comes every day on three Western channels." He came up with this himself and thought it quite profound. Perhaps that was why he quoted it so frequently.

Herr Gellert's house gave testimony to his wealth. It was big, roomy, and surprisingly bohemian, which Lisette attributed to his four former wives, all of them older than Herr Gellert.

There was Rikka, whom he married just before the war. She died of a gallbladder disease shortly after the birth of their son, Herr Gellert's only offspring. The boy was twenty-three years old now, a jeweler in Munich. Herr Gellert hadn't spoken to him since the boy ran away from home at age eighteen, this rather than to become a Communist.

After Rikka, he married Hertha. She was a full twenty years older than he. Her first husband, a Nazi general, had been killed during the march to Stalingrad. Supposedly she had married Waldemar because he was immediately available.

Then there was his third wife, Verina. Recently widowed and moody, Verina was very wealthy. After just six months of marriage, she left Herr Gellert in exchange for a dashing young lieutenant.

Finally there was Katharina, a nurse Herr Gellert had met at the hospital where he had his gallbladder removed. They were married ten years when Katharina died of food poisoning. Two weeks after her funeral Herr Gellert began courting Lisette.

"I was never meant to be alone," he once told her. "I have to have a wife."

Lisette was convinced Herr Gellert loved her, in his own stiff German way. She would be the first woman he married who was younger than himself. And she was certain that every one of them had contributed their own little touches to the house.

The room in which they sat had a cream-colored Chinese rug. There was a grand piano, though Herr Gellert didn't know how to play it. A Chinese scroll and amateur pastoral paintings adorned the wall. She thought perhaps they were Katharina's, but she'd never looked at them closely enough to check the artist's signature. A bronze nude by Fritz Cremer, which was completely out of place for the man who owned the house, stood in the corner. Probably it was Verina's. There had to be a story behind it, and someday she'd ask, maybe while she was having it removed.

Hundreds of books lined a floor-to-ceiling bookcase. An antique chair with bowed legs and an oval back had been positioned beside studio windows, closed off at the moment by drapes. A display of Coke bottles neatly lined the mantel of the fireplace. Knowing Herr Gellert's passion for Coca-Cola, Lisette was certain they were his contribution to the room's decor. The sitting area for this room was the center, where there were two chairs and an end table with a lamp and Herr Gellert's pipe and tobacco tin.

It was here Lisette spent every Friday and Sunday evening with the man she would someday marry.

Herr Gellert cleared his throat, his way of letting her know he was about to say something, much like the tapping on the factory microphone just before an announcement.

"There's something I'd like you to do for me," he said.

"You have but to ask, Waldemar." She'd only been calling him by his first name for a month or so, and it still wasn't easy for her.

"Have you been to our store in Pankow?"

"Why on earth would I go all the way to Pankow to buy shoes when I can get them at the factory?"

Herr Gellert stared at her.

"No, dear," Lisette said. "I haven't been to the Pankow store."

"I want you to go there." He picked up a folded slip of paper from beside his tobacco tin and handed it to her.

Lisette leaned forward and took it from him. She unfolded it and saw a series of numbers that she recognized as shoe model numbers. Next to them were written a range of shoe sizes.

Two strong puffs of smoke appeared, then, "We suspect the manager is doctoring his books."

Lisette lowered the slip of paper. "You want me to spy on him?"

"We've made a few surprise visits, but apparently someone's tipping him off. I'm doing this little project on my own."

Lisette found it hard to believe what she was hearing. "Waldemar, I wouldn't be comfortable doing this," she said.

"You go as a customer. You walk in, ask for a pair of shoes. Ask for the wrong size. Then when they don't fit, the salesman will step into the back looking for another size. You grow impatient and so wander into the back room to look for the shoes yourself. When you're back there, check the numbers on that paper. Similar scenarios happen all the time. No one will think anything of it."

Again, Lisette couldn't believe they were having this conversation. "It sounds very much like spying to me. I'm not a spy."

"I want you to do this, dear," he insisted. "No one will suspect you. You're the most unassuming person I know."

By the way he held his pipe and looked at her, she could tell the discussion was over. And even though she still didn't want to do it, Lisette knew she would.

Saturday, August 19, 1961

Lisette took the S-Bahn to Pankow. Leaving the station, she then walked five blocks to get to the store. A familiar Schönner's Shoes sign hung over its entrance in two-foot-high block letters with a black shadow that made the name appear to be rising from a white background.

"I can't believe I'm doing this," she mumbled. It had been her constant refrain since the night before. Neither could Mady or Elyse believe she'd let Herr Gellert talk her into the covert errand. Tomcat offered to accompany her, but while Lisette would have liked the company, she had declined. She didn't want to take him away from

Elyse, for they'd had so little time to spend together.

Lisette managed to find the courage by telling herself that she'd done espionage before. What was Ramah Cabin if not wartime espionage? Only her spying credentials were phony and she knew it. She'd taken care of the children; that qualified her as a *hausfrau,* not an undercover agent.

She'd considered not going at all, imagining herself telling Waldemar she couldn't do it. How would he react? That was the problem. She didn't know. It frightened her that she didn't know, and it frightened her even more to find out.

So here she was. On the train she'd taken out the slip of paper and held it tightly. There was nothing left to do but go inside. A bell jingled as she opened the store's front door.

The place appeared empty. As casually as her legs would allow, she strolled over to a display of women's shoes. She recognized the style, also the cheap material. She picked up a pair of brown walking shoes. The stitching was poor, probably one of the new girls at the factory.

"Looking for something comfortable?"

A middle-aged man with thinning hair raked across his scalp appeared from behind a curtain that separated the showroom from the stock. Above the curtain hung a sign: No Admittance, Employees Only. The man wore a short-sleeved white shirt with a brown-checked tie.

Lisette handed him the shoe and asked to see a pair one size smaller than the size she wore. The salesman took the shoe from her. He glanced at her feet but said nothing. Obviously he'd sold shoes long enough to know better than to challenge a woman when she gave him her shoe size.

He disappeared into the back. Lisette pretended to look at another shoe, doing her best not to look conspicuous. But there was nothing inconspicuous about the rate at which her heart was pounding. That was when she formulated a new plan—to buy a pair of shoes and get out of the store as fast as she could. Later she would think of something to tell Waldemar.

The salesman reappeared. Lisette took a seat, and it came as no surprise to either of them when the shoes didn't fit. She asked to try another size, her actual size. The salesman nodded as if to say he knew that this was the correct size all along when the telephone rang.

He excused himself and answered it.

For a person committed to the original plan, things couldn't have worked out better. The fact that the salesman had answered the phone himself was a good indication he was here working alone. The phone call was an excellent distraction, a tailor-made excuse for her to feign impatience and go exploring. But for a person who was committed to abandoning the original plan, the ringing of the telephone couldn't have come at a worse time.

Then things got worse still. The salesman turned his back on her, hunched over, and spoke low, indicating he would be on the telephone for a while.

"Rats," Lisette mumbled.

She got up and moved toward the back of the store. A cloth curtain separated her from the stock. She quickly shoved the curtain aside and stepped into the back room.

"I grew tired of waiting for you," she said, practicing her line. "I grew tired of waiting for you." She then thought of another card she could play if she had to. It was obvious the salesman was taking a personal call, something she could threaten to tell upper management, that is, if it came to that.

Lisette checked the four-digit numbers on the slip of paper Herr Gellert had given her. The stock on the front shelves was three digits. She worked her way farther back. She could still hear the salesman talking on the phone.

Three rows deeper into the stock room the numbers on the shoe boxes added another digit. She needed 2743. After coming to the end of the row, she saw she was still in the 26s. So she rounded the shelves to the next aisle. As she did, she pulled up short.

There was another worker in the middle of the aisle. He was bent over, stocking boxes on the bottom shelf. A baggy white shirt—too large for him—was cinched at the waist with a belt, also too large. He didn't appear to know she was standing behind him.

Lisette's instincts screamed at her to back away quietly and return to the showroom part of the store. But a voice in her mind stopped her. She guessed it to be the voice of Herr Gellert, telling her first to scan the numbers and then leave. She found herself unable to make a decision.

"Can I help you?"

Lisette froze. She forgot her lines. Her mind had but a single thought—run! Unfortunately, while her mind was working, her legs were not. Some spy she turned out to be.

On some level she was aware that the man had turned to stand and face her. Lisette's gaze was fixed on the floor, however, like a frightened child caught in a naughty act.

"Is this the size you're looking for?"

He reached for the shoe she held in her hand. But as he did, he didn't take the shoe. Instead, he reached past it and touched her hand.

A familiar touch. This wasn't the first time this hand had touched her. She knew this the instant it made contact. Lisette stared at the hand and the sight awoke in her a host of slumbering memories. But it couldn't be!

She looked up. She almost didn't recognize him; he was so thin, a ghost of his former self.

Chapter 10

Lisette burst through the door, breathless. Elyse and Tomcat were sitting on the couch. Elyse removed her hand from Tomcat's knee and placed it in her lap. Tomcat turned toward the sound of the door opening, one bare foot covering the other. As it turned out, their embarrassment went unnoticed.

"Is your mother here?" Lisette asked between gasps.

"In the kitchen. Is something wrong?"

Lisette fought to catch her breath. She could only imagine how frightening her sudden, disheveled appearance looked. Herr Puttkamer was probably beside himself with curiosity.

Mady appeared from the kitchen, wiping her hands on a dish towel. "What's the commotion?"

Lisette fell back against the door, still recovering but also not knowing where to start.

"Dear? Is something wrong?" Mady asked, worried now. "The shoe store! Something happened, didn't it? You never should have gone."

"You got caught!" Elyse cried. "You got caught, didn't you?"

Lisette knew what she wanted to say; she just didn't have the breath to say it. Or the control. For just when she thought she could talk again, her emotions welled up and choked the words.

"Over here, dear," Mady said.

Elyse and Tomcat relinquished the couch.

Lisette was weeping now.

Mady started saying unkind things about a man who would send a woman to do his dirty work for him.

Lisette shook her head. She held up a hand. "I saw him!" she gasped, then was overtaken by another wave of sobs.

"Saw who?" Mady asked.

They waited for Lisette to answer, the three of them standing over her. Mady and Elyse exchanged pained sympathetic glances. Tomcat put his hand on Lisette's shoulder.

"Kon . . . Konrad," Lisette managed to say.

"Konrad!" Mady repeated in disbelief.

"Are you sure?" Elyse said.

"Where did you see him?" Mady asked. "On the street? On the train? How far away were you? Are you sure it was him, or was it just—"

"He touched me," Lisette said.

After that, it was all tears, as though those three words alone were holding the dam in place. Lisette went back to weeping and couldn't stop. Mady sat down beside her on the sofa. Elyse ran for tissues. Tomcat stood by helplessly.

"Don't rush it, dear," Mady said. "When you're ready."

It took a while, but finally Lisette said, "It was him."

"Where?" Elyse asked.

"Are you sure it was him?" Mady said.

"Yes. We talked," Lisette said. "At the shoe store. He works there."

"Oh, my dear," Mady said, holding her tighter.

Lisette went through one tissue, then another.

"Where has he been all these years?" Elyse asked. "Has he been looking for you?"

Lisette looked up and said, "He's been living in Berlin for seven years!"

Supper was a subdued meal of vegetable soup, bread, and jam. Lisette was feeling better, though she was drained, the way a person gets after being out in the sun too long.

She told them that her conversation with Konrad had been brief. No sooner had she recognized him when the other worker got off the phone.

"Finding me in the back room, he shouted, 'Didn't you see the sign over the door?' "

She said he yelled at Konrad for not enforcing the rules of the store. Konrad showed no emotion but instead seemed to absorb the man's anger. He made no effort to defend or explain himself. The worker told him to get back to work and he did.

"Konrad turned around, got down on his knees, and continued stacking shoe boxes like I wasn't there," Lisette said.

"Did he tell you where he was living?" Mady asked.

"The salesman wouldn't have let him even if he'd tried. He was too busy shoving me out of the back room."

"Did Konrad at least seem glad to see you?" asked Elyse.

Lisette began to weep again, softly. "I almost didn't recognize him. He's so thin. His eyes were hollow. Lifeless."

All evening Tomcat remained strangely quiet.

Sunday, August 20, 1961

It was Lisette who discovered that Tomcat had left them. She was usually the first one up in the morning, and this morning was no exception. She awoke with a headache, residue from the previous day's emotions. As she reached for her housecoat, her first thought was that the temperature was cooler. She hoped that the heat wave had finally played itself out.

She went into the kitchen and put a flame under the teakettle, then checked the refrigerator to see if there was enough cheese for everyone for breakfast. With a young man in the house, food disappeared quickly.

Stepping lightly, she peeked into the living room to see if he was awake. The sofa had been vacated, the sheets and blanket folded and stacked neatly. Lisette assumed he'd stepped out to use the common facilities in the hallway so busied herself with making tea while awaiting his return. Mady then appeared, calling over her shoulder to Elyse, telling her it was time to get dressed for church.

Still no Tomcat, so Lisette went to check on him. Adjusting her housecoat, she stepped into the hall and smelled cigarette smoke.

Herr Puttkamer was hacking away behind the door to his flat. She went to the door of the men's facility and knocked.

"Tomcat? Are you in there?"

From the other side of the door came a phlegmy throat clearing, followed by a man's voice. "I'm the only one in here, lady."

The voice didn't belong to Tomcat.

Lisette felt a prickling of concern. As the day progressed, it would grow.

She walked to the end of the hall. "Herr Puttkamer, have you seen the young man who's been staying with us?"

No response. Maybe Herr Puttkamer wasn't home. A nasty convulsive cough told her otherwise. Everyone knew Herr Puttkamer lived with his eye glued to the peephole. He alone thought he was unobtrusive.

"Herr Puttkamer?"

"No one's come out your door," Herr Puttkamer said. A reluctant admission.

"How long have you been up, if you don't mind my asking?"

"I do mind. None of your business."

"Thank you, Herr Puttkamer," Lisette said.

She walked to her front door.

"Since four o'clock," Puttkamer yelled.

"Thank you, Herr Puttkamer."

Elyse was upset over Tomcat's disappearance. She wanted to go looking for him right then, but her mother said there was probably a perfectly normal explanation and that they should get ready for church. Tomcat could take care of himself and would probably be waiting for them on the doorstep when they returned home from church.

They ate breakfast in silence.

It was a typical Sunday for a socialist country. The pews of the church were mostly empty. During the decade following the war, churches watched their attendance shrink steadily. There was a time when eighty percent of the German population attended church. Now it was more like thirty percent in East Germany. Baptisms, confirmations, and church weddings dropped as well. Had it not been for contributions and gifts coming from West German churches, the churches in East Germany probably wouldn't have survived.

Attending church services was a point of contention between

Lisette and her intended, Herr Gellert. He saw no need for churches. He said the state had replaced them. But while he didn't approve of Lisette's going to church, he didn't forbid her from going either. Lisette wondered if that would remain the case once they were married.

Following the service, Elyse danced around anxiously as Mady and Lisette stood and talked to women friends whom they saw only once a week. When they finally made it home, Tomcat was not waiting for them on the doorstep, nor was he waiting for them in the hallway, nor had he managed somehow to get back into the flat—all scenarios Elyse had imagined during the sermon.

Mady and Lisette were now less cavalier in their attitudes about Tomcat's mysterious disappearance. The three women skipped lunch, changed into more comfortable clothing, and walked the streets around the apartment complex in search of Tomcat.

They saw no sign of him.

"We should call K7," Elyse suggested.

"Why would he go back there?" Mady said. "That's where he ran away from."

"But maybe Herr What's-his-name will know where to look for him," Elyse said.

"They've probably been looking for him since he escaped," said Lisette. "Besides, didn't Tomcat say Herr Witzell knew he would come here?"

"Also, we have no phone number," Mady added. "I don't think they list phone numbers for those kinds of institutions."

"We've got to do something!" Elyse cried, giving voice to her feeling of exasperation. "Maybe somebody kidnapped him."

"Unlikely," Lisette said. "If they did, would they fold the bedding?"

Mady said, "The only places associated with him that we know of are K7 and here."

"And Konrad," Lisette said.

"Of course! He could have gone to Pankow!" Mady said.

Elyse started heading toward the door. "Let's go!"

"Do you really think he'd try to find Konrad?" Mady said.

"It's possible," Lisette replied, though it was clear from the look on her face that the thought of seeing Konrad again so soon was a painful prospect.

"You stay here," said Mady. "We'll go."

"No." Lisette got up despite the weight on her shoulders. "I'm going with you."

Chapter 11

Armed with determination, the three women stormed through the door of Schönner's Shoes in Pankow. Mady was the vanguard while Lisette brought up the rear. When the salesman spotted her, he was not pleased. He placed his hands on his hips, prepared to do battle.

Mady fired the opening salvo. "We're here to see Konrad Reichmann."

It wasn't a request. She was moving toward the curtained doorway as she spoke, the one that led to the restricted back room.

Herr Salesman positioned himself between the invading force and the back room curtain. "This is a shoe store, not a social club! You can talk to him after his shift."

"We're looking for a missing person," Elyse said, "and Konrad may know where he is."

The salesman was unmoved. "I fail to see how that is any concern of mine."

Mady stepped to one side to flank him. "We'll only be a minute."

He blocked her. "Get out of my store!"

During this confrontation, Lisette had walked quietly behind the counter to the phone. She picked it up and began dialing.

"What are you doing?" the salesman shouted. "Put that phone down!" He started toward her, then realized he was leaving the doorway unprotected and moved back. He glared at Lisette, who was using a piece of company equipment.

"She's calling Herr Gellert," Elyse said.

"That name means nothing to me," the salesman said. "But if you don't leave right now, I'll call Herr *Vopo*." He chuckled, apparently thinking himself witty for his personalization of the People's Police.

"Herr Gellert is a Party leader and supervisor at the Schönner factory," Mady said. "He suspects you of stealing from the company. Lisette here has a list of stock items to check. I imagine she's calling to report that you're being less than cooperative."

The salesman's face blanched. Suddenly the phone became a greater priority to him than the doorway. He abandoned his post to stop Lisette from making the call.

The doorway now unobstructed, Mady pushed aside the curtain and stepped into the stockroom. Elyse was right behind her. Two rows down they found Konrad with a box of shoes under each arm.

"Mady," he said, as though it had been days and not years since he'd last seen her.

Mady couldn't believe her eyes. Konrad was sickly thin. Lisette had warned her, but no amount of warning could have prepared her for this. He looked strikingly like Josef shortly before he died, a victim of Nazi experimental drugs that ate away at his insides, leaving him little more than skin and bones.

"Konrad." She acknowledged him with barely a whisper.

"You shouldn't be back here," he said. "They don't like it when customers come back here."

"We're looking for Tomcat," Elyse said. "Have you seen him?" She too was taken aback by his appearance.

Konrad cocked his head.

"This is Elyse," Mady said.

"Elyse?" Konrad said, staring at her. His eyes filled with tears. "Elyse," he said again.

"Konrad, we need your help," Mady said. "We think Tomcat may have come looking for you. Have you seen him?"

At the sound of the boy's name Konrad's eyes gave up several tears.

"Tomcat?"

"Yes. Have you seen him?" Elyse asked again.

Konrad had trouble answering. Finally with difficulty he managed to say, "No, I've not seen him."

The three women returned to their flat, deflated more by Konrad's appearance than by their disappointment over not finding Tomcat. Nevertheless, the immediate task was to locate him.

Elyse resurrected the idea of calling K7, but Mady was still resistant to this. Only as a last resort, she said. In spite of the kind things Tomcat had told them about the administrator, K7 was a government agency, and any contact with the government that could be avoided should be avoided.

However, with each passing hour the weight of anxiety became heavier, and Elyse took it upon herself to regularly announce the amount of time that had passed since Lisette discovered Tomcat was gone missing.

"He's been gone eight hours now."

"Ten hours and no word. Nothing."

Images of Tomcat haunted them individually. Tomcat lying helpless in a gutter. Tomcat sprawled out on the street, hit by a car. Tomcat trusting a stranger for a ride, only to be abducted or robbed or stabbed. None of them gave voice to their visions, even though they knew they shared them.

So it was no surprise that they all jumped when there was a knock at the door. Elyse rushed to answer it, with Mady and Lisette close behind her.

"Konrad!" Elyse said.

He stood in the doorway, shoulders slumped, eyes downcast, waiting for an invitation or instruction.

"Come in," Mady said, glancing at Lisette.

Konrad shuffled as he walked.

"Oh!" Lisette cried. "This is Sunday! What time is it?"

She hurried about, gathering her things.

"That's right," Elyse said. "Herr Gellert."

Lisette rushed past Konrad and out the door. "I have to go," she said.

"It's Sunday," Elyse said by way of explanation to Konrad. "Lisette always spends Sunday evenings with Herr Gellert."

Mady said, "Herr Gellert is—"

"I know who Herr Gellert is," Konrad said. "He and Lisette are getting married."

He spoke without emotion. Mady couldn't help but wonder how he knew these things, or how long he'd known them, or why he knew and hadn't said anything or called or sent a message or stopped by the flat before now since he obviously knew where they lived! She attempted to stop the growing avalanche of emotion with civility. "Come in. Have a seat," she said.

He took the seat Lisette had been sitting in. He sat on the edge with his back straight, hands on his knees, head bowed. He didn't look eager to tell them the reason for his call or to say anything, for that matter.

"I suppose your manager yelled at you after we left," Mady said.

"It doesn't matter," Konrad said without looking up. "I no longer work there."

"He released you?" Elyse said.

"I'll talk to Herr Gellert tomorrow," Mady said. "I'm certain he can—"

"I wasn't released," Konrad interrupted. He looked up at Mady. "I quit."

Mady was sitting on the end of the sofa closest to him. Elyse was beside her. "Well, I'm sure you had your reasons," Mady said, hoping he'd explain them to her. She found it difficult to look at him. There was no doubt it was Konrad. The voice. The mannerisms. His face and hair. All these were familiar. But at the moment it was hard for her to imagine that the man in her flat was once the cocky boy she'd known as a leader in the Hitler Youth organization or the broad-shouldered, proud SS soldier. "How did you find us?" she asked.

"I knew where you lived."

Mady wanted to ask for how long. It was a question that begged to be answered.

"Tell me about Tomcat," Konrad said. "When did you see him last?"

Elyse filled him in. She told him of Tomcat's sudden reappearance into their lives and equally sudden disappearance. Konrad asked questions. He seemed particularly impressed with Tomcat's ability to get around. She told him everything that had happened right up to the moment he knocked on their door.

"Does he still meow?" Konrad asked with a hint of a smile that looked like it was painful to make.

"No," Elyse said, smiling easily.

After a moment Konrad said, "I think I know where Tomcat is."

"You do?" Elyse said.

"He returned to K7."

"Doubtful," Mady said.

"No, I'm certain of it."

Mady wasn't convinced.

Konrad didn't seem concerned whether Mady was convinced or not. She had to coax him for an explanation.

"If Elyse's narrative is correct," Konrad said, "he told you where he'd be."

Mady shook her head. "Maybe you heard something we didn't."

"What does he call them? The Hadamar Six?"

Elyse nodded eagerly. She wanted to believe Konrad. "That's right. Viktor, Annie, Hermann—"

"And he wanted you to rescue them."

"Yes, but . . ." Mady said.

Konrad said, "He went back to K7 to be rescued."

Elyse grinned. Mady didn't. "I think you're reading too much into that," she said. "Besides, as I told him myself, it makes no sense for us to pull them out of there. They have food, clothing, a man who's looking out for them. And we don't have the resources, the space, not to mention the funds to house eight adults."

"Eight?" said Elyse.

"Six young people, counting you, plus Lisette and me," Mady said.

"Lisette is getting married. She'll be leaving."

"Eight, seven, what does it matter? We don't have the means to care for that many people. Anyway, I'm still not convinced that Tomcat returned to K7."

"There's no doubt about that," Konrad said. "That's where he's at. He left right after learning that Lisette found me at the store."

"The next morning!" Elyse said.

"He knew that once I discovered where they were, I'd come for them."

"Tomcat said you'd rescue them!" Elyse said excitedly.

"Tomcat was right," Konrad said.

Mady was shaking her head emphatically. "Isn't anybody listening? Do you have any idea how much it costs to feed and clothe and house that many? We can barely get by with just the three of us!"

"We won't have to do it for long," Konrad said.

"What do you mean?"

"Getting them out of K7 is only the first step. We're going to get them out of East Germany."

Mady stared at him openmouthed.

Konrad continued, "Human beings were never meant to live behind locked doors and barbed-wire fences, whether that be an institution, a walled city, or a concentration camp. God created mankind to live free. I'm going to set the Hadamar children free once and for all. It's what Pastor Schumacher would have wanted for them. It's what he'd do. I'm going to finish what Josef began."

Chapter 12

Friday, September 1, 1961

A white panel truck, its headlights turned off, coasted to a stop in the night shadow of a stately old tree. 10:22 P.M. The moon was of generous size, though not yet full, and K7 could be seen a hundred yards off from the driver's side window.

"It looks depressing," Elyse said from the passenger seat.

Floodlights bathed the gray block building with a yellowish glow. From behind mesh grating, streaked and dirty windows reflected artificial light. The compound, a dirt expanse that boasted few weeds, had been established with a chain link perimeter fence and a gate that was closed and padlocked. There was no sign, only a large *K7*, printed in black, fastened to the upper right corner of the building.

The building's obscurity was by design. For a people who prided themselves on being superior, the residents of K7 were seen as a blemish, and like all blemishes, state blemishes were covered up to keep them from becoming an embarrassment.

Lisette crawled from the back of the truck to see for herself. "Lord have mercy," she said.

From even farther back, in a dark corner of the windowless truck, came Konrad's voice. "They won't be in there much longer. What time is it?"

"We have six minutes," Mady said.

Tomcat had prepped them for this mission. Mady claimed it was unintentional, that he was just telling them about his life at K7. Konrad disagreed. He insisted Tomcat knew exactly what he was doing by providing them every detail they needed to plan an escape.

They knew exactly when the compound lights would be switched off—10:30 P.M. They knew that the Hadamar children were kept together at the end of the east wing. They even knew that Tomcat's room was second from the end on the left and that his bed was the farthest of three beds from the door. They knew security was light. Why wouldn't it be? Who would break *into* a mental institution? Hadamar was a fortress compared to K7, but then, Hadamar was a secret research facility, one with a definite military presence. The only secret at K7 was that a socialist population had the same physical and mental maladies as the rest of the world.

Tomcat had also given them a daily schedule. They knew the front gate was locked at 9:00 P.M. and that the guards watched television from 10:30 to 1:00 A.M., when the stations went off the air. A check of the TV program guide told them which shows were an hour long and which ones a half hour. Regardless, commercials came every quarter hour, and the orderlies ran to the bathroom during the commercials.

Based on Tomcat's information, Konrad had formulated a rescue plan. If all went like it should, they would be in and out of the building in ten minutes' time. They would enter the building at 10:58 P.M. and have five minutes to locate Tomcat and the others. Another five minutes and Mady would be driving a truckload of Hadamar survivors down the road leading away from the K7 facility.

Penetration of the building would occur through the east wing door when an orderly hauled the trash outside to the back of the building. Tomcat had mentioned that this was a detail normally requiring two orderlies—one to carry the trash, another to hold the door, which was self-locking. However, oftentimes an orderly would use a wedge of wood to prop the door open, thus reducing the task to a one-man operation and freeing up the other to continue watching television.

Konrad and Lisette would make entry through the propped-open door. The five-minute delay between entry and escape gave the trash man time to return; it also allowed for top-of-the-hour commercials to conclude and the next television show to begin. There were three TV stations. A check of the program guide indicated that the eleven o'clock choices were *Sky King, Fury,* and *Roy Rogers*. It being late-night television, all of them were reruns of popular 1950s episodes.

10:30 P.M. The compound lights went out.

"Let's go," Konrad said.

He opened the back doors of the truck, jumped out, and turned to assist Lisette, but she climbed out on her own. Konrad grabbed a canvas bag stuffed with goodies and made his way toward the fence. Lisette followed. As they passed the front of the truck, Konrad heard the words, "God be with you." It was Elyse. So much like her father, Konrad thought.

At the fence Konrad crouched low, unzipped the canvas bag, and produced a pair of heavy-duty wire cutters, large enough to snap open a good-sized lock. They made short work of the chain link fence. Lisette stood at a distance and watched him. He hissed and motioned her to get down.

Tossing the wire cutters back into the bag, Konrad took out a revolver and tucked it into his waistband.

"A gun? You brought a gun?" Lisette said.

"An equalizer."

"Who do you think you're going to shoot? What if one of the kids gets hit?"

Konrad sighed. "It's not loaded, okay?"

"Then why bring it?"

"Just trust me. Let's go." He peeled back the fence, holding it for Lisette to cross under. Lisette didn't move.

"I'm not going in there if you take that gun," she said. "What if one of the orderlies sees it and starts shooting at us?"

"Orderlies don't carry guns!" Konrad said in a loud whisper.

Lisette crossed her arms.

Konrad sighed and said, "There will be three, maybe four orderlies. Most of these guys are built like tanks. They have huge upper bodies to lift bedridden patients. In case you haven't noticed, I'm not exactly in the best physical shape. Should something go wrong and we have to face a number of them, we wouldn't stand a chance." He pulled the gun out. "This will hold them off, not hurt them." He removed the clip. "See? I told you—it's empty. Any questions?"

Lisette lowered her arms. "Was it so hard to explain that to me?"

Konrad peeled back the fence for a second time. Lisette ducked through.

"Why didn't you explain that to me on the ride over here?" she asked. "We had plenty of time. But then, you're not big on communication, are you? If the last seven years are any indication."

Konrad gritted his teeth and followed her under the fence, leaving the canvas bag outside the perimeter. He'd been on hundreds of missions but never with a partner who was so chatty.

The night was warm and humid. They followed the fence to the closest corner of the building. Konrad checked his directions. He saw the east-wing door, the one Tomcat said was used to take out the trash.

He motioned Lisette to follow him. She did so with ease. While his step was no longer a shuffle like it was in the shoe store, to call it spry or even average for his age would be a lie. They took up a position just around the corner from the door.

"We made good time," Konrad said, his breathing labored. "We have about twenty minutes before someone comes out with the trash."

"Any other surprises you're keeping from me?" Lisette wanted to know. "We have the time. Tell me, are you married? Do you have children?"

Konrad shushed her.

For twenty minutes they sat next to each other, leaning against the rough brick wall in painful silence.

10:58 came and went. No trash-carrying orderly appeared. Then 11:00 . . . 11:03 . . . The television programs had started by now.

"Maybe they don't take the trash out on Friday nights," Lisette said.

11:05.

"We could come back tomorrow. Maybe they take it out on Saturdays," she said.

Konrad remained stone still, his attention focused on the east-wing door. This was strange—according to the women, Tomcat had emphasized that Herr Witzell had every aspect of the operation of K7 on a very strict schedule. Tomorrow was unacceptable. The fence had been cut. If they left now and someone discovered the hole in the fence, the element of surprise would be compromised. But to complete their mission tonight, someone had to come out that door.

11:10.

"Maybe they changed routines," said Lisette. "Maybe the morning shift takes out the trash now."

11:14.

She jumped when the side door flew open. Konrad peeked around the corner. A man wearing white stooped down and shoved a wooden wedge under the door to keep it open. He ducked back inside and reappeared almost instantaneously, lugging a large trash can with both hands. He scurried down the three concrete steps and went sprinting to the back of the building. Apparently he was trying to squeeze the chore into the time it took the network to air its commercials.

There wasn't time to say anything. Konrad grabbed Lisette's hand and pulled her around the corner, up the stairs, and into the hallway. Outside, he could hear the clanging of trash can lids.

They had seconds to disappear before the orderly would vault up the steps, grab the wooden wedge, and run right into them. The hall was lined with doors. Tomcat's room was second from the end, but from the sound of the approaching footsteps they didn't have time to get to the second door. Konrad reached for the first door, hoping it wasn't locked.

The doorknob turned and the door swung open. Konrad pulled Lisette inside and closed the door behind them just as a thump sounded on the landing. The creak of the door followed. It closed. The orderly's feet pounded down the hallway.

Konrad's eyes had yet to adjust to the absence of light in the room. As they did, he saw three beds. There was a rustle of covers as a little girl sat up in the middle bed. Suddenly he got worried. Would the child scream?

Lisette stepped toward the girl. "Do you have to go to the bathroom?" she asked.

"No," a tiny voice replied.

"Then lie down and go back to sleep."

She spoke with motherly authority. It did the trick. Without so much as a murmur, the little figure plopped back down against her pillow.

"Good girl," Lisette said. "We'll check on you again in a little while."

She opened the door and they stepped into the corridor.

"You're good," Konrad said.

"Years of practice."

The corridor was empty. Male voices could be heard halfway down the corridor, intermixed with the sounds of *Sky King* coming from the TV. Somewhere in the distance Konrad could swear he heard Frank Sinatra singing.

They stepped silently to the second door, behind which they expected to find Tomcat. Konrad placed his hand on the knob, then looked back at Lisette. For an instant he was struck by doubt. What if he was wrong? What if Tomcat hadn't returned to K7? How would he break the news to Elyse?

Opening the door, he stepped inside with Lisette close on his heels. Tomcat had said the third bed was his. Konrad and Lisette made their way quietly the length of the room. A figure in pajamas lay sleeping in the bed, one of healthy size, and male. The bedclothes were crumpled up at the foot of the bed. Not until they were next to the bed did Konrad see it was indeed Tomcat.

He let out a sigh.

"Let me," Lisette said. She touched his shoulder.

Tomcat stirred. He opened his eyes and smiled.

"Lisette," he said.

"How does he know?" Konrad whispered.

"And Konrad!" Tomcat sat up with a grin. "I knew you'd come!"

The lights switched on.

A round figure smoking a cigar stood in the doorway.

"So did I," the man said.

"Something's gone wrong," Elyse said. She sat forward in her seat to get a better look around her mother. They'd seen no movement in the K7 facility since the orderly leaped the stairs and shut the door.

"Give them time," Mady replied. She drummed the steering wheel with her fingers. "They got in late."

"But they know where everyone is! They should be out by now."

"It's not time to panic. If something had gone wrong, there would be lights and sirens and such."

"That's what happens in the movies, Mother."

Mady turned to her, a serious look on her face. "If something does go wrong, I want you to get out of the truck and run."

"What?"

"You heard me."

"And go where?"

"Make your way back to the flat."

"And do what, exactly?"

"Wait for us."

"Mother, that's ridiculous."

"At least you'll be safe."

"Alone too—and it wouldn't be safe there for very long."

Mady thought about this. "You could go to Herr Gellert's," she said.

Elyse's eyes grew wide. "Herr Gellert? I'd live by myself before I went to . . . No, I know where to go. I'd get word to Herr Parker. I could stay with him."

"Out of the question! Park lives in America."

Elyse wasn't serious. She just wanted to get back at her mother for suggesting she could live with Herr Gellert, and she knew that mentioning Herr Parker's name would do it. And yet for some reason the idea stayed wedged in her mind.

At that moment the lights in the compound clicked on.

"Is it time to panic now?" Elyse said.

The office in which Lisette and Konrad found themselves was thick with cigar smoke. Either Herr Witzell had been here for hours waiting for them or he belonged to a cigar smoker's club and they'd just held a meeting in this room.

When he'd caught them in Tomcat's dorm room, he brought plenty of muscle with him. Five big orderlies backed him up.

Konrad took out his gun.

"Everyone calm down," Witzell said. He was speaking to the orderlies, not to Konrad. "He's not going to shoot anybody."

"Don't count on it," said Konrad. "You're going to step back, and we're going to take five childr—" he still thought of them as children—"five inmates with us. Our choice. Nobody gets hurt."

Witzell just stood there and grinned at him, which didn't sit well with Konrad.

"You think I'm kidding?"

"Frankly, yes." He then began walking toward Konrad, his hand outstretched. "You know you're not going to use that gun. It's not even loaded, is it? Hand it over, Konrad."

Lisette gasped.

Konrad's eyes darted from person to person. Soon Witzell was upon him.

Konrad's bluff had been called, and he had little recourse but to hand over the gun. Witzell ordered that Konrad and Lisette be escorted to his office, saying that he'd be there in a few minutes. When they left the room, Witzell was talking to Tomcat.

Now in Witzell's office an orderly stood inside the door glaring at them. There was little they could do. Even if they were somehow able to overpower the white shirt with the bulging muscles posted at the door, two more were probably waiting for them outside.

Konrad leaned closer to Lisette and said, "Let's hope Mady figured out what's happened and drove away."

"No talking!" the orderly barked.

"I didn't hear any instructions forbidding us to talk," Lisette said to the orderly. "Were you really given those instructions, or do you just like to make up rules as you go along?"

The oddest look came over the orderly's face. He opened his mouth to speak but said nothing.

Then the door opened and Witzell walked in. "They weren't going to walk them out of here," he said to two orderlies behind him. "There's a vehicle nearby. Find it, and bring whoever is in it to me. Go."

The orderlies turned to carry out their orders.

"Herr Witzell," Lisette said. "Let me get them."

Her offer threw Witzell off balance.

"Lisette!" Konrad said. "What are you doing?"

Ignoring Konrad, she said to Witzell, "If you send your goons out there, you'll only scare them away. Let me go. I'll bring them in."

At first Konrad couldn't figure out what she was up to. And then her plan dawned on him. It was risky, but still it might work. She was going to warn Mady, possibly even try to escape herself. What was the worst that could happen? They'd catch her and bring her back. Konrad wondered why he hadn't thought of the idea.

Witzell narrowed his eyes as he studied her. Oddly enough, he smiled, and there was a glint in his eyes.

"Fine. Do it," he said.

Without so much as a glance Konrad's way, Lisette stood and walked out of the room.

After she was gone, Witzell said to Konrad, "Would you like to listen to a little Sinatra while we wait?"

"Look!" Elyse shouted.

She pointed to the side door, the one through which Konrad and Lisette had entered the building.

Mady reached for the ignition switch without taking her eyes off the door.

Two men appeared. Both in white. Both muscular. They came out inspecting the perimeter fence and beyond.

"This isn't good," Mady said.

Lisette emerged next.

"Oh no, they've got Lisette!" Elyse said.

"Run!" Mady said. "Get out and run!"

"Mother, I'm not going to leave you."

"Run!"

"No!"

"Elyse . . ."

"Look! Lisette's waving."

Elyse was right. Lisette was waving. Not only waving but motioning for them to come to her.

"You don't think they've brainwashed her . . ." Elyse said.

Mady scoffed. "She's only been in there thirty minutes!"

Now Lisette was calling.

"What do we do?" Elyse said.

Mady removed the keys from the ignition and opened the door. "We stick together," she said. "We've always stuck together, and no matter what happens, we'll stick together now."

"But you wanted me to run."

"I panicked. It was the mother in me."

"So we stick together?"

"We stick together."

Witzell and Konrad were sitting in silence when they walked in. Konrad didn't care much for Sinatra.

Lisette entered first, then Elyse, then Mady.

Only Mady didn't get far inside the door. She stopped moving the moment she laid eyes on Witzell.

Lisette provided the introductions. "Elyse, I'd like you to meet your grandfather."

Chapter 13

Matthew "Park" Parker strolled down Bruin Walk with briefcase in hand. The descending Southern California sun felt particularly good after being cooped up with a roomful of pompous university professors for nearly two hours.

The worst part of being a professor was having to associate with other professors. He'd never known such a petty, disagreeable bunch. The meetings prior to the start of a new semester were unbearable. As he did every year, Emory Clarkson complained about his room assignments. Grey bemoaned the intellectual level of this year's incoming freshmen. Adele Ramsey tried to pawn off her sponsorship of the Young Philosophers' Club. There were no takers. And Adrian Lindsey bored them with tenure lists, medical plans, and updates on retirement packages, none of it encouraging.

Between reports on the trash problem on campus, the debate about dress code and hair length, and the scheduled arrival of an accreditation review team, about the only bright moment of the afternoon was when the Bruin cheerleaders burst into the room to rally the faculty for the upcoming football season.

The Blue and Gold had not fared well in 1960. While their record on the gridiron was a respectable 7-2-1, they failed to earn an invitation to a bowl game. Park had attended only one game last year, the one versus North Carolina State. It had been billed as an offensive shootout between two quarterbacks who were bound for the pros: Billy Kilmer for UCLA and Roman Gabriel for NC State. And while it failed to live up to its billing, UCLA won 7-0, resulting in a leap up the national standings. It appeared as though the team was on the verge of turning the season into something memorable, but two weeks later they suffered a crushing loss to crosstown rival USC and the bottom fell out of the Bruins' hopes for a Rose Bowl berth, or any post-season play for that matter. Now it looked like the 1961 season was going to be much better than last year.

With the faculty building behind him, Park headed across campus. He had parked his '56 Plymouth Belvedere—two-tone aqua and white, with fins and push-button automatic transmission—in a parking lot next to the tennis courts. This particular morning he tossed his tennis racket into the trunk in hopes of picking up a match before dinner. His chances were slim. This being the start of Labor Day weekend, the campus was deserted.

No matter. It was enough just to be outside. Although a hot holiday weekend had been forecasted, today was picture-perfect. He walked into an ocean breeze as the afternoon shadows were beginning to stretch.

"Professor Parker!"

Park had just entered Bruin Plaza. He turned to see who was calling his name and then wished he hadn't.

"Professor!"

A lanky young man loped toward him. Park continued walking. The student fell in step beside him. "Professor," he said. Then in a hushed voice, "Comrade."

"What are you doing here, Ferrell? Everyone else has left for the holiday."

"I was waiting for you."

My lucky day, Park thought.

Whenever Park saw Ferrell Welch, he thought of grease. The UCLA senior never washed his hair. Black and shiny, it fell straight to his collar, then flipped up. His beard was splotchy, his clothes always wrinkled and dirty. His personality and ethics were slippery, and he spoke in a smooth, snake oil salesman kind of way. A pair of gold wire-rimmed glasses completed the ensemble of this walking three-day-old French fry.

"You were there, man!"

"Where?"

"Berlin, man! You were there when the Wall went up!"

"Yeah, guess I was."

"The Party's having a meeting on the nineteenth," Ferrell said. "I want you to give us a rundown of what you saw. That, and your tour of the factory."

Park stopped and stared at him.

Ferrell grinned at him—the grin of a weasel.

"You know about that?" Park said.

"Didn't anyone tell you?" Ferrell replied. "I was appointed campus chairman. I'm lining up programs for the year."

A blond co-ed ran up behind Ferrell. "There you are!" she squealed. She hooked Ferrell's arm.

"This is Weena," Ferrell said. "She's a freshman, and I recruited her. Well, Professor? How about it? The nineteenth good for you?"

"Let me think for a moment," Park said, "new fall schedule and all." He was really trying to think of a good enough excuse to put Ferrell off.

"Ferrell, sweetie," Weena cooed, "the nineteenth is . . ." She cupped his ear and whispered.

"I know," Ferrell said. "It's all right. Professor Parker is one of us."

Weena's eyes lit up. "You're a Communist too?"

Park threw his briefcase onto the front seat of his car and climbed in after it. The tennis courts were empty, except for a skinny kid and his girlfriend, who couldn't keep the ball in the court. Just as well—he wasn't in the mood for tennis anymore.

Releasing the parking brake, he punched *D* for drive, eased from the curb, and headed south on Veteran Avenue. He needed to clear his head. Maybe he'd drive down to San Diego for the weekend.

He made a mental note to enter the nineteenth on his appointment calendar before he forgot it. Ferrell Welch would never believe him if he said the meeting had slipped his mind.

He had to be cautious. He wasn't afraid of Ferrell, which was probably a mistake because it was the slippery ones who were most dangerous. Actually it was the whole Communist infrastructure that was frightening. The right hand always knew what the left hand was doing. Always.

They knew about Lisette and Elyse.

In itself, that came as no surprise. Anybody who was a member of the Communist Party doing the things he was doing, who wasn't aware he was under constant surveillance, was a fool. It was how the underbelly types used that information—that was what infuriated him.

Park had taken too long coming up with an excuse. Ferrell got suspicious.

Ferrell goosed his thought process by saying, "How was your meal at Café Lorenz? I hear their pastries are to die for. I also hear that you enjoyed the company of a couple of ladies at your table."

Someone had briefed Ferrell for reasons Park couldn't fathom. Ferrell knew that after watching the girls cross the border, Park had entered East Germany himself and that afterward he'd been given a tour of the Warnow-Werft shipyard factory. But what irritated Park most was the smirky way Ferrell disclosed the information. Like so many others in the Party, his preferred method of persuasion was blackmail.

"The trip to East Berlin, the tour, all a matter of record," Park said. "Just doing my job for the Party. As for the girls at the Café Lorenz, they're none of your business, so you can just shut up about them!"

"Golly! That wasn't very nice, Professor," Weena said.

Park regretted the outburst. It wasn't smart to humiliate little weasels in front of their girlfriends. Little weasels grew up to be big weasels.

Park was convinced that it was people like Ferrell Welch who would doom the Communist Party. What was it about socialism that seemed to breed his type? Or at least attract them.

Ferrell Welch was no mystery to Park. He'd been given his own briefing about the boy. Ferrell was a blue blood of sorts, recruited by the legendary Walter Thaelmann. A German physicist, Thaelmann escaped the FBI's net following a dramatic midair explosion of an airliner over Nebraska in 1954. With meticulous care and using modern scientific methods, the FBI examined hundreds of pieces of the plane's debris and what had been recovered of its cargo and the personal effects of passengers. They found evidence of an explosion, that the explosion had occurred in the luggage hold, as well as remnants of the suitcase in which the bomb had been placed. They then investigated the backgrounds of all forty-four victims, established a link to the bomber, and arrested him. He later confessed to the deed, and both the FBI and the state took their bows for a job well done. Only they never established the source of the explosives. That source, and the mastermind behind the plot, was Walter Thaelmann.

After the bombing, Thaelmann moved to Glendale, California, where he moved next door to a television repairman named Welch, who had a wife, Audra, and three sons, the youngest by the name of Ferrell. In his senior year at Glendale High, Ferrell took a blue ribbon in the science fair, something to do with plastics and electrical conductivity. Thaelmann introduced himself, befriended the boy, talked science—and Marx and Lenin and Hegel—with him. Ferrell always had something of a smart-alecky rebel streak in him and so took to Communism without hesitating.

At UCLA Ferrell Welch's grades floundered. He became frustrated, then angry, and needed to find something he could do that would make him feel good about himself, like he belonged somewhere. Communism always had a place for his kind.

Ferrell's claim to fame was that he saw Nikita Khrushchev in 1958 when the premier toured Los Angeles. To hear Ferrell tell it, Khrushchev came to the West Coast to see him.

But while Ferrell Welch may imagine himself someday doing what William Z. Foster and Earl Browder could not do—become the first Communist Party president of the United States—in reality he was nothing but a guppy in the ocean of Communism, and one day a real socialist shark with huge teeth would surely swallow him up.

Meanwhile, when it came to Ferrell, Park knew he had to put his personal feelings aside. Out of duty he would do his part for the Party. He'd speak at the meeting on the nineteenth. He would narrate his impressions of August 13, the day the Wall went up. He would portray it as a heroic stand by Premier Khrushchev to defeat the fascist intent of a bumbling, youthful President Kennedy. He would predict that now that East Germany was closed off to the forces of evil which sought to destroy her, the state had a chance to prosper like never before. He would tell them that in East Germany the world would witness the glory of socialism.

"Progress through work builds socialism," Park muttered. "Workers of the world, unite."

Chapter 14

The last time any of them had seen Reverend Wilhelm Olbricht, he was hijacking the truck they were using to rescue the Hadamar children following a standoff on a stone bridge. None of them had heard from him again.

That was twenty-one years ago. Elyse was an infant at the time, Konrad young and cocky, the poster boy of Nazi Youth. Mady had just discovered how much she loved her husband. Josef was still alive; however, the experimental drugs were circulating in his system and before long would bring about his death.

It was the first time Mady stood up to her father, choosing Josef over him.

"I suppose you're wondering what I'm doing here," Witzell said. Now that they knew his identity, he sounded very much like Reverend Olbricht.

Konrad and Lisette occupied the only two chairs in the room, other than the one behind the desk. Elyse stood with her back to the wall a few feet inside the doorway. Mady leaned against the closed door, her arms folded. There were no orderlies in the room. Witzell had dismissed them, told those who were not working the usual graveyard shift to go home.

Witzell's eyes kept gravitating to Elyse. They were a grandfather's eyes when he looked at her. And she stared back at him. It wasn't every day one's grandfather climbed out of his grave to have a chat.

He reached for her with cupped hands.

She backed away, closer to her mother.

Witzell pulled back. He took no offense. If anything, his face registered understanding. "Your hearing," he said. "Which ear can you hear out of?"

Elyse raised a hand and lightly touched her left ear.

"And the other ear. Any hearing at all?"

Elyse shook her head.

"But you've learned to read lips," he said.

"She's had no formal training at it," Mady snapped. "Are you going to tell us what's going on?"

By the way Witzell looked at Mady, it was clear he could spend the next hour doing nothing but reacquainting himself with her face. For their sake, hers mostly, he resisted. He stepped back behind the desk and pulled the chair out.

"Would you like to sit down, Elyse?"

Elyse shook her head.

"Mady?"

"Just get on with it."

Witzell looked at the chair, then shoved it back under the desk. "Where to begin?" he said, flipping open the lid of his humidor and then closing it again without removing a cigar. "Where to begin?" he repeated. "Reducing two decades to a few sentences is not easy." He laughed nervously. "On the bridge. If you'll recall, I quoted the Party line about certain lives not worth the living. Then standing there on that bridge at Hadamar were my daughter and son-in-law, and Konrad"—he nodded at Konrad—"and Neff and Ernst . . ."

He broke off, paused for a second.

"By the way, have you kept in touch with Neff and Ernst?" he asked Konrad.

"Neff was killed," Konrad said.

Witzell sighed heavily. "So many of them."

"Ernst is in America," Lisette said. "He married a French woman."

"Doing something scientific, I suppose."

"Building rockets."

Witzell beamed. Wagging a finger between Konrad and Lisette, he said, "I suppose you two are married by now."

"Hardly," Lisette said.

"Long story," Konrad added.

"Let's just get on with it!" Mady said again.

"Of course, of course." It took Witzell a moment to find his mental place marker. When he did he continued, "I got nearly fifty kilometers north of Hadamar before they caught up with me. They were looking for the truck. Naturally they were surprised to find me driving it. They brought me to the Hadamar facility, interrogated me, then locked me up for nine days. It gave me time to sort through everything, and I came to some conclusions. The obvious being that Josef had been right all along and that I'd been living my life in fear. Trying to play it safe, thinking that by doing so I was protecting my family when, in reality, all I'd done was sold my soul to the devil. In short, I came to see that it was I who was living a life not worth living. And so, in that holding cell at the Hadamar facility, I came to the realization that Wilhelm Olbricht had to die.

"I got on my knees before God and put Olbricht to death. Knowing what a weak man I am, I knew that if I went home and tried to pick up where I left off, the old Olbricht would sooner or later return. For the first time I understood the necessity of the Old Testament practice of taking a new name. You recall, don't you? At a turning point in his life, Abram became Abraham and his wife Sarai became Sarah."

"Jacob became Israel," Lisette said.

Witzell smiled. "Your pastor would be proud of you. So I took my first and last initials and reversed them. Wilhelm Olbricht, WO to OW. From that, I fashioned a new name. Otto, my grandfather's name, and Witzell, one of my seminary professors I greatly admired. While the Nazis captured Wilhelm Olbricht, they released Otto Witzell. Next, I went to Leipzig and joined the resistance league."

"You just abandoned Mother?" Mady said.

"Edda," Witzell said. He lowered his eyes. "She loved being the wife of a minister. It wasn't going to be easy for her to be the wife of an outlaw."

"So you just let her worry herself to death?"

"The plan was for me to establish myself in Leipzig. Get a house. Establish an identity. I thought if she could see the changes . . . she was never very good at conceptualizing things. Only I proved to be a lousy resistance fighter. I was captured within weeks and spent the remainder of the war years in Dachau. A political prisoner. By the time I tracked your mother to Cologne, she'd already passed on."

"I'm so sorry," Lisette said.

Konrad fidgeted in his chair, positioning and repositioning himself, trying to get comfortable. It was difficult for him to sit for any period of time. Some people took his fidgeting for lack of interest. It wasn't.

"Following the war," Witzell said, "I wanted to use my ministerial skills to help people adjust to the changes, particularly children. This being confession time, I guess now is as good as any time to tell you this."

He looked directly at Mady.

"On the Hadamar bridge you told me that I could spend the rest of my life trying to be like Josef and still never measure up to him. You were right. I've spent every day of my life since Dachau doing just that.

"So imagine my surprise when, working with the Berlin relief agencies to place war orphans, I came across a list of five children who had recently arrived, all disabled, and all sharing the same last name—Schumacher." His eyes teared. "It was as if God was giving me a second chance. A chance to put right my wrongs. What better way to honor Josef Schumacher than to reunite him with his children?

"Of course, I learned that Josef was dead, and I found no trace of any of you."

"We tried every means possible to find the children," Mady said flatly.

"I don't doubt you did, dear," Witzell said.

No further explanation was needed or, by the way Mady's jaw worked back and forth, wanted. Everyone in the room knew the chaos of postwar Berlin.

"About that same time, I was appointed to this post at K7, and I arranged to bring the children here. That was about fifteen years ago. At one point there was an effort to take them away from me. I never knew the source, only that pressure was brought to bear on certain individuals in the agency. However, I managed to call in a few favors and maintained custody of the children. I know they don't belong at a facility like this, but it was the only way I could keep them all together."

"Tomcat speaks highly of you," Lisette said.

Witzell smiled. "He's my boy," he said. "We listen to Sinatra music together."

"So that's what that is all about," Elyse said, more to herself than anyone else. When she saw everyone looking at her, she said, "He asked me if I liked Herr Sinatra's music."

"Do the children know who you are?" Mady asked.

"They know me only as Herr Witzell."

"Yet you were evidently waiting for us tonight," Konrad said.

"Yes," Witzell said. "Given the nature of our government, it's difficult to make inquiries without raising suspicion. So, while I've been searching for you all these years, I've had to do it quietly and patiently, and as funds would allow."

"Funds?" Mady said.

"Anonymous information has a price. About six months ago I purchased a list of three names, all of them M. Schumacher. It was a list of workers. One worked at a music conservatory, another at the Intershop in Alexanderplatz, and one at Schönner's shoe factory. In order to keep a low profile, I enrolled for piano lessons at the music conservatory. Imagine that! At my age, at the conservatory, they laughed me out of the building."

"You're not good at undercover work, are you?" Konrad said.

Witzell took this in the humor in which it was given. "I then managed to get my hands on some Western currency and went to the Intershop," he continued.

"You could have been arrested for having such currency and for going into the Intershop!" Elyse said.

Witzell shrugged. "I couldn't ask someone else to take that risk for me," he said. "But as you can surmise, it was the third name on the list that led me to you. I sat outside the factory at quitting time. After five days I spotted Lisette." He looked at Mady and added, "You and this beautiful vision of a granddaughter were right behind her."

"You followed us home," Mady said. "You stalked us like a Stasi agent."

If Witzell had plans to tell them that he used a retired Stasi agent to make contact with them, he jettisoned the idea now.

"What was I to do? March up to you and say, 'Hello, dear. What have you been up to?'"

"Instead, you put a blind boy in danger," Mady said.

"I had him followed," Witzell replied. He decided now wasn't the time to confess that they lost Tomcat for several hours.

"Wait, I'm not following," Lisette said. "Why Tomcat?"

"Yeah, why Tomcat?" Elyse echoed.

Witzell said, "Twice he'd escaped and went looking for you on his own. This time I let him overhear a conversation. That's how he got your address. Believe me when I tell you, if I thought it was dangerous to him, I never would have involved him."

"So why did you?" Mady asked.

"I was afraid." Witzell sank into his chair and leaned back. "I was afraid if I suddenly appeared on your doorstep, you'd slam the door in my face. Scott—Tomcat's legal name is Scott Schumacher, which has made the paper work much simpler. Tomcat was my emissary. I was hoping that if he told you that I, Witzell, was a decent sort, when you met Witzell and found out it was me, you might at least give me a chance."

Like a lawyer making his final argument to a jury, Wilhelm Olbricht, alias Otto Witzell, rested his case and awaited the verdict.

"Can we see the children?" Mady asked.

"Of course."

She turned and reached for the door handle.

"Can I ask you something first?" her father said.

Mady turned around, and in one motion her arms folded across her chest.

"What are your plans for the children?" he asked. "If you'd succeeded in taking them from K7, what were you going to do?"

"Get them out of East Germany," Konrad said.

It was Witzell's turn to be surprised. "Well, that's certainly a new wrinkle," he said. "I'm going to want to hear more."

It was a discussion that would have to wait. Now it was time for a reunion.

At Witzell's orders, the lights in the common room were turned on, causing something of a crisis among the night-shift staff, who grumbled their objections loud enough to be heard. Some objected to the hour. It was past midnight. Others objected to Witzell hosting a band of criminals. Weren't these the people who were caught breaking in? The loudest objections, however, came from the orderlies, whose TV watching had been interrupted.

Acting as host, Witzell led them to the common room. Lisette followed closest behind him, down the hallway, around a corner, a short distance, then one more corner. Having recognized him first as Olbricht, she'd had more time to adjust to his identity, or possibly she wanted to keep a few steps ahead of Konrad. Mady trailed at a good distance.

The room was more than adequate to hold all of them. White walls. Hospital-shiny green tiles on the floor. Overly bright lights. Wire mesh covered the windows, a reminder that this wasn't the rec room at some church or club.

They didn't have to stand around awkwardly for long. A grinning Tomcat was ushered into the room by an orderly.

"Everyone sound out so I know where you're at," he said happily.

In turn, each said something. Tomcat had his bearings instantly. He went straight to Elyse, took her by the hands, and whispered something in her ear. He didn't have to think which was the better ear for hearing.

Smiling, she nodded.

"Yes?" he asked.

"Yes," Elyse said.

"Herr Witzell?"

"Yes, Tomcat?"

"Would it be all right if Elyse and I woke the others up and brought them to the common room?"

"If there are no objections," Witzell said, looking to the others.

There were none.

Tomcat took Elyse by the hand and led her out the door and down the hallway.

"Every time I see him do something like that, it amazes me," Witzell said.

The next few minutes passed with Witzell stealing glances at Mady, and Mady ignoring him with concentrated effort.

The first of the Hadamar children to arrive could be heard coming down the corridor, which was uncharacteristic of her, but this was an unusual night. The door opened and Marlene appeared, flanked by Elyse and Tomcat.

"Fräulein Lisette! Frau Schumacher!" she screamed, her speech slurred more than usual from the excitement.

Lisette reached her first, giving her a fierce hug. Mady was next. Then Konrad.

Short of stature, Marlene had matured nicely, having filled out and become a woman now.

Tomcat and Elyse joined hands and raced out to deliver another late-night reunion.

A short time passed before they arrived with a limping but happy Hermann. His hair stuck up at several places on his head like brown sun flares.

"You could have at least given him time to comb his hair," Witzell said, laughing.

Next to arrive was Viktor. He was so happy, he cried. And when he hugged Lisette, he buried his face against her chest so hard she wondered if they'd ever be able to pry him off.

They woke Annie last. She arrived with a bit of swagger, probably in reaction to Tomcat tormenting her all the way down the corridor. He held her arm—the one with the shriveled hand—above the elbow, which made it look like he was the prison guard and she the inmate.

"And who didn't think I could do it? Bet you want to eat those words now, huh, Annie? Because I did it. I said I'd do it, and I did it!"

"Tomcat," Witzell said, "be a gentleman."

While the common room easily swallowed their little group, they managed to fill it with sound, so much so that a couple of sleepy residents appeared at the doorway wondering why they hadn't heard about the party.

Witzell stood off to one side and observed, the picture of male satisfaction. Konrad was in the middle of it all, though he was so overwhelmed at times he appeared frightened. Elyse was the center of attention with her having been the one left out all these years. Tomcat flitted between her and Konrad. Lisette and Mady sat next to each other in chairs against the wall, mostly watching, occasionally leaning in to each other to share an observation. Much of the time Lisette sat with the fingers of both hands covering her mouth. A half-dozen used tissues lay in her lap. The tears flowed freely that night. Mady shed her fair share and even laughed, more than she'd laughed in a long time. Never once did she look at her father. And though she seemed to be enjoying herself, there was a dark undercurrent of emotion just beneath the surface.

Memories of the past dominated the conversation.

"Remember when it was Marlene's turn to be Aaron, and Fräulein Lisette couldn't get her to stop crying long enough to tell us where we were going?" Tomcat said.

"And then someone said that if she kept up her crying, she'd cause a flood?" Elyse said.

"I said that," Viktor said, beaming.

"You did not," Annie argued. "Hermann said it."

"I said it!" Viktor argued.

"And someone else said, 'That's all right. Moses parted the waters once; he can do it again!' "

"Then I said that!" Viktor cried.

"You didn't say anything, Viktor," Annie snapped. "You were too busy grabbing on to Fräulein Lisette's leg because you were so scared."

"All of us started laughing then," Elyse said. "Even Marlene. She was laughing so hard, she couldn't talk."

"Remember the Christmas that Elyse and Annie fought over who was going to be the Virgin Mary?" Marlene said.

"Those bathrobes we wore as shepherds," Hermann said. "Where in the Bible does it say the shepherds wore bathrobes? Did they wear shower caps too?"

"I was a shepherd! I remember!" Viktor cried.

"You were not," Annie groused. "You were one of the sheep."

They all laughed. Even Viktor.

And so it went until nearly dawn. As the reunion wound down, the K7 residents returned to their rooms complaining that they weren't going to get any sleep now. Still acting as host, Witzell walked the four rescuers out to their rescue truck and stood there as they drove off. A casual observer never would have guessed a rescue attempt had occurred earlier.

When they reached the flat on Kellerstrasse, Konrad was offered the couch. He refused. While he didn't say it, he'd overdosed on socializing and needed to be alone. So he took the truck and drove home.

Elyse went to bed echoing the complaint of the K7 residents, that it was useless to think they'd get any sleep tonight. As Lisette and Mady lay under the covers in their own beds, as though it was a normal night, they each tried to make sense out of what had just happened and what would happen now.

Chapter 15

Sunday, September 3, 1961

Konrad watched with veiled amusement as the little Wartburg sedan sputtered up the hill. He'd always associated Reverend Olbricht with big automobiles, the kind with plenty of power and a deep rumbling sound. In fact, one of the joys of his life had been the unexpected treat of driving Olbricht's Essex Super Six on the day of the Hadamar rescue. Now, to see him laboriously climbing the hill in a little yellow Wartburg, which had all the power of two mice on a treadmill, Konrad found it hard not to laugh. He wished Neff were here to see it.

The car finally pulled to a stop and was enveloped by a cloud of dust as Witzell got out. "It belongs to the institution," he explained before Konrad had a chance to say anything.

With his ever-present cigar sticking out the side of his mouth, Witzell walked to the front of the cabin. Squinting against the afternoon sun, he looked it over.

"This is it?" he asked.

When Witzell learned the details of the original escape plan, he insisted on examining the proposed living quarters before proceeding any further.

Konrad stood on the front porch that stretched all the way around the cabin. Four six-foot-wide wooden steps separated him from the approaching Olbricht. Or Witzell, he corrected himself. It would take time for Konrad to see him as anything other than Reverend Olbricht.

The steps creaked as Witzell groaned his way up them. He held out his hand to Konrad. To shake, or did he need help? Konrad took it and never was quite sure which it was, because it turned out to be a little of both.

"Yep, yep," Witzell said, looking around. "Nice breeze here."

Konrad led him inside. The tour lasted ten minutes. Konrad showed him around both upstairs and downstairs. All the while, the only thing Witzell said was, "Yep, yep." Except in the room in which Konrad had been sleeping.

"No mattress?" Witzell said, pointing with his cigar at the blankets in the corner.

"I've tried," Konrad said. "Too soft."

"Yep, yep. Mind if we sit on the porch?"

Konrad secured two chairs, and the two men sat at an angle to each other, overlooking dense forest and the deeply rutted dirt road that led back down the mountain.

"Tomcat is the hero of K7," Witzell said.

"He's one of a kind, isn't he?"

"Takes a shine to you. They're calling you 'rad. Do you know what that's all about?"

"That's what the kids called me at Ramah Cabin. I believe it was Tomcat's first word."

Witzell relit his cigar, which had gone out. He offered one to Konrad.

"Thanks. No."

"Josef never cared much for cigars either. Guess there's no hope for the younger generation."

Konrad chuckled.

"I miss him something fierce," Witzell said. "Had always hoped I'd have a chance to make it up to him for what I did to him."

The breeze gusted and rolled three leaves in front of them.

"Some sins you just have to live with," Witzell said.

"You can make it up to Mady and Elyse."

"God willing."

Konrad didn't envy him. Getting back into Mady's good graces would be a difficult task.

"Rustic," Witzell said with a circular wave of his hand.

"Yeah."

"Looks like it's been decorated by a man who's spent too many years in a Russian gulag."

Konrad laughed. "That bad?"

"We can do better."

It felt strange to be sitting on the porch with Reverend Olbricht. He was the Reichmanns' pastor before Josef. Konrad remembered him being a thundering preacher, prone to stomping around and pounding the podium. Konrad's father had always liked Reverend Olbricht. Supported him openly. He hadn't felt the same for Josef, however. Konrad wondered if Olbricht knew his father was dead, that he'd been murdered by a renegade SS officer who was out for revenge against Konrad.

"What was it like in the gulag?" Witzell asked.

"Pretty much like Dachau, I suspect."

"It helps to talk about it."

Konrad didn't want to talk about it. He couldn't get over the fact that he was sitting here with Reverend Olbricht. It reminded him of how it felt to be a child sitting with the grown-ups. *If only Pastor Schumacher could see us now,* he thought. *Me and his father-in-law mentor sitting on a porch, jawin' away the afternoon.*

"You're scared, aren't you?" Witzell said.

Konrad didn't answer.

"Blankets for a bed in the corner of your room. This cabin, miles from anywhere. Back seven years without so much as a hello to Lisette."

"The cabin is for the children."

"And Lisette?"

From the cool of the shade, Konrad stared out into the bright sunlight. Witzell matched his gaze, puffing serenely on his cigar, not letting the matter drop. Konrad remembered talk of Olbricht resembling a bulldog, both in appearance and temperament. *Some things just don't change,* he thought.

Olbricht said, "With Mady, I wasn't so much afraid that she'd hate me. That was pretty much assured. It was the anguish I'd cause her by suddenly showing up in her life again. I've been dead to her all these years. She's made her peace with that. Letting her know I'm alive is an overture of sorts. Stepping into her life means she has to deal with my existence again. Only, it's not the same relationship. It can't be. We're both different people now. She's no longer a little girl. I'm not the same man she knew as her father. Will we even like each other? I don't know. However, I did know that I was about to stir things up, that which was settled and done with, and there was a side of me that urged me to leave things alone. In some ways she was better off not knowing I was alive."

"So why did you do it?"

"I keep telling myself it was for the Hadamar children. I won't be around forever. My health is failing. Someone needs to look after them." He took two puffs, then added, "But I think if I was honest with myself, I'd have to say that part of me did it for me. I finally got to the place where my desire to make amends with my daughter and granddaughter outweighed the discomfort I knew it would bring them. Selfish, wouldn't you say?"

But Konrad didn't say. He didn't say anything for a long time. But then, neither did Witzell. The bulldog was biding his time. It was Konrad who finally broke the silence.

"I'm not the same man Lisette fell in love with," he said.

"Yep, yep."

More silence.

"She's not the same girl I fell in love with."

"Yep."

Konrad stared at the porch planks. "I saw a man kissing her in front of the opera house. He's old. A Communist. Lisette's going to marry him."

"Is she now?"

"She'll be better off with him."

"Probably."

More staring at the planks. They were old, worn, dirty. Someone needed to strip them down to fresh wood and refinish them.

"I'm not the same man I used to be."

"You already said that."

"It's true."

"Didn't say it wasn't."

"I've changed."

"Being a prisoner of war will do that to a man."

"You don't know . . . I mean, you know—Dachau was no spring holiday for you."

Witzell chuckled. "No, no spring holiday."

"But these were the Russians. And I had this . . ." He pulled up his shirt-sleeve. The SS tattoo was still prominent on his arm. "It singled us out for special attention, if you know what I mean."

"Don't know that I do. Tell me about it."

Konrad stared at the old bulldog. All of a sudden Konrad was aching to talk about it. Yet at the same time he didn't want to talk about it. Better to keep some things locked away in the past, like old family secrets no one acknowledged. He was afraid he'd foul up the present with the past. He didn't want to open the door to the gulag for fear the filthy rotten stench of it—the murderous ways, the hate, the fear and desperation there—would spill into this world and spoil it as well. No, he couldn't do that to Lisette. That was why he'd kept silent all these years. Better to keep that door shut. Locked tight.

And yet . . .

The door was bulging. The hinges were creaking, threatening to give way. How much longer could he keep it closed?

Some days it was easy. Other days it was all he could do to keep everything from spilling out and messing everything up. And now here was Witzell, fiddling with the latch.

"He 'giveth songs in the night,'" Witzell said.

"Beg pardon?"

"The thought kept me living from one day to the next in Dachau. It's from the Psalms. 'Yet the Lord will command his lovingkindness in the day time, and in the night his song shall be with me.' It was worst at night, wasn't it? Hope is hard to come by in the dark. Time seems to stop. The grip of fear grows hideously strong. To fight back, I sang silently to myself. I remembered the great hymns. I was reminded of God's love, his strength, his provision. It was these songs in the night that helped me to survive."

Witzell's bulldog face grew somber with the memory. Konrad understood.

"After treating my chest wound, they took me to a field camp that held twelve thousand other soldiers," Konrad said. "There were no tents. For two months, as the war wound down, we lived in a swampy meadow, penned in by barbed wire. It was a weeding-out process. They left us there to see if we'd die."

Konrad could tell Witzell had done this before. He knew better than to ask questions at this point, or to comment. The old preacher sat back in his chair, worked his cigar, and stared off into the distance, nodding occasionally to indicate he was listening.

"I nearly died. Infection set in. Captured German doctors did their best to treat us, but they weren't given any medical supplies, so there wasn't much they could do. We were fed thin vegetable soup once a day, a stale biscuit every third day. After a while, there were few who could still stand on their feet. Hundreds died every day.

"After two months of lying there, we were surrounded by Russian soldiers and ordered to stand. They were shipping us out. It was a sorry sight. Many of us had to learn to walk all over again. The once proud Waffen SS was now a herd of broken, filthy, coughing, diseased, limping cattle. It's strange how your mind works at times like that. Here we were, staggering to our deaths for all we knew, and all I could think about was parading down Unter den Linden, columns of us in our Hitler Youth uniforms.

"They marched us to a relocation center just outside Stalingrad. Thousands more died along the way. They were the lucky ones, as it turned out. They loaded us onto cattle cars, closed the doors. Then we just sat there. Day after day we sat there, not moving. After five days of this, they opened the door and off-loaded us. For a week we stayed there under armed guard beside the tracks. They then loaded us into the cars again. This time we began moving down the tracks. They took us into the heart of Russia.

"Oransky number seventy-four. Gorky province—four hundred kilometers east of Moscow. We were laborers for Soviet reparations projects, postwar reconstruction—railroads, roads, canals, forestry, mining, agriculture, construction of houses and other buildings. As you would expect, conditions were inhuman, unhealthy, and deadly. You can't say they didn't warn us. No sooner had we exited the train when we stood before the commandant of the camp, who explained the terms under which we could live. He said, 'Make no mistake. We represent in ourselves organized terror. This must be understood very clearly.' The next morning he set out to prove it.

"To stimulate our enthusiasm for work—and to cull the camp population by killing off the weak—every morning when we were called to work detail, we were made to run outside the barracks and form a line. The last man to line up was declared a laggard, and he was shot.

"One day a railroad tie fell on my foot and broke a few toes. I never received any medical treatment, and it was all I could do to stand, let alone compete for a space in line. For a month Gren Laufer . . . a Pankow boy, as it turned out. He lived on Klaustaler Strasse."

"Over by Panke River," Witzell said.

"That's right. Gren was a Luftwaffe colonel during the war. We became close. Would reminisce about home. Anyway, for a month, Gren carried me to the line for morning roll call."

"I'm sure you would have done the same for him."

"I did." Konrad's voice turned ominous. "About a year later there was an accident. A bulldozer kicked up a metal reinforcing rod. It went through Gren's left calf. Didn't break the bone or anything, but infection set in. Not only was it next to impossible for him to walk, he was often delirious. One morning roll call he was out of his mind with fever. When I tried to help him up, he kept fighting me off. I managed to wrestle him out the door, but again he pushed me away. Everyone else was in line and here we were—wrestling on the ground, with me trying to force Gren into line, him screaming and pushing me away. The guards decided to make sport of us. They separated us. Then we were commanded to race for the last position in line.

"The signal was given. I made no attempt to run. Out of his mind, Gren turned on me, and then, when a guard grabbed him, he turned on the guard. When the guards saw there wasn't going to be a race, they ordered me into line. They would've shot me if I hadn't obeyed. I knew then I wouldn't be able to save Gren."

Witzell said, "They shot him."

Konrad's silence confirmed Witzell's statement.

"The guards knew Gren and I were friends. They thought it amusing to give me death detail with him in it. I had to dispose of the bodies of the men who died. They made us fix a wooden marker to the left leg of each of the dead with his number printed on it. Then we had to pull out any teeth that had gold fillings before the bodies were carted outside the camp for burial in a mass grave."

Witzell closed his eyes.

Konrad took a deep breath before continuing. "I have a recurring nightmare," he said. "I'm holding Gren. Cradling his head in my lap. My hand is gripping a pair of pliers."

Witzell wiped his eyes with the back of his hand.

They sat in silence for a while.

"Then—I think it was '52—we heard rumors that all prisoners would be released sometime within the next year. Some kind of general amnesty. Well, we'd heard rumors before. Not until they started shipping some of us out did we believe them. They didn't seem to be in any hurry about it. The SS officers were the last to be released. I was released in 1955.

"Thinking back on it, of all the cruel and inhuman things the Soviets did to me, the cruelest was setting me free."

Witzell looked at the end of his cigar, which was a stub now. He tossed it to the ground. He stood and stretched, stared off into the distance. "Give it time," he said.

Konrad nodded. "Yeah."

Witzell stomped his feet. To look at him, he'd found a line of ants and was determined to stomp them into oblivion. In reality there were no ants, only the feeling of ants in his legs. The stomping was an attempt to coax his blood back into circulation.

Konrad stood and did a stretching routine of his own. "So what do you think?" he asked, jerking a thumb at the cabin.

Witzell turned and gave the structure one final look. "We can do better."

With that, he waddled down the steps toward his car. Konrad stood at the top of the steps having no more idea about the status of the cabin than when Witzell first arrived.

The old preacher pulled open the driver's side door. He pointed to the other side. "Get in," he said.

Konrad descended the steps. He opened the passenger side door, still finding it humorous that Reverend Wilhelm Olbricht would be driving this rattletrap.

"Where are we going?"

"To do better," Witzell said.

Chapter 16

Monday, September 4, 1961

They met at Witzell's house. Had they met at the flat, Herr Puttkamer would have suspected them of plotting the overthrow of Communism. By the time the others arrived, Konrad was already there. Having spent Sunday evening with Witzell, he'd decided to stay over.

Otto Witzell was waiting for the women at the S-Bahn station when the train pulled in. From there, it was a three kilometer drive in his Wartburg to the outskirts of town. Mady had expected to find a two-room flat. Instead what she saw when she climbed out of the car was a sizable house.

"How many bedrooms?" Mady asked while looking up at the house.

"Five," Witzell replied.

"And you live here all by yourself?"

Elyse and Lisette exited the car from the back seat.

"Wow," Elyse said. "Look, Lisette. It's bigger than Herr Gellert's house!"

Lisette stared at the house and said nothing. She'd hardly said a word since getting off work, not during the walk home, or supper, or during the train ride.

"For seven years I shared it with Ulla," Witzell said.

"Ulla?" Mady asked.

"My second wife. She passed on two years ago." He watched Mady's reaction closely.

Her face turned to stone. "You had a second wife?" she said without looking at him.

"Mady, I didn't know where you were."

"Was she like Mother?"

Witzell calmly said, "Edda was more social; you know how your mother came alive around people. Ulla didn't mind being alone. It wasn't a hardship on her when I worked late. She occupied herself with puzzles. Jigsaws mostly, but also word puzzles."

Mady remembered how her mother's exuberance brought out the social side of her theologian husband. Sometimes she had to drag him out of his study when guests arrived. She'd walk him around the room initiating conversations. Mady always thought it was similar to taking a book from a shelf and blowing off the dust. Once her father opened up he could be quite entertaining. Ulla, apparently, left him on the shelf.

Mady hated the sound of the woman's name. Especially the way her father spoke it with tenderness. To Mady, Ulla would always be the other woman.

"This way, ladies," Witzell said cheerfully, ushering them up the stone walkway.

He deposited them in a tastefully furnished living room while he went to inform Konrad of their arrival.

Elyse flopped back comfortably in a stuffed chair. "This is nice," she said, taking it all in.

Lisette sat on the edge of her chair, her hands folded in her lap atop her purse.

Mady didn't sit down.

"As you know," Witzell said, returning, "yesterday I went to inspect Konrad's cabin."

"He concluded we could do better," Konrad said, following Witzell into the room.

"Better?" Mady said. "You must be mistaking us for people with money. I never would have agreed to this plan had there not been a house with suitable—"

Konrad cut her off. "This is better," he said. "This." He held up both hands and made a sweeping motion to indicate the house. "This is the new Ramah Cabin."

"You planned all along to move the children here," Lisette said.

"I wish you'd quit calling them *children,*" Elyse said. "We're not children anymore."

"Sorry, dear," said Lisette, reaching over and touching Elyse's hand.

"Was Ulla aware of your plans?" Mady asked.

"I kept no secrets from my wife."

"And was she going to cook and clean for the children?"

The question was a legitimate one. It was Mady's tone that made it belligerent.

"We're not children!" Elyse muttered under her breath.

"They've been taught living skills," Witzell said patiently. "However, at times they do require supervision. That was one of the reasons I hoped to find you. They can't stay at K7 forever."

"Why?" Mady challenged him. "They're safe there, aren't they? They have food. Shelter. Clothing."

"But they won't always have me," Witzell said. "I'm well past retirement age. A new administrator would split them up. They don't really belong at K7."

"I still don't see why you need us," Mady said. "As you said, they have living skills, and now this house. You've looked after them all these years. It sounds to me as if you have it all figured out."

Witzell looked at his hands. "Look at me. I'm an old man, and my health is beginning to fail."

It was a while before anyone spoke.

"We *do* want to help, Reverend Olbricht," Lisette said. "What can we do?"

Witzell didn't correct her for using his former name and occupation. It seemed fitting for her to use it. "Thank you, dear," he said. "You can help me with the Hadamar children."

"Of course we will," Lisette said.

"Don't make promises you can't keep," Konrad said.

The fact that his comment stung Lisette was obvious to everyone.

"Konrad Reichmann," she said with a tremor, "what would possess you to say something like that?"

"I don't know, but let me ask you this—what will Herr Gellert say when you tell him you have to take care of some disabled children? After the wedding, is he going to let you come over here and stay the night if needed?"

Lisette didn't answer. Possibly because she didn't have an answer. Herr Gellert knew nothing of all this. Yet that didn't stop Lisette from glaring at Konrad.

"We're not children!" Elyse insisted once again. "We don't need someone to stay the night with us."

"What makes you think you'll be staying here?" Mady said. "You have your own bed, at home with me."

Witzell stepped into the middle of their little circle. "Providing living space for the Hadamar chil—" he stopped and looked at his granddaughter—"for the former residents of Hadamar—"

"They call themselves the Hadamar Six," Elyse said.

"Six?"

"They include me."

"Ah! And so they should."

"You're not staying here, young lady," Mady insisted.

Witzell began again. "Providing living space for the Hadamar Six is only one of the obstacles we face."

"We still have to get them out of East Berlin," Konrad said.

"Before we try to crack that nut," said Witzell, "we first have to deal with government paper work and the Stasi."

"The Stasi?" Mady said.

Witzell's bushy gray eyebrows shot up. "Ever since I obtained a guardianship of sorts, I've known that my monthly reports have been passed on to state security offices."

"What is their interest in the children?" Mady said.

Elyse glared at her mother, who, she was almost sure, was calling them children just to make her angry.

Witzell said, "I don't know. There's no reason the Stasi should be interested in a mental institution. I don't know who is requesting the reports. All I know is that my reports are forwarded every month."

"They have their reasons, you can be certain of that," Konrad said.

"And then there are the reports themselves," Witzell said. "Had you been successful in snatching them the other night, their disappearance would have created all kinds of inquiries and investigations. As we all know, the socialist system keeps track of its citizens. Disappearances would not go uninvestigated. Had you been successful, you would have had all manner of government forces trying to track you down."

"We didn't take that into consideration," Lisette said.

Witzell let them chew on this for a while, then said, "But I believe I've come up with an answer, both to the Stasi problem and to the government record problem."

"Tell us," Lisette said.

"We know that as long as they are alive, there will be paper work kept on them. But what if they were to die?"

Witzell had given this much thought. He would tell the K7 staff that they were going to be transferred to other facilities. No one would question the announcement. They knew the inmates in question didn't belong at K7 in the first place.

Then, in intervals, Witzell would announce their departures to the staff. However, the official paper work would tell a different story altogether. His report to the government would indicate they'd died. He would file the appropriate death certificate. As long as he wasn't greedy about it and reported the deaths over a suitable period of time, they would not set off any alarms. People died in mental facilities all the time—a service to the state, for it meant one less nonworker mouth to feed, one less blemish to hide on the East German visage of superiority. As for the Stasi, whatever their interest in K7, these five individuals would drop off their radar screen.

"Then this house becomes a staging area to get them out of East Germany," Konrad said.

"One thing at a time," Mady said.

"We need to start planning for it now," Konrad argued. "Getting a bunch of disabled kids over the Wall isn't going to be easy."

"Did you hear about that one man," Elyse said, "Gunter something?"

"Litwin," said Lisette. "Gunter Litwin."

"He was shot by a border guard while trying to climb over the Wall," Elyse said. "He got all tangled up in the barbed wire."

"We can talk about this later," Mady said.

"They just left him there to bleed to death," Elyse continued. "But I also heard that a woman made it across successfully by jumping out a window near the Wall."

"Later!" Mady said, her voice rising.

Elyse matched her gaze, but not for long. She slumped back in her chair and folded her arms.

"Still, we need to start thinking about it," Konrad said.

"Maybe I should show you the rest of the house," Witzell offered.

Following Witzell from room to room proved interesting. Elyse stayed close to her grandfather, avoiding her mother, Lisette kept Mady between her and Konrad so she wouldn't get caught in a room alone with him, and Mady kept at a distance from her father. Konrad often found himself standing alone in a room, yet he didn't mind. He didn't have anything to say to anyone anyway.

As for the house itself, they found it spacious. The five would have more room and better facilities here than they were accustomed to at K7.

The tour completed, Mady asked, "When do we start?"

"Tomcat will be the first to die," Konrad said.

It was meant to be humorous but didn't come off that way.

Witzell said, "I asked Konrad to move in immediately. Tomcat appears to be the best choice to start."

Mady began to object, then stopped midsentence. She gathered up her things. "Do we have a ride back to the train, or do we have to walk?"

Witzell pulled car keys from his pocket.

That night, Mady couldn't wait to be alone. Lisette and Elyse seemed to take forever getting ready for bed.

"You staying up?" Lisette asked.

"For a while."

"I don't know why you insist on calling us children," Elyse said. She didn't kiss her mother good-night.

"Would you like company?" Lisette asked.

"Let's have hot cereal for breakfast," Mady replied.

Lisette nodded and went to bed.

Finally alone, Mady sat in the dark. She could stew better when it was dark. She wanted to stew. She'd waited to stew. So stew she did. There were no tears, just anger.

One by one, she went over the events since Tomcat made his grand entrance back into their lives. She studied each incident, reliving the events, replaying the dialogue.

Her chest rose and fell with force. By the time she progressed to today's events, the furnace of her anger was stoked and the fire blazing.

She was angry with her father for presuming on her life, for barging back in when he was supposed to be dead, and for having a wife who wasn't her mother. She was angry at Konrad for pushing, pushing, always pushing, never taking into consideration the danger or the consequences if they got caught. She was angry at Elyse for being insufferable. She was angry at Lisette, because Mady knew she was losing Lisette to Herr Gellert.

But she was mostly angry with herself. She was angry over her attitude. Angry with her anger. It seemed all she ever did was attack the people who were closest to her when all she really wanted was to love them.

Tears came despite her efforts to fight them back.

More than anything, she wanted to throw her arms around her father's neck and call him Daddy—to talk about old times and to tell him that she would always be there for him, that nothing would ever separate them again.

She wanted to embrace Konrad because, though she didn't know exactly what he'd endured since his stand at Ramah Cabin, she knew it must have been horrible to take a broad-shouldered young man and reduce him to a thin, hunched-over wreck who looked twice his age. Every time she looked at him, he reminded her of Josef, and she wanted to cry. She wanted to thank him for giving them time to escape Ramah Cabin even though he knew it would probably cost him his life. And from the looks of him, it had.

She wanted to take Lisette aside and talk to her, woman to woman, friend to friend, to tell her she was making a mistake in marrying Herr Gellert, to tell her to give Konrad time, that he still loved her and that she wasn't fooling anyone by pretending she didn't love him in return.

And she wanted to hold Elyse like she used to hold her when Elyse was a child. Mady could feel her little girl slipping away, and it hurt. It hurt so badly.

Going back to that night in the K7 common room, she wanted to pull every one of those children to her bosom and fly away with them to safety, far out of reach of a state that despised them yet would never release them willingly.

She thought of what lay ahead for them. It brought back

memories. Horrible, wretched, painful memories. Memories of things she never wanted to think about again.

Mady was afraid, shaken to the core of her being. She didn't know if she could do this again. She didn't know if she had the strength. She knew she didn't have the courage; the storage chest that held that commodity had been emptied long ago. Yet they were going to want to depend on her, and all she could think about was how she wanted to climb under the covers and hide and never get out of bed again. Because then she wouldn't disappoint anyone.

And then, for some reason, she thought of Park, and her anger flared because all of this was his fault. Had he kept his promise, the children never would have been torn from her arms. Had he kept his promise to them and had the Americans give them shelter, in all likelihood right now they'd be living on the freedom side of the Berlin Wall.

Park had let them down.

He let her down.

Just when she trusted him, just when she thought there might be something between them, he turned his back on them and, thinking only of himself, went home to America, the land of plenty, leaving her and the children to starve, or be killed, or be crushed between opposing armies, or be violated by marauding anarchists.

She would never forgive him for that.

Her hatred for Park made her strong, goading her into survival mode, enough to entertain a plan to rescue the children.

Chapter 17

Tuesday, September 12, 1961

Mady Schumacher's reacting in fear came as no surprise to Konrad. He'd seen it before. More than seen it, in fact; he'd lived it every day in the gulag. He also survived it. Many hadn't.

Like Dyakonov, the political dissident who feared retaliation for stealing another prisoner's piece of bread. He had every right to be afraid. The bread he stole belonged to Fabrizio, an Italian weight lifter who had beaten men to death for far lesser offenses. Dyakonov saved him the trouble. He stuck a wooden stake in his own gut before Fabrizio could get to him.

Then there was Seppanen, whose fear got the best of him one day for no apparent reason, at least none that was apparent to Konrad. Seppanen broke rank and made a run for it across an open field in broad daylight. He didn't get far. Did he really expect he would? He was gunned down before he took a dozen strides.

And Cegielski, the collaborator whose nerves were steady enough during the building of an escape tunnel but who fell apart the night of the escape. His cries alerted the guards, who heard screaming coming from the ground beneath their feet.

One of the strangest, though, was Eisenbein, who had said his good-byes and then turned over on his bunk, his face to the wall. By morning he was dead. Best anyone could figure, he simply willed himself to die.

The Russians may have confined them and worked them and

abused them, but it was fear that stalked the prisoners. Giving in to fear meant death. A person had to fight it. Every day. Steady on, as the English often said.

For Konrad that meant swinging his legs over the side of the bunk every morning and, in defiance of fear, slapping the floor with his feet, getting himself up, and facing down another day.

In this respect, living in East Berlin behind the Wall had been no different than living in the Russian gulag. That's why Konrad pressed Mady. She wanted to lie in bed and turn her face to the wall, just like Eisenbein. Konrad wasn't going to let her.

The first of the K7 inmates died on schedule. Otto Witzell signed Scott Schumacher's death certificate and sent it to administration headquarters. That same day, Tomcat moved into his new home, now called Ramah Cabin, despite the fact that it didn't look like a cabin at all.

The week preceding Tomcat's death, Konrad had the spacious house to himself. It was a palace compared to his place in the hills. Witzell worked all day and usually late into the night. When he did come home he and Konrad would talk. Konrad grew to admire the man, though at first this had proved difficult due to Witzell's being largely responsible for Josef's death. Now, the way Konrad saw it, Witzell had paid his penance and had more than redeemed himself in his caring for the Hadamar children. Besides, in happier days, hadn't the man been Josef's teacher, his mentor? Occasionally Witzell would say something that rang a familiar bell, and Konrad would realize he'd first heard it from Josef, who had learned it from Witzell.

Konrad was anxious about Tomcat's arrival. He didn't know if he was ready to be social all day long. His concerns proved unfounded. He and Tomcat understood each other. They both required their time alone.

When they were together, it was Konrad's task to acquaint Tomcat with the layout of the house. Konrad would describe the room, and then he'd lead Tomcat through it, noting any unusual projections or obstacles. Tomcat would read the floor surfaces for landmarks and test distances with outstretched hands. He was a quick study. Within a week he was navigating most of the rooms with ease.

Within a month he could move anywhere in the house as well as a sighted person, better in the dark.

Not long after Tomcat's moving in, Lisette, Mady, and Elyse started coming over in the evenings, Lisette less often than the others. For three, sometimes four nights a week she would spend her evenings with Herr Gellert. From what little Konrad overheard, the couple's wedding plans were progressing, although he didn't know the exact date of the wedding. It was to be a civil ceremony because Herr Gellert wouldn't even entertain the idea of getting married in a church.

On the nights Lisette visited Ramah Cabin, she cleaned. This was Lisette's way of coping, not only with the stress of Konrad and the reappearance of the Hadamar Six, but with life in socialist East Germany with its long list of restrictions, the constant surveillance, and the suppression of speech. Some people responded with a feeling of helplessness, allowing themselves to become dependent on the system. Others complained constantly that nothing worked anymore. Still others grew fatalistic. Lisette cleaned, as if to say, "We may not be free, but we're going to be clean."

Either that, or Lisette cleaned to avoid being with Konrad. Regardless, she did a good job of it—both with the cleaning and avoiding him.

Mady moved about Ramah Cabin, preparing for each new addition in a friendly, polite, methodical fashion. She rarely laughed or showed emotion. Mady put everything in order, and Lisette spit-polished it.

It was the Hadamar Six who brought the place to life. Elyse especially. She breathed life into the house, possibly because there was so much catching up to do.

The first two weeks it was just her and Tomcat. Romantic sparks jumped between them. The only time they quarreled was when Tomcat tried to force Sinatra music on her. He'd badger her until she agreed to listen to one of his LPs.

"Give it a chance. You'll like this next song. Millions of fans can't all be wrong," he would tell her.

Elyse only pretended to listen. After a couple of songs, she'd yawn, then get up to do important things like search for a nail file. When the record finally ended, Tomcat would ask what she thought of it. She'd be honest with him, and Tomcat's feelings would get hurt.

Then Elyse would insist he listen to her music. She owned three singles: "It's Now or Never" by Elvis Presley, "I'm Sorry" by Brenda Lee, and "Cathy's Clown" by the Everly Brothers. Tomcat didn't like any of them.

One night, believing she could find some modern music Tomcat would like, she asked her mother for permission to turn on the radio.

"It's not our radio," Mady said. "It belongs to Herr Witzell." She insisted on calling him Herr Witzell and that Elyse do the same, expressly forbidding Elyse from calling him Grandfather or Grandpa.

Elyse asked Herr Witzell for permission to listen to the radio, and he told her the house was hers now as well as his and that she should treat it as such. Yet when Mady heard the radio playing, she made Elyse turn it off.

"What if it breaks?" she said.

"Then we'll get it fixed," Witzell replied, coming to his granddaughter's aid.

"I still don't want her playing with it," Mady insisted. She gave her father one of those "this is a parent thing so don't interfere" looks.

Witzell folded. "Best do what your mother says," he told his granddaughter.

Marlene was the next resident of K7 to die and move to Ramah Cabin. She was followed a week and a half later by Hermann, then Viktor, who was so glad to see Tomcat again that he burst into tears. At first he begged Tomcat to go back home with him to the institution. It took a united effort to convince him that Ramah Cabin was his new home.

Their days were spent in a daily regimen of chores; their evenings were their own. With the radio off-limits and with no television—Witzell had no use for one and, when alive, Ulla preferred her puzzles—Elyse took it upon herself to broaden the life experiences of the former residents of K7, who had been living their lives behind cinder-block walls. She told them what it was like to shop at Alexanderplatz, what it was like to work at a factory, and of course all about the pastry and sausages at Café Lorenz. She also described incidents in her life, like the time she auditioned at the State Conservatory of Music, that she was turned down because her improvisational skills were below standard, and also about the time one of her teachers slapped her at school.

"It was in the eighth grade," she said, "about three weeks into the new year. For some reason, we were given a new teacher in our composition class."

Viktor, Marlene, Hermann, and Tomcat all sat around her as she told the story.

"The new teacher's name was Herr Zollner. He was totally bald. I mean, there wasn't a hair on his head. And the skin on top was so smooth it looked like an egg."

Viktor laughed.

"Really!" Elyse insisted. "I remember looking up once while we were taking a test and he was sitting at his desk reading a book. His head was so shiny I could see the light reflected on the top. Not just the glare, I mean the fixture!"

She paused for Viktor to laugh. He did.

"Frau Holz was our old teacher. She was kind. I liked her. But I guess she wasn't strict enough, which was why they replaced her with Herr Zollner. The first day he told us there would be changes. Drastic changes. He said he knew that some of us were doing our homework during school recess and that this practice would stop immediately."

"Why couldn't you do homework during recess?" Marlene asked.

"It was the rule."

"Why was it a rule?"

"I don't know. They didn't explain the rules to us; they just expected us to obey them. And Herr Zollner warned us not to try anything on him, for he could tell how long ago something had been written by the ink. He said he wouldn't accept any work that was done in pencil or ball-point pen."

"Wow. That's strict," Marlene said.

"Too strict," Tomcat said.

"He even memorized our names and the seating order the first day," Elyse said. "But the way he did it was really creepy. He walked down each row, stopped at each desk, and made us look him in the eyes. Then he said your name three times, really slow, while staring into your eyes. He told us that if we broke any of the rules, we would be punished with a severe whipping."

Viktor got scared. He was hugging his knees.

"Maybe Viktor shouldn't hear this," Marlene said.

"You all right, Viktor?" Tomcat asked.

"Yeah."

But he didn't stop hugging himself.

"Should I go on?" Elyse said.

"He's fine," Tomcat said. "If he wasn't, he'd tell me."

"Kurt Kluepke got whipped once," Elyse said.

"What for?" Marlene asked.

"Cheating. We didn't see it. But we heard it. Kurt started crying. He begged Herr Zollner to stop. It was awful."

"Herr Zollner sounds like a horrible man," Marlene said.

"After a few weeks he got nicer. He even joked with us a little. So we thought we'd play a little prank—not a bad prank, just playing around."

"Uh-oh," Hermann said, anticipating what would come next.

Elyse continued, "We waited for Herr Zollner to leave the room. Then we pulled the shades and stuck candles in our inkwells and lit them. It really looked cool! Then we waited for Herr Zollner to return. The door opened. It was him."

She paused.

"What happened?" Hermann asked.

Elyse smiled, drawing out the suspense.

"Well," she said, "at first he just stood there. We couldn't see his face because the hallway light behind him was too bright. Then he switched on the lights, and he was so angry that his face and neck had turned purple!"

Viktor began rocking back and forth.

"He let out this terrible roar, stormed into the classroom, and brought up the window shades—so hard that one of them came down and hit the floor. He shouted at us to stand beside our desks and blow out the candles. He ordered everyone who had a candle to form a line outside in the hall."

"Did you have a candle on your desk?" Marlene asked.

"Everyone did," Elyse said.

"Did you get a whippin'?" Viktor asked. He looked like he was about to cry.

"That's what I'm going to tell you next, Viktor," Elyse said.

"Herr Zollner led us into an empty classroom. All I could think about was Kurt Kluepke and how he kept begging Herr Zollner to stop beating him."

"What happened?" Marlene asked. She pulled her legs up against her and started to hug them just like Viktor.

"Herr Zollner made us walk past him single file. He made us look him in the eyes just like he did when he memorized our names. Then, when we were looking him in the eyes, he slapped us on the cheek."

"Did he slap you?" Tomcat said.

"He slapped all of us."

"Did you tell Frau Schumacher?" Hermann asked.

"Not right away," Elyse said. "I told her about a year later. I was afraid she'd get angry with me for pulling a prank on Herr Zollner."

"Did she?" Tomcat asked.

"Yeah," Elyse said. "But she didn't punish me or anything."

"Herr Zollner sounds like a horrible, horrible man," Marlene said.

"I hate him!" Viktor cried.

"Really, he wasn't so bad after that," Elyse said. "I learned a lot from him. I think he liked me."

Chapter 18

Tuesday, October 24, 1961

Annie was the last to die to K7 and be reborn to new life in the new Ramah Cabin. As he did for all the others, K7 administrator Otto Witzell filed the requisite death certificate. The deaths occurred more quickly than he had originally planned. He'd run into an unexpected complication—the children themselves. With each departure, those who were left became restless and lonely. They sought companionship with the friendlier members of the staff. And while they hadn't been informed of Witzell's duplicity—like the staff, they'd simply been told they were being transferred to another facility—they knew enough about Ramah Cabin to raise suspicion among the more intelligent staff members. Witzell knew it would be foolish of him to think that his facility was free of state informants.

His answer to this unexpected glitch was to stage a small epidemic. Nothing too scary. Something he could knock out with the appropriate drugs but not before there were several fatalities. Three to be exact. Witzell chose viral pneumonia, a common threat among hospital and institution patients.

According to his report, Hermann and Viktor showed the first symptoms. They were too far gone before the disease was diagnosed. They died within a day of each other. Annie caught it too and, as the report read, they thought they'd reached her in time. She lingered for a few days, and then she too succumbed.

The night of Annie's death they had a party at the new Ramah

Cabin. It was only the second time in over sixteen years that they'd all been together. Possibly from a sense of relief, or possibly because he'd managed to fulfill his dream of reuniting Josef's children with Mady, Witzell was jollier than anyone remembered seeing him. Mady too was uncharacteristically joyous. And there was nothing that gave a father greater pleasure than to see his daughter happy, especially knowing that he was the one who caused it.

Holding a cup of fruit punch, Mady joined Lisette, who stood at the edge of the room holding her own cup as she watched, listened, and did a lot of smiling.

"Remind you of anything?" Mady said.

"I was just thinking the same thing," Lisette replied. "Christmas 1939, at your house."

"They're older than you were," Mady said.

Lisette laughed. "Just as loud, though."

"I think they're louder. And it appears they don't get along with each other any better than you did."

Mady motioned across the room with her cup. Elyse and Annie were going at it. Tomcat stood nearby, trying to stay out of it, but Annie kept pulling him in by grabbing his arm.

"Good thing it's October," Lisette said. "They don't have a Christmas tree to knock over."

"Poor Kaiser," Mady said.

She and Lisette laughed at the memory.

"I wonder what happened to Kaiser," Lisette said.

He was left behind when they fled the first Ramah Cabin, and like so many animals, he probably became a casualty of war. But that didn't stop one or the other of them from occasionally posing the question. As always, it hung in the air unanswered, like a haunting refrain.

The argument between Elyse and Annie got louder. Only a few words managed to find their way through the din to Mady and Lisette. Two in particular made Mady stiffen.

Uncle Parker.

"Now, why would a grown man send a young woman a package like that?" Mady said. "You'd think he'd have more sense."

"He meant nothing by it, Mady. I think it's sweet. He promised her he'd send copies of the photographs he took at Café Lorenz."

"But did he have to send her all that other junk? Look. It's causing a rift. We don't need that."

Park's package was delivered to the flat the day before Annie arrived at Ramah Cabin. Besides the photos, it contained packages of gum, Jell-O, a tin of cocoa, Nescafé, and a box of Tobler chocolates—all coveted items in East Germany. There were only two ways someone on this side of the Wall could get these things. They could be purchased at an Intershop, which carried an assortment of Western items, such as nylon stockings, Marlboro cigarettes, Maxwell House coffee, Lux soap, and Johnny Walker whiskey. But Intershops accepted only Western currency, illegal for East Germans to carry. The other way was for a westerner to ship the items in.

"Do you know she's telling everyone he's her rich uncle who lives in America?" Mady said.

"It's harmless," Lisette said. "Her friend Ericka has a rich American uncle."

"That's different. Elyse is no relation to Park, and I don't like her telling people he's her uncle."

Lisette knew better than to continue trying when Mady had made up her mind on something.

"I wonder where Gael is," she said.

"Gael Wissing? I haven't thought of her in years."

"She's probably not Wissing any longer. I'm sure she's got her hooks in some man by now."

"At least we know it's not Konrad," Mady said.

"Not that she didn't try."

"And Willi. What ever happened to Willi? Does Konrad know where his brother is?"

It was Lisette's turn to stiffen. "I wouldn't know," she said.

At that moment Willi Reichmann was sauntering down the darkened corridor of the state security offices known and feared as Stasi. Willi felt no fear. By the way he walked, an observer might conclude he was a high-level supervisor or a top agent. By his dress, the observer would have to go with agent. Undercover.

The first thing anyone noticed about Willi was the patch he wore over his right eye, which only partly covered a scar that ran through his eyebrow. It was his combat badge, along with his left hand, which was frozen in a clawlike shape. To disguise it he used a cane, fixing the handle in such a way that it appeared his hand was gripping it. The next thing that drew an observer's eye—and Willi loved to draw attention to himself—was a black beret, the kind Frenchmen and Spaniards wore, and a summer overcoat that flared dramatically as he walked.

However, there was no one to observe him and that was odd, given the fact the Stasi were big on surveillance. These were low-level administrative offices, and should he happen upon a guard who gave him trouble—he'd have to be new not to recognize Willi—a phone call would straighten everything out. He could get the information he was after during office hours, no questions asked. He'd been blackmailing this particular records officer for years now. They had a comfortable working arrangement. Nevertheless, Willi liked to make the occasional unannounced after-hours check, just to make sure his informant was giving him accurate information.

Willi stopped in front of the records office. He reached into his pocket and pulled out a pick tool and made short work of the lock. Inside, he knew exactly where he was going and where to find what he was looking for. He walked between rows of desks to the back of the room, picked another lock, and was inside a small office, barely large enough for the desk to fit. He pulled out the chair and sat, picking a third lock, a desk drawer, illuminating it with a penlight he held in his teeth. He removed three file folders and plopped them down on the desk, the penlight still in his mouth. He opened the first file folder. Four sheets of paper into it he found what he was searching for. On both sides of the penlight, the corners of his mouth stretched into a grin.

In his good hand he held a copy of a certificate of death.

"And Annie makes five," he said.

Chapter 19

Wednesday, October 25, 1961

"On the news last night they showed a border guard escaping to the West," Konrad said. "It might have been at Friedrichstrasse, I couldn't tell for sure. He was standing there with his rifle shouldered, looking at the barbed wire, glancing away, looking again. You could see he was thinking about it. Then he just dropped his rifle and jumped through the wire in three steps."

"What did the other guards do?" Mady asked.

"Nothing. Took them by surprise."

"A dated film clip," Witzell said. "It's harder now and getting harder all the time. Every time someone makes it across, the guards make it harder for the next person."

"And those who don't make it?" Mady asked.

"Prison," Witzell said. "They're charged with political crimes against the state."

Four of them sat in the living room, the same four in the same room they met in the day Mady and Lisette first saw the house. A thick cloud of cigar smoke circled over them. To someone just walking in, it might appear they were playing some kind of parlor word game, boys against girls. But this was no game, though the seating arrangement was most definitely adversarial.

This was the night they broke the news to the former residents of K7—that Witzell's home was but a staging place for their next move, one that would take them out of East Berlin.

The news came as a shock. That was expected. While the residents of K7 weren't totally ignorant of current events, neither were they politically savvy. For they had been sheltered for so long.

After being informed of the general plan, they were told to go to a different part of the house while specific plans were discussed.

"They're treating us like we're children!" Annie said.

"They always do!" Elyse said. It was the first thing she and Annie agreed on since Annie had moved into the house.

"They're the leaders," said Tomcat. "Like generals in an army. Say what you want, I trust them."

Elyse and the others didn't go far; they stayed close enough to hear most of what was being said.

"We don't know what we're up against," Mady began. "And from what I've heard, they won't let you get close enough to the Wall to get a good look at it."

"What about the people with houses in sight of the Wall?" Konrad said.

"Everyone within a kilometer or two has been moved out. The people living there now are staunch Communists and they all know each other. They report any strangers they see."

"I may be able to get a look at the Wall," Witzell said. "I know one of the border guards. Helped him get the job. I could pay him a visit, possibly get something of a tour."

"Wouldn't he be suspicious?" Mady asked.

"The boy likes to brag. If I showed him a little interest, who knows?"

"It's a start," Konrad said.

Lisette, who had yet to contribute to the discussion, sat with a far-off look in her eyes. It was obvious her mind was elsewhere. Konrad wondered if she'd brought Herr Gellert with her to the meeting, at least his spirit. Was she wondering what his reaction would be if he knew she was involved in an attempt to get over the Wall?

Just then a horrible thought came to mind. He saw them climbing over the Wall to freedom. He brought up the rear. As he slung a leg over the Wall, he looked back. There was Lisette, waving goodbye to him. Of course she wouldn't be coming with them. She'd be

Frau Gellert by then. But not until now did the thought have emotions attached to it.

Konrad looked at her.

Lisette was looking at him.

Were they thinking the same thing?

"I want to say something," Elyse said. She stood a good two meters outside the perimeter of the seating area.

Turning her head, Mady said, "Elyse, you were told to leave the room. Go join the others." Having dealt with the interruption, she turned her attention back to the others. In her mind the matter was settled.

"We should contact Herr Parker," Elyse said. "He'll help us."

"Elyse! This doesn't concern you!" Mady barked.

"Who's Herr Parker?" Konrad asked.

"You know him," Lisette said, joining in. "The American colonel who was Josef's contact at Ramah Cabin."

"You still have contact with him?" Konrad said.

"Just recently. We met up with him at Café Lorenz in the Western sector," Lisette said.

"The day the border closed," Elyse added. "He wanted to help us then. He said he could, and I believe him."

"Elyse! That's enough," Mady said.

"But—"

"I said, that's enough!"

In a huff, Elyse turned to leave.

"Thank you, dear," Witzell called after her in his grandpa voice. "It was helpful."

"I'll not have anything to do with that man!" Mady snapped.

"It's worth considering," Konrad said.

"No, it's not worth considering. The man can't be trusted. He abandoned us once; we'd be foolish to trust him again."

"He abandoned you?" Konrad asked. "He didn't strike me as the kind of man—"

"You weren't there," Mady said.

Konrad looked to Lisette, who didn't appear to have anything to add.

"Still," Konrad said, "it helps to have someone on the outside. Think of this as a prison break, because that's exactly what it is.

Having a contact like Herr Parker may spell the difference between success and failure."

Mady was adamant when she said, "I'll tell you what it will spell. It'll spell certain failure if you think you can depend on him. It's not an option. Not as far as I'm concerned."

In tears, Elyse stormed through the room where the others were sitting. A person would have to be a blind man not to see that she was in no mood to talk to anyone. Maybe that was why Tomcat got up and followed her. Elyse stormed down the hallway and out of the house.

"Elyse?"

"Not now, Tomcat."

He reached out. His hand found the back of her shoulder. She flinched, and for a second he thought she was going to shrug it off. She didn't.

"It'll be okay," he said.

"She treats me like that all the time! For once, I wish she'd listen to me," Elyse said.

"Konrad listened. So did Herr Witzell."

Elyse sniffed. She turned and Tomcat dropped his hand. He wanted to keep it on her shoulder and even place his other hand on her other shoulder but didn't think now was the best time to make such a bold overture.

"Thank you for coming after me."

"I was concerned."

For a time they stood there and neither one spoke. Inside, they could hear voices. Mady's was strong, insistent. Witzell's was calming, reasoning.

Elyse was no longer sniffing. Tomcat could feel her nearness. She was looking at him; he could sense it.

"Tomcat?"

"Yeah?"

"Do you ever think about us?"

"Sometimes."

It was a lie, but something held him back from telling the truth. He thought about her all the time.

"When you think about us, what do you think?"

"I think about what it was like back at Ramah Cabin when we were kids."

Elyse giggled. It was a wonderful sound. Much better than sniffling. "I think about that too," she said.

"And I think about us when I listen to Sinatra songs."

"Ugh! Let's not bring Frankie-boy into this. You know how I feel about him."

Bringing Frankie-boy into it was a mistake. Tomcat knew it the moment the words left his lips, only he was trying hard to be truthful with her.

"And I think about us whenever I think about Konrad and Lisette."

"You do? Why?"

"Because I think they belong together."

There was a moment of silence. Then a sniffle. Why a sniffle? Tomcat thought they'd moved past the sniffles.

"Really?" Elyse said. Her voice trembled slightly.

"Well, yeah. I've always thought Konrad and Lisette belong together. I think they know it too."

"You think *we* belong together."

"Well . . . yeah."

A hand touched his shoulder. It was warm—fever warm. Then he felt her breath a moment, just before he felt her lips.

"All I'm saying is that we need to know exactly what we're up against before we start making plans," Mady said.

"Is that really what you think?" Konrad said. "Or are you just using that as an excuse to put off planning an escape?"

"I think Mady's right," Lisette said. "Let's get more information."

"I'll arrange to meet up with my contact. It shouldn't be too difficult getting him to give a tour of—"

A movement caught their eye and they realized they weren't alone.

The others stared. Konrad stood.

"Looks like a reunion party," Willi said.

"And we weren't invited," his companion added.

"Gael? Is that you?" Lisette said.

"Don't let us interrupt," Willi said, grinning with a grin too wide to be friendly. "You were about to take a tour."

Witzell stood. "I could have sworn I locked the front door," he said.

Gael made a throwing motion with her hand. "Oh, locks don't stop Willi," she said airily. "He just lets himself in. Doesn't even carry keys anymore."

"Too clumsy," Willi said. "Keys just slow you down."

"Since you're already in," Witzell said, "would you care to sit down?"

With Gael at his side, Willi stepped inside the circle of chairs and the two of them sat on the sofa. "Thank you, Reverend Olbricht. Oops. Forgive me. I meant, Herr Witzell. It's so hard to keep track of people's names these days, isn't it?"

"Same ol' Willi," Konrad said.

"Same ol' Willi," Willi mimicked. "But you, dear brother . . . it looks like you've been on a diet. Lost a few pounds, haven't you?"

Lisette chimed in. "Gael! It's been years. But it looks like you and Willi have kept in touch."

"She doesn't let me touch her as often as I used to," Willi said with a wink.

"We're married," Gael explained.

"Oh . . . ?" Lisette stammered. "Well, that comes as a . . ."

"A shock?" Willi said. "That the gorgeous Gael Wissing would stoop to marry a one-eyed cripple?"

"Willi, I didn't mean . . ." Lisette said.

"Does it help to know that I'm rich?" Willi said. "Sheds a new light on things, wouldn't you say?"

Gael sat beside him this entire time smiling indifferently. Apparently she'd sat through this one-man vaudeville routine more than once.

She wore expensive clothes that had a Western flare. That was the odd thing about many wealthy Communists. On the one hand they spouted the evils of capitalism, while on the other they made a show of their Western possessions. They owned blue jeans, Paper Mate pens, and Superman comic books, drank Ovaltine, and loved Coca-Cola.

Konrad noticed that, while it was true that Gael had retained her figure, perhaps because, as they would come to learn later, she'd never given birth, still she showed signs of aging, particularly in the amount of makeup she used to cover up wrinkles, and facial skin had lost its firmness and begun to sag. He had always thought Gael pretty, fun to be with, and flirtatious—not such terrible things to a young man. After a while one got tired of her, however. A person couldn't be around her for very long before she began talking about money, usually with her spending it. Before and during the war, her father had plenty of money to keep her happy. Konrad wondered if he still did under the Communists. Probably not. It appeared that Willi had filled that role in Gael's life, and Konrad had to wonder where the money was coming from. Even so, it was a little disheartening to see Gael looking like a cheap imitation of herself. He had always thought of her as the cream of the group. The cream had definitely curdled.

Willi looked the same. He still wore that irritating smirk he had when a boy, except for the times their father wiped it off his face with the back of his hand. Willi remained thin and wiry, his cheeks hollow. It was still painful for Konrad to see him wounded. The eye patch. The gnarled hand with the cane that was vintage Willi. As a boy, he was always carrying a stick and swatting things with it—trees, buildings, fences, any animal that came within striking distance, and occasionally people. He remembered once, following a Hitler Youth meeting, when Willi whacked Neff in the shins a good one. Neff would have taken Willi's head off if Konrad hadn't stopped him. That didn't happen too often, because Willi was the runt and he knew it. Their father used to say that it was a good thing Willi wasn't born a cat, for they drowned the runts of the litter. But what Willi couldn't get with talent or good looks or strength, he got through devious means and cunning.

Look at us now, Konrad thought. Who would have figured it would turn out this way? Willi, the one with money. Married. A decorated war hero. While Konrad had what? Nothing.

"To business," Willi said, rapping the floor three times as though calling a meeting to order. He cocked his head and smiled as something behind Mady caught his eye. He raised his cane, calling with it. "Come, come, little ones. Uncle Willi is here!"

Annie and Viktor had their heads poked around the doorway. They stepped out hesitantly at first, then a little more boldly when they saw Witzell nodding his head that it was all right. The fact that he wasn't smiling may have accounted for the absence of enthusiasm displayed on their faces.

"Ally ally out come free!" Willi called to them. "Don't you have a hug for your Uncle Willi? Don't you remember me? I'm the one who brought you all the goodies at the cabin. I was your guardian angel, remember? Your savior when you were starving."

He counted out loud as they walked out.

"One, two . . . come, I know there's more. That's it . . . three, four. Where are the others? The blind boy. Where's the blind boy, the one who was always meowing. What did you call him? Cat-boy?"

"Tomcat," Mady said.

"Ally ally out come free, Tomcat!" Willi called again.

Tomcat appeared in the doorway. He was holding Elyse by the hand.

"That's five . . . and six! Of course, little Ellie! Look, Gael, it's little Ellie! You remember, Pastor Josef's little girl."

"Elyse," Mady said.

But Willi wasn't listening. He was waving the cane horizontally now. "Line up, line up! I want to see you all. Oh my, look at you! You've all grown so much. You're not children anymore! You've all grown up."

Willi spread his arms wide, his cane extending so far that Witzell had to move his head to keep from being hit by it. "Look at you! You all look so healthy," he said. "Not a one of you looks dead."

Beside him Gael wore a wicked smile. Willi had evidently filled her in before they arrived.

Willi said to Witzell, "I must say, Reverend, in a way I'm pleased to see them in such good health. I thought for a while there you were killing them off."

"The reports to the Stasi," Witzell said.

Willi laughed. "Very good, Reverend Olbricht."

"You're Stasi?" Konrad said.

"No! Of course not," Willi said. "However, I have worked for them on occasion. And they for me."

"Still collaborating. Up to your old tricks," Konrad said.

"Tricks? No. Game. But then, it's all a game, isn't it? Winners and losers. The winners get all the money while the losers get themselves killed." He leaned forward and spoke as if sharing a secret. "The key, dear brother, is to play with the winners and then beat them at their own game." He winked.

"No matter who you have to sell out," Konrad said. "You were going to hand Ernst over to them."

"You were conscious, were you?" Willi said. "Couldn't quite tell. Thought you might be dead. The timing was wrong on that one. A valuable lesson, and one which cost me dearly."

"The children," Mady said, attempting to bring the discussion back to the present. "How did you find out about them and K7?"

"We're not children!" Elyse snapped behind her.

Willi gazed at Mady. He didn't answer immediately. He leaned on his cane, resting his chin on it. His whole demeanor softened. "You know, you look as ravishing as ever. For some people the years are unkind." He nodded toward his wife. Gael scrunched her nose at him like a defiant two-year-old. Willi ignored her. "For others such as yourself, the years are kind. More than kind. You are more beautiful now than ever."

The way he leered at her made everyone uncomfortable. But Willi didn't seem to notice, or he did and was enjoying it. Mady matched his gaze with an unblinking gaze of her own. If she was uncomfortable, she refused to give him the satisfaction by showing it.

Willi then sat abruptly back on the sofa and answered Mady's question. "On occasion," he said, "it has been advantageous for the Stasi to use the services of psychiatric institutions such as K7."

Witzell nodded that this was true, though he didn't look too pleased about it.

Willi continued, "Sometimes they need someone to disappear, but they don't want to kill them. A mental institution is handy for such arrangements. Or sometimes they want to torture someone, but instead of clubs and fists, they use drugs. Reverend Olbricht, you're familiar with this practice, aren't you? Isn't that what you did to Josef Schumacher at the Hadamar facility?"

"Willi!" Lisette cried. "That was uncalled for!"

Willi feigned innocence. "What? I thought everyone knew about that."

"It's all right, Lisette," Witzell said.

Willi laughed. He looked at Lisette and shook his head. "Sweet, sweet Lisette. Some people never change, do they? They never grow up. They refuse to recognize the unpleasantries of the world." He snapped his fingers. "But then, I could be wrong about that. I understand you're doing a little collaboration of your own. With a Communist at the shoe factory. A Herr Gellert, if I'm not mistaken. Very out of character for you, Lisette, I must say. Always thought you and Konrad would someday get married. Although you always have been attracted to the strong Party types, haven't you? Nazi. Communist. What difference does it make?"

Lisette's face reddened.

"Leave her alone, Willi," Konrad said.

The Willi smirk appeared.

"You tracked the children to K7," Mady prompted him.

"Not exactly," Willi said. "Actually, I wasn't looking for them. Just browsing through some documents late one night and happened to see their names. Five orphans, all by the name of Schumacher, and I thought to myself, What are the chances of that? There they were on the list—Annie Schumacher, Viktor Schumacher . . . you get the idea. After that, well, it just sort of became a hobby of mine. I tried to have them relocated to a place where I could keep an eye on them."

"You're all heart," Konrad said.

"So you were the one I was fighting," Witzell said.

"I was the one," Willi replied. "But you beat me that round. And I don't like to lose. So I thought I'd better do a little digging to find out about my opponent. Imagine my surprise when I discovered that Otto Witzell is none other than ol' Reverend Olbricht, fresh from Dachau concentration camp. And I thought, What is it about these misfits? They're some kind of magnet, because they keep attracting people I know to them. That's when I arranged to keep an eye on them, just out of curiosity. To see who else might show up. Now, I have only one question for you. What took everyone so long? I mean, sixteen years!"

"We don't have the resources of the Stasi," Konrad said.

"Your loss," said Willi. "If you're going to play the game, you have to make contact with the right people."

"This is no game, Willi," Mady said.

Willi leaned forward in all earnestness. "Then . . . what is it, my dear? What exactly is going on here? And don't say it's none of my business. I make everything my business. That's how I make my living."

"It's my doing," Herr Witzell confessed. "I had two objectives. To redeem myself for wrongs committed against Josef Schumacher by caring for the children he rescued from that death house Hadamar, and, God willing, to somehow reunite them with my daughter and granddaughter. These objectives were purely personal. They are no threat to the state."

"Unconvincing, Herr Witzell," Willi said. "Though I must say the reference to Saint Josef of Pankow almost brought a tear to my eye. Only what you've said doesn't explain the elaborate ruse behind the phony death certificates. Don't get me wrong, I love a good ruse. But there's something more going on here. I can smell it."

"I think that foul odor you smell," Konrad said, "you brought with you."

Willi pointed to his brother, his good hand in the shape of a pistol. He shot it. "Good one, brother." He stood. Gael stood with him. "I can't tell you how much fun this has been," Willi said. "We'll have to do it again sometime. Soon. Just think of me as nosy ol' Uncle Willi, who loves a good puzzle and who is determined to solve this one."

He turned to leave, then swung back around.

"By the way, I expect the population here to remain constant. Understand me? No more fake deaths, or runaways, or eloping." He winked at Elyse. She blushed and let go of Tomcat's hand. "I'll be dropping in from time to time to see how everyone's doing." He waved a hand. "Don't bother to show me to the door. I know the way."

Gael smiled and wiggled her fingers good-bye. She looked bored.

The door was heard closing. Outside a car engine started, and they were gone.

Chapter 20

With the closing of the door, Mady directed the Hadamar Six to the other room for the second time that night. While they went grumbling as before, this time they were gabbing about "Uncle Willi."

"That puts an end to our plans," Mady said.

"Maybe not," Konrad said.

"What do you mean? You heard him. How are we going to do what we planned to do with him snooping around? It was dangerous enough before. But now . . ."

"Mady's right," Witzell said. "I've seen his type. All he has to do is say the right word to the right person and we all can end up in prison. The Stasi doesn't care if it's true or not."

But Konrad wasn't ready to give up just yet. "All I'm saying is that there may be a way around this. Let's not make any hasty decisions. Let's think about it for a few days."

"Konrad, this isn't the time to resurrect a personal rivalry with your brother. Lives are at stake here."

"I know what's at stake," Konrad said. "I also know this isn't the time to crawl under the bed and hide just because Willi Reichmann paid us a visit."

Voices were growing heated.

Witzell raised a calming hand. "There's nothing more we can do tonight," he said.

Mady looked to Lisette. "You've been quiet all night," she said. "What do you think, Lisette?"

Lisette didn't say anything. She didn't look at anyone. Instead, she stood and left the room.

It was late when Mady inserted the key into the door of the flat. Elyse was right behind her, asleep on her feet. Lisette was third in line, having not said a word all the way home.

A rapping sound came from the end of the hallway. Someone was knocking on a door, but no one else was in the hall.

"It's just us, Herr Puttkamer," Mady said. "We're sorry if we woke you." Turning back to the task of opening the door, she muttered under her breath, "Doesn't that buzzard ever go to sleep?"

Rap. Rap. Rap. Rap. Rap.

There it was again.

"Good night, Herr Puttkamer," Elyse said sleepily.

Mady had the door open now.

Rap. Rap. Rap. Rap. Rap.

"I think he wants something," Lisette said.

"He wants to annoy us," Mady said. "That's what he wants."

"He's just lonely," Elyse said.

"Small wonder," Mady said. "Who would live with such a man?"

Rap. Rap. Rap. Rap. Rap.

"Herr Puttkamer, do you want something?" Lisette called, covering half the distance between their door and his.

Rap. Rap. Rap. Rap. Rap.

"Herr Puttkamer?"

She walked the other half of the way, moving close to the peephole so Herr Puttkamer could get a good look at her. "Herr Puttkamer?" Lisette said. "Do you need help?"

Mady and Elyse had joined her, leaving the door to their flat standing open. When all three of them were in front of the door, Herr Puttkamer spoke.

"It's late," he said.

"We're sorry if we disturbed you, Herr Puttkamer," Lisette said. "We're going to bed now. We won't disturb you anymore."

"I know you're up to something," Puttkamer said.

The three women exchanged glances, each with the single thought, *How much could he know?*

"Three single women coming and going at all hours of the night. It's unnatural. Suspicious, if you ask me."

Another exchange of glances, this time with poker faces, fully aware that there was an old man with his eye glued to the peephole and watching their every move from a fisheye perspective.

Lisette said, "We're three Christian women, Herr Puttkamer. We're not doing anything immoral."

"As if it were any of his business!" Elyse whispered a little too loudly.

Both Lisette and Mady warned her with quick, alarmed glances.

"My brother-in-law had tenants like you," Puttkamer said. "Always coming and going at all hours of the day and night. He called the Stasi and guess what they found?"

"What did they find, Herr Puttkamer?" Lisette said.

"Escape plans. They were planning an escape over the Wall. They were building a submarine, of all the fool things. The Stasi found the plans hidden in a flour jar in the kitchen."

No glances were exchanged. Lucky guess or not, Puttkamer was wise to them.

"I have a mind to call the Stasi, to see what they'd find in your kitchen," Puttkamer said.

Mady stepped forward. "They'd find flour, Herr Puttkamer. Flour and a floor that needs waxing."

"Then how do you explain all the coming and going? Until a few months ago, you were regular as clockwork."

"It's my father," Mady said. "Elyse's grandfather. We lost track of each other during the war and haven't seen him since Elyse was a baby. For fifteen years he's been looking for us, and he just found us. We've been spending our evenings with him. Catching up."

The other side of the door was silent. Herr Puttkamer was chewing on this.

"His name is Herr Witzell," Mady offered. "Otto Witzell. He's the administrator at K7, a psychiatric institution just outside the city. Sometimes we get carried away and just manage to catch the last train home. We're sorry if we disturbed you."

She waited for a response. There was none.

"Herr Puttkamer?" Mady said. "Are you still there?"

For all they knew, her story put the old man to sleep.

Mady motioned with her finger, and the three of them walked back down the hallway.

"I'll be keeping an eye on you," Puttkamer called behind them.

"Thank you for your concern, Herr Puttkamer," Lisette said.

The door to their flat closed behind them.

"Do you think that was wise—giving him your father's name?" Lisette asked Mady.

"It's a risk. If the old buzzard does place a call, hopefully whoever looks into it will find enough truth to satisfy them before digging too deep."

"You're right, it's a risk," Lisette said.

"Do we have to get up and go to work in the morning?" Elyse said. "Can't we instead send word that we're sick and then sleep in?"

Lisette lay in her bed. She raised her head. The alarm clock on the bureau across the room had fluorescent numbers and hands, but it was too far away for her to make out the time. She could hear both Mady and Elyse on the other side of the room. Their breathing was steady. Rhythmic. They were unaware that Lisette had not slept, nor probably would she sleep at all tonight.

The window curtains glowed around the edges. It was getting light outside. Lisette heaved a sigh. It was going to be a long day at work. Her production count would be down, and Herr Gellert would say something about that. He always did when it was down. If the count was up, he wouldn't bother mentioning it.

Willi's unexpected visit had started her thinking, bringing up the issue she'd been avoiding. Namely, what exactly was she doing? In a way, Willi had done her a favor. He was forcing her to make a decision she knew she was going to have to make sooner or later. She couldn't continue seeing Herr Gellert and help the children escape from East Germany. She couldn't keep putting him off. She had to choose between them. The sooner, the better.

All through the night Lisette had weighed the pros and cons. She loved the children. She loved seeing them again, catching up with them, seeing how they'd grown, how their personalities had developed. She loved seeing Elyse reunited with them. Elyse completed them, and they all added a dimension to her life that she had been lacking.

Lisette placed being with the children on the pro side of her mental ledger. The balancing con to that positive was that they would be leaving and she would be staying. Add to that Herr Gellert's reaction to them if she told him about them. Oh, how she wanted to tell him about them. About Viktor's rib-crushing hugs, Marlene's sugary disposition, Annie's "look you in the eye and tell you just what she thinks" approach to life, and Hermann's physical competitiveness, in spite of his foot. And Tomcat—amazing Tomcat. More than once during an evening with Herr Gellert, one of their names was on the tip of her tongue and she had to swallow it. She hated that she had to keep this side of her life a secret to Herr Gellert. But he wouldn't understand. He wouldn't be sympathetic. She knew that if he knew, he'd turn them in. Everything was black and white to him. Sometimes Lisette admired people like that. Their lives were so much simpler. But they could be cruel as well. And she was afraid that one night her tongue would slip and Herr Gellert would find out and the children would suffer for it. She wouldn't be able to live with herself if that were to happen. So that was a definite con.

But she also had to list Herr Gellert on the pro side. He gave her security. As Herr Gellert's wife, she would never be on the wrong side of the law, like she had been all that time hiding the children from the Nazis. Like she was again now, hiding them from the Soviet authorities, and none too well now that Willi knew about them. Every day she approached Herr Witzell's house wondering if the Stasi or the People's Police were waiting to arrest her. She never had to wonder such a thing when visiting Herr Gellert's house. She also would never have to wonder if there would be enough money for food and clothing, or whether or not they would have a roof over their heads. So many years she'd had to live with these uncertainties. Battling ladies in line for a bit of meat or fruit. And she was tired of it. To live with the assurance of having one's daily needs met, why, that was heaven, wasn't it?

Besides, what did she have to contribute to an escape operation? Mady and Konrad were the leaders. Although they were often at odds with each other, in the end they both wanted the same thing—for the children to be safe. And Witzell was there now to help mediate between them if needed. He too had the children's best interests in mind. He'd gotten them this far, kept them together and provided a house for them. He had resources. Watching him with the children, they obviously loved him; she could see it in their eyes. Likewise, he loved them, knew them, and in ways Lisette no longer knew them. Before, it had been her task to take care of the children while Mady charted the appropriate course. But the children were older now; they could take care of themselves. And Herr Witzell was their encouragement. They no longer needed Lisette. She wasn't trying to be humble. It was a fact.

Then there was Konrad. What column did he fit in? The pro side for the children. He was getting stronger every day. She could see him emerging from his hermit hole and interacting with others more and more. He was once again taking the lead in things. This whole episode with Witzell and Tomcat and the children had been good for him. Some of the old Konrad was beginning to show around the edges.

But her and Konrad? Con. For the simple reason he didn't want her. He'd made this evident with his hiding from her for the last seven years. Had it not been for Herr Gellert sending her to that Pankow shoe store, Konrad would still be there in the back room, sorting and shelving shoes. And while she was just as certain Herr Gellert didn't love her—he did as much as he was able, but the only thing Herr Gellert truly loved was production reports that showed an increase—at least he *wanted* her. Which was more than she could say for Herr Konrad Reichmann.

Added all up, what did it mean? That she posed a danger to the escape plan; that she served no useful purpose. Plus the man she loved no longer loved her.

Did she just think of that? Her own words surprised her.

Lisette began to weep softly.

She did still love Konrad.

The alarm clock went off. Lisette jumped, startled by the intrusion.

Mady groaned. Throwing back the covers, she rose and hit the button that stopped the annoying jangle. "Lisette? You still in bed? Are you feeling ill?"

"Just slept in," Lisette lied.

"Come on, Elyse," Mady said. "Time to get up. It's another day."

Chapter 21

The elation following Herr Witzell's successful transfer of the K7 residents to Ramah Cabin dissipated quickly with the appearance of Willi Reichmann. But it was Lisette who delivered the knockout blow when she announced the next day she wouldn't be coming to Ramah Cabin anymore.

Dry-eyed, she gave her reasons. She told them how proud she was of them and how much she loved seeing them again, but also how difficult it was for her not to speak of them to Herr Gellert. It wasn't right for her to keep secrets from her future husband. That led to the next admission—which she said should have been obvious from the first, yet even she had avoided admitting it to herself. She wouldn't be leaving with them. They would be escaping to West Berlin, and she would have to stay in East Berlin.

This was all she told them. She didn't tell them of her feelings of uselessness, with them not needing her anymore, for she had nothing really to contribute. Nor did she tell them how much it hurt for her to be around Konrad, watching him become stronger, becoming once again the Konrad she had loved for so many years, and knowing that he no longer loved her. These were personal matters. She didn't even share them privately with Mady.

Naturally there were objections and tears, but Lisette remained strong. The only time she cried was when Tomcat hugged her and pleaded with her to reconsider and told her now that he'd found her after all these years, he couldn't bear to lose her again. Konrad stood at a distance, leaning against the wall, his hands in his pockets, with no expression on his face.

When Lisette walked out the door of Ramah Cabin that day, she did so alone and without exchanging words with Konrad. Mady and Elyse stayed behind, wisely deciding not to leave the two men to deal with the emotional aftermath alone. A depression settled over the house like a funeral pall. On returning to their flat that night, Mady and Elyse found a note from Lisette saying that she'd gone to Herr Gellert's for the evening. It wasn't until one o'clock in the morning that they heard his Mercedes outside the apartment complex and the door to the flat opening and closing as Lisette slipped in and then quietly dressed for bed in the dark.

Herr Witzell made his announcement a week later. He wanted to make it clear to everyone that he, too, never intended to leave East Germany. He would help them to escape to the other side, but he wouldn't be joining them. "I'm too old for that sort of thing," he said. He assured them all that he'd cooperate fully and use every resource available to him to help them in carrying out the plan.

"And then what?" Mady said. "When Willi sees that we're gone, he'll crucify you."

"I'll disappear before that time," Witzell replied, pleased that she was concerned for him. "I've changed identities before; I can do it again. That's why I'm telling you now. I've already started the process. Someday, without any warning, I'll just disappear."

"Where will you go, Grandpa?" Elyse asked, not caring that her mother disapproved of her using the endearing name for him.

Witzell cupped her cheek with a withered hand. "It's best you don't know any of the details," he said.

"But it's not fair!" Elyse said.

"We can't expect life to be fair in a world where evil men hold the reins of power," Witzell said.

"Then what do we do?"

Witzell cupped her other cheek so that now he cradled his granddaughter's face in his hands. "We place our trust in the One who is above all earthly powers."

The winter of '61 iced the streets and froze more than the ground that year; it froze all talk of escape among those at Ramah Cabin.

Konrad organized the residents into work parties that rotated between food preparation, kitchen detail, and housecleaning.

Four paychecks supported the house. Witzell went to work like always, though they suspected that just as he'd used a portion of his time to plan for Ramah Cabin, he now was hard at work laying the groundwork for a new identity. Mady, Elyse, and Lisette continued working at the shoe factory, contributing to the house as much of their earnings as possible. After work, Mady and Elyse spent the evenings at Ramah Cabin. The frequency of Lisette's evenings spent with Herr Gellert increased, although it wasn't uncommon for Mady and Elyse to return to the flat and find her there. They suspected she spent three or four evenings a week alone. Respecting her privacy, they didn't ask.

Just like he said he would, Willi dropped in frequently and always unannounced. Gael didn't return with him, something that wasn't surprising given the fact she appeared so bored during their first visit.

While at Ramah Cabin, Willi became Mady's shadow. Wherever she went, he followed. Regardless of who was in the room at the time, his focus remained solely on her, at times leaning close and whispering in her ear. It was clear by the way he looked at her that his boyhood obsession with Mady had never gone away. Only he was no longer a boy. From the moment Willi walked through the door until the moment he left, when he would insist that she walk him out to his Mercedes, he stalked her.

Once when Willi was not present, Witzell and Konrad took Mady aside. At first she insisted that she could take care of Willi, that they shouldn't concern themselves. When they pressed, however, she admitted he was making indecent advances toward her, but she didn't want the others, especially Elyse, to know about it.

She told them that Willi had admitted to her that the only reason he was allowing Ramah Cabin to continue operating was because of her—that for her sake he would look the other way. He then let her know that he expected "friendly favors" from her in return. *"I take great risks obtaining and concealing information,"* he told her. *"But there's always a price to pay. It's important you know that, Mady. There's always a price."* She asked him what would happen if a person was unable to pay the price. To this he responded, *"That's not an option. Please don't test me on this, Mady."*

After hearing about this exchange, Konrad devised a plan whereby Mady and Willi would never be alone together. He informed the others that despite Herr Willi's busy schedule, he came to Ramah Cabin with the purpose of seeing them, only he was painfully shy about expressing himself. It had something to do with a tragic war experience. So it was important that whenever he was in the house they go out of their way to show him how much he was appreciated.

As expected, the Hadamar Six responded. They brought Willi cookies and coffee or tea. They asked him questions. They sang for him and sometimes performed little skits for his entertainment. And when they weren't nearby, Konrad was.

Christmas arrived, and Lisette joined them. The Communist Herr Gellert had no need for the holiday, so it was easy for Lisette to get away. Later she confided in Mady that Gellert made it clear that this would be the last Christmas she would celebrate.

Santa Claus himself couldn't have brought more joy to the house. Stories of Christmas at the first Ramah Cabin were thick in the air. Elyse walking around the house singing "O Tannenbaum" at the top of her lungs. Tomcat batting the tree's ornaments. The fighting over whose turn it was to play Mary while the Christmas story was read aloud.

That evening, when Konrad saw Lisette sitting alone, he went to her and wished her a blessed Christmas. They had a pleasant chat, avoiding any talk of Herr Gellert and the future. They shared memories of their own. Of Neff, the jokester. Of Ernst, who was always an easy laugh for Neff's jokes. Of Josef and Mady and the Christmas at their house when Josef did his best to present a devotion, giving them each a personalized gold medallion with a Scripture verse inscribed on it. And of Konrad and Willi knocking the tree over and scaring Kaiser the cat from the room.

"Do you still have your coin?" Lisette asked Konrad.

"Of course. You?"

"Of course."

How innocent those days were. How much had changed with the war and with Germany's fall from power. How many ugly days, days of hardship, had separated them from that Christmas so long ago.

How much they missed Josef. And Neff too. Konrad felt a fresh pang of guilt over Neff's death. He'd never forgiven himself for failing to protect him, even though now he knew the chances of any of them surviving the war had been slim. The fact that so many of them were still alive was a miracle.

Konrad thanked Lisette for coming. He told her that this little trip down memory lane with her was the best Christmas present he'd been given in a long time.

On New Year's Day Lisette didn't come to Ramah Cabin. Instead, she spent the holiday with Herr Gellert.

Konrad spent the holiday remembering New Year's Day eighteen years ago. He and Lisette were taking down the Christmas tree at Ramah Cabin when she said she had an idea. She got a bowl from the kitchen and told him to sit on the floor. She sat opposite him, placing the bowl between them. She gave him a piece of paper and a pencil and told him to write down something he hoped would happen in the coming year. She did the same. Then she instructed him to fold the paper twice and place it in the bowl.

She lit the two pieces of paper on fire.

He wanted to know what she'd written on her paper, and she said he'd have to wait until the next New Year's Day, when they'd know for sure if their wish had come true or not. Konrad remembered how beautiful Lisette looked and how he had leaned forward to kiss her, and also how she had recoiled. He remembered the pain in his gut. He'd become reacquainted with that pain. He now felt it every time he saw or thought of Lisette.

New Year's 1945, one year after Lisette burned their wishes in a bowl, Konrad confronted her, wanting to know what she'd hoped for. Lisette pretended she didn't remember, but Konrad wouldn't let her off the hook. He finally dragged it out of her.

She said, "My wish was that before the year was over, you would find a woman who would make you happy."

When she pressed him to reveal his wish, he said he couldn't remember a time when she wasn't part of his life and that he never wanted that to change. "My wish was that we would always be together."

He still wished it.

Konrad wondered what Lisette and Herr Gellert were doing to celebrate the new year.

As the ground thawed and the earth shrugged off its white winter coat for one of springtime green, talk of escaping to freedom was revived.

They heard of successful escapes from Western radio and television. Failures were broadcast persistently over East German channels. While these attempts provided a point of discussion, they did little else. For the most part, escapes were attempted by one or two persons. They had to find a way to get eight people across, six of them with some form of disability. They had to take into consideration hearing problems, blindness, a clubfoot, a shriveled arm, less than perfect speech, and a grown man with a child's mind. And it had to be all at once. Willi's surprise visits precluded any plan that provided for any sort of time-released escape. One person missing, and Willi would know something was up.

To add to their list of challenges, with each escape attempt the border agents grew wiser and as a result increased the difficulty for those who dared to follow. The Wall was upgraded. Border guards reluctant to shoot their own were swiftly replaced with those who had no qualms about killing East Germans. Towers were built, dogs trained, and kill zones established. The longer the residents of Ramah Cabin delayed, the harder their escape would be.

The plan for Witzell to contact his former employee, now guard, was resurrected. And while Witzell was willing to do this, he feared his report would be the final nail in the coffin of their escape hopes.

Chapter 22

Saturday, June 23, 1962

Otto Witzell worked the ground around his roses. Besides puzzles, Ulla had liked roses, though she was never that skilled at growing them. She had a tendency to water them to death. For the sake of the roses, Witzell took over, and he found he enjoyed it. It felt good to work outdoors with the sun on his back, and he took pride in showing off the fruits of his labor, greater pride than he thought a grown man should take in such things.

This particular morning he was out enjoying the sun, the smell of freshly overturned earth, and mostly the quiet. That was something he and Konrad had found they shared in common. As much as Witzell loved Josef's children, they were a noisy bunch, and there sometimes came a point when his ears ached so much from all the noise he thought they'd bleed. So he'd come out to the garden for a reprieve.

He found the lack of sound to be a unique sensation. At times there was nothing like it. Especially on a day like today. The morning sun. Fresh air. And quiet. The combination was a potent elixir that not everyone knew how to enjoy.

A dying breed, those who loved silence. Most people needed some kind of noise going on at all times. Radio. Television. Music. Not Witzell. After experiencing a time of silence, he found good music to sound even better. Periods of not talking made talking more meaningful. Too much noise was not a healthy thing, and too much of a houseful of people who had known one another all their lives was too much of a good thing.

Witzell straightened up and stretched his back when he saw them walking toward the house. "Lisette! How good to see you!" He let the garden hoe drop and pulled at the fingers of his gloves.

Walking beside Lisette was a man whom Witzell didn't recognize. Tall. Close-cropped hair. He moved with an easy stride. Lisette looked comfortable next to him.

"Herr Witzell!" Lisette waved.

As he approached, Witzell took a good look at the man. There was something about him that reminded Witzell of the American actor John Wayne.

"Look who showed up on our doorstep," Lisette said, stepping inside Ramah Cabin.

Elyse, Tomcat, and Annie were cleaning the front room. Elyse and Tomcat held dustrags. Annie had a broom in her hand.

Elyse looked puzzled. "Lisette? I thought you weren't . . . Herr Parker!" She dropped the dustrag and ran to Park, throwing her arms around him and giving him a hug.

Her reaction surprised Park and turned his face red. Her reaction seemed to have surprised Elyse too. Now that Elyse had her arms around him, she wasn't quite sure what to do with him.

Konrad rescued her. Coming from the back of the house, he greeted their guest, giving Elyse a chance to release him and step aside so the two men could shake hands.

"Colonel Parker," Konrad said.

Park held out his hand but didn't return the personal greeting.

"You probably don't remember me," Konrad said.

"Of course he remembers you, Konrad!" Lisette said.

"Konrad . . ." Park said as the two men shook hands. "Yes, now I remember you."

Mady appeared wiping her hands with a dish towel, drawn to the room by the commotion. When she saw who it was, she stopped.

Park looked up and saw her standing there. It was the first time he'd seen her since the day she and the children left the American army encampment back in 1945.

"Mady," he said.

How many times had he imagined seeing her again? The setting was usually a little more romantic than dustrags, brooms, and dish towels. Sometimes it was a chance meeting on the street, such as along Unter den Linden or Freidrichstrasse. Sometimes at a place like Café Lorenz. He'd look up from his cup of coffee and see her just as he'd remembered her. She never aged in his re-creations, which was foolish now that he saw her again, because as a mature woman she was more beautiful than ever, even holding a dish towel. In his fantasies she'd smile a smile that would wash over him, leaving him warm and fulfilled, and in that moment all of their differences and all the intervening years would dissolve.

Standing in the doorway, Mady looked at him, her hands twisting the towel. Then she turned and disappeared to the back of the house.

"You'll have to forgive the reception," Konrad said. "To see you here . . . to put it bluntly, you are one of the last people we would expect to see."

Park sat down on the edge of a chair, his forearms resting on his knees. "I would have called," he said, "but Mady . . . and Lisette and Elyse don't have a telephone. At least, not that I know of."

"We don't," Elyse said. She sat on the sofa next to her grandfather. She had been allowed to stay, appealing to her grandfather when Mady called from the back that everyone should return to their chores. Annie and Tomcat were sent to a different room, while Lisette, Witzell, and Konrad entertained their guest.

"I think what Konrad means to say is that we're surprised you're in East Berlin," Witzell said. "We don't see many westerners."

Park didn't answer at first. "Mady has your eyes," he said to Witzell. "There's a distinct family resemblance." He glanced down at his hands. "My apologies," he stammered. "Yes. Given the world climate, I understand what you're saying."

They waited for further explanation. When none came, Konrad asked, "Are you a diplomat?"

"No, I'm a professor. Of philosophy. At a university in California. UCLA. The Bruins. Maybe you've heard of it?"

Konrad sat back. "A philosophy professor?" he said.

Park looked at Lisette. "Why does everyone say that? Is it so hard to believe?"

"Forgive me, Colonel Parker," Konrad said, "but the last time I saw you, you were in charge of a military op behind enemy lines.

And you looked and acted the part. You just don't strike me as a professor of philosophy."

"What can I say? That's what I am."

"Even so," said Witzell, "what would a California professor be doing in Communist East Berlin?"

Park sat up. "Officially? Translating the great German philosophers."

"And unofficially?" Konrad said.

Park's face turned serious. "I'm here to help get you out of East Berlin."

Whether Mady had been listening the entire time or it was just coincidence, she chose that moment to come out and join the conversation.

"What makes you think we wish to leave?" she said. "And even if we did, what makes you think we need your help?"

She stood facing Park the way a mother would stand when demanding an answer from a wayward son, one that had better be good.

But Park was more amused than offended. If he knew her better, that might not have been so. "I know what life is like on this side of the Wall," he explained. "I also know what it's like on the other side. You'd be fools to want to stay."

Shouts came from the back of the house, both male and female. A cry of frustration, followed by a cry of dismay. Herman appeared in the doorway, his shirt soaked and splotched with dish-soap bubbles. There were bubbles on his face too, with one patch on his chin looking like a white goatee.

"Frau Schumacher!" he wailed. "Look what Marlene did to me!"

"He started it!" Marlene shouted from behind him. "He kept putting the dishes back into the water, saying 'You missed a spot! You missed a spot!' when they were perfectly clean!"

With an exasperated sigh, Mady pointed toward the kitchen. Hermann turned. Mady was on his heels.

"We're not children," Konrad teased.

Lisette and Witzell laughed. Elyse apparently didn't think it was funny.

Minutes later Mady returned.

"Look, Mady," Park said, "you have every right to hate me, but we knew there were no guarantees when we took the children to the

American base. I did what I could, but the decision wasn't mine."

"You should have left us at the house," Mady said.

"Mady, you don't know that," Lisette said. "At the time, going with Park seemed our only hope."

"It didn't take long to find out that our hopes were misplaced, did it?" Mady said.

"Think what you want," Park said. "But I'm a man of my word. I fully intended to take the children to safety, and that's my intention now. I made a vow to your husband and I intend to keep it."

"You're seventeen years too late," Mady said.

Park stood, and a stern look came over his features. "For seventeen years I've had little else on my mind other than fulfilling that promise!"

"I'll bet you have," Mady said. "I'm sure you've spent one anguished night after another while living in the land of plenty."

Park had a comeback. He started to say it, then swallowed it. He sat back down.

"If you were to help us," Witzell said, "how would you do it?"

It took Park a moment before the question registered. He hadn't yet finished stewing over the exchange with Mady.

"How?" Witzell repeated.

"By walking them across. One at a time."

Chapter 23

A car rumbled outside. Its approach was fast, accompanied by the creaking of the undercarriage as it dipped and rocked up the uneven road.

Mady sat closest to the house's front window. She peered out. "It's Willi," she announced. "Take him to the back. Lisette, you do it."

It wasn't lost on Park that the entire time he'd been at Ramah Cabin, Mady had yet to say his name. But from the quickness with which everyone stood and scattered, the more immediate concern seemed to be the person approaching in the car.

Mady returned to the kitchen. Konrad disappeared down the hallway. Witzell threw open the front door and stood there while pulling on his garden gloves. "Just in time to help me hoe around my roses!" he said to Willi, whoever Willi was. From where he was, Park couldn't see him.

Lisette took Park by the hand and led him to the back of the house, to a bedroom with three beds. She shut the door behind them.

If a similar scene had occurred in an American house, Park would have been amused and curious. But this was East Germany. Hiding and concealment were a way of life here. Those who were smart kept the volume on their televisions and radios low. They kept their private lives private and, above all else, never spoke their minds outside of their own homes. Whoever this Willi was, if Mady and the others thought it best for Park to hide, Park knew it was for everyone's safety.

Park found a straight-backed chair that had been placed in a corner of the bedroom. It had a pair of trousers hung over it and a pair of shoes shoved beneath. He sat down. Lisette paced, wringing her hands, staring at the floor. Occasional glances at the closed door indicated she was trying to listen to what was going on down the hallway. At one point she stopped, pressed her ear to the door, and held her breath.

Park surveyed the room. There were two windows, both of them open. A slight breeze moved the thin curtains. He got up and crossed the room and pulled aside the curtains of one window. The back of the house faced the edge of a forest—a forest with a rising slope. Though he still didn't know the extent of the threat, he felt it wise to have an escape route planned.

Lisette became calmer now, moved away from the door on tiptoe. "He's with Mady in the kitchen," she whispered.

"Are you in danger?"

"Willi doesn't carry a weapon," Lisette said. "Konrad asked him once. He's always been afraid of guns. He does have a cane he likes to whack things with. He's been doing that since he was a little boy."

"You know him?"

"He's Konrad's younger brother."

"So he's not dangerous."

Lisette thought about that. "It's who he works with that makes him dangerous."

"Stasi?"

Lisette nodded. "Willi makes his living as a snitch. That and blackmail, apparently."

"And you say he's Konrad's brother?"

"Yeah, but the two of them are as different as night and day." She sat on the edge of one of the beds. She appeared more relaxed.

"So," Park said, "when's the wedding?"

Lisette tensed visibly, her eyes downcast. "I don't know exactly, but he is pressing me. But now I have a question for you," she said with a hesitant glance his direction. She didn't ask the question immediately. Park waited.

"Back at the American camp, when they sent us away. What happened?"

Park pursed his lips and stared at the floor.

"You don't have to answer," Lisette said.

"It's a fair question."

It was a scene in his life that had haunted him by night and consumed countless hours of thought over the years. Each time he replayed it, he thought of something else he might have done that would have altered the outcome.

"They wanted a scientist," he began.

"We knew that going in," Lisette said. "You warned us that taking the children was risky, and not just because of the trip."

"Did I? That part's a little fuzzy for me. I remember assuring you that you'd be taken care of."

Lisette smiled. "That's what you wanted for us."

"Command could smell victory by then. The great land grab was on. The Russians were coming in hordes, and it was a race to see who would get what first." Park sighed heavily. "The children were simply in the way. My commander said they'd slow us down and that they weren't our problem. *'We're not a baby-sitting service,'* he said. *'Besides, they're just a bunch of . . .'* Well, you were the enemy."

Lisette smiled, and Park was struck by the sweetness of her face. It was the eyes. Always friendly. Warm. Nonthreatening. She had a way of making a person feel that no matter what they did or said, she would never think less of them. Park understood why the children loved her so. Yet it also made him feel worse for having let down such a good-hearted woman.

"I volunteered to make you my responsibility. Again my commander refused, insisting it wasn't our problem. The thing is, you weren't a problem. It would've been nothing for us to put you, Mady, and the children somewhere safe and out of the way. He just didn't want to do it. He was one of those men who would make a snap decision and then stick to it no matter what. So he'd made his decision, and he didn't like me challenging it."

"Did you get in trouble?"

"I did after I slugged him."

Lisette's eyebrows shot up. "You hit your commanding officer?"

"He had it coming. The more I argued, the angrier he got. He ordered me out of his tent. I wouldn't go. He called for guards. They arrested me."

"When did you hit him?"

"As I was being led out, he said something about Mady. You don't need to know the details. I took exception to it, broke free, and slugged him."

"Park!"

"It earned me time in the stockade. I thought for sure he'd press charges, that I'd be court-martialed and dishonorably discharged, but by then I didn't care. I couldn't believe how much we'd lost our focus. Two German women and a half-dozen disabled children were never the enemy. You were as much victims of the mustached monster as the rest of Europe. And we kept saying we were here to fight for liberty and justice, to do what was right. Why couldn't we extend a little of that to you?"

"Were you court-martialed?"

"It was the end of the war. So much was going on, what with all the German POWs and securing territory and keeping two armies who had a head of steam by now from crashing into each other like opposing tidal waves. I guess a punch between two men didn't seem like much at the time. Or maybe it just fell between the cracks. All I know is that I was released and told to rejoin my unit."

"But it wasn't nothing," Lisette said.

Park grinned. "You're right. Striking a commanding officer is a—"

"That's not what I meant," Lisette said. "What I mean is that you did something. You didn't just abandon us. You fought for us."

"I didn't do enough," Park said.

From beyond the door came footsteps approaching fast across the hardwood floor. Park had time to take but a single step toward the window when the doorknob rattled and the door swung open.

Lisette faced the door, her hands to her mouth, expecting the worst.

Konrad entered. He closed the door behind him.

"He's going to be here awhile," Konrad said. To Park he said, "It's best you leave the house."

Park looked at his watch. "For how long?"

"We never know."

"What's beyond the trees out back?"

"More trees."

"How about if I wait in the trees until nightfall. If he's still here then, I'll make my way back to the city."

"Avoid the access road. We're the only ones who use it. The main road—"

"I know where it is."

Konrad nodded.

"Should I take Lisette with me?" Park asked. "She'll be safe with me."

"Not necessary," said Konrad. "Her presence is easier to explain." When Park had one leg out the bedroom window, Konrad said, "I want to hear more of your plan."

Park nodded and sprinted up the side of the hill, feeling his age with every step. Although he'd kept in sufficient shape to play tennis, with each passing year his aging muscles complained a little louder. Working his way a safe distance beyond the tree line, he found a spot that concealed him while at the same time afforded him a good view of the back of the cabin.

He squatted, his heart pounding from the sudden exertion. From the excitement too. He was too old for this sort of operation. The fact that he was hiding in a German forest, that if he was caught he would go to prison—these things brought back a flood of memories of his former life, which now seemed as far from the UCLA campus as the Earth was from the next galaxy.

As it turned out, Park had to wait only a couple of hours until Willi's old Mercedes rattled to life and roared down the hill in a cloud of dust. Even after losing sight of the car, Park could hear it turn onto the main road. Then the sound of the engine finally faded until he could hear it no more. He waited an additional thirty minutes before walking out of the woods.

But should he climb back through the bedroom window or go around to the front door? After weighing this for a moment, Park decided it would be best for him to walk around the house to the front. Herr Witzell had apparently finished his work. The ground around each of the rosebushes had been dug into wells. A ring of standing water encircled them.

Witzell answered the door. "Ah! You didn't leave us."

When they were all once again convened in the front room, they explained Willi to him and by doing so confirmed that they too had at least considered attempting to get the children over the Wall. Mady sat with them, next to Lisette. Park couldn't help but wonder if Lisette had said anything to her about their conversation in the bedroom earlier.

"I'm afraid that complicates things," Park said, now that he understood Willi's role.

"How so?" Konrad asked.

Park didn't want to say. When he first arrived, he thought he had a workable plan. Not anymore. He'd even gone and told them he had a plan. Now it was a bad one and he didn't want to admit it. He was afraid of Mady's reaction.

"I have access to student visas," he said.

They looked at him. Waited for more.

"The plan was to smuggle the visas in, then use them one at a time to get the children out."

"Posing as American college students," Konrad said.

"That was the idea."

"You would cross the border with each of them?" Witzell asked.

"Yes, but it would have to be one, possibly two at a time. I couldn't exactly make it a field trip."

"Field trip?" Lisette said.

"Something elementary schools do in the States. The entire class goes on a trip. To the zoo. A museum."

"His plan won't work," Mady said.

Park winced. It wasn't what she'd said—he already knew the plan wouldn't work now—it was that she'd been so quick to point it out and that she had yet to call him by name. Not even "Your plan won't work," but *"His plan won't work."*

Witzell said, "You still haven't told us how you get across the border. There are strict limits to student visas. Can you really come and go as easily as you say you can?"

Park was impressed by Witzell. "I'm sorry, I can't tell you that," Park said.

"Are you a diplomat?" Konrad said.

"We have no diplomatic relations with the West," Witzell said.

"Then how?" Mady said. Her eyes were steely.

"I can't tell you," Park said. "You'll just have to . . ."

He didn't finish the sentence. He never should have begun it. He knew it was a mistake the moment he started it, but there was no taking it back now.

"We've heard this before," Mady said.

"Mady . . ." Lisette put a hand on Mady's arm.

"Mady's right," said Park. He looked at his watch. He stood to leave.

The others stood too. Mady left the room. Park said his good-byes to those who were left behind.

"Would you like me to walk back with you?" Lisette asked.

"Lisette?" Mady called from the back. "I need your help with something."

"That's all right. I know my way back," Park said.

He wanted to assure them that he wasn't going to give up, that he'd think of something, but heaping promises on top of disappointment didn't seem the wisest course of action.

Matthew Parker walked back to the train that would carry him to Berlin.

Chapter 24

Sunday, June 24, 1962

It was a coincidence that Park saw them on Sunday morning. Mady, wearing a floral print dress and white hat and gloves, walked a few steps ahead of Lisette and Elyse, who were also looking cleaned and pressed for Sunday services. Especially Elyse. Her hair shone in the sunlight and bounced in a carefree manner that matched her stride. Park couldn't be certain, but he thought Lisette was wearing the same dress she'd had on the day he saw her at Café Lorenz.

From across the street Park took a step back, placing a tree between himself and them in the off chance they might turn his way and see him.

The precaution proved unnecessary. Their minds were on church as they turned up the walkway toward a small stone building with its doors propped open. An elderly man in a gray suit and thinning white hair greeted them and handed them a program or song sheet or something along those lines from a stack in his hand. He'd done the same to the couple who had entered the church before the three women. Mady and Elyse disappeared under the archway that framed the door. Lisette stopped to say something to the man in the gray suit. His head went back as he laughed. He then leaned closer to Lisette and said something apparently he wanted only her to hear. She laughed and touched his arm, and then she too walked under the arch.

The man in the gray suit remained at his post for five more

minutes. Only one other person came—a young man, early thirties maybe, with a swaying necktie, a white shirt, no coat. Piano music could be heard coming from inside. The gray suit stepped halfway toward the street, looked up the street then down, turned, and walked under the archway. From the stack in his hand, it looked like he was expecting a much larger attendance.

"Sheep in search of a shepherd."

The voice startled him, even though he recognized it. Park chastised himself for letting the man sneak up on him like this. It was careless, the kind of carelessness that could get a man killed.

"Herr Koehler," Park said.

The man he greeted was also wearing a gray suit, only his looked like he'd worn it for a week, slept in it also. The man's collar was undone and his tie pulled loose. Definitely not a churchgoer but more like what Park knew him to be: an academic, and the man who had recruited Park as a spy.

Koehler looked up at Park. He had to, for he was a good foot shorter and another foot rounder. He squinted, then shielded his eyes. "Let's find someplace shady," he suggested.

A block down the street they found a coffeehouse. Park offered to buy. Koehler ordered a large coffee and then took only three sips from it. They sat in a corner in the back.

"Have an interesting day yesterday?" Koehler asked.

Park looked at him. Koehler didn't care whether or not his day had been interesting. Park had given the man tailing him the slip, and now Koehler wanted Park to account for his whereabouts.

"Should I walk slower? Would that help?" Park said. He knew better than to get smart. Communists had no sense of humor. Especially on their own turf. They were the top dogs and made the most of it, preferring snarling and snapping to satire.

Koehler's eyes flashed angrily. "Herr Parker, need I remind you—"

"Forgive me," Park said, trying his best to sound contrite. "An American weakness. Flippancy is funny to Americans."

"Not to us."

"Yes, I can see that."

Koehler glared at him, suspecting Park was being flippant again but not sure. "I spent the afternoon with a friend," Park said. "A female friend."

Koehler frowned in disapproval. "How did you meet her?"

"We've known each other since the war."

Koehler reached into his inside coat pocket and pulled out a pad and pencil. "Her name."

It wasn't a request.

"Herr Koehler, I would prefer that you keep her out of this."

Koehler's pencil was poised over the blank top sheet. He waited.

With a show of reluctance, Park gave the man what he wanted. Name. Address. Details. Then he answered a list of questions that had undoubtedly been memorized from some Communist interrogators' manual. Was she a member of the Communist Party? Had he ever heard her make remarks about the Party or its leaders? Had she ever done or said anything that would make him question her loyalty?

Park gave his lady friend a good report, knowing that they would investigate her. Only when they did, they wouldn't find her. The information was fictitious. They would come back to him. That was to be expected. He would show surprise and dismay over her disappearance. This would be looked at as suspicious, but then, they were always suspicious, so what did it matter?

"Remember, you are a guest in this country," Koehler warned.

"An invited guest," Park said. There was a time to be contrite and a time to take a stand. "Remember, you invited me to this party," he added.

Park could tell Koehler didn't like his tone, but there was no arguing the fact. It was he who had approached the American Matthew Parker, who was then a student at Frankfurt University studying philosophy. Like now, they spent hours over coffee, discussing the merits of socialism and the inevitable collapse of capitalism. It was Koehler who had questioned Park about the growing student movement in the United States and about the American Communist Party, of which Park was a member. It was Koehler who had invited Park to write a paper on the potential of the student movement. And it was Koehler who had, based on a review of the paper, recruited Park to select potential students who could be brought to East Germany to be shown the wonders of socialism firsthand and who could return to the States as missionaries of Communism.

Koehler nodded a concession of sorts. It was obvious he was still concerned about Park's disappearing act yesterday. Park was his recruit, and Koehler had higher-ups to answer to.

"Do you have any progress to report?" Koehler asked.

"I spoke to a group on campus about my visit to the shipyard factory," Park said.

"Yes, we know. You were received well."

Park wasn't surprised at the admission that even at UCLA he was being watched. "There are some promising prospects that I will follow up over the summer." Park sat up straight, animated by a revelation. He knew how to get the Hadamar Six out of East Germany!

"What is it?" Koehler asked.

Park smiled. "I was just thinking about the seed that has been planted. You know, come fall semester, I think we're going to start seeing fruit. In fact, I'm sure of it."

Following their meeting, Koehler was most insistent that Park allow them to house him for the duration of his stay. Koehler wasn't fooling anyone. But then, he didn't make any great pretense about it either, which made Park grateful in a way, even if it did provide another annoying obstacle.

From the coffeehouse they walked two blocks to Koehler's car, a tan Mercedes that had seen better days, and Koehler gave Park a lift to a small house where an elderly couple lived. Party loyalists, possibly with Stasi ties. Koehler introduced them as Herr Nikolai Popitz and his wife, Hilde. The couple led Park to a back bedroom and closed the door. They might just as well have put him in a jail cell.

The Popitzes were friendly enough. He was short and thin, with bushy white hair on both sides of his head. The top of his head was bald and freckled. Frau Popitz appeared matronly, outweighing her husband by at least fifty pounds. She had gray hair and two double chins and spoke in an unnatural falsetto voice.

They fed Park a lunch consisting of cabbage soup, homemade bread, and jam. Frau Popitz fussed over him as if he were a real guest. That afternoon, when Park mentioned he wanted to take a walk, Herr Popitz said it was a stellar idea and decided to accompany Park. The old man was good for no more than half a kilometer before they had to turn back.

Every time Park opened his door, one of the Popitzes popped up. It was automatic. Too automatic. Park discovered why. At the top of the doorjamb there was installed a metal plate. Opening the door tripped an electrical circuit that sounded an alarm of some kind, probably a bell or buzzer, though Park himself never heard one. He checked the only window in his room. If there was a metal plate, he couldn't tell because he couldn't get the window open. It had been painted or nailed shut. Either way, the only way out through the window was to break the glass.

This created a real dilemma for Park. Having figured out a way to get the Hadamar Six out of East Berlin, he was eager to share the new plan with Mady, to share it with all of them—Konrad, Lisette, Elyse, and the others. But to do that, he was going to have to break out of his minimum-security prison and then sneak back in without Herr and Frau Popitz knowing he ever left.

The remainder of the afternoon Park worked on the problem.

"What were you thinking?" Mady yelled.

For the second day she was on the warpath, a term Neff would have used, being a fan of movie Westerns.

"The last thing we need right now is another distraction! And that's all he is—a distraction!"

"I thought he could help," Elyse said, angry at her mother and angry at herself for crying like a little girl while her mother yelled at her.

They were in the kitchen. Mady had dismissed Tomcat and Annie from kitchen detail so she could yell at Elyse. Mady washed. Elyse dried. When the dishes were done, Mady started on stove parts, canister lids, the cookie jar, anything else in the kitchen that could possibly fit in the sink. She needed more time to yell.

"He can help us!" Elyse said. "Besides, I like him. I think he's a kind and caring man."

"You don't know him. An afternoon at Café Lorenz with him and you think you know him? You don't know him."

"Lisette likes him!"

That was the wrong thing to say. It only made Mady angrier, possibly because she didn't have an adequate rebuttal. Lisette had known Park for as long as Mady. And it was true; Lisette did like Park.

Soap suds sloshed over the sides of the sink as Mady scrubbed the stove's burners. "Just be quiet and do your work," she said. She plopped the last burner in the dish drainer and turned to see what else she could find to wash.

Park complained to Herr Popitz about the window, saying it was stuffy in the room and when he went to open the window to let in the breeze, he was unable to.

Herr Popitz laughed. "That window hasn't been opened since Stalin's funeral." He made it sound as though Stalin had lain in state in the room.

"Is there something we can do about it?" Park asked. He explained that he lived near the Pacific coast and had grown used to having a breeze blowing in order to get to sleep.

Popitz nodded with understanding. "I think we can do something about that," he said. "Wait right here." The old man disappeared. A few minutes later he returned with an old electric fan under his arm. It was a table model. Black and dusty. It looked like it was a relic of the war, possibly the First World War. The electrical cord was frayed in several places, a fire waiting to ignite. Herr Popitz handed the fan to Park and said, "The wife and I used this on our honeymoon."

Park didn't know exactly what the man meant by that. He didn't ask. Park thanked him and returned to his room. He plugged in the fan. He didn't expect it to work, but it did, sending dust into Park's face. After sneezing a couple of times, Park examined the fan more closely. It was exactly what he needed.

The fan was on when Herr Popitz came to the door to say goodnight. Park waited an hour, then went to work. Taking his penknife from his pocket, he pried off the circular cover that fit over the prongs, exposing two screws. He unscrewed them, freeing the exposed ends of the electrical wire. Next, he removed the cover screws for the motor. Inside, the electrical wire was soldered. It didn't matter, for he could splice the wire at that end when he was done with it.

With the electrical cord free, Park stripped the insulation from the motor-side ends. He grabbed a wooden chair at the end of the bed and stood on it.

Having second thoughts, he put the chair back and stuffed the wire under the bed, angry with himself that he hadn't thought of this plan earlier.

He went to the door and opened it. As expected, a few seconds later Herr Popitz appeared, rubbing his eyes. "Looking for something?" he said.

"One too many cups of your lovely wife's tea, I'm afraid," Park said.

Popitz nodded. "You know where it is."

"Thank you," Park said, pressing past the old man and making his way down the hall. He prayed that Herr Popitz would not be so nosy as to take a peek in the room and see that the fan was off. If he should inspect it . . .

Park stood in the bathroom an appropriate length of time. When he came out, Herr Popitz was just where he left him. Park thanked him again, and each man turned to his own room.

"By the way," Popitz said, "how's that fan working for you?"

"Just what I needed," Park said.

"The wife and I used that fan on our honeymoon," Popitz said.

Inside the room again, Park paced for a good half hour before grabbing the chair again and placing it next to the door. Retrieving the wire from under the mattress, he stood on the chair. In the gap between the top of the door and bottom of the jamb, Park could see two metal plates. He wondered who installed them. The Stasi, or Herr Popitz in an attempt to control a wayward son or daughter.

With his penknife, Park forced one end of the wire under the first plate. He tested it to make sure it would hold. He repeated the process with the second plate and then stepped down off the chair. He switched off the room light.

Gripping the doorknob, he muttered, "The moment of truth."

He pulled open the door and waited. No lights came on. No one appeared.

He stepped into the hallway, closing his bedroom door behind him. From the end of the hall he could hear snoring. Then a throat clearing. He waited and only the snoring continued. The throat clearing was definitely Herr Popitz, which meant it was his wife who was snoring.

Park checked the front door for contacts, then the street for watchful eyes, before easing his way into the night air.

Ramah Cabin was dark when Park arrived. No surprise really. It was well past midnight. His instincts still on high alert, he didn't approach the house immediately but waited and watched for any suspicious movement or the flare of a match by a bored sentry. He didn't expect anyone to be watching the house, but that was when he had to be most careful. In his enthusiasm to see Mady again, he'd played it a little too loose and it landed him in the Popitz jail. He wouldn't make that mistake again.

After a time Park made a slow search of the perimeter and surroundings. All was quiet. Satisfied, he approached the front door and knocked. The sound echoed in the nearby woods.

No one answered. Should he wait longer? Should he knock again? Park's heart began racing. He raised his hand to knock again when a forced whisper came from the other side of the door.

"Who is it?"

"It's Park. Matthew Parker. Colonel Mat—"

The lock clicked. The door opened a crack, hesitating as Park's identity was confirmed, and then opened wide enough for a man to enter. Witzell stood in the doorway in his pants and undershirt. "Trouble?" he said, looking over Park's shoulder.

"No."

"It's late."

"My apologies, but it was difficult for me to get away. I'd feel more comfortable explaining inside."

Witzell looked him over again as though seeing him for the first time. Then he stepped back and let Park in.

Konrad was standing in the middle of the front room, dressed like Witzell except for his belt, which wasn't buckled. Neither of the men had a weapon, something that surprised Park.

"I've come up with a plan," Park said.

"Couldn't it wait until tomorrow?" Konrad said.

"I leave tomorrow. It has to be tonight."

Witzell and Konrad looked at each other and arrived at a silent consensus. Witzell switched on a light, and the three of them sat.

"It would be best if Mady and Lisette heard this too," Park said.

Konrad looked confused. "That would mean going to their flat and getting them."

Park felt like a fool. He knew they didn't stay the night here. What was he thinking? Ever since he'd crossed the border with

Mady's address in his pocket, he'd acted like a muddleheaded idiot.

"You're not very good at this, are you?" Witzell said.

"I used to be," Park replied. "The rules have changed. And there are more distractions now."

"You said you have a plan," Konrad said.

Park interlaced his fingers. He really wanted Mady to be here to hear this. "Okay," he said. "Here it is: doubles."

"Doubles," Konrad repeated.

"The original plan will work; all we need are doubles. Matched sets. It'll work like the old briefcase switch. We both have identical briefcases. We meet in a public place. The switch is made, and I take the original back to the States with me."

"And the double . . . ?" Konrad said.

"Comes back here with you so that Will is none the wiser."

"Willi," Witzell corrected him.

"Right."

"You bring the doubles in from outside?" Konrad said.

"Affirmative. I recruit them, train them, bring them in on a student visa. The switch is made, and I take a replacement student back with me. The double stays here."

"Lives here?" Konrad said.

"Temporarily," Park explained. "Long enough for us to get everybody out."

"Then what happens to them?"

"That's the good part," Park said, enjoying telling his plan. "The original idea was for me to smuggle student visas in with an entry stamp. We'll do that to get the doubles out. Once the children are safe in the States, I'll smuggle the visas back in and they can walk out on their own."

"Where will the children stay in the States?" Witzell asked.

"I was thinking we could—"

"With Ernst and his wife," interrupted Konrad.

"Your scientist friend?" Park said. "Even better."

Witzell liked that idea. He was nodding. His next thought furrowed his brow. "And you can recruit these doubles? Young men and women who would be willing to do this?"

"Students. Yes, I think I can."

"Who have the same disabilities as our children?"

"A challenge, but doable."

Witzell sat back, stared at Park, and said, "Maybe it's time you tell us exactly who you are, Herr Parker."

Monday, June 25, 1962

Matthew Parker's flight departed from the Templehoff airport right on schedule. The ticket in his suit pocket listed his itinerary as Stockholm, New York, Denver, Los Angeles. He reclined his seat and closed his eyes.

Last night, after revealing his plan to Witzell and Konrad, he'd made it back to the Popitz house shortly before dawn, finding everything just as he'd left it, including Hilde's snoring. Closing his bedroom door, he removed the wires from the frame, spliced them to the fan, and tested it. Just as good as before.

Koehler just happened to stop by the house about the time he was leaving. His recruiter graciously volunteered to drive Park to the border. Park commented on how kind everyone was in East Berlin.

Now on the freedom side of the border, Park took a deep breath. Finally the years of preparation were paying off and he had something tangible to work with.

Chapter 25

"You expect me to believe that Colonel Matthew Parker is a Communist?" Mady said.

"It does stretch credibility," Lisette agreed. Since she was about to marry one, she spoke with authority. "But then, no more than to think of him as a philosophy professor."

"He said he despises philosophy," Witzell said with a chuckle, "always has. If you'd seen his face, well, that much was believable."

"Did you believe him?" Lisette asked Konrad.

"Once you hear the whole story, it makes sense," Konrad said.

While Park was winging his way west over the Atlantic, Mady and Lisette sat in the front room of Ramah Cabin listening to Konrad relate the events of the night before. Witzell had picked the three women up at the factory after work. They all squeezed into his yellow Wartburg sedan and drove directly to Ramah Cabin. Going up the hill, the car sputtered and so did Witzell, griping that these little Marx-mobiles, as he called them, had no power.

Konrad relayed Park's story to them as he remembered it. Lisette had already told them about his narrow escape with a court-martial. Mady was unimpressed.

"He said that his one goal since the war has been to make good on his promise to see that the children of Ramah Cabin are safe," Konrad began.

"Now, see? Right there," Mady interrupted. "Why? Why would

he do that? He knows nothing of these children. He barely knows any of us. Why would a man go to such lengths?"

"You think he has ulterior motives?" Witzell asked.

"Yes, I do."

"And they would be . . . ?"

Mady fidgeted. She didn't have an answer. Her thought process had never gone that far down the road. Having spent all her time fussing and fuming over Park's inability to protect them once they'd reached the American camp was as far as she'd ever gone with it. She had no plausible explanation as to why he'd returned.

"I'd put that same question to you," she said. "Why? What's in it for him?"

"Park said he made a vow to Josef to do all that was within his power to protect the kids," Konrad said.

"That's convenient, since Josef isn't here to confirm that," Mady said.

Witzell leaned forward, his forearms on his legs. "Is that so hard to believe, Mady?"

It was Reverend Wilhelm Olbricht who was speaking now. Just the way he spoke Mady's name, he became her father again.

"Look at us," Olbricht said. "Who among us isn't here because of Josef Schumacher? If it wasn't for Josef, would I be here?"

Lisette said, "I first came to Ramah Cabin because of him, and you too, Mady."

"Pastor Schumacher believed in me when I was nothing more than a Nazi thug," said Konrad. "He entrusted those children to me just before he died. That's not a responsibility I take lightly."

"Josef touched so many lives," Olbricht said. "Is it so hard to believe that he touched one more?"

When Mady had no reply, Konrad continued.

"Park said that following the war, he tried to get a position with the diplomatic corps. He was hoping to use diplomatic channels to get the children out of Soviet hands and possibly to America. But then things heated up between the Soviets and the Allies, and no diplomatic relationships were established or ever would be established, at least not anytime soon. After wasting several years going down a blind alley, as he put it, he decided he'd have to go it alone."

"To be the Lone Ranger, he said," Witzell added. He was Witzell again.

"About that time, things were heating up in America with the Communist Party, with trials and testimonies to Congress, that sort of thing. He enrolled in university to study philosophy."

"Even though he hated it?" Lisette said.

"He had his reasons," Konrad said. "And he also joined the American Communist Party."

"Was he still working for the government?" Lisette asked.

"He's not on the payroll. Again, his words. But he sends reports to them. His observations and impressions of the Party—an insider's view. After he got his degree in philosophy, he requested further studies on socialism and Marxism here in Germany."

"He studied at Frankfurt," Witzell said.

"Knowing they'd investigate his background and see that he was a member of the Communist Party," Konrad said. "Also, knowing that philosophy students tend to be . . . what was his word?"

"'Flaky,' I think he said," Witzell replied.

"Right, flaky," said Konrad. "And sure enough, after a couple of years of study here, he was contacted. First, they approached him and asked him to write a paper of his impression of the student movement in America. Then they asked him to recruit students, ones who could be swayed to adopt socialism. Leaders. Writers. Those who might someday have the potential to influence policy or great masses of people."

"That's why he's able to come and go across the border so readily," Witzell said.

"However, he's still under watch. Naturally. He had to sneak out late last night to tell us his plan," Konrad said.

"You mentioned doubles," Lisette said.

Konrad went on to outline Park's plan to the women with as much detail as he'd been given.

"So we'd house a group of American strangers and hope Willi doesn't notice?" Mady said. "And what if he does?"

"No one said it would not involve some risk," Konrad said.

"What do you think of the plan, Herr Witzell?" Lisette asked.

"It would mean we wouldn't have to attempt a mass escape over the Wall," he said.

Mady was shaking her head.

"Another man was shot and killed last night," Lisette said. "He tried to escape using a ladder."

Mady continued shaking her head.

"I think it's worth exploring," Konrad said.

Still shaking her head, Mady said, "What do we actually have? More promises. So what do we do in the meantime?"

"He asked us to wait until he returns," Witzell said.

"That doesn't seem wise," Mady said. "I say we move ahead with our own plan. If we sit around here on our hands waiting for Colonel Parker to return, we may be waiting another seventeen years."

"He'll be back," Lisette said.

"He'll be back," Konrad said.

"How can you be so certain?" Mady asked.

"He's sweet on you," Lisette said.

Mady sputtered, taken aback. "Don't be ridiculous."

"Oh, he's sweet on you," Konrad agreed. "No doubt about it."

Witzell nodded. "A father notices these things. He's definitely attracted to you, Mady."

"I've heard enough of this nonsense!" Mady said. She left the room.

Chapter 26

Tuesday, July 3, 1962

Horst Fricke was the kind of man who specialized in everything Otto Witzell despised in a person. Normally Witzell would avoid such a man, taking precautions in the same way, for example, one would take precautions against coming into contact with a flu virus. But there were two problems to this approach. First, Witzell's theology and training. As a Christian he'd been taught to respect all of God's children, even the disagreeable ones, no matter how obnoxious, rude, or revolting. As a minister it was expected of him to be kind to all persons. Over the course of Witzell's ministry—that is, the ministry of the Reverend Wilhelm Olbricht—there had been several persons with whom these professional expectations were sorely tested. Though none so great as with Horst Fricke. The second problem that kept Witzell from avoiding the man was that Fricke had information Witzell needed.

So, for the sake of Mady and the others, for two days before his scheduled meeting with Fricke, Witzell spent hours on his knees praying for the spirit and strength of Jesus for the coming ordeal. As it turned out, two days of prayer was barely adequate for him to muster enough graciousness to survive one afternoon with Horst Fricke.

He was to meet Fricke at a watchtower on Kieler Strasse in the Mitte district. It had been years since he'd been in this part of town. It seemed like another lifetime. He and Edda had found a delightful little chocolate shop on Kieler Strasse in the days they were courting, where they would stop after spending the day walking in the park at Tiergarten. The shop was owned by a very round, very jolly couple, the Rehses. For some reason, they took a great liking to Otto—Wilhelm then—and Edda.

"I knew the two of you were in love the moment you walked through the door!" Frau Rehse, Irina, said to them one day.

Her husband, Wolfgang, would come from the back room, throw his hands up in excitement, and his face would turn red. A memorable man, Wolfgang, with a huge white mustache that turned to gray at its waxed tips. He would give Wilhelm a one-armed hug, laugh, and growl like a bear. He always asked Wilhelm how his studies were progressing, commenting that Germany needed more men of God like Wilhelm.

Wolfgang and Irina Rehse. Witzell smiled, cheered by the memory.

He recalled how Irina would always put an extra piece of chocolate in their bag, insisting that he and Edda share it. *"A couple can face any difficulty in marriage if they share something sweet every day,"* Irina told them.

From the looks of them, and not just their mutual size, Wolfgang and Irina had shared a lot of sweets between them in their lives.

Witzell's destination rose up before him like a concrete monster. The Kieler Strasse watchtower. How out of place it looked here, on what was once Wolfgang and Irina Rehse's street. Stark. Gray. Smooth concrete walls stretched up to meet horizontal windows on all sides. Not many feet above the windows, a flat roof with railing and spotlights. Witzell thought of Dachau. This was something that belonged in a concentration camp, not along a city street.

The thought had struck him with force. Suddenly he was back in the concentration camp. Dachau. East Berlin. What difference was there? The accommodations were better, but that didn't change the fact that he wasn't free to go as he pleased. If he tried to walk past that bunkerlike tower to Tiergarten today, he'd be shot in the back, just as surely as if he'd tried to walk out of the concentration camp.

This was different. It was worse.

He had been sent to Dachau because, in following his conscience, he found himself having to violate a law, knowing full well that if he got caught he'd have to pay the price for what he had done.

What laws had Mady broken? Or Elyse? Or any of the children? Why must they live in the shadow of this deadly gray monster?

Until this moment Witzell had been lukewarm about an escape effort. It had been their idea, not his.

Now it was his.

A door at the base of the tower swung open. Horst Fricke saw him. Fricke looked at Witzell, then tapped his wristwatch. He wiped his nose with an index finger, hitched up his pants, and disappeared back into the monster's belly.

Reluctantly, Witzell climbed out of the car.

Otto Witzell sat with his tired feet propped up on a stool. His feet were swollen from all the walking, and his head ached from being out in the sun all day. That, and from being around Horst Fricke. But the worst part of the day was yet to come. He had to tell Mady and the others what he'd seen.

Konrad and Lisette had just walked through the door. Konrad had taken Witzell's car to the station to pick her up. While Mady and Elyse had come straight from work, Lisette had stayed behind to talk to Herr Gellert. Entering the room, both Konrad and Lisette appeared to be out of sorts. Konrad was speaking. He was finishing a sentence as they walked in.

". . . thinking of them," he said angrily. He looked up to see Witzell sitting with his bare feet resting on the stool. Whatever the two of them were talking about between the station and the house came to an abrupt halt.

Mady was the last to join them. She motioned with her head to the rooms behind her. "They're playing Parcheesi," she said of the others while taking a seat. "Did you find out anything useful?" she asked Witzell.

Her father winced and repositioned his elevated feet. It was difficult to know if the wince had been because of foot pain or because the information he held wasn't good, or both.

"I met up with Horst at Kieler Strasse," he said. "Have any of you been down there recently? A huge concrete tower has been built there. It's imposing, and depressing. Of course I had to sign in. Then Horst's supervisor questioned me. They're not letting people even get near the Wall, not without proper authorization."

"What did you tell him?" Mady said.

"They'd already checked my credentials before I arrived, so he knew about my being the administrator at K7. I simply told him the truth—that I was Horst's previous employer, that I learned he wanted to be a border guard and so I helped him to get the position, and that now I was interested in seeing how he was doing. I omitted the part that my interest in getting Horst transferred from K7 was to get rid of him."

"Was Horst grateful to you?" Lisette asked.

Witzell laughed. "You don't know Horst. *Grateful* is not in his vocabulary. He's as self-possessed and obnoxious as he ever was, only now he has deadly authority. It's frightening. Anyway, that worked to our advantage. After I was questioned, the other guards pretty much left us alone, happy that I was taking Horst off their hands for a day. They obviously don't care much for him."

Witzell repositioned his feet again; he was delaying giving the bad news.

"As it turned out, Horst proved to be a pretty good tour guide, in his own sick way. The way he speaks of the Wall, you'd think he'd designed it himself. He showed me a portion of the Wall in that area of the city, and then we took a ride outside the city to a remote section of the Wall where he's been stationed."

"Good," Konrad said. "I was wondering about the outlying areas. The more remote, the better."

"Maybe the more obvious, the better," Mady countered. "I heard that two men went over the Wall with a simple ladder."

"And nobody stopped them?" Lisette asked.

"That's the point," Mady said. "They were just two ordinary looking men with a ladder. The next thing anyone knew, they were over the Wall and free."

"That couldn't happen now," Witzell said.

"All I'm saying is, let's not try to hatch some kind of elaborate plot if something simple will work," Mady said.

Witzell didn't disagree with her, but neither was he enthusiastic about her approach. "Let me tell you what I saw," he said, "then we can decide."

Unable to find a comfortable position with the stool, he slid his feet off and straightened himself in the chair, steeling himself to deliver the news. Leaning forward, Witzell let the information spill out.

"In the city, the Wall is made of concrete slabs with barbed wire on top. According to Horst, it cuts through one hundred ninety-two streets, thirty-two railway lines, eight S-Bahn tracks, and four underground lines, as well as several rivers and lakes. At the checkpoints concrete barriers have been erected so that any cars passing through must do a slow zigzag to prevent them from picking up speed. Cars are stopped, papers are checked, and mirrors and dogs are used to locate secret compartments. As for the Wall itself, while several lorries have been used to crash through at certain points, that's no longer possible. Antivehicle trenches and antitank barriers have been constructed to prevent any more attempts."

"What's it like out in the country? Any better?" Konrad asked.

"There's a five-kilometer border zone that parallels the Wall. Only select people can live within that zone. They all know each other and are trained to report immediately anyone they don't recognize. Special authorization is needed to enter the zone. The closer you get to the Wall, there are other zones set up—each one more dangerous than the last, with each specifically designed for that area. The obstacles are many, like mesh fencing, signal fencing, and electric fences. There are zones that have upturned spikes and trip alarms. One section has a zone of soft dirt that's been carefully prepared to reveal footprints. There are towers, bunkers, dogs, floodlights, and a death strip fifteen meters wide. It's all mined."

"Oh my," Lisette said.

"As for the guards," Witzell continued, "apparently at first, many of the guards were reluctant to shoot their own citizens. They've since been replaced. Now guards who shoot people trying to escape are given a medal, a cash reward, and an all-expenses-paid holiday."

"And they have no shortage of guards, I'm sure," Mady said.

"As abhorrent as Horst Fricke is," Witzell said, "he's not unique. He told me one story that set him to laughing so hard he had to steady himself against the Wall at one point to keep from falling over. Apparently in some places—Horst was manning the Wall at Kreuzberg at the time—the Wall's built back several meters from the actual demarcation line. There are signs posted to this effect. Still, they'll occasionally get someone on the West side who thinks the Wall is the actual border. Horst and his buddies would wait on this side of the

Wall for some unsuspecting person or daredevil, whichever the case, to come across the border. When they did, a guard would bolt out and arrest them. What got Horst to laughing was the surprised look on one old man's face—someone they went after, knocked to the ground, and kicked a few times, as Horst said, 'Just for the fun of it.'"

Konrad closed his eyes, feeling the sting of shame as he relived a regrettable part of his past.

"Well, that's it," Mady said. "It's over."

"It's not over," Konrad said.

"Automatic firing systems? Land mines?" she said. "How are we going to get six disabled children through all that?"

"Maybe we don't have to get them over it," Konrad said. "Let's see what—"

"Don't say it!" Mady raised a warning finger. "Whatever you do, don't say the name Park. We're not going to risk our lives on his promises." Turning to her father she said, "What's the penalty if we get caught?"

Witzell looked at her with sad eyes. "Anyone caught organizing to assist others in escaping is sentenced to life in prison."

"Oh my," Lisette said again.

"We've got to try," Konrad said.

"How?" Mady shot back. "Tie a rope around their waists and lead them across?"

"I don't know. But we've got to try."

"Lisette," Mady said, "you be the voice of reason here. After hearing all this, what do you think?"

Lisette looked to be on the verge of tears. She said, "I shouldn't be here."

Chapter 27

"How do you think they took the news?" Konrad asked.

The car bounced onto the main road in a swirl of dust. Until now Lisette had been holding herself in place with a hand on the dashboard. She didn't look at him as she spoke.

"As well as can be expected, I guess. It's hard to tell," she said. "I can't read them like I used to."

"And whose fault is that?" Konrad snapped.

"Fault?" Lisette looked at him. "Fault? It has to be someone's fault?"

"Didn't you see their faces?" Konrad said. "Did you have to tell them you'd probably never see them again?"

"I told them the truth!" Lisette said. "It had to be said. What else was I to do? Just walk away and leave them wondering?"

Konrad squeezed the steering wheel as he drove. "Yeah, you're right. Everybody feels so much better now."

Lisette began to cry. "This is hard on me too, you know," she said.

"I'm sure your rich Communist husband will find a way to comfort you."

"Konrad Reichmann! What an ugly thing to say!"

That was where he was driving her, to Gellert's house. For a while they fell silent, both of them too angry to speak.

"Stop the car," Lisette said.

Konrad looked around them. Nothing but businesses and small shops. "I said I'd take you . . ." The next word caught in his throat. He made another run at it. "I said I'd take you home, and I will. Just point the way."

"Pull over here," Lisette insisted.

"But . . ."

"Herr Gellert lives nearby. I'll walk the rest of the way." She gathered her things. Her right hand gripped the door handle.

"I'll take you to the house."

"Konrad, pull over. Now."

With a jerk of the wheel, Konrad made a sharp exit from throughway traffic, a little too fast. The car jolted as it came in contact with the curb. He left the engine running. "Tell me," he said, "are you ashamed of me, or of him?"

"Don't be childish." Lisette opened the door.

Konrad grabbed her arm.

"Let go!" Lisette cried.

But he held tight. "It's me, isn't it? You're ashamed to introduce me to him."

"Afraid is more like it," Lisette said. "I'm afraid you'll make a fool of yourself."

She made a second attempt to climb out of the car. He wouldn't let her.

"Lisette . . ."

"I said, let go of me!" she shouted.

"Please, Lisette . . . don't go."

"Herr Gellert is expecting me."

"That's not what I meant."

She stopped struggling. Sitting on the edge of the seat with one foot on the curb, she looked at him.

"I meant don't marry this man," Konrad said.

"I don't see how it's any concern of yours. You don't even know him."

Konrad released his grip.

Lisette exited the car. She adjusted her dress and put a hand on the car door to close it.

"He's not right for you, Lisette," Konrad said.

For a moment she just stood there, her hand on the door like a statue. She stood so her face was hidden from Konrad by the roof of the small car.

"That's great," she finally said. "Just great. What gives you the right, Reichmann?"

Konrad bent low, trying to see her face. He still couldn't.

Then she stooped down to look him in the eye. "All these years . . ." she sputtered, "all these years . . ." She couldn't get past the three words. Each time she said them, she got angrier.

Konrad tried to help her out. "It's just that I always thought we'd get back together, Lisette. You know, eventually. And I think it took Herr Gellert—"

"That's what you always thought, did you? Is that what you were thinking while you spent all those days marching around the country while I waited for you at home like a heartsick little girl, hoping for Der Führer's pride and joy to show up or maybe send a letter? Is that what you were thinking when you went off on your own personal vendetta against Der Führer? Is that what you were thinking for seven years—" her voice broke—"for seven years living within kilometers of me, while all the time I thought you were dead? Is it, Herr Reichmann? That someday we would get together?"

"The only reason I took that job at the shoe store was to be near you," Konrad said.

"What? To be near me? That's rich!"

"Yes, to be near you. I saw how you were. You'd moved on. You had a job. You had Mady and Elyse. You had Herr Gellert. You had a normal life. What did I have to offer you? Life in a Soviet gulag? Believe me, Lisette, I may have walked away from it, but it's still a part of me. Every night I'm back there again, reliving it." His emotion caught up with him.

"Konrad . . ." Tears welled up in Lisette's eyes. "Konrad, all you had to do was—"

"Please! Don't tell me what I should have done," Konrad said. "Life's a lot simpler when you're sitting in a rich man's parlor, Lisette. Don't you think I beat myself up every day telling myself what I should do? I don't need any advice from you."

"Then what, Konrad? What is it that you want from me?"

A pain in Konrad's chest constricted his breathing. He couldn't think. "I don't know," he blurted. He reached across the seat and grabbed the door handle. Just before slamming the door shut, he said, "You're fiancé's waiting for you."

He rammed the car into gear and roared off in a cloud of blue-black smoke that smelled of oil. In the rearview mirror he saw Lisette standing on the curb, her hands helplessly at her sides. She was crying.

With the Parcheesi game back in full swing in the boys' bedroom, Elyse and Tomcat sat on the floor opposite each other, cross-legged. It was a rule that the boys weren't allowed in the girls' room, but Elyse didn't feel like playing Parcheesi after the family meeting. Besides, they were sitting on the floor and the door was open. Who could object to that?

Lovable Viktor saw them go in the room and followed them. He wanted to sit on the floor too. Elyse asked him to leave. Politely. Viktor's feelings got hurt, so Tomcat took him aside and managed to smooth things over with him. The boy worshiped Tomcat.

"How are you taking the news?" he said, joining Elyse again on the floor.

"Which news? About staying? Or Lisette's news?"

"Which one's bothering you?"

For a boy, Tomcat was insightful. He had an extraordinary ability to sense a person's mood.

"Lisette's news is disturbing, of course, but it's different for me. I still get to see her. At work. And at home, that is, until she gets married."

"But . . ."

Elyse smiled. "But, I guess I always hoped that something would happen and she wouldn't marry Herr Gellert."

"Is he a bad man?"

"Not bad. Not really. He's our boss. He's always pushing for us to work faster." She did a poor imitation of a man's voice. "'Production is down! Unacceptable, people! Unacceptable! Are we losing our focus here? Do I need to remind you that we're working in the greatest socialist state in the world?' I think the thing that bothers me most is that he really believes that. These things are important to him."

"Yet isn't that what you're supposed to be doing—making shoes?"

Elyse sighed. "Spoken like someone who's never worked in a factory," she said. She touched his hand. "I didn't mean that in a bad way, Tomcat. It's just that Herr Gellert is more concerned about making shoes than he is about the people who make them. And I'm afraid that's how he's going to be with Lisette. And I think Lisette deserves better."

Tomcat nodded.

"As for staying here, I guess I'm disappointed. I was hoping that we all might get to go to America, but I never really believed that would happen. You know what I mean?"

"I know."

"How about you? Are you disappointed we'll be staying here?"

Tomcat shrugged. "I like living here better than living at K7. The orderlies here are nicer."

Elyse laughed.

"There is one thing I miss, though."

"Don't say it," Elyse warned.

"I really miss—"

"Don't say it!" She leaned forward and put her hand over his mouth.

His words were muffled, but they still came through. "I miss Herr Witzell's Frank Sinatra records."

They were both giggling now. Tomcat really did miss listening to Sinatra. Even though they had a record player and Witzell had a couple of Sinatra LPs, nobody would let Tomcat play them. His choice of music was always drowned out by a chorus of boos.

"But I'd give up Sinatra for you any day," Tomcat said.

Elyse's lips formed a grateful pout. "What a sweet thing to say," she said.

She gripped his hand. He gripped back and pulled her closer to him. An invitation, and one she was eager to accept. Elyse's eyes closed. She didn't know why, they just did. Possibly to heighten the sensation, which it did, because she could feel the warmth of Tomcat's lips and breath, heightening the anticipation of what was to come.

"Can I come in now?" Viktor asked. "They won't let me play Parcheesi. They said I don't play right."

It was twilight. Witzell and Mady walked among his roses. Mady had picked up a stone and was tumbling it back and forth from hand to hand.

"I didn't want the others to hear us," Witzell said, explaining why he'd asked her to step outside. They walked in separate rows, speaking over the roses. "I want you to know how proud I am of you," he said.

Mady allowed herself half a smile. "I can see why you wouldn't want the children to hear that."

Witzell chuckled. "A sharp tongue. Even when you were a little girl. You got it from your mother."

"I suppose next you're going to tell me you were always the mellow one."

"I wouldn't presume. There were times when I thought you knew me better than your mother did. You certainly knew how to handle me."

"All little girls know how to handle their fathers," Mady said. "Is that what you wanted to tell me? Because I have a sink full of potatoes in the kitchen waiting to be peeled."

She couldn't have hurt him more had she hit him with the stone. The potatoes were only an excuse not to be with him. Mady didn't peel potatoes; that was the kind of work she had the younger ones do. She'd searched for a reason to leave Witzell standing among the roses by himself, and a sink of potatoes was as handy of an excuse as any.

Despite the blow, Witzell continued. He had something he needed to say.

"When you were little . . ." he began.

Mady sighed, a little too loudly.

"I would do anything to protect you. I sacrificed my theology, my personal beliefs, my very soul trying to protect you."

"Don't put all that on my doorstep," Mady snapped. "You were afraid, plain and simple. You had too much to lose. The Nazis intimidated you, and you gave in. I had nothing to do with it!"

"You had everything to do with it!" Witzell said, raising his voice. "Do you think I was afraid for my own life? I was afraid for you and your mother. I cooperated, thinking that by doing so I could protect you from harm."

"Is that why you turned on Josef? To protect me?"

"Yes!" Witzell said, his face red, his eyes teary. "Yes! Yes, yes . . ." Each yes came out sounding softer. "He was reckless, and his recklessness put you—put all of us—in danger. I did what I did for you."

"You killed my husband!"

Witzell was so distraught, he could barely remain standing. But there was nothing to lean against, only rosebushes and Mady, and neither of them would hold him up right now.

"Do you want to know the worst part?" Witzell said.

"What, worse than killing Josef?"

Witzell nodded sadly. "The worst part is that you didn't need my protection. You were strong enough to protect yourself, only I didn't see it at the time."

Mady said nothing. She plucked at the petals of a rose.

"Look at all you've been through. You've endured more hardship and suffering in your lifetime than any woman should ever have to. And you've survived. War. Death. Famine. Exposure to the elements. Abandoned and on your own. Yet you survived."

"Turnip Winter."

"What?"

"Mother told me once about Turnip Winter and the shortages following the First World War. She said I should count myself fortunate that I didn't have to live through it."

"But you did, and with six children. You kept them alive. Safe. Together. Even though they don't share the same blood, they're closer than most families."

"They fight like brothers and sisters."

"Then finish the job."

Mady turned on him. "What did you say?"

"You heard me. You've come this far. Now finish the job. Konrad's right. There's no place in East Germany for these children."

"It doesn't seem to me like we have a choice," Mady said. "You saw with your own eyes what we're up against."

"Yes, I did. I saw the Wall. I saw the guards. I saw the towers, the barbed wire. You know what else I saw? Dachau. I saw Dachau all over again. I saw that my daughter and my granddaughter are stuck behind the walls of a concentration camp the size of a city, and I didn't like it."

"It appears to be our lot in life."

"That's fear talking," Witzell said.

"I can't believe you said that!"

"I speak from experience. For years I cowered before it, letting it rule my life like some sadistic taskmaster. And now you're doing the same thing."

"I have potatoes to peel," Mady said. She started walking toward the house.

"I lost you for twenty years because of my fear, Mady. I lost you when I thought I was protecting you. Don't make the same mistake."

Mady didn't comment. She continued walking instead.

"There'll come a point," he called after her, "when, as evil as it is, the concentration camp becomes comfortable because there's an order to it, you know your place, you know what's expected of you. Talk to Konrad. He knows. He told me once that the worst thing the Soviets ever did to him was to set him free. That's you, Mady. You're afraid of freedom. You like it here. You can be angry and blame everyone for putting you here. Here, you're a martyr."

She'd reached the front door.

"You'd rather nurse your anger than be happy. You'd even sacrifice the happiness of everyone inside that house just so you won't have to give up your anger and your precious martyrdom. Why are you afraid of allowing yourself to be happy, Mady? Have you asked yourself that?"

Mady turned on him and said, "What does happiness have to do with anything in this world?"

"I don't see why I have to go with you," Gael said, pulling a compact mirror from her purse and checking her makeup.

There was a small glop of mascara in the corner of her eye. She picked at it with the nail of her little finger until it was gone. The Mercedes took a bump at a high rate of speed, and she nearly poked herself in the eye.

"You always drive too fast," she complained.

Willi steered with the heel of his crippled hand while he smoked a cigarette with his good hand. His cane lay on the seat between them.

Though dusk was fast approaching, there remained enough ambient light to see into the trees and catch an occasional view on the passenger's side of the road.

"I'm always going someplace or other with your friends," Willi said. "It's time you returned the favor."

Gael dropped the compact into her purse and grimaced. "I've known these people as long as you have. Except your brother. And since when have you considered them your friends? We both know the only reason you go over there is to fawn over Mady Schumacher. It's sickening, and I don't want to spend all evening watching you."

From the beginning their marriage had been one of convenience. Romance had nothing to do with it. They had each allowed the other their dalliances, without question and without jealousy. Gael didn't object to his going after Mady. She didn't care. Except with Mady he'd become obsessed with telling Gael everything he thought about Mady, everything they talked about. Now he wanted her to witness their conversations or whatever they happened to be doing together, which probably was nothing. She was certain there was nothing going on between Mady and Willi. Because of Mady, of course. The attraction was completely one-sided. Willi was just fooling himself. No, worse than that. He was making a fool of himself. And while there was some amusement to be had in watching Willi humiliate himself, Gael didn't want to give up an entire evening to see it.

"What's this?" Willi said. He was looking in his rearview mirror. A car had come up behind them and was flashing its lights.

Gael turned in her seat to get a better look. "Who is it?"

Willi studied the image in the mirror. "It's Toad. I wonder what he wants."

"Toad?"

"Georg Zaisser. He works with me."

"What does he want?"

"How should I know?" Willi pulled the car off the road onto a dirt turnout. They'd been climbing steadily and had reached an elevation of about two thousand feet. The horizon had not yet surrendered the last of its color; a strip of pink and blue still lined a distant ridge.

"Don't get too close to the edge!" Gael said, leaning back in her seat as though that would stop them from going over.

Willi braked to a stop. He pulled the keys from the ignition and opened the door. "I'll be right back."

"Hurry," Gael said. "I have needs, if you know what I mean."

"Just sit back and enjoy the view," Willi said.

Toad was climbing out of his car. His straight, oily hair was blowing every which way, something that seemed of no concern to him. Matters of hygiene seemed of no importance either. His shirt and pants were unbelievably wrinkled and dirty, and his shoes were untied.

"How fast were you going?" Toad said, looking a bit agitated. "I had the thing floored and I still almost didn't catch up with you!"

"Keep your voice down," Willi said. "She'll hear you."

In the car, Gael watched as Willi spoke with the other man. She didn't recognize him. But then, she didn't concern herself with Willi's business. She didn't even know exactly what he did, only that he brought home plenty of money and then gave her some of it without her having to put up too much of a fuss. Occasionally he took her to nice restaurants too. There were times when he was gone for a week or two, but not often. Most evenings she had someone to talk to and someone to protect her when she got scared, although he sometimes ridiculed her for her fear. They slept in separate bedrooms, and he was usually gone by the time she climbed out of bed, which was usually around noon.

The two men walked to the back of the Mercedes, where Willi opened the trunk and she lost sight of them.

"That's an old one," Toad said.

"It was my father's," Willi said as he hefted the rifle from the trunk. He checked to see if it was loaded. It was.

Toad's eyes lit up. He always got excited during an operation, like a little boy on Christmas morning.

Willi stepped back from the car, keeping more to the driver's side. He set his feet and rolled his shoulders to get the kinks out. With a smooth movement that came only with practice and expertise, especially considering his disability, Willi Reichmann raised the rifle barrel with his crippled arm. His good hand pulled the stock against his shoulder with his finger reaching for the trigger. He was steady, his breathing calm. He nodded to Toad, who was still standing near the open trunk, only to the side now. At the signal Toad slammed the trunk shut.

Gael had her compact mirror out again, checking her makeup, her little finger back to the corner of her eye.

The report of the rifle and the shattering of the back window of the Mercedes sounded simultaneously. Gael slumped forward in her seat. While she was almost certainly dead, Willi took pleasure in firing three more rounds into the back of her seat.

Toad started clapping. The half-wit was actually clapping. "Divorce, Willi-style!" he laughed. He thought he was awfully funny. "Get it? Divorce, Willi-style. Pretty good, huh?"

"Put this in your car," Willi said, handing the rifle to Toad.

Willi wasn't laughing. He was at work. He moved with businesslike efficiency. Rushing forward, he pulled open the driver's-side door, returned the keys to the ignition, and started the engine. He didn't look at his dead wife. Instead, after releasing the parking brake, Willi slammed the door and then hollered at Toad, "Help me with this!"

The two men pushed the car over the edge of the turnout, the very edge that Gael was afraid Willi had driven too close to. They watched the car plunge down the steep slope, clearing a path through the brush and small trees. Gaining momentum, it tumbled all the way down to the rocky base of the mountain.

Willi stood there, staring down at his mangled Mercedes. "Come on, come on," he muttered.

A flicker of flame appeared.

"Come on!"

He'd filled the fuel tank just before they set out tonight.

"Come on!"

Toad stood next to him, looking at the car as if it were a feature film.

The car erupted into flame.

Toad clapped.

Turning to Toad, Willi said, "I'll pick up the rifle from you Saturday."

"Saturday," Toad said.

"Only one thing left to do," Willi said.

Toad took a step back.

Willi walked to the edge of the turnout, his back to Toad. The moment his shoes reached the brink, his businesslike demeanor vanished. He began to shake—violent tremors that shook his entire frame. Then he began to giggle. "Do it," he ordered Toad without looking back.

"You sure?"

Willi's giggles became uncontrollable. "Do it!"

"You're gonna hold it against me if I do," Toad complained, genuinely afraid. "Can't you just, you know, take one more step?"

Perspiration trickled down the sides of Willi's face. His eyes were closed. He was half laughing, half crying. He'd begun to inch away from the edge. "I said, do it! Do it! Do it!"

After a few seconds' hesitation, Toad rushed up behind Willi and shoved him over the edge. He didn't wait around to see what happened. After skidding to a stop, Toad reversed his direction and ran back to his car. He tossed the rifle onto the front seat, jumped in, and sped off, the rear tires making a rooster tail in the dirt.

When Witzell went to answer the front door that evening, he found Willi standing there, his clothes and flesh torn in numerous places. He was covered with dirt and wore only one shoe. His left eye, the good one, was black and blue, and the patch was missing from the other eye, revealing a horrible scar.

Willi told a nightmarish tale that began with his pulling his car onto the turnout. Gael had insisted. The sky was so beautiful at twilight, she wanted to stop and enjoy it. One thing led to another. She became amorous and in her enthusiasm accidentally knocked the car into gear. Willi explained that if he'd had two good hands, he might have been able to regain control of the car. But with one hand being useless . . . The car inched over the side. The last thing Willi remembered before waking up at the base was Gael's screams. He himself was thrown clear of the wreckage. Gael wasn't.

Willi got the reaction he wanted from his Ramah Cabin audience. They were shocked. Saddened. Sympathetic. He'd hoped for a more emotional response from Mady, but in time that would come. Now that Gael was out of the way, Mady would be more open to his advances, in time. And Willi had plenty of that. No one was going anywhere.

Chapter 28

Tuesday, August 21, 1962

Ramah Cabin had settled into its new routine. Konrad managed the house during the day, doing his best to keep the residents occupied and productive. Witzell kept regular hours at the K7 facility, with no more of the late nights that had once characterized his work schedule. Working at the shoe factory during the day, Mady and Elyse took the train and were later picked up by Witzell on his way home.

Willi's visits became more frequent. He visited four nights a week: Monday, Wednesday, Thursday, and Saturday. No one knew the reason why these nights and no others, nor did anyone know what Willi did the other three nights of the week. When he came, he usually brought gifts such as flowers, chocolates, or coffee, all of which had to be purchased illegally at an Intershop.

It didn't take long for Willi to grow wise to their plan to keep him from being alone with Mady. He began pulling Mady into empty rooms, closing the doors, and blocking them from the inside with whatever was handy—a chair, a wastebasket, a typewriter. He discouraged any attempted intrusions with curses, until Mady finally informed everyone that she could handle Willi and didn't need rescuing. No one knew what went on behind the closed doors. Mady never spoke of it.

The new routine didn't include Lisette. Mady and Elyse saw her at the factory on workdays. They reported she was well and that she'd been spending every evening with Herr Gellert. She spoke as if she and Herr Gellert were already married. She talked about the house, the meals they shared together, of Gellert's goal for making the factory a model of socialist production, along with his views of recent events. He thought President Kennedy was a typical tough-talking westerner but an intellectual lightweight who would plunge the world into another war; that the Soviet Union space achievements were evidence that there were no equals in the world to Communist scientists; and that Valeri Brumel's world high-jump record of 7 feet 5 inches was proof that Communist men were physically superior to Americans. Herr Gellert was all Lisette talked about anymore, and with that being the case, their days at the factory were spent largely in silence.

Mady was fixing a stew for supper. She had planned to use stock she'd made the night before and had left instructions for the vegetables to be cut and placed in the stock over a low flame by mid-afternoon. However, when she walked into the kitchen after work, the oven was cold and the vegetables sat on the counter untouched. Elyse had gone to the back of the house to see where everyone was. Something was supposed to be simmering, and since supper wasn't, Mady was.

She was looking around for an explanation when she heard the front door close. Thinking it was Konrad, she headed that direction seeking answers, and they'd better be good ones.

"You," she said, surprised. She would get no explanation for the uncooked vegetables from the man standing in the darkened entryway just inside the front door.

"Mady," Park said.

Elyse stood beside him.

Why was it that certain people had a knack for showing up when she least wanted to see them? Park was the last person Mady wanted to talk to right now.

"Have I come at a bad time?" Park asked.

Mady started to answer. No words came. Something wasn't right, something she couldn't put her finger on. And it had to do with Elyse, not with Park, though it galled her that he'd returned just like everyone had predicted he would.

Not Elyse! That wasn't her daughter standing next to Park!

Tomcat emerged from the hallway. "Did I hear Colonel Parker's voice?" he said.

"Hello, Tomcat," Park said.

Elyse smiled. A pretty smile. But it wasn't Elyse's smile. Mady's mind started swimming; she had to grab hold of something solid.

Tomcat moved to Mady's side. "Isn't someone going to introduce me to our guest?" he asked.

"Impressive," said Park.

Mady stared at the girl beside Park. The resemblance to Elyse was uncanny.

"Tomcat has no visual clues to throw him off," Park added.

"Why? Does she look like Elyse?" Tomcat asked.

"Yes," Mady said with a faraway voice. "Yes, she does."

"Cool," Tomcat said.

The uncut, uncooked vegetables were forgotten for the moment, though the issue would come up again when there was no stew at suppertime. Tomcat called everyone from the back to see the new Elyse, including the original Elyse.

A few minutes later Konrad and Witzell walked through the front door.

"Whose car is that out front? Would you look at that," Witzell said, catching sight of the two versions of his granddaughter.

Konrad was equally dumbfounded. "Colonel Parker, you did it," he said. "You said you could do it, and you did."

"Everyone," Park said, "I'd like you to meet Sharon Lewis. Miss Lewis is a journalism student at UCLA."

There ensued a general hubbub as everyone greeted her. Witzell stepped forward.

"Welcome to Ramah Cabin, Miss Lewis," he said. "Allow me to make introductions. I'm—"

"Please," Park interrupted him. "Let's allow Miss Lewis to do it."

Witzell was intrigued, as were the others.

"Very well," Sharon Lewis said. She approached Witzell. "Herr Witzell," she said. "Or should I say, Reverend Olbricht? But then, I'd call you Grandfather, wouldn't I?"

One by one, she went around the room.

"Herr Reichmann, Konrad." Sharon offered him her hand.

"Frau Schumacher. Mady. Mother. If I may . . ." She hugged Mady.

"Now, let's see . . ." she said. "Viktor, you're easy—you're the sweet one."

Viktor blushed.

Annie pulled her left hand behind her back and angled herself so Sharon Lewis couldn't see it. Marlene was standing as she often did with her hands behind her back. But Sharon wasn't fooled.

"Marlene and Annie," she said, identifying them correctly. "Hermann. Are you as lucky at Parcheesi as they say you are?"

"He cheats," Annie said.

"And Tomcat," Sharon said. "You're even more handsome than Park said you were."

It was Tomcat's turn to blush. At first, Elyse laughed with the rest of them. Then she stopped laughing. Rather abruptly.

"I don't see Fräulein Lisette," Sharon Lewis said, looking around.

"She's . . . not here tonight," Konrad said.

Sharon walked over to Elyse. "You know . . . all of a sudden my mind went blank. Who are you?"

Everyone broke into laughter, especially Viktor, who thought it was the funniest joke he'd ever heard in his life. He was happy to have two Elyses in the room. It was remarkable. For Elyse, it was the strangest sensation to see her mirror image take on a third dimension, a voice, and a personality.

Following dinner—sausage sandwiches, for it was too late to cook vegetables now—the conversation took on a more serious tone. The fun and games were over. They all knew why Park had brought Sharon Lewis to Ramah Cabin, and thoughts of escape and the feelings of danger that accompany such an endeavor were now very much present.

They found Sharon to be an articulate young woman. Park explained how he got her into East Germany.

"She's here to study the German labor movement," he said, "under a *Studienbesuch,* a study visit. The Communist Party is interested in cultivating select American students who have an interest in history and are leaning toward socialism."

"Do you lean toward socialism, Miss Lewis?" Witzell asked.

"Yes," she said, convincingly and without hesitation. Then she smiled. "Officially, that is. And especially while I'm on this side of the Wall. If you were to ask me that question while I was standing in Bruin Plaza, I'd probably give you a different answer."

"Bruin Plaza?" Konrad said.

"The university campus in California," Park said.

"You're here under what arrangements?" Witzell asked.

Park answered, "Student visas are issued at the border for up to six to eight weeks. My contacts are particularly interested in journalism students. They arrange tours for the students that include meeting with local labor officials, members of the Socialist Unity Party, university professors, local German-Soviet Friendship Societies, a visit to the Lenin Museum and monuments of the German labor movement, such as Karl Liebknecht's home in Leipzig and the Museum of German History. They've even offered to make certain library and archive materials available."

"The last time you were here, Colonel Parker," Konrad said, "you had to sneak back here at night. How is it that you can travel so openly now?"

It was a valid question, its seriousness reflected in Konrad's eyes. Movement within Communist East Germany was restricted and regulated. The only persons who enjoyed freedom of movement were trusted Communist officials.

"We've been here since the third of August," Park said. "Because I am an official supervisor, or guide, I'm given the privilege of moving around freely. The car out front, for example. And I'm responsible for Miss Lewis's movement. However, it would be unwise of me to think that such a privilege is not under constant surveillance."

"A wise assumption," Witzell said.

"Our shadow—that's what we've been calling him—fell asleep at the university," Sharon Lewis said, giggling.

"After six hours in the archives," Park added. "I imagine we'll have a fresh replacement by morning."

"Why would you do this?" Mady asked.

There was not even a hint of friendliness in her voice. It was a straightforward question, asked in a cold, hard tone. She leaned forward for an answer, staring unblinking at the girl who had her daughter's face.

Sharon Lewis met her gaze. "If you think I'm doing this as a lark, or a game, or for some thrill or sense of adventure, you couldn't be more wrong, Frau Schumacher. Am I frightened? I'm scared to death. I have no illusions. If I'm caught, I'll most likely go to Hohenschonhausen prison. How do I know that? The last story I researched was of John Strickmann, a twenty-five-year-old son of a University of Vermont professor of psychology. He was captured here in Berlin and convicted in a closed court for allegedly trying to help East Germans get over the Wall. He was supposedly here writing a paper on the Communist playwright Bertolt Brecht. According to his father, Strickmann was positively impressed with Communism. Yet he made the mistake of expressing openly that he thought the Communist regime in East Berlin would collapse if Moscow decided to pull its twenty divisions out of East Germany. He was arrested for slander, and the elderly couple he was staying with testified—probably under pressure—that he offered to help them escape to the West. So yes, Frau Schumacher, I am fully aware of what I am doing here and the risk that it entails."

"But *why*? Why would you do it?" Mady said.

Until now, Sharon Lewis had been an emotional rock. Self-assured and steady. Asked this question, her eyes glazed with tears and her voice grew husky.

"Because Professor Parker told me about you. About what the Nazis tried to do to you. . . ." She paused, looking at each of the Hadamar Six. "And how your husband rescued them. I can't imagine what it's been like for you all these years. But I know one thing. I want to be a part of any effort that will get you to freedom, because I think you deserve that much."

"One more question," Mady said.

"Ask as many questions as you wish."

"Can you sew?"

"A little," Sharon said.

"Have you ever sewed shoes in a factory?"

"No."

Chapter 29

Mady had a problem with Park's escape plan—it just might work. The American replica of her daughter proved to be charming, intelligent, and brave. To the casual observer she could easily pass for Elyse. At the factory, Mady and Lisette could cover for her while she got acquainted with the machine and routine. It would probably involve some sick days; the girl's fingers were soft and smooth—those of a journalist, not a factory seamstress. Personal interaction would be risky, but that was limited at the factory anyway. They could sit "Elyse" between them. They usually came straight from the factory to Ramah Cabin. It could work. And that was the problem.

"Why Elyse?" Mady asked.

"I'm not sure I understand," Park replied.

"Why Elyse? Why did you choose her for your little experiment?"

"Someone had to be first. As far as finding a replacement, her hearing disability isn't visible, so she's the safest choice for a trial run. Besides, I had pictures of her."

"Oh?" Mady made it sound like there was something wrong with his having pictures of her daughter.

"From Café Lorenz," he explained. "The afternoon we met there. With Lisette."

With each question, Mady felt Elyse slipping away from her, and there was nothing she could do about it. "What if something goes wrong?"

"Like what?"

Mady waved a hand. "Anything. I don't know. Fingerprints, a slip of the tongue, anything."

"Unless she commits some kind of crime, taking her fingerprints is unlikely. The authorities already have Miss Lewis's fingerprints on file. I've tried to think of everything. But I won't kid you. Any attempt we make is going to be risky."

Slipping. Slipping. It was as though Park had greased everything, and Mady couldn't hold on much longer.

"You're being unusually quiet," Mady said to Elyse, who was sitting on the floor, huddled next to Tomcat. There weren't enough chairs for everyone.

"You mean besides the eerie feeling of seeing myself sitting on the sofa? Other than that, in a way it's exciting, and in another way, frightening."

"What are you scared of?" Mady said.

"Not the actual crossing," said Elyse. "I mean, look at us, we can easily use each other's photo identities. And it's not like I'll be doing this alone. Herr Parker will be there with me, and I trust him."

"It would be best if you began calling me Professor Parker," Park said. "Herr Parker probably wouldn't raise any eyebrows, but since our relationship is professor-student, Professor Parker is safest."

He thinks of all the details, Mady thought. More grease.

Elyse nodded, taking his instruction.

"Then what scares you?" Mady repeated.

"Leaving all of you," Elyse said, tears edging her eyes. She felt for Tomcat's hand and found it, but she was looking at her mother. "I've never been away from you and Lisette in my life, and I've just found Tomcat and Viktor and everyone else again. It's hard thinking about leaving all of you."

"But we'll be right behind you," said Tomcat.

"Will they?" Mady asked Park.

Park sighed. "It won't be easy. It's not as if I can advertise in the newspapers. It'll take some time. And I'll need to get pictures. I brought my camera. But yes. I think I can find doubles for everyone. Not everyone will match up as easily as Elyse, but I have some ideas. Possibly Herr Witzell can help with some of them."

"Whatever I can do to help," Witzell offered.

"Frau Schumacher . . . I mean, Mother," Sharon Lewis said. "If

Elyse should start calling him Professor Parker, then I guess I should start calling you Mother. If anyone can do it, Professor Parker can."

"Well, considering what we've learned about the Wall," Konrad said, "it sounds like the best plan for success."

Everyone's trying to take my baby away from me, Mady thought. She looked at her father, who was looking at her. She knew what he was thinking. He'd tried to protect her and had lost her as a result. She was doing the same thing with Elyse. But how could she give Elyse up and still have her at the same time? Slipping. Slipping. Her baby was slipping out of her hands.

"What about Viktor?" Mady said. "You can find a retarded university student who wants to study Marxist history?"

It was her last remaining card to play. Eliminate one from the rescue effort and the whole scheme could possibly crumble.

Park sighed and said, "Viktor is a unique challenge. We'll probably have to go a different route with him. The student angle won't work. I have some contacts that I'm exploring, which involve a medical angle. That's one of the things I wanted to talk to Herr Witzell about."

"A medical angle?" Mady said. "You can't be more specific?"

"Not at present."

"Until you *can* be more specific," Mady said, "I think it's best we wait."

Park winced. "That may not be possible."

Mady folded her arms. She had the distinct impression she wasn't going to like what Park was going to say next.

Park rubbed flat hands together. "Sharon's visa is good through Monday."

"Monday?" Mady cried. "That's less than a week away."

Park looked at her with sympathetic eyes. "We'll need to make the exchange Sunday. I know it's not much time, but we have to work with what we've been given."

"Considering all you've done, Colonel Parker," Konrad said, "we can make the necessary arrangements by then."

Mady glared at Konrad and Park. Such a simple decision for them to make. They had no idea of the turmoil she was feeling. Already they were talking about how the exchange would be handled.

"One thing more," Park said, standing. He looked to Sharon.

"Oh, the dirt," she said.

She rummaged in her handbag and produced four letters and a plastic bag of dirt. Park distributed the letters. One to Mady, one to Konrad, one to Elyse. "And this one's for Lisette," Park said, holding up the remaining letter.

"I'll see that she gets it," Elyse said.

"They're from Ernst," Park said. "He and Rachelle are excited about having each of you join them at their home in Huntsville, Alabama. It's large enough for about half of you. They're looking for a larger place along Cedar Ridge so they can accommodate all of you. It's beautiful country. Trees. Lakes. Friendly people. You'll love it, and them too. They're a wonderful couple. And they sent this." Park held up the bag.

Sharon Lewis began to laugh. "You wouldn't believe the attention a bag of dirt can get at the border. It held us up for two hours."

"Apparently not everyone brings dirt with them into East Berlin," Park said.

"One inspector smelled it," Sharon said, laughing, "putting his nose against it, then he tasted it!"

"Compliments of Ernst and Rachelle Ehrenberg," Park said. He stood to one side and poured the dirt onto the hardwood floor.

Mady gasped. Had Lisette been there, she would have gasped too, only louder.

"Come here," Park said, spreading the dirt around with the toe of his shoe. "A little ceremony. This was Ernst's idea."

Unsure as to what they were doing, everyone stood. Park motioned and urged them to join him. "Everyone on the dirt," he said.

It was like a party game. There were smiles, glances, smirks, raised eyebrows. They had to press in close for everyone to fit. This was accompanied by a crunching sound as they all found a section of dirt on which to stand.

Park said, "Ernst wants you to know that this dirt came from Cedar Ridge, near his home. It's there he will purchase a home where all of you can live. He said he'll call it Freedom House. He wants you to know you are now standing on free soil, and that someday we will once again stand together on Cedar Ridge soil in America. I give you my pledge not to rest until that day."

Sunday, August 26, 1962

Park checked his watch.

11:44 A.M.

It was time. They had arrived well after Mady and Elyse were to arrive at church, just so no one would happen to see the two identical women. Elyse was attending the worship service. In one minute she would go to the lady's room, and three minutes later she would leave the church through a side door where she was to join Park. At 11:46 A.M. Sharon Lewis would enter the church and take Elyse's seat next to Mady, who would be sitting on the right-hand side near the back, where they always sat. The two women were wearing identical clothing.

Park signaled to Sharon, who stood around the corner just out of sight of the church building. "Ready?" he asked.

Sharon took a deep breath.

"I want you to know that you are an impressive young woman," Park said.

"Thank you, Professor."

"I'll get you out."

"I know you will."

With a nod she walked across the street. Soon she'd disappeared through the side door. A minute later she appeared again, only it wasn't her. It was Elyse.

It took a moment for her to spot Park. When she did, she made a beeline for him, hurrying a little too much.

"Is that her?"

The voice beside him startled Park. He turned to see Herr Koehler sauntering toward him, looking as disheveled as ever, smoking a cigarette. Park looked at Elyse coming toward them. There was no time to warn her.

"Miss Lewis?" Park said.

Koehler shoved a hand inside his waistband, tucking in a bulging portion of his shirt. He made no attempt to tuck in all the other bulges that encircled his midsection.

"I've heard a lot about her," Koehler said, watching Elyse approach them.

Now Elyse saw that Park wasn't alone. She stopped in the middle of the street.

Keep coming, keep coming! Park urged her silently. He couldn't say anything or motion to her without appearing suspicious. Maybe he'd thought it loud enough, because Elyse continued walking toward them, her step appearing confident. Park was proud of her. She was close enough now so that Park could call to her.

"Miss Lewis!" he said, raising a beckoning hand, "I have someone I want you to meet. A pleasant surprise, really. I didn't think you'd get to meet him this trip."

Elyse smiled warmly.

"Miss Lewis, this is Herr Koehler."

"It's an honor to make your acquaintance, Herr Koehler," Elyse said. At least Park thought it was Elyse. She looked more like Elyse than Sharon, but at the moment he couldn't be certain.

"Miss Lewis," Herr Koehler said. "Come! Let me buy you both a cup of coffee!" He motioned in the direction of the same coffeehouse he and Park had met in previously.

"We have a schedule to keep," Park said. "But then, who am I to remind you of German efficiency?"

"Your train doesn't leave until 1:00 P.M.," Koehler said. "I'll see that you get there in time."

"Very well," said Park. "Miss Lewis, would you like to stop for coffee?"

She laughed. "It's been my salvation on many a long night, typing one thesis or another."

Good answer, Park thought. It was Elyse, wasn't it?

Park was quick in heading to their table. He took the seat facing the window and offered his student the seat at the end. With the other end shoved against the wall, Herr Koehler had no choice but to sit with his back to the window.

Koehler smiled too much. Park couldn't be sure what type of game the man was playing here.

"Tell me, Fräulein Lewis," he said, caressing the handle of his coffee cup with one finger, "what do you think of our Wall?"

Park watched them both intently, working hard to mask his growing nervousness over the situation.

"And the shooting of your own citizens who attempt to cross it?" Miss Lewis added.

She sat straight-backed in her chair and looked him in the eye when she'd said it, unafraid of his reaction. Or did she simply not realize the power this man had over their lives? When Koehler's smile faded, Park's heart nearly stopped its beating.

"The Wall's there, of course," she continued, "and the Western press makes much of the unfortunate deaths of those who attempt to cross the Wall illegally. They are unfortunate, aren't they?" She reached across the table and touched Koehler's hand. "While I deplore the loss of life, I feel those who are attempting to escape and also the Western press, that both are missing the larger picture."

Behind Koehler, on the other side of the window, church was letting out. The same old man in the same gray suit stood at the doorway greeting people as they left. Park watched while he listened to the table conversation. Mady appeared. Behind her was Elyse. The girl stopped to greet the old man. She said something. He laughed. She laughed. Then she took her mother's arm. Lisette stepped out and joined them. Still laughing, Elyse walked between them. Happy. Carefree. Perfectly at ease.

At the table, Miss Lewis was still talking. "But the important thing to know about life on this side of the Wall," she said, "is that with the Wall you have now established your own identity as a state. Before you were Germans. Now you are citizens of the GDR. Personally I think it will be exciting to watch you raise the first generation of GDR citizens, with no holdovers from the past, no memories of the fascist years, of war and those difficult times. They will be a generation of faith, true believers in the Party."

Koehler sat back. He was clearly impressed with her, and not just with her attractive looks. "And what are your thoughts on capitalism, Fräulein Lewis?" he asked.

She didn't answer immediately, choosing instead to take a sip of coffee, her eyes distant as she formulated her thoughts.

"A very wasteful system," she said finally.

"What sort of waste?"

"People," she said. "Unemployment mainly. But there's also a great waste of raw materials. And food. Food especially. For example, the destroying of milk or certain crops to inflate prices."

Park glanced at his watch.

Koehler took the hint. As they stood to leave, he said to Park, "A word. Alone." He turned and left the coffeehouse, and Park followed him.

Outside, Koehler grabbed Park's arm and pulled him into an

alley on the side of the building. Park's military training kicked in. He scanned the alley for an escape route. But getting out of the alley was the least of his concerns. Getting them out of East Germany was another story entirely.

Koehler was in his face. "Outstanding!" he said through clenched teeth. "Simply outstanding. And you found her at UCLA?"

Park was taken aback by the man's aggressive enthusiasm. "Yes," he said by way of an answer.

Koehler nodded. "Are there others like her?"

"I believe there are. One in particular. She's sharp, but there's a problem."

"Problem?"

"She's . . . deformed."

Koehler grimaced. "Deformed? How?"

"One arm. It's not fully developed."

Koehler thought about this a moment. "But she's like this one?" he said, pointing a thumb toward the coffeehouse.

"Mentally, she's Sharon Lewis's equal. Only more determined. All her life she's been rejected. She dreams of a society in which all workers are valued and equal."

Park knew all the buttons to push. He only hoped it was enough.

Koehler was nodding.

"An excellent writer," Park added.

"Outstanding! We can work with that," Koehler said. "Possibly use it as a commentary on the poor state of the American health system. Better yet, the total disregard capitalists have for the safety of their workers. All right, bring her over." He then slapped Park on the shoulder and said, "You get the girl. I'll bring the car around."

During the ride to the station where they would board the train that would take them to the border crossing, Koehler did most of the talking. Actually it was a lecture on socialism. He was all smiles again by the time he left them.

They boarded the train and were several minutes into the ride when Park turned to the girl sitting next to him. "Elyse?" he said.

She gave him a huge smile.

"I really wasn't sure! You were amazing back there."

With the excitement behind them, Elyse's hands began to shake. Park took one of them and held it securely in his. "After that performance," he said, "crossing the border will be a breeze."

Elyse smiled, assured but still frightened. "When I saw him standing with you, I almost turned around and ran back into the church."

"I saw you hesitate."

"But all morning I've been thinking about how much fun Miss Lewis seemed to be having all this week pretending she was me, and I thought it might be fun to pretend being her, since I didn't have much of a choice anyway." She laughed nervously.

"Well, you did an excellent impression of Sharon Lewis. And your command of the facts! Koehler was impressed, but I have to say, no more than I."

Elyse smiled. "All those workers' meetings, all that Party propaganda, I guess something good finally came from them."

Mady thought the first day would be the hardest. She was wrong. As they walked out of the church, to everyone else it was Elyse beside her, their arms linked. But it wasn't. It was an American stranger whom she'd known for less than a week. The arm entwining her arm did not feel like Elyse's. Her stride was not Elyse's stride. Maybe from a distance, her eyes looked like Elyse's eyes, but whenever Mady looked into them, another woman, not Elyse, looked back at her.

The afternoon was subdued as Ramah Cabin held its breath for news that they all knew would not come today, or tomorrow. The truth was, they didn't know when it would come, or how. There was no phone service between the East and West sectors of the city. So it wasn't as easy as picking up a phone in West Berlin and saying, "Hi, Mother! We made it safely. Wish you were here!"

All Mady could do was wonder where her daughter was now. They were at the border, she would tell herself. Standing in line. The authorities would ask to see her visa. They'd compare the picture to the person standing in front of them. They'd ask questions. They'd be suspicious of everything. That was what these people were trained to do. They were good at it. They looked for signs of nervousness, lack of eye contact, or eyes that were too bold. At the slightest suspicion, they could haul Elyse away to a holding room, separate her from Park. Interrogate her. What would Elyse do then? What would she say? She knew nothing of life in California or the campus of the

Bruisers. Would they be able to tell the difference between a native of America and a native German as easily as she could tell the difference between Elyse and Sharon Lewis?

Throughout the afternoon and into the night and next morning Mady tortured herself with horrific scenarios of Elyse being hauled off to jail, of Vopos roaring up the road and raiding Ramah Cabin because Park and Elyse had failed in their first escape attempt. Mady didn't care what happened to her. After what she'd been through, she couldn't imagine surviving alone in prison would be any more difficult than surviving in war-torn Germany during the days of anarchy, trying to feed a half-dozen starving kids without getting shot. She was more concerned about what would happen to Elyse and the other children. God knew they deserved better. They had never done anything to harm anyone. Yet all their lives they'd lived in a world populated with people who wanted to separate them and abuse them just because they were different.

Probably the worst moment was early Monday morning. Mady had stayed the night at Ramah Cabin. She'd managed to doze off shortly before dawn.

She awoke to someone calling her name.

She opened her eyes.

It was Elyse.

And for a split second Elyse was home again. Safe. All the talk about leaving had been a dream. Everything was made right again. Everything was as it should be.

"Shouldn't we be leaving for the factory?"

That face.

Not Elyse.

Sharon.

Reality came flooding back. Park's arrival with the imposter from California. Standing on the dirt. Less than a week to say good-bye. The Sunday service. Elyse standing up during the sermon. Excusing herself. Giving her mother one final glance. A scared smile. Then her walking out. A short time later, an American returning and sitting next to her. And smiling at her. Not Elyse.

"How much time do I have to get ready?"

The crush of reality made it hard for Mady to speak.

"Half hour," she managed to say.

It was going to be an impossibly long day. Her first full day without Elyse, without knowing where Elyse was or how she was doing.

Wednesday, September 5, 1962

Lisette walked into Ramah Cabin carrying a parcel.

"What a pleasant surprise!" Witzell said upon seeing her. "It's been too long."

"Where's Mady?" Lisette asked.

"Here." Mady appeared. She looked at the box in Lisette's hand.

"It's for Elyse," Lisette said. "From America." She handed Mady the box.

Soon everyone in the house was gathered together in the front room, Lisette being the main attraction. Until they saw the box addressed to Elyse. The return address read *E. Ehrenberg, Huntsville, Alabama.*

"Open it!" Lisette demanded of Mady. "I've been dying to see ever since I got it from Herr Puttkamer."

"Herr Puttkamer?"

"They attempted to deliver it while we were at work. Herr Puttkamer intercepted it."

Mady studied the parcel. "Did he open it?"

"I don't think so," said Lisette. "I examined it all the way over here on the train. It's still sealed."

Mady pulled at the tape. She was too slow for Viktor, who was the most excited. Sharon Lewis stood at a distance, watching. Konrad was more preoccupied with looking at Lisette than he was with the contents of the box. Everyone else pressed to see what was in the box.

One flap came up. Then the second.

"Move aside. I can't see! I can't see!" Tomcat shouted.

Everyone laughed. Mady reached into the box and rummaged around. "There's the usual," she said for Tomcat's benefit. "Chocolates. Coffee. Comic books."

"What kind of comic books?"

"Superman!" Hermann cried. Mady was going too slow for him too.

"And there's an envelope," Mady said. She opened it. "Photos. Oh . . ."

She couldn't continue. She raised a hand to stifle her sobs. With the other hand shaking, she stared at the top photo.

Lisette picked up the commentary, though she herself was having trouble speaking. "It's . . . Ernst and Rachelle Ehrenberg," she said. "And it looks like they're standing in front of their house." She turned to Mady. "Look how they've aged! Ernst looks good, and Rachelle is still ravishing, but . . . we haven't aged that much, have we?"

"Who else?" Tomcat shouted.

"Sorry," Lisette said. "Colonel Parker is there with them. And Elyse. She looks happy."

Chapter 30

Thursday, September 20, 1962

Tomcat was next.

Park found a broad-shouldered blond surfer, a second-year student at UCLA by the name of Fletcher Green. While he didn't have the altruistic streak of Sharon Lewis, he was something of a rebel and an adventurer who was eager for a challenge. Perhaps too eager. Most importantly, Fletcher bore a striking resemblance to Tomcat, so Park decided to gamble on him.

His father, Blake Green, a local car dealer, made a fortune through his advertising on late-night television, stunts like living in a cage suspended above the car lot until his salespeople sold a thousand cars, or dying the skin of his sales staff just so he could deliver the pitch, "I'm Blake Green, and if we can't put you in a new car, we're all blue!" It took three weeks for his staff to shed the last tint of blue; the final week they looked like the walking dead. But Blake Green moved more cars in that three-week period than at any other time in franchise history.

When his son, Fletcher, was two years old, Green used him for one of his commercials by dressing the toddler in a diaper, cowboy hat, and chaps and strapping him to the back of a pig while the porker wandered around the lot among selected car models. Not only did Blake Green sell a lot of cars with the gimmick, he received hundreds of letters and postcards telling him how adorable his son looked riding that pig.

Blake Green's nightly television antics made Fletcher something of a celebrity among his classmates in elementary school. In junior high and high school, however, his father became an embarrassment, one that just wouldn't go away. Fletcher rebelled. He ran away from home. He shoplifted clothes when he had plenty of money to pay for them. He started an underground organization on his high school campus called The Young Communists, not because he believed in socialism, for at the time he didn't have a grasp of what it meant to be a Communist. He got involved with the Party because he knew it would get a rise out of his teachers and especially his father.

Fletcher's great love, though, was surfing. He spent most days and weekends at the beach, frequently skipping classes. He and his father had grown distant. In the last two years they'd spoken to each other only twice, and it was Fletcher who placed both calls.

When Fletcher walked into Park's Introduction to Philosophy class in the fall of 1962, Park instantly recognized a possible double for Tomcat. Through a number of personal interviews with Fletcher, Park's initial reluctance began to vanish. Beneath a troubled surface, he found the heart of an idealistic young man who was loyal to his friends and who wanted his life to count for something.

The next step was the riskiest. Park described the mission but in general terms. Fletcher's first reaction was that there was a camera hidden somewhere in the room, with him being the object of a prank. After Park assured him of the reality and the dangers of the situation, Fletcher thought about it a moment, then said, "Outa sight, man. When do we go?"

They started with a crash course in the basics of the German language. Park's plan was that when going in, an American student who spoke little German was unlikely to draw undue attention given the circumstances of Park's assignment. Later, when coming out, with a different set of officials, Park would instruct them that the American student was to speak German only. All part of his training.

Of course Fletcher wasn't blind. He didn't need to be. The most crucial part of the ruse would depend on Tomcat's ability to act as a sighted person. When at Ramah Cabin, Sharon Lewis, who spoke passable German, could serve as Fletcher's translator. And the part Fletcher liked best, probably because it suited his surfer lifestyle—he would go barefoot.

Before leaving for Germany, Park purchased duplicate conservative clothing for Tomcat and Fletcher. White shirt. Black pants. Thin tie. No American rock or beer T-shirts that might catch the eye of a German postal inspector. He shipped Tomcat's clothes to him in a package filled with goodies, along with a note.

> *I've told Uncle Fred all about that little shop on the eastern side of Alexanderplatz. He's interested in the rack of postcards in the back corner. Just what he's looking for, he says. Remind me to pick some up for him during my next visit. Parker*

He thought it best to keep the exchanges public. Park didn't want to risk leading anyone to Ramah Cabin. A date and time was established in a separate letter. He sent this letter to Herr Otto Witzell at the K7 address.

Matthew "Park" Parker sat on a bench in the Alexanderplatz square and watched as Fletcher Green disappeared into the shop with the postcards. Strictly speaking, Park was in violation of his orders. He wasn't supposed to let his students out of his sight. For anyone watching—and there was always someone watching—he rubbed his legs as though they were sore, then stretched and leaned back on the bench like he was tired. It was a good thing the watchers couldn't monitor his heart rate, because it was pounding so fast that it was almost a steady hum.

Elyse had been the easy rescue. Her impairment was minimal and unseen. Tomcat posed a greater challenge. Not as great as Viktor's, but dangerous just the same.

Park resisted looking at his watch. Though he knew Fletcher had entered the store only seconds ago, for some reason he had a tremendous urge to check his watch to see exactly how many seconds it had been.

Just then, Fletcher reappeared. He stepped out of the shop and into the bright sunlight. Even though he was wearing dark sunglasses, he raised his hand to shield his eyes.

"Well, I'll be . . ." Park muttered.

Fletcher continued walking forward, slightly off course.

Park stood. "Find what you're looking for?" he called.

A slight adjustment and Fletcher moved straight toward him.

"Are those the cards Uncle Fred is looking for? I wasn't quite sure. I was hoping you could tell since you saw his collection the last time you were over at the house."

He was rambling, but with a purpose.

Fletcher drew to within a meter of Park and stopped. "The cards are similar," he said, "but they don't match his collection. Maybe we can look elsewhere."

Park stepped closer, whispered, "That bit with the sun? Inspiring."

Tomcat replied, "Something I've been practicing."

"Are you all right? We can still turn back."

"Thanks, Professor Parker," Tomcat said with a calm voice. "But I think I've seen enough. I'm anxious to get back to the States." In a low voice, he added, "Stay close and keep talking. With these shoes on, I'm blind as a bat."

Tomcat knew he was facing a window, but because he had no sensory input beyond the glass, all of his impressions came from within the train compartment. His voice and breath bounced against the glass and back into his face when he spoke. The seat felt sticky. To his right, a woman was cracking her gum as she chewed, spearmint flavor; to his left, a man was reading a newspaper. He could hear the pages being turned. A newspaper has a sound all its own. Other than that, the air in the compartment was stale, the train noisy and monotonous. Tomcat was nervous. Mostly because of the shoes. His toes squirmed in vain to free themselves, to feel something other than the dark, cramped quarters in which they were confined.

He forced himself to think of something else.

"Are we close to the Wall?" he asked.

"It's within sight," Park said in a low voice.

"Is it as frightening as Herr Witzell described it?"

"It's imposing. No doubt about that," Park said. "But it's nothing to us. We're going to walk out the front door."

The train slowed. Tomcat's shoulder bumped into Park as the train's brakes complained with a high-pitched scream.

Park said, "Do you know who you are?"

In anticipation of an interview, Tomcat had been reviewing the information about Fletcher Green that Park had sent to him—names, places, background, vital statistics. Unlike Elyse, Tomcat never had a chance to get to know his double, having met him for just a few seconds in the postcard shop.

"Game day, man. You're up."

This was the extent of his contact with Fletcher Green, who smelled of suntan lotion.

In answer to Park's question, Tomcat said, "My name's Fletcher Green, man."

"Drop the 'man.'"

Park's voice had become tense. Tomcat was just trying to be funny. He knew better than to call an East German official "man." East German officials were notorious for their lack of humor, especially American humor. While a flippant remark might not land a person behind bars, it certainly could delay their crossing and the approval of their passports for hours, if not days.

The train pulled to a stop.

Park stood.

Tomcat grabbed his luggage. "Looks like we're up, m . . ." He dropped the last word, though the temptation to act like a California surfer was strong.

Park moved forward with a slow exiting-the-train shuffle. Tomcat followed suit, matching his shuffling. Clearing his throat, Park tapped a handrail as he turned right to leave the train. Out on the platform he began whistling. Tomcat didn't recognize the tune, though he knew it was nothing Sinatra would ever sing. He followed the prearranged sounds, keeping Park close. He'd practiced this at Ramah Cabin as well—wearing shoes, following people around. Only once with Annie, she deliberately walked him into a corner. Of course, she swore she didn't do it on purpose. Tomcat didn't believe her.

"Get out your visa," Park said, moving closer to Tomcat. "We go down these steps and through that second door over there."

It was the kind of comment a supervisor would make to a student. Park was alerting him to the steps. Shoulder to shoulder now, Tomcat followed a half step behind, his elbow brushing Park's arm, noting each step down.

Tomcat's neck and upper back began to ache from the tension. He told himself to relax. If he was too tense, he'd draw attention to himself. And suspicion. The last thing one wanted to do around people who were trained to be suspicious was to act suspicious.

They entered a hallway that, to Park, was incredibly dirty. It was cold, and the walls had more scratches on them than paint. Considering the extent the Communist Party went to show a modern face to the public—particularly in their new apartment complexes and shopping centers like the Alexanderplatz—Park was certain the depressing atmosphere of the border crossing was deliberate and for effect. They knew what they were doing, because it worked. He and Tomcat entered a queue thirty or so people in length.

The long wait to be scrutinized had begun.

"We're together," Park said, setting his luggage down, the signal to stop. He slapped his passport on the counter.

Taking his visa from his front shirt pocket, Tomcat placed it on the counter next to Park's passport. The man standing on the other side of the counter—Tomcat knew it was a man, and fairly young, because he'd been listening to his incessant monotone for nearly an hour while standing in line—smelled of horseradish and corned beef.

"It's an old picture," Park said.

The agent was scrutinizing Park. Tomcat had been told that the agent would be paying special attention to a person's nose, ears, and chin. Never having seen the picture on the visa, Tomcat had to trust Park that the features in the photo resembled his own.

"Foster Grants," the agent said.

The tone of his voice indicated he was impressed, maybe even envious, of Fletcher Green's sunglasses.

"Remove them, Herr Green."

"Sorry. Can't." Tomcat said.

"Corneal scratch," Park explained. "We were on a tour of the chemical factory in Mahlsdorf."

"Instead of weaving, I should have ducked," Tomcat said with a wry smile.

The agent didn't laugh.

Tomcat fished in his front pocket and produced a folded piece of paper. He unfolded it, held it up as if to make sure it was the right paper, even though he had only the one piece of paper in the pocket with his visa. He realized it was upside down, quickly turned it right side up, and handed it to the agent. It was a note from an East German doctor, compliments of Herr Witzell.

There was a moment of silence, followed by the agent calling for his supervisor.

Park sniffed. His feet shuffled. No signal. He was just nervous. If the border agents saw the white shields of Tomcat's blind eyes, it was all over.

More than one set of footsteps approached from the far side of the counter.

"What's the problem?" The new voice sounded like it was itching for an excuse to exert its authority.

"He says he can't remove his sunglasses," the agent said.

"For medical reasons," Park said. "He has a note from an East German physician. There's certainly no need for armed guards."

That explained the multiple footsteps.

"Remove the sunglasses," the supervisor demanded.

"Even in this light, removing his glasses may cause permanent damage to his eyes," Park argued.

There was a shuffle of feet.

"I must protest this action!" Park shouted.

The supervisor must have given some sort of signal. Tomcat could hear someone circling the counter and coming toward him. The next thing he knew, the Foster Grants were being removed from his face.

Tomcat closed his eyes.

Silence.

The guard said nothing. Neither did the agents. Park was silent too.

Did they suspect something? Did the guard catch a glimpse of his eyes before the glasses came off?

Tomcat swallowed hard. The wait was interminable, the anticipation excruciating. Should he say something? Were they expecting him to say something? What were they doing? He could feel the guard's presence on one side and Park's on the other, so he knew they hadn't all suddenly disappeared. Behind him someone in line coughed. Coming from the other side of the counter he heard typewriters clicking, muted conversations, people moving about. But those closest to him, the ones who would determine where Tomcat would go next—across the border or to prison—remained eerily quiet.

Tomcat could feel perspiration forming on his upper lip.

"Foster Grants," the agent said with authority.

Tomcat breathed easier. They were examining the sunglasses. Not him, the sunglasses.

"Hold out your hand," Park said.

For a moment Tomcat was confused. It was the kind of thing a sighted person would say to a blind person, but he was pretending to be sighted, so why would Park say something like . . . That's right! Distracted by the comfortableness of his lack of sight, Tomcat remembered he was a blind person pretending to be a sighted person who, temporarily, couldn't see.

He held out his hand and felt the sunglasses placed in them. Tomcat put the glasses back on, mentally reminding himself to open his eyes, for it mattered not to him if he walked around with his eyes open or shut.

"That line," the agent said, pointing.

"The longest one?" Park said. He had turned his back on Tomcat, who turned to follow.

"Our papers," Tomcat said.

"Next," the agent said loudly.

"They keep them for now," Park explained.

Tomcat followed the voice.

"Our next stop is currency exchange."

They queued up in line and performed what Park explained as the bureaucratic shuffle—a slow dance with one's luggage.

"Too many James Bond novels," Park whispered. "They almost looked disappointed they didn't find a transmitter in the frames."

Tomcat smiled with relief.

"We're not out of the woods yet," Park warned. "And what was that with the prescription? How did you know it was upside down?"

Tomcat's smile widened. "Nice touch, don't you think? The upper right-hand corner was folded over. Not much. Just enough."

They shuffled forward another half meter.

"Uh-oh," Park said.

"What?"

"I've been keeping an eye on our papers. Ours have been diverted."

"Trouble?"

"Possibly."

At the currency exchange counter, they had to account for every penny of Western currency. Upon entry, travelers had to make a declaration in writing that detailed how much foreign currency they were taking with them. Their receipts and remaining currency would need to match that declaration when they returned across the border. Inside East Germany a visitor had to guard the declaration with his life. Lose it, and he might never be able to leave again. It was against the law for East German citizens to have Western currency.

After matching their currency to their declaration, Park and Tomcat were taken to a waiting room. This was where they would wait. And wait. And wait.

There weren't enough couches or straight-backed chairs to accommodate everyone, so Park and Tomcat stood. Tomcat made sure he kept his head moving, advice he'd received from Konrad. *"You keep your head too still,"* Konrad had told him. *"When people are waiting, they look at the walls, the lights, each other, the floor."* So Tomcat turned his face toward the buzz of the overhead lights, or toward the clearing of a throat, or the scrape of a chair, or the opening of the door through which person after person was eventually summoned.

Park quietly explained that once a person's name was called, another agent started scrutinizing, once again matching person to photo. The person was then sent to customs, which could mean anything from a check of one's luggage for stashed currency or forbidden books to a body search. After those encouraging words, they returned to nervous silence.

"I think she likes you," Park said.

"Who?"

"How old are you?" Park asked, obviously not addressing Tomcat. A pause. The answer must have come by way of fingers, because Park said, "Four? You're a big girl."

Tomcat looked in the direction Park was speaking. He grinned.

"Ah. She's shy," Park said.

Three hours later their names were called. They were led past the customs line and down a deserted corridor. Tomcat followed Park's footsteps. Three turns and . . .

"Why the police?" Park asked.

"Herr Parker, this way. Herr Green, follow Officer Thunert."

"This way, Herr Green," a smooth baritone voice said.

"I would like an explanation," Park said. "This student is my responsibility. If there's a problem, I want to know what it is."

"This way, Herr Green." Same voice, only this time a gripping hand accompanied it, a vise grip that discouraged discussion. Tomcat was nearly lifted off his feet.

The sound of Park's protesting grew fainter as Tomcat was forced to walk down another corridor.

"Herr Green," the baritone voice announced.

Tomcat was pulled at a right angle and tossed into a room. The door closed behind him and locked. Rarely was Tomcat aware of his blindness. He was now. Having been thrust into the room, he didn't know if he was alone or if half the Kremlin was in the room with him. From the sound of the door, it wasn't a large room. He listened for breathing or other signs of life. There were none. The air hit his nostrils as stale with smoke. It seemed he was alone. But someone could be sitting or standing quietly in a corner, observing him, and he wouldn't know it. Or they could be observing him through one of those one-way-glass windows. He couldn't act blind.

But he was blind. And with shoes on.

"What is this?" he said.

The question became his radar, a signal sent out to see if anyone would respond. He kept his head moving, just as Konrad taught him, as though he were looking at everything. He was hoping for a sound, something he could zero in on.

His radar hit nothing. Not one ping. No voice. No movement detected.

He considered sending out another question, then thought better of it. If someone had been in the room and he failed to direct the question at the person, or persons, they'd know for sure he was blind. And if nobody was in the room and he spoke as if someone were, they'd know he was blind—that or crazy.

It was best for him just to wait, to stand here and do nothing. Pretend to look at nothing. Silent defiance. If they were watching, let them interpret it as passive resistance.

He folded his arms and cocked a hip. His mouth became a thin line of disgust. He didn't move to the left or to the right.

After a half hour, he concluded he was alone in the room. Still, he stood.

An hour passed. Then another thirty minutes.

The lock behind him clicked. The door creaked open. He turned to face . . . what? Who? A cigarette smoker, he could tell that at least.

"Sit, Herr Green."

Whoever it was strode past him with hurried, authoritative steps. He heard a folder or packet of papers hit the top of a table. A chair scraped the floor, and the man gave out a grunt as he sat down.

"Sit, Herr Green," he said again, this time more sternly.

The man was facing him. That meant there was probably a table between them and a chair on his side.

"What's this about?" Tomcat said, pointing his face toward the voice.

"The interrogation will not begin until you sit down."

Tomcat took a step closer, gauging the distance between himself and the man by the sound of his voice. But how large was the table? He unfolded his arms and hooked his thumbs in his belt, American cowboy style. He did it mainly to feel in front of himself. His hands touched nothing.

"Do I have to call the guard?" the man said.

Tomcat inched forward. "I don't want any trouble."

"Then sit down!" the man shouted.

The back of Tomcat's knuckles encountered a chair. He knew it was a chair and not the edge of the table because it rocked forward when he made contact. Making a show of resignation, he pulled the chair out and sat.

An exasperated sigh came from the other side of the table, along with the sound of a folder being opened and pages turned.

"Is something wrong with my visa?" Tomcat asked.

"Name."

Tomcat pretended to look at the ceiling, his impression of American rebellion.

"Name!" his interrogator shouted.

"Green, Fletcher H."

"Full name."

Tomcat thought about protesting again but didn't want to overdo it. "Fletcher Hyram Green."

"You're a U.S. citizen?"

"Yes."

"You live in California?"

"Yes."

"Glendora?"

"Yes."

"Street address 3458 Belmont Drive?"

The number was wrong. A misprint? A test?

"3488."

"You're a student at the University of California, Los Angeles?"

"Yes."

"Major?"

"Social science. That's my declared major. I'm considering—"

"Father's name."

Tomcat's mind went blank.

"Father's name?"

Tomcat couldn't think of it. He knew it on the train. But now it was gone. Vanished. Just like that. He grasped for details, hoping that one would prompt the name to appear again, the way a magician pulled flowers out of a sleeve or made a coin appear from behind a person's ear.

Fletcher Green's mother's name was Lois. Lois Green. Lois and . . . It wasn't coming. He tried reversing the order of the names but it still wasn't coming to him. *The man was a car salesman. A television celebrity. Mr. Green. My name is . . . Green, and I can get you a great deal on a used car. . . . What's his name?*

"Herr Green," the interrogator said, "if you'd prefer, we can hold this discussion in a prison cell."

The Greens have lived in Southern California since 1946. His first car lot was on Century Boulevard. Fifteen cars. Now he has more than three thousand cars. . . .

"Guard!"

"Blake!" Tomcat said. "My father's name is Blake Edward Green. Edward after his father's brother."

A guard entered. The interrogator told him to stay in case Herr Green's memory suddenly became vague again. As it turned out, his presence wasn't needed. Tomcat was quick with the rest of the information about the Greens.

While answering questions, Tomcat could hear Park's voice in the distance. He sounded rooms away. He was shouting.

"Guard, see if the doctor is in the hallway."

A cold shiver went up Tomcat's spine.

"Herr Green, remove your sunglasses."

"You're aware that—"

"I'm aware. Remove your sunglasses."

"I have—"

"Corneal abrasions. I read the report."

Tomcat's heart started racing. It was all he could do to keep his voice from quivering. "I must protest. I don't see the purpose of this."

"The GDR regrets any injury you may have incurred while visiting our Mahldorf factory. We feel responsible. It is our desire to assess the situation and provide you with any medical attention you might require. We'd hate to return you to your own country broken, so to speak."

Broken. It sounded more like a promise than an apology.

"I prefer to have my own doctor—"

"Herr Green, this is not a matter of preference. Remove your sunglasses."

The polite tone was but a thin veneer, a shiny surface on an enforcer's bludgeon, with every "Herr Green" spoken as a threatening wave of the club.

The door behind the interrogator opened. The interrogator stood. "Herr Green, this is Dr. Podgorny."

"Remain seated," the new voice insisted. Something heavy hit the table, probably a medical bag. "Please, turn off the lights," he said.

A switch clicked.

Tomcat felt the sunglasses being lifted from his face. He grabbed them, holding them in place.

"I must insist," Tomcat said. "My father's medical plan . . . in the States . . ."

"Herr Green, I'll not ask you again," said the interrogator. Gone was the thin veneer of politeness. The bludgeon was all that was left.

The sunglasses were lifted from Tomcat's face. He closed his eyes.

"Now then . . ." The doctor leaned into him. Tomcat could feel the man's warm breath and then the doctor's hand touching his face, his finger on the upper eyelid, a thumb on the lower lid.

There was nothing Tomcat could do to stop him. A simple parting motion of the man's thumb and finger and he would know that Tomcat was not Fletcher Green. Everyone would know. At that moment an image of Elyse flashed in his mind, the way she would look when she heard the news that he'd been arrested at the border.

The door to the room slammed open.

"Remove your hands from that boy!"

Park!

Never before had Tomcat been so relieved to hear someone's voice.

The doctor stepped back.

"Guard!" the interrogator shouted.

But a new voice countermanded the interrogator. "That'll be all."

Three words and it was over. Tomcat didn't know who the new voice was. He didn't care. All he cared about was that the interrogator and the doctor and the guard recognized the man's authority.

"We'll discuss this later," the new voice said. "Herr Parker, Herr Green. This guard will take you to customs."

Tomcat felt blindly on the table for his sunglasses. Like before, at first the act alarmed him. It took a minute for him to remember that his actions were normal for a man with his eyes closed. He found the sunglasses and slipped them on. Park was at his side, gripping his arm just above the elbow, helping him up.

Tomcat was grateful for the help. His wits had fled him when the doctor was about to learn his secret.

Without a word to anyone, Park led Tomcat out into the hall. They followed the thudding heels of boots on a tile floor. Two right turns. A door. Soon they were once again standing in a line.

Tomcat never knew how much he loved waiting in line until that moment. It beat the alternative any day of the week.

Not until they were on West Berlin soil did Tomcat learn how Park had fought until they allowed him to place a call to his Party contact, a Herr Koehler. While he was given a stern lecture for not reporting the incident to Koehler immediately, Park managed to convince Koehler that Fletcher Green's famous Hollywood father—an exaggeration—would not take kindly to his son being injured, then detained against his will for something that was no fault of his own. He added that the resulting publicity would also severely damage Park's chances of enlisting more students. For added measure Park intimated that Fletcher Green's incredibly wealthy father could be quite generous in his expression of gratitude.

A bluff. But it worked.

Two weeks later another package was delivered to Ramah Cabin, to avoid the chance of it falling into snoopy Herr Puttkamer's hands.

The package contained the usual goodies, and a photo. This one showed Ernst and Rachelle Ehrenberg, as before, with Elyse and a grinning Tomcat, his arm draped casually over Elyse Schumacher's shoulders. Another resident of Ramah Cabin stood on free soil.

Chapter 31

By November 1962, all but Viktor had crossed over from East Germany to Freedom House in Huntsville, Alabama. Unanticipated problems arose among the Americans staying at Ramah Cabin. While their devotion to the cause remained steadfast, their bickering and complaining over shortages and lack of amenities was getting on everyone's nerves. Sharon Lewis had experienced coffee and chocolate withdrawal. Fletcher Green turned surly over the absence of television and rock and roll music. At times the whole operation nearly collapsed for want of a good old-fashioned American hamburger. Most nights Viktor cried himself to sleep. He missed Tomcat and Elyse and the others.

Witzell's pastoral skills were tested daily as he mediated bathroom privileges and disputes over the work schedule. One night he surprised everyone with a backyard barbecue and his interpretation of a hamburger. His effort to accommodate the Ramah Cabin guests did not go unnoticed. Konrad was the only one who groused about the barbecue. He said he'd eaten his share of outdoor meals during the war.

In the States, Park had succeeded in finding the doubles but not without determined effort and persistence. The enlistment of each double was a story in itself.

Marlene's and Hermann's doubles crossed together as boyfriend and girlfriend. Park located Marlene's double by acting on a lead he'd gotten from Sharon Lewis. They had attended the same high school in Santa Barbara, just up the coast from Los Angeles. Darlene Narducci was a senior when Sharon was a freshman, secretary of the Associated Student Body, and had participated in a student exchange program with a Brazilian school between her junior and senior years. Her hair, general build, and height were a close match to Marlene. The last Sharon had heard was that Darlene planned to be a foreign missionary following graduation. Sharon didn't know which country.

Park began his search for Darlene at the high school. He got lucky. She still lived in the area, working as a cashier at a local supermarket. Darlene remembered Sharon. They were on the pep squad together. She became enthusiastic after learning of Sharon's part in the Ramah Cabin rescue effort and appeared to be sympathetic concerning the mission. She was also fascinated that she looked like someone who lived in Germany, and she seemed a strong candidate for a double, that is, until Park showed her Marlene's picture.

"What's that?" Darlene asked, pointing to Marlene's upper lip.

That was when Park nearly lost her. Darlene proved to be vainer than Sharon knew or had let on. Park appealed to the spirit of a woman who would consider becoming a missionary. It was at this point that he learned her missionary career was short-lived due to an unhappy romance with a fellow missionary. It took three trips to the UCLA Medical Center, where Darlene was shown the reversible procedure that would simulate a harelip; the reversible part had to be emphasized repeatedly. Finally Park won her over. He managed to convince her that few people were given a chance to do something of this magnitude to help someone less fortunate than themselves. Then he made her a deal. Undergo the procedure, and if within three days she changed her mind, the procedure would then be reversed, no questions asked. One successful late-night intervention two days later and Park had his Marlene.

Park had to call on the Alton Bell Hollywood talent agency to find his Hermann. Realizing the futility of trolling the student unions after visiting nearly two dozen college campuses, he thought, Why not let Hermann find me? Alton Bell, a Normandy war veteran, was only too glad to assist him. Together they fabricated a casting call for a movie about an American football player who infiltrates East Germany to rescue his kidnapped girlfriend, whose father is an

American diplomat in Berlin. When Park explained that America didn't have diplomatic ties with East Germany, Bell shrugged it off.

"We're dealing with actors here, not political scientists," he said. "Besides, this is Hollywood. If we say an American diplomat is trapped in East Germany, who's going to argue with us?"

Over three hundred men applied for the lead role of Hermann. The young man who got the part was actually a college football player, ironically for the University of Southern California—UCLA's biggest rival. He was persuaded to play Hermann in exchange for lifetime representation by the Alton Bell agency when he returned. One simulated football injury complete with leg cast later, this to hide Hermann's clubfoot on the return journey, and Park had his Hermann.

Annie's crossing, as expected, proved to be even more difficult. Where did one find a twenty-two-year-old woman with a shriveled left hand? Park found her after spending countless hours at the UCLA Medical Center, sitting outside the prosthetics department. He tried the more direct route—asking to review the center's records—but no amount of talking could get them to share anything with him other than an introduction to a security guard.

He spotted Connie Hayes one afternoon just after finishing his third cup of horrible hospital coffee. She was slightly taller than Annie. The hair color was wrong, though that was an easy thing to change. And she was older than Annie, eight years as it turned out, so a makeup job would be needed to play down the age difference. He found out one other thing about her almost immediately: she hated men.

Park had to do a lot of fast talking to this unemployed telephone operator just to convince her that he wasn't someone who was looking to pick up women. Having recently come out of an ugly divorce, her second, Connie Hayes listened only after Park showed her a picture of Annie and told her that he was trying to help Annie to be able to lead a normal, independent life. It took his credentials, pictures of all of the Hadamar Six, and the persistence of a pit bull just to get her into a Denny's restaurant where he presented his case while she ate a chicken-fried-steak dinner—the price for her time, for she said she at least wanted to get a meal out of the deal.

It wasn't until halfway through the meal, as he was nearing the end of his argument, that Park realized to his horror that his efforts had been in vain. The realization came when Connie Hayes poured cream into her coffee. She poured it with her left hand. Her *good* left hand. Annie's good hand was her right hand.

In his enthusiasm to find a woman with a shriveled hand, one who looked remotely like Annie, Park had missed this rather obvious difference. His heart sank, and not just because he was out five bucks for Connie's meal.

Whether it was weariness or just plain desperation, Park decided to press forward. Connie, however, was still reluctant. It took a trip to Huntsville, Alabama, to convince her. She refused to believe him until she saw Freedom House and the people in the pictures with her own eyes, those who had already made it to America. She insisted they meet her at the airport, and if they weren't there when she stepped off the plane, she was going to turn around, step right back on, and fly home.

Seeing Elyse and Tomcat standing hand-in-hand at the airport to meet her, the last of Connie Hayes's resistance dissolved. She started to cry and didn't stop for two hours. Now all Park had to do was figure out how he was going to explain the fact that she had the wrong arm disfigured.

He considered bribing the visa official to print "left arm" rather than "right arm" in the space provided to record any unusual physical characteristics. It was risky, especially considering the student visas were obtained at the East German border. Too risky, he concluded. He ultimately decided to go with what he had. Maybe they'd get lucky.

They didn't.

Crossing into East Berlin went without incident, as did the exchange that was made at Heinrich's Bookstore on Unter den Linden. Their luck ran out at the border. The official at the counter performed the usual check, comparing Annie's ears, nose, and chin to the photo. He squinted once. Was the age difference noticeable? If so, it wasn't enough for him to refuse passage.

He started to stamp the visa while telling them to move to the currency exchange line when the stamp hovered midair.

He put the stamp down. "It says here, 'right arm.'"

This time Park was quick to call Herr Koehler. Park blamed the discrepancy on the visa official, insisting it wasn't Annie's fault the man didn't know his right from his left. It was a reasonable argument, but Koehler sensed there might be more going on here.

"Do you think I'm playing games?" Park argued. "I told you about this woman some time ago. This is a simple misprint."

Park wanted to keep this between himself and Koehler. The last thing he wanted was for Herr Koehler to quiz Annie like he'd quizzed Elyse earlier.

Koehler summarized: "An eye incident at a factory. A harelip. A football injury. And now this? You expect me to believe all these American students are flawed like this?"

Park was ready for him. He'd anticipated their having this argument at some time or another. The success of his argument would depend on how much Koehler swallowed the steady dose of anti-American propaganda the Communists fed the general public.

"Sadly," Park lamented, "the health of American youth is extremely poor, what with all the hours spent in front of television sets, a diet high in sugar, lack of exercise, and a society that values decadence over sacrifice and hard work. You'd be surprised at the ratio of the disabled and unfit in the general populace. It's alarmingly high, much higher than is publicly known. The government suppresses these figures, fearful that it will weaken its image in the international community."

Koehler nodded knowingly, as though he had suspected as much all along. He lit a cigarette. Looked at Annie. Then at her visa.

She crossed over without further incident.

Annie would be the last of the six to cross on a student visa, however. Even if Park could find someone with Down's syndrome who matched Viktor and was willing to take the risk, he couldn't risk involving Koehler in another crossing. The doubles plan had gone as far as it could. Park would have to find another way to get Viktor out of East Germany.

That fall, Willi had increased his visits to Ramah Cabin to five nights a week. And he had started waiting for Mady outside the factory when she got off work, sitting in his Isetta, a sleek sports car with no back seat.

Two things disturbed Mady about this; a third disgusted her. The first thing that disturbed her was that he'd been able to obtain a car so quickly, let alone a new sports car. It was general knowledge that a person had to wait eight years just to buy a small Wartburg sedan like Herr Witzell's, a car that broke down every two weeks and for which spare parts were impossible to find. For the privilege of car ownership, they paid dearly. Yet somehow Willi had purchased a sports car within weeks following Gael's death. The second thing that disturbed Mady was that the car seated only two—the driver and one passenger. How convenient. Elyse and Lisette had to take the train home.

What disgusted her was Willi's behavior when they were alone. He was bold and openly offensive, telling her that he'd fantasized about being with her since he was a youth, and now that they were both unattached adults, he saw no reason why his fantasies could not become reality.

His boorish behavior continued at Ramah Cabin. He insisted they eat alone and spend their evenings alone. Some nights he took her out of the house. Mady never said where he'd take her or what they did, but they never returned before two the next morning, and Mady's clothes smelled of cigarettes and booze, though the smell of alcohol was never on her breath.

One day Konrad confronted Willi, telling him to leave Mady be, to back off from pursuing her. The next night Mady came home with a bruise on her face. She blamed it on Konrad, saying he'd only made things worse. She insisted that he and everyone else stay out of her affairs, that she was handling it, and that this was a price she was willing to pay for the safety of Viktor and the students, which was growing more and more precarious.

With the increase of doubles in the house came an increase in the risk of detection, such as when Mady and Willi passed by a closed door behind which English was being spoken. She was almost certain that Willi heard and took note. Another time, Willi made a comment about Tomcat's double.

"That blind kid . . ." he said.

"Tomcat," Mady said.

"What's with the sunglasses? When did he start wearing them?"

"You know how impressionable young people are," Mady laughed. "Actually, it's Elyse's fault. She made a comment, something about how with sunglasses on he'd look like James Dean. And now he won't take them off. He combs his hair a lot now too. You remember what it was like at his age."

That seemed to smooth things over, at least for the time being. But after Willi left that day, they had a meeting where Mady stressed how important it was for each of them to stay in character all the time. None of them were exact doubles, she reminded them. So they were to stay out of sight as much as possible whenever Willi was around, and they were to speak German only. No exceptions.

Despite their efforts, slipups were bound to happen. Viktor nearly blew their cover one night when Willi brought Mady home at a late hour. Willi was drunk and louder than usual. He knocked over a lamp, and the sound of the crash woke up Viktor. Viktor appeared half asleep, mumbling about how he missed Tomcat, the real Tomcat.

Mady covered. She couldn't remember exactly what she said, but somehow she was able to get Viktor back to bed and Willi out of the house. Just as he was leaving, she saw that Willi had a peculiar look in his eye. Seeds had been planted, seeds that would eventually bear the fruit of realization. Mady was certain. It was just a matter of time.

Chapter 32

Saturday, November 10, 1962

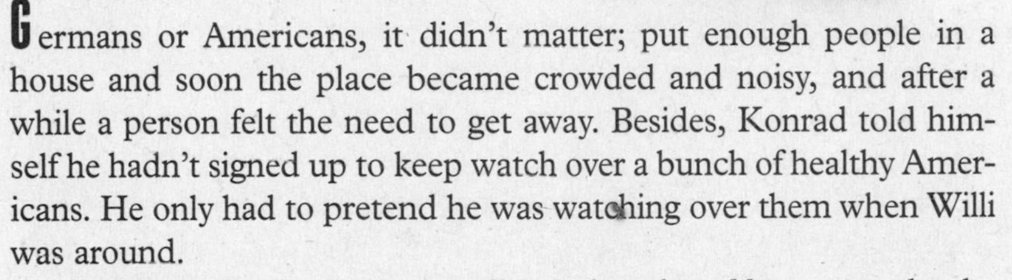

Germans or Americans, it didn't matter; put enough people in a house and soon the place became crowded and noisy, and after a while a person felt the need to get away. Besides, Konrad told himself he hadn't signed up to keep watch over a bunch of healthy Americans. He only had to pretend he was watching over them when Willi was around.

So during the day he took walks. At least he *told* everyone that he was taking a walk, and there was enough truth in the statement to keep his conscience satisfied. He didn't feel it was necessary to tell anyone his walks were to the S-Bahn station, and from there he took the train downtown. He carried along a camera with a telephoto lens. This wasn't the camera with the cross hairs, the one Neff had designed; that camera was lost the day of the showdown with Krahl at the original Ramah Cabin. This new camera wasn't as good, but it was good enough for Konrad's purposes.

Today, stepping off the train, newly fallen snow crunched under his boots. A stiff breeze whipped around the station, slapping Konrad's cheeks red and stinging his hands.

He muttered under his breath like an old man. Why did the cold affect him so much these days? This was nothing compared to the winters on the Russian front, yet he couldn't remember his skin and bones hurting so much because of a little snow. As a boy he used to make sport of the way old people complained about the winter.

Could it be he was one of them now?

Konrad winced with each aching step as he descended to street level. Avoiding major streets, he walked randomly up one street and down another, never the same way two days in a row but always eventually making his way west.

He surveyed the buildings as he went. Finding one abandoned, or overcrowded so a new face would go unnoticed, or with easy access, he would make his way to the roof. There he became a sniper again, setting up a blind. His target was the Wall, his weapon the camera.

Day after day he studied it. Photographed it. He noted the position and schedule of the guards. When he felt confident he knew one section, he'd move on to the next, and in this way he would systematically work his way the length of the Wall, at least the portion within the city.

It wasn't that he didn't trust Park to be able to keep his promise to get all the children out. He did. But if his army training had taught him anything, it was that no plan was perfect, that the unexpected should never take one by surprise, and that a contingency plan should be in place.

Konrad didn't have a contingency plan yet, but observing and gathering facts was the first step toward coming up with one. Anyway, after a week of listening to the cooped-up Americans of Ramah Cabin, he needed a distraction, even if that meant lying on a rooftop in the snow.

The late morning sunlight filtered through high clouds. Konrad took a reading with a light meter, set the aperture and shutter speed, and pressing the camera to his eye, picked up his observation of the Wall from where he'd left off last time.

"Herr Reichmann? Do you have a moment?"

Sharon Lewis stood in Konrad's bedroom doorway. He finished returning his camera to the top shelf of the closet and then shut the closet door. His stomach grumbled. They were clearing the lunch dishes when he'd walked in. He'd have to scrounge something up on his own.

Konrad turned to face the young lady. He no longer looked at Sharon and saw Elyse. The two might look alike, but he'd spent enough time now with the American girl to know she and Elyse were nothing like each other. Whereas Elyse was happy, flirtatious, and often silly, her American counterpart was serious and studious. Not that Sharon wasn't pleasant to be around, for she had a winning smile and was accommodating to a fault. She was just so obviously not Elyse. And if this was true for Konrad, it was probably true for the others. If not now, in time.

"What do you need, fräulein?" Konrad said.

"Just a moment of your time," Sharon said. "It's about Lisette."

"Go on."

"As you know, I spend a lot of hours sitting beside her at the factory."

"How's that going?"

Sharon held up her blistered hands. "Painfully," she laughed. "Lisette and Mady have been wonderful covering for me. Anyway, we talk a lot. About lots of things. And sometimes, because I look like Elyse and all, sometimes I think Lisette forgets I'm not her and she tells me things, personal things, that I don't think she'd tell me otherwise."

"Such as?"

Sharon shook her head. "I don't feel at liberty to tell you the things she says, it's just that . . ."

"You felt I needed to know that you and Lisette talk at work," Konrad said.

"I know it's none of my business," Sharon Lewis said.

"That's correct, fräulein. It's none of your business. Is there anything else?"

"No, sir. Nothing else." She turned to leave, took a half step, then was back in the doorway. She spoke quickly, wanting to get everything out before he cut her off. "Only that she's not happy, and I get the impression she's painted herself into a corner and now she doesn't know how to get out, but she desperately wants to get out. She doesn't say it in so many words, but a woman can tell, and I know that if you'd just throw her some kind of rope, anything that she could grab on to, she'd cling to it and—"

"Good night, fräulein," Konrad said.

Sharon Lewis started to say more, but the look on Konrad's face communicated that wasn't such a good idea.

Herr Gellert was just finishing his pipe lighting ritual. The bowl resembling an old man with bushy eyebrows had been stuffed and packed, the match struck, the sucking and hissing noises had lasted longer than usual, and now he was in the *aaaahhhh* phase.

Lisette sat catercorner to him with an unfinished piece of embroidery in her lap and a novel she was reading lying on the table situated between their chairs. His pipe burning to his satisfaction, Herr Gellert reached for the weekly production report that he'd set on top of Lisette's book before he'd lit his pipe. With a now-let's-get-down-to-business sigh, he settled back in his chair, concentrating on the report before him.

It was a typical Saturday evening for the couple. They sat in their chairs, the same chairs they always sat in. Lisette took in the room. She could get used to this, she thought. They'd had a nice meal. Luxurious compared to her meals at the Kellerstrasse flat. Here all was quiet. Pleasant. She felt relaxed, warm, and safe. Yes, she could get used to this.

She usually read in the evenings. A book Herr Gellert had approved, something he'd insisted on. When it came to fiction, at first they had disagreed. Herr Gellert was of the opinion that novels were made up of cleverly contrived lies intended to influence weak minds. Lisette appealed to the great Russian novelists Tolstoy and Dostoevsky, arguing that they were still highly revered in the Soviet Union. Herr Gellert had no adequate response to this, so he allowed her to read select works. She was currently reading Dostoevsky's *The Brothers Karamazov,* but for some reason she found Ivan Karamazov's refusal to recognize God, despite the fact he admitted to God's existence, a little tedious tonight.

On nights she didn't feel like reading, she embroidered instead. It had been Pastor Schumacher's secret pastime, which Mady had picked up following the Hadamar incident when Josef could no longer do it. Lisette thought it might be just the diversion she needed. However, after a long day working the sewing machine at the factory, her hands were often too tired to hold a needle. Even now, on Saturday, she found no joy in her project.

So rather than reading or embroidering, she sat listening to Herr Gellert make hissing noises with his pipe, planning what she'd wear to church in the morning.

The downstairs helper—who didn't like being called a maid—interrupted them.

"A gentleman to see you, sir," she said. "A Herr Reichmann."

Gellert pulled his eyes away from the production report. He didn't like to be interrupted. His brow furrowed the way it always did when he was interrupted.

"Herr Reichmann," the helper repeated.

Lisette's heart leaped. Suddenly she no longer felt tired. Konrad? Or it could be Willi, though she didn't know why Willi would show up at Herr Gellert's house. But then, she didn't know any good reason why Konrad would visit them either.

She looked at Herr Gellert. He was studying her.

"Remember, I told you about—" she began.

"I know who Herr Reichmann is," he said flatly.

"It could be Willi Reichmann . . ." Lisette hastened to say.

"Show Herr Reichmann in," Gellert said.

Lisette folded her embroidery and set it aside. She smoothed her dress and sat up in the chair. She considered standing but thought that might appear eager, considering that Herr Gellert remained seated. Out of the corner of her eye, she saw that he was staring at her, and he was not amused.

"Herr Reichmann," the helper announced.

Konrad entered the room, immediately distracted by the clutter of displayed wealth.

"Come in, Herr Reichmann," said Gellert, motioning with his pipe. He didn't stand or offer his hand. And because Herr Gellert didn't stand, neither did Lisette.

Konrad moved from the polished wooden floor to the cream-colored Chinese rug. He acknowledged Herr Gellert with a nod and Lisette with a glance.

"Konrad, what are you doing here?" Lisette asked.

"It's obvious, isn't it?" Gellert said. "Herr Reichmann has come to attempt to steal you away from me."

"There's nothing between me and Konrad," Lisette said.

"Lisette, dear," Gellert said. "Go upstairs to the bedroom and get me a fresh pouch of tobacco."

Lisette frowned. It embarrassed her that Gellert implied she was familiar with his bedroom. She was. She'd been in the room before. She'd entered it to fetch Herr Gellert's tobacco. He told her where he kept it and she'd retrieved it for him. But for him to ask her now, in front of Konrad, well, it implied a familiarity that wasn't . . . she hadn't . . . *they* hadn't . . .

"You know where I keep it, dear," Gellert said. "The upper left drawer of the bureau, next to my—"

"I know where it is," Lisette snapped. "Now?"

"I'm sure Herr Reichmann will excuse you, won't you, Herr Reichmann?"

Lisette stood. She would have to cross in front of Konrad to leave the room. As she did, there would be a moment when her back would be to Herr Gellert and she'd be facing Konrad. She was ready for him. Konrad would find this so funny, so hilarious. He was busting at the seams to hold it in, she was certain of it. And she had an expression ready for him, one which would warn him to keep his mouth shut if he knew what was good for him.

She timed it just right.

But Konrad wasn't busting at the seams. There was no sign of levity, no amusement in his eyes, no tugging at the corners of his mouth. It was too late for her to change her expression; he'd already seen it and absorbed it. Now she felt horrible.

She hurried up the stairs, keeping an ear cocked in the direction of Konrad and Herr Gellert. Yet neither man spoke. She was certain Herr Gellert was waiting until she was out of earshot.

What was he planning to say to Konrad in her absence? How would Konrad respond? What had Konrad come here for anyway?

Lisette reached the top of the landing and paused. Still no voices below!

Herr Gellert's bedroom was located at the far end of a long hallway. She hurried toward it, hurrying without running. She didn't want to appear to be a child.

Throwing open the bedroom door, she crossed the room to his bureau and opened the drawer. There was no pouch of tobacco inside. But there was always an extra pouch.

Then she remembered that earlier this evening Herr Gellert had told his helper he was out of tobacco. He knew he was out of tobacco, but he sent her up here anyway!

Furious, Lisette shoved the bureau drawer closed and retraced her steps, faster than before, to the landing and down the stairs, doing her utmost to project her hearing into the drawing room and to descend the steps as quietly as possible so they didn't know she was coming. She expected to hear shouts. If not shouts, then a low, intense exchange. Instead she heard nothing. Not a sound other than the ticking of the mantel clock.

She reentered the drawing room.

Konrad hadn't moved.

Herr Gellert hadn't moved.

Had they just stared at each other the entire time she was gone?

"There is no pouch in your drawer, dear," Lisette said as pleasantly as she could manage, though with great difficulty because her anger and exertion combined to restrict her breath. "Remember? You reminded the maid you were out."

"So I did," Gellert said.

Lisette took her seat. She examined Konrad's face. It was just as she'd left it. He was staring at Herr Gellert, and Gellert was staring back at him. Herr Gellert seemed to be looking for a challenge, but Konrad had obviously not come here to fight.

"Konrad?" Lisette said.

"Right about now, my dear, Herr Reichmann is feeling a bit overwhelmed. While he came, I'm sure, with a passionate appeal, one that he no doubt prepared and rehearsed to perfection, now in the presence of reality, his words have vanished like so much fiction. While he imagined himself eloquent, and while he imagined that you would succumb to his passion and leave this very night, vowing never to step foot again in this house, the moment he entered this room his imaginings evaporated. Isn't that right, Herr Reichmann?"

Konrad made no attempt to say anything.

"You see, dear," Gellert said, adopting the tone of a detective who had just solved a murder, "your Herr Reichmann began second-guessing himself the moment he saw this house. Once inside, he couldn't help but notice all the finery, and he's since been taking stock of himself. But then, that's what you do best, isn't it, Herr Reichmann? You're used to taking stock of things, the same way you took stock in that little shoe store in Pankow."

Lisette objected. "Herr Gellert, you're being rude."

"Not rude, dear. Just observant. You see, once you found your Herr Reichmann in the back of that store, I did a little checking."

"You investigated him?" Lisette asked, shocked.

"It's always wise to know one's competition," Gellert said. "You still have your SS tattoo, do you?" he said to Konrad. "May I see it?"

Konrad appeared to consider the request for a moment, and then he removed his coat and rolled up his sleeve. The tattoo that had been a source of pride in his youth, and a lightning rod for all kinds of abuse in the Soviet prison system, was still prominent.

Gellert leaned forward in his chair to get a better look.

"You see, dear," he said, settling back in his chair, "it's when I discovered he was SS and had been in a Soviet prison camp and had stocked shoes in obscurity that I dismissed him outright. Look at him. He stands there like a whipped dog; his once proud fascism, the terror of all Europe, has met its match in socialism and a superior Communist system."

"Konrad, say something!" Lisette said.

Konrad looked at her. He didn't speak.

"There's nothing for him to say," Gellert said. "All he can think about right now is how badly he wants to get out of here. That coming here was a mistake. But that's good. He knows that now. And in a way, it's good that he came. He'll no longer fill his mind with delusions of things he can never have. He'll be a better man for having come here."

"Konrad?"

"It's all right, Herr Reichmann," said Gellert, taking up his production report. "You did the honorable thing. Console yourself with that. I'm sure you can find your own way out." Gellert turned his attention to his report.

Konrad stood in the same place he'd been standing since walking into the room. When he stepped off the Chinese rug, Lisette could see the impression his shoes had made. Two perfect imprints. Until now he hadn't shuffled, or moved an inch, since he'd stepped onto it.

He made his way to the front door.

Lisette watched him turn the corner and disappear into the entryway. She fidgeted as she heard the front door open. Unable to stop herself, she jumped up from her chair and went after him.

"Lisette!" Gellert called after her.

She knew she'd pay for it, but she continued after Konrad. He was at the bottom of the front steps when she reached the door.

"Konrad!"

He stopped. Turned.

"Why did you come here?"

He just looked at her.

"Say something!" she shouted. "Say something! This is crazy!"

Konrad said nothing; he just kept looking at her.

She stared back at him. She couldn't remember looking into his eyes like this, not since she'd found him in Pankow. There had been casual glances but never a lingering gaze like this one. It reminded her of the way they'd looked at each other a long time ago, New Year's 1945, while sitting on the floor of Ramah Cabin. Just the two of them. This was the look they shared just before they kissed. This was Konrad as only she knew him.

Lisette screamed in frustration, stormed back inside the house, and slammed the door shut.

Chapter 33

Sunday, November 11, 1962

Following his afternoon walk—the kind he made with a camera on the rooftops of downtown Berlin—Konrad opened the door to Ramah Cabin and was met by an assault force of two angry women.

"What did you do to Lisette?" Mady shouted.

"She was in tears during the entire worship service," Sharon Lewis added.

Not having been in a combat situation for over fifteen years, Konrad's reaction time had become rusty. He'd just finished shooting a roll of film and was headed to the basement, where he had set up a makeshift darkroom. He remembered that he was low on developer and was wondering if there was still enough in the box to mix a batch for a single roll of film when Mady and Sharon jumped him, guns blazing.

"I didn't do anything to Lisette." The words stumbled from Konrad's mouth.

"What did you say to her?" Mady said.

"I didn't say anything."

That was the truth.

Sharon Lewis picked up the cross-examination. "But you went over to Herr Gellert's last night."

"What did she tell you?" Konrad said, interested now.

"She was crying so hard she couldn't tell us anything," said Mady. "She sniffled all through the service, then broke down afterward when we asked her what was wrong. All we got out of her was that you showed up at Herr Gellert's house last night, and then she ran off."

"Did you?" Sharon Lewis asked.

The element of surprise having worn off, Konrad determined that the flow of information in this discussion would go only one direction. He excused himself, wedging his way between the two women. He hadn't seen the others until now, but there was a group of Americans and Viktor watching the drama from a distance. If the room had a slope, they'd be in the balcony.

Mady wasn't ready for the scene to end.

"Konrad, something happened last night."

Konrad kept walking. Over his shoulder he said, "I went over there. Nothing happened."

"You went over there? Why?" Mady demanded to know.

"To see for myself."

"To see what for yourself?"

But Konrad's part in this impromptu drama was over. He exited upstage, toward the basement. But not before hearing the dialogue of the two remaining actors on stage.

"Why would he go over there?" Mady said.

"I think it's partly my fault," Sharon said. "I told him he should go talk to Lisette, but I didn't think he'd storm Herr Gellert's house."

"Talk to Lisette, I agree. But privately—not in Herr Gellert's front room."

"Definitely not with him there."

"Of course not."

"Men can be so dense."

"Honey, you don't know the half of it."

Konrad was stretched out on his bed when he heard a sharp knock at the door. Three raps. Not timid.

He looked up from the book he was reading. *Of Human Bondage* by W. Somerset Maugham. He'd found it in one of Park's packages, along with a couple of Graham Greene novels. Reading the novel in English was slow going for him. His interest in English had been spurred on by the arrival of the Americans, and he'd considered asking Sharon Lewis to help him with the novel, until he read enough of the back cover to learn that it was the story of Philip Carey's obsession with a pale waitress named Mildred.

He slipped the paperback under his pillow. "Can it wait until morning?" he shouted at the door.

The door swung open. Mady stood there. "No, it can't," she said.

Her eyes were hard, her mouth a thin line. She stepped aside. Lisette crossed the threshold. Her hands were folded in front of her, and her eyes were red, her cheeks marked with tear tracks.

Konrad threw his legs over the side of the bed and stood up.

Scowling at Konrad, Mady left and closed the door, leaving it open just a crack. The swing of the door forced Lisette to step farther into the room, closer to Konrad, which she did only with the greatest reluctance.

They stood there facing each other, a meter or so apart, with neither one looking at the other.

Finally Lisette said, "Why did you come?"

Konrad didn't want to have this discussion. Not now. Probably not ever. Seeing Lisette in that man's house, sitting there all cozy in the parlor, looking every bit the married couple, had crushed Konrad's heart. Standing on that Chinese rug in that Communist's house, watching Lisette take a familiar path upstairs and return to her place in the parlor next to that man, the man who would make her his wife, the man who would be the father of her children—it had done something to Konrad. It had smothered all the feelings he had for Lisette.

"Well?" Lisette said. "Are you going to say something, or are you just going to stand there like you did at Herr Gellert's house?"

Konrad wanted just to stand there. He was afraid that if he said anything, it would only hurt her worse. But by not saying anything, he was hurting both of them.

Lisette waited for an answer.

"I had to see for myself," Konrad said softly.

"See what, Konrad?" Lisette spat. "How rich Herr Gellert is? Tell me."

"I wanted to see if you were happy."

"Happy?" Lisette cried. "I have news for you, Konrad Reichmann, my happiness is none of your concern. You gave up any right to my happiness years ago."

"Herr Gellert didn't appear all that upset with my visit."

"*I* was upset with your visit!" Lisette said, crying now. "You had no right to barge into our lives like that!"

"Our lives." She said, "Our lives." Lisette and Waldemar. They were an *our* now. Of course they were. But hearing Lisette say it out loud was a fresh jab at an open wound.

"Do you want me to apologize? Is that it?" Konrad asked.

Lisette stared at him. Her chin began to quiver. She turned her back on him and ran from the room.

Lisette stayed the night at Ramah Cabin. And the next night. And the next. Each day after work she arrived at the house with Sharon Lewis and Mady. She spent her evenings avoiding Konrad. She took up residence with the girls in their room.

It wasn't until the fourth night when Sharon Lewis saw Konrad covertly watching Lisette that the American slid beside him and whispered, "She left Herr Gellert. The wedding's off."

Shortly after this, Mady and Lisette moved out of their flat on Kellerstrasse and into Ramah Cabin.

Mady had just about had her fill of the Reichmann boys. While she felt a definite relief that Lisette had broken things off with Herr Gellert, that didn't excuse Konrad's boorish behavior in the matter. He'd hurt Lisette deeply, and if Mady were a man she'd take him out back to the woodpile and give him a good thrashing.

As for Willi, his advances were progressing beyond the mixture of sweet talk and crude innuendo he'd used up to now. He was getting impatient with her always keeping him at a distance. He knew he was being played. She knew he knew it. But his attraction to her was strong enough to keep him coming back.

Each time he did, however, he pressed for more from her. He'd begun cornering her, or backing her against walls, pinning her there, groping, forcing kisses on her. Each encounter grew increasingly more revolting. Mady kept telling herself that she had to hold out just a while longer. Any day now Park would return with a double for Viktor and then they could all clear out. The Americans could take their visas and cross back over the border. After that, what could

Willi do? The threat to the group was his leverage. Once that threat was gone . . .

Mady's only hope was that she could hold Willi at bay until Park showed up with Viktor's double.

He'd surprised her, Park had. Unlike the time before, this time he'd come through for them just like he said he would. She had to give him credit for his persistence. Once home in America, he could have forgotten all about them. But instead Park came back for them. That said something about the man.

And though she'd never admit it to anyone, she found herself looking forward to his appearances, as brief as they were. She got nervous and excited right along with the others each time it was their turn to cross. Yet, since Tomcat's crossing, the excitement far outweighed any nervousness. Park had proved himself someone who could be trusted with their care. Of course, the unexpected could still happen. This was dangerous business. There were no guarantees. But if anyone could handle it, Park could. Mady knew that now.

Lisette had told her about Park striking his commanding officer, about the stockade and his narrowly averting a court-martial. He'd interceded for them. It didn't make the nightmare that followed any less horrifying, yet he did try. She had to give him credit.

As for everyone saying Park was sweet on her, well, she no longer found that as repulsive as she once had. In fact, it was kind of nice. The thought that someone found her attractive resurrected feelings she hadn't had since she was young. Eons ago. In a different world. Now, with the pressure of the group's safety starting to lessen, Mady found herself occasionally thinking about what it would be like to sit down with Park and just talk, or to go out to dinner with him, or spend a casual afternoon with him by a lake, or walk together in a park.

Why not? she asked herself when feelings of guilt arose. It would feel good to get away and not have to worry about production goals, or secrets, or meals, or all the things that anchored her body, mind, heart, and soul to this drab, fear-riddled East German existence.

"This is it," Park said.

He spoke to his passenger as they pulled up in front of Ramah Cabin, all the while checking the grounds for an extra car—an indication Willi Reichmann might be present. He also checked the rearview mirror for any headlights or other signs they'd been followed.

His hands were clammy on the steering wheel. He felt sick to his stomach. Sneaking away to Ramah Cabin involved great risk. Yet the circumstances were extraordinary, so against his better judgment, he decided he had to take the chance. Park had tried to come up with a better location for this particular exchange, but given its potentially explosive nature, he thought it best to make the exchange in a controlled environment.

"Nice house," Alex said, peering through the double layer of darkness and a dirty windshield.

"Your home for the next few months, should everything go well," Park said.

"It has a garden."

"A passion you and Herr Witzell have in common."

Park opened his door. The moon was full. He checked the road again. Nothing but the swirling wisps of blue-gray dust caused by his own arrival. Beyond that, darkness. He listened. Something under the hood of the car was hissing.

He and Alex approached the house. All the windows were dark.

"It's a shame we have to wake them," Alex said.

"Couldn't be helped."

Park took a deep breath. Of all the crossings, this would prove to be the most difficult.

He knocked on the front door.

Chapter 34

Park had to knock a second time before there was any response from within Ramah Cabin.

"Who is it?" came from beyond the door.

"Konrad?"

He took a chance. The voice sounded too young to be Witzell.

"Konrad? It's Park."

The latch sounded. The door opened a crack. Eyes peered at them out of the darkness. Before opening the door farther, Konrad turned to someone behind him.

"It's me, Park," he said.

Konrad opened the door but then froze halfway, his eyes wide. "I don't believe it!" he said, looking shocked.

"This is Alex," Park said. "Alex Moffett."

It took several seconds for Konrad to regain his senses enough to back away and let them in.

A light switched on.

Witzell stood behind Konrad. His eyes were just as wide as Konrad's, his mouth just as open. Dumbfounded, he stared at their late-night guest.

"Alex Moffett," Park repeated the introduction.

"You'd better get Mady and Lisette," Konrad said.

Witzell nodded and backed into a wall. The jolt brought him back to himself. He disappeared down the dim hallway.

A moment later they could hear him knocking on a door, calling Mady's name. While they couldn't hear what was said from inside Mady and Lisette's room, they heard Witzell say, "It's Park. You'd better come see for yourself."

By now Konrad was awake and in control of himself. He wore a silly grin.

Witzell reappeared. Mady was on his heels, tying the belt of her housecoat. Lisette was right behind her.

Mady stopped suddenly when she looked up. So suddenly, Lisette ran into her.

If Mady's first reaction was any indication as to whether or not she would approve of Park's plan, it wasn't promising.

"What's this?" she said. She'd barked the words.

Behind her, Lisette's reaction was similar to what Konrad and Witzell's had been.

Mady grabbed the ties of her housecoat and yanked. Hard. She stepped forward to stare into a mirror image of herself.

"Mady Schumacher, Alexandra Moffett. Alex, this is Mady Schumacher."

"Pleased to meet you," the woman said, extending her hand.

Mady ignored it. Her attention was solely on Park. "I think you'd better explain yourself, Colonel Parker," she said. "And it had better be good."

"You were supposed to bring a double for Viktor," Mady said.

Park sat next to Mady's look-alike on the sofa. Mady sat directly opposite them. Witzell, Konrad, and Lisette—none of the Americans had ventured out of their rooms—took up places on both sides to watch the spectacle. Their expressions bordered on outright laughter, which, for Mady's sake, they held in. As the words flew back and forth between Park and Mady, the spectators' eyes moved back and forth like at a tennis match, comparing the two Madys.

Alexandra Moffett sat straight-backed on the sofa, her hands demurely in her lap. Her hair had been pulled up, revealing a graceful neck. She wore a brown skirt and jacket combination. Her legs crossed at the ankles. She appeared calm. Occasionally her eyes flashed at something Mady said. There was an obvious intelligence behind them—and a bit of anger, which she was keeping in check. At least for now. She let Park do all the talking.

The real Mady kept gripping and adjusting her faded floral-print housecoat, pulling at the ties with ferocity. Mady's hair was down and disheveled, looking like a woman who had just been dragged from her bed. Her skin wasn't as smooth as her counterpart's complexion, and her bare feet clawed at the tassels of the throw rug.

Park sat on the edge of the sofa, leaning forward, his elbows on his knees, his hands open and extended as he tried to explain the situation.

"You know we can't walk Viktor across the border like the others," he began.

"Old news," Mady said, doing her best to keep her eyes on Park and not on the woman seated next to him.

"Yes, I'm just saying that . . . well, I've tried, and I haven't been able to come up with a—"

"Tried? How? What have you done?"

Park's hands orchestrated his argument. "You have to understand. After Annie, we had to approach this whole thing from a different direction."

"Again, old news."

"We needed to come up with a plausible reason for bringing a boy with Viktor's condition into East Germany. I've risked consulting several medical experts at the med school, and"—his left hand motioned to Witzell—"I've consulted with your father, and so far we haven't been able to find a plausible reason that won't draw a lot of attention to itself. I'm sorry."

"You're sorry. That's it?"

"Mady," Witzell said, "you're being a little hard on—"

"No, I don't think I am," Mady said. "Once again Colonel Parker has made promises he can't keep." To her father she said, "You of all people should understand what's at stake. For years you kept the children together. Now Colonel Parker has succeeded in splitting them apart onto two continents, abandoning poor Viktor. Who's going to tell him? He's going to be heartbroken."

"I haven't abandoned him," Park insisted, a little heated. "We'll find a way. I just haven't found it yet."

"In the meantime, you've found something else."

Park and Alex exchanged glances.

"I just thought—"

"It's pretty obvious what you were thinking!" Mady said.

"Hold on," said Konrad. "I don't know about the rest of you, but I'm curious to know what Park was thinking."

Park looked at Konrad. He couldn't tell if Konrad was coming to his defense or handing him a rope to hang himself.

"I'd like to hear his explanation," Lisette added.

"It's the next logical step," Park said as matter-of-factly as he could manage. "We get the children out, and the rest of you follow. I've been keeping an eye open for doubles for each of you."

"That was never the plan," Mady said.

"You're wrong. That has always been the plan. Back in '45 and now. Then it included you and Lisette. Now we've added Herr Witzell and Konrad."

"You've been looking for an American who looks like me?" Konrad said.

"That or a reasonable facsimile."

"I never agreed to go to America," Mady said. "And even if I did, I would never go unless I was taking Viktor with me."

She was leaving no room for discussion, that much was obvious.

"It's just that, with most of the others already in the States, and with Konrad and Lisette and Herr Witzell still here for Viktor, I was thinking . . ."

"Yes, I can see what you were thinking," Mady said, this time not avoiding looking directly at Alex Moffett.

By now Alex was ready for the challenge. She started to say something, but Park stopped her.

"Just like the others," Park said in all seriousness, "she has risked her life coming here, leaving a lucrative practice."

"Practice?" Witzell said.

"I'm an ophthalmologist," Alex said.

Witzell raised his eyebrows at Park—he was impressed.

"What exactly is your role?" Mady said to her. "I'd like to know what Park said to you to get you to agree to this."

"Professor Parker can be very persuasive," Alex said. "He's a man with high ideals. Very passionate."

Now Mady raised her eyebrows.

Konrad and Lisette snickered.

Alexandra Moffett took exception to this. Standing, she said, "I don't pretend to know all that is going on here, or all that has gone on in the past between you, but let me tell you this: whenever

Professor Parker spoke of you—all of you—he did so with the utmost respect and decency. You may not appreciate that, but this man has dedicated himself to getting every single one of you out of East Germany, and every single time he crosses the border, he does so knowing that he may never come out again. That may not mean much to you, but let me tell you, there are few men in this world who would repeatedly risk capture and prison, and I think you're fortunate to have a man like him who is willing to do that for you!"

Her chest rose and fell from the exertion of the outburst. No one said anything. No one was smirking now.

To Park she said, "I'll wait for you out in the car." With that she got up and left.

Mady stood. Park did too.

Mady didn't look at him. She didn't say anything more to him. She just turned and went back to her bedroom.

Park said to her back, "I'll keep trying to figure a way to get Viktor out."

Excusing himself, he headed for the door.

The TWA flight out of Tempelhof took off on schedule. As the plane taxied to the end of the runway, the sound of the engines filled the compartment, making conversation difficult.

Park and Alex Moffett were strapped into adjoining seats. Outside their window, the lights of West Berlin shone bright against the backdrop of night.

There was a roar of engines and the plane picked up speed, pressing the passengers back into their seats. Next came a gentle lifting sensation and they were airborne.

"I'm sorry to have dragged you halfway around the world for nothing," Park said, adding an apologetic smile.

Alex smiled sweetly. She didn't know it, but it tore at Park's heart. It wasn't the first time. Working closely with Alexandra Moffett for this operation had been a very difficult thing for Park. Every time he looked at her, he saw Mady. Every time she smiled at him, it was as if he was living his dreams. When she laughed at something he said, it was Mady sharing that moment with him. There were times, unguarded moments, when she would catch him by surprise and he had to reject the impulse to take her in his arms, to declare his love for her.

"Maybe it wasn't for nothing," Alex said. She placed her hand on top of his.

He looked at her hand, then in her eyes.

"These last few weeks have been special for me," Alex said.

She spoke the words with Mady's lips.

"I don't know what your relationship is with that woman," she said. "From what little I saw, there's something between you."

"Animosity," Park said. "That's what it is."

"I wouldn't be so sure. Regardless, I want you to know that in the time I've known you, I've come to have feelings for you."

Park knew it was dangerous to look at her. He couldn't help himself. The words. The face. Her willingness. Sitting right next to him was everything he wanted.

Only, it was a mirage.

It wasn't Mady.

The next morning Mady made it official. "We're on our own to get Viktor out," she said.

Witzell disagreed. "Park may come through yet."

"I'm with Mady on this one," Konrad said. "If Park is able to come up with a plan to get Viktor out, fine. In the meantime, it's up to us to develop a plan of our own. In my room I have photographs of the Wall."

He went to his room to retrieve them. Moments later, black-and-white photographs of the Berlin Wall were spread before them on the table.

"We could be arrested simply for having these photos," Witzell said. "Lisette, go to the window and watch for Willi. How much time before he shows up?"

Mady looked at the clock. "Thirty minutes to an hour."

Lisette went to the window while Mady, Konrad, and Witzell examined the pictures. Periodically Witzell would point out a feature from his tour. The more they studied the pictures, the more impossible it seemed they'd ever be able to devise a plan to breach the Wall.

"I've been taking walks too," Lisette said, holding back the curtain slightly as she spoke. "Early evenings when Herr Gellert was at the factory and I was alone. Mostly in Pankow. I wanted to see the old church. The house I grew up in." She smiled, visualizing it. "It has a happy family living in it now. Once, I even got a ride to the original Ramah Cabin. I couldn't tell if it's owned by a family or an organization of some kind. There were no signs."

The others picked up one photograph after another as they listened to her.

"I mainly went to visit Pastor Schumacher's grave."

Mady looked up. So did Konrad. They'd buried him in an unmarked grave, but it came as no surprise to them that Lisette was able to locate it.

"That night I dreamed about Pastor Schumacher. I was standing near his grave when all of a sudden he was standing next to me. It wasn't scary, though. I don't think I could ever be afraid of Pastor Schumacher."

None of them were looking at photos now.

"Then he climbed into his grave and sat in it like you would a bathtub. And then he looked up at me and stretched out his arms, as though he wanted me to join him."

"Oh, Lisette," Mady said, "don't read too much into something like that. It was just a dream."

Lisette looked at her. "I know, but still, I got to thinking about it, and I think Pastor Schumacher was trying to tell me that dying isn't the frightening experience we make it out to be, that when it comes our turn to die, he'll be there to see us safely across."

After a moment or two, the three began looking at photos again but in a much more somber mood.

"I don't even know why I thought of that now," Lisette said. "Maybe because of Herr Parker, the way he's been helping the others cross the border . . . Pastor Schumacher will be there to help us cross over to our new life in heaven."

"I don't think that's it," Konrad said. He straightened up, holding a photo in his hand. "I don't think that's it at all."

"Do you have something?" Witzell asked.

"I know how to get Viktor across the border."

Chapter 35

The winter of 1962 was a difficult one. Not so much due to the weather. It was a time of retrenching and preparation for a new escape effort come springtime. But mostly it was a time of reflection.

The Americans experienced cabin fever. It was their first holiday season outside of the States. And while Mady's and Lisette's attempt to help them celebrate the American holiday of Thanksgiving with a turkey was appreciated, the side dishes of lentil-and-sausage soup and sauerkraut reminded them they were far from home. Christmas turned out better, since it was a holiday shared by both cultures, though in East Germany it was officially discouraged. Their hosts took them shopping, which backfired. The shelves of the stores lay bare and depressing. With what little they could find, they had an exchange of gifts. They sang carols and decorated a tree with lights and tinsel. Still, homesickness was a common illness that year at Ramah Cabin, exacerbated by there being no word from Park indicating how much longer they would need to stay.

Viktor's emotions swung from elation, from the extra attention he was getting, to depression. It was the first holiday season he'd spent apart from the others. He received a package from the States filled with Christmas presents bought at Macy's. Each of the others sent him a letter or a Christmas card. Included was a picture of all of them standing with Ernst and Rachelle in front of a huge Christmas tree. On the back of the photo was an inscription that said, *Next year together at FH.* Whoever had written it didn't risk spelling out Freedom House for fear it might give too much away to the East German postal inspectors.

Mady muddled through the holidays in a subdued mood. Having Lisette around the house again was good for her. As for the men in her life, she managed to find a balance. Willi's visits were taken like castor oil. They were a necessary unpleasantness. She was calling Herr Witzell "Father" more frequently and began kissing him goodnight on the cheek. He, of course, relished the change. As for Konrad, his brilliant escape plan had redeemed him in her eyes, and it wasn't uncommon to sec the two of them huddled together refining the details of the plan.

The holidays were hardest on Lisette and Konrad, since their closest times in the past occurred at this time of year. The youth Christmas party at Pastor Schumacher's house when he'd given them each coins with personalized inscriptions and when the boys knocked over the tree roughhousing—*"Poor Kaiser!"*—and Lisette tuned the radio to what she thought was Christmas music, only to learn it was the forbidden BBC channel. And New Year's of '44 after Neff was killed, and '45 when they shared their New Year's wishes and Konrad told Lisette she was the woman who would make him happy.

Lisette took a short walk by herself on the last day of 1962. Bundled against the cold, she left a trail of crunched footprints that meandered through the trees. She took with her the coin Josef had designed for her, the coin that had the inscription, "She shall rejoice in time to come." The dear man.

He knew of her unhappy homelife when he selected the text. It was his promise to her that her life would not always be a whirlwind of strife. She grinned, wondering what Pastor Schumacher would say to her if he knew that, twenty-some years later, she still hadn't found the joy he predicted.

It was this coin and the realization that she never would have found joy with Herr Gellert that convinced her to leave the night of Konrad's silent visit. That, and one thing more. The way Konrad stood there in Herr Gellert's parlor, unmoving, refusing to react to Herr Gellert's goading. How unlike the old Konrad. The old Konrad would have traded blow for blow. Fists, if necessary. The Konrad who stood in Herr Gellert's parlor was a different Konrad. The thing that had struck Lisette so profoundly that night was that in him she saw the image of Pastor Schumacher. Not a physical likeness. But the moral strength. The kind that didn't need a barrage of boasts or posturing to prove itself. That night she saw in Konrad moral strength woven into the very fabric of his being.

When her anger cooled enough for her to recognize it, she knew that she would find her happiness with him or not at all.

As they all ushered in 1963 with toasts by firelight, Lisette caught Konrad staring at her. His eyes, like hers, were wet with memories.

Chapter 36

Friday, March 22, 1963

Seated on a wooden stool next to a window overlooking Wilmersdorfer Strasse, in West Germany, Willi Reichmann glanced down at the street. It resembled a beehive that had been poked.

He chuckled. He'd done that once when he was young—poked a beehive with a stick. He wasn't after honey or anything; he just saw it and thought it would be fun to poke it. It proved to be a mistake. Twenty-seven bites. He'd counted them. He was swollen and sick to his stomach for days. The thing he remembered most about the beehive, though, wasn't so much the beestings but the stinging of his father's tongue. While the bees did their worst in one day, Herr Reichmann belittled his son in every public setting imaginable for weeks.

But that was in the past. He'd learned his lesson. So had his father, for the beehive incident and more. Willi knew now that if someone was going to poke a beehive, that person had better take precautions.

He disassembled the rifle, set it in a wooden box, lowered the box into a long wooden trough, then arranged nine boxes of key blanks side by side on top of it. He turned on his stool to face a whirling grindstone, lowered safety goggles to protect his one good eye, and with sparks flying, continued cutting a blank to match the master key.

Setting the finished key aside, he reached for another blank. He didn't look out the window. No need to. He'd seen the scene often enough. All that was left for him to do was to wait for the police.

As he waited, he thought of Mady. All morning he'd been looking forward to this time when, his work done, he could concentrate on her. He had yet to figure out what it was about her that so captivated him. All he knew was that he'd always felt this way about her. It wasn't uncommon for a young man to develop feelings for an older woman. It amused him now to think that for him it was the pastor's wife. Most boys, however, grew beyond their first infatuation by turning their attention to younger, available girls. Willi hadn't.

While his army buddies were yearning over the girls they left behind or paying for companionship, Willi couldn't get his mind off of Mady. Returning from the front, his first thought was that he wanted to see her. And when he learned that her husband had been pumped full of drugs for his part in some cockeyed plan to rescue a bunch of retards, Willi's heart leaped at the thought that Pastor Schumacher would probably die young. The joy came from the realization that he could then have Mady all to himself.

The day Josef Schumacher died was a happy day for Willi. Immediately he started looking for ways to swoop in and win Mady's heart. By this time, Hitler was on the ropes and there were shortages of just about everything. With Willi being heavily involved in the black market, he began using food and supplies to make himself the hero and put Mady in a position to thank him. Just when he thought he was making progress, the war ended and messed up everything.

Mady disappeared. Willi consoled himself by marrying Gael Wissing. She was nothing like Mady, but she was attractive enough. Soon Willi became well off, gaining much personal profit through collaborating with the invading Soviets. While Germany suffered the pangs of national guilt and lived among the ruins of their once-proud cities, boiling the ends of furniture to make glue soup, Willi and Gael Reichmann dined on pheasant and drank fine wines, paying for it all with Soviet rubles that Willi had earned by turning in wanted German military leaders.

Then, when he thought he'd given up hope of ever seeing Mady again, while doing a little late-night, after-hours snooping at Stasi headquarters, he came across some papers that indicated Mady's retards were still alive. He tracked them down, and though he didn't find Mady, he found her father—surprise, surprise; he was supposed to be dead—and knew that all he had to do was to keep an eye on these kids. He pinned his hopes on the fact that if Mady was still alive, eventually she'd be drawn back to the kids, sort of like how Gael was drawn to jewelry.

As it turned out, he was right. Willi's obsession found new life.

The door to the key shop flew open with a bang. Four policemen, guns drawn, burst in. Willi pretended to act surprised. For effect, he kicked over a box of key blanks. They scattered noisily across the floor.

Willi slowly raised his hands.

"Herr Kippenberger?" the first policeman through the door asked.

"Like on the door," Willi said.

The door, the one that had just been kicked in, had Kippenberger's Keys printed on it in gold letters. Willi had leased the space and moved in six months earlier.

The police looked around the room, leading with their guns. Behind counters and stacks of boxes. In closets.

"Has anyone been here recently?"

"*Nein*."

"Did you hear anything? See anything?"

"*Nein*. Only that there seems to be a disturbance of some sort on the street." He looked out the window. "Is that man, the one lying in the snow, hurt badly?"

The police took one last look around.

"Let's go," the leader ordered.

"Is he anyone important?" Willi called after them.

He received no answer. He didn't need one. The man lying in the snow was dead. Willi knew more about the deceased than the police who were slamming their way into the office one door down.

The man lying in the snow was Alfred Kleiber, thirty-two years old. He had a wife, Ingrid, and three sons, Wolfgang, Franz, and Walther. He was a West German navy captain, commander of a military counterespionage group. A year ago he had approached a border barrier waving an envelope and persuaded an East German guard to take it. It was a letter offering his services to the Stasi, purporting that he could deliver details of Poseidon missile sites, the top secret locations of U.S. tactical nuclear weapons in West Germany, with map coordinates that would enable the Soviets to retarget their weapons, ensuring accuracy within a hundred meters. He would do this for a price, of course.

Unknown to Kleiber, the Stasi had a mole in West Germany with the ability to confirm the coordinates. The coordinates didn't check out. It was an attempt to pass on West German disinformation. The Stasi sent Willi to take care of Kleiber.

Willi knew things about the man that even Ingrid, his wife, didn't know. For example, he knew that Kleiber had a mistress—Adelheid Klar, a brunette bombshell who wore high heels that sculpted the calves of her legs—and that Kleiber kept her in an apartment on Wilmersdorfer Strasse. That he visited her every Friday at two o'clock in the afternoon for a couple of hours before going home for the weekend. Except for today. Alfred Kleiber would not be keeping today's scheduled rendezvous with Adelheid.

Willi peered out the window. The police had established a perimeter around the body to keep a small but growing crowd away. He looked for Adelheid. Did she know yet? Or was she brooding in her apartment, angry that her lover was late? He was reaching for another key blank when his stomach grumbled. Unlike earlier days when killing upset his stomach, now it actually made him hungry. This too brought a chuckle. He'd grown up in so many ways since his youth in Pankow. Those who knew him when he was young and skinny wouldn't believe what he was capable of today.

Funny the way things turned out. Actually it was Konrad who had been trained to be a killer, while Willi was afraid of guns. War changes things. Now Konrad couldn't kill and Willi made his living as an assassin. Well, that was where the big money was. His regular flow of cash came from selling information and from blackmail payoffs.

It was at Stalingrad that Willi learned there was profit in killing. It still amazed him how profitable it could be. And how simple. Of course, in the trenches at Stalingrad, he was still a scared little boy when he tossed the grenade into his own trench. The plan was simple enough. Wound himself and then get sent back home before the Russians killed him. And he still thought he had it figured right if Georgy Bauer hadn't turned around unexpectedly. Pudgy Georgy. If he wasn't a comical sight! Georgy staring wide-eyed as the grenade bounced off his chest. It was the last surprise Georgy ever had. As for Willi, the shrapnel hit him in the face and arm instead of the leg.

When Willi regained consciousness, he saw there was one other survivor—Rudy Reck, their point man. Willi owed him a paycheck and a half for a bad luck streak in a card game. Rudy was minus one leg. He knew that Willi had thrown the grenade; he was staring at Willi with murderous eyes. What else could Willi do? His own right eye filled with blood and one hand rendered useless, he managed to sling Rudy over his shoulder. Rudy was losing blood fast. To keep him from talking to anyone, Willi made a circuitous route toward the rear of where their unit had been dug in. A medic spotted him wandering and came to his aid. Willi wrestled him for Rudy, thinking Rudy might still be alive. The medic took Willi's actions for shock. And when he finally got Rudy away from Willi, Rudy was dead.

That was when the army rewarded Willi and sent him home a hero. A Silver Wound Badge and an Iron Cross, Second Class. And all Willi had to do for it was to toss a grenade in his own trench.

Only once since then had he killed for something other than profit—well, twice if he counted Gael, but he hardly thought of her anymore. He killed once for revenge. For a lifetime of ridicule, and physical and verbal abuse. Willi killed his father.

Konrad thought Krahl had done it. After Willi returned from the front a wounded war hero, his father actually began to show him some respect. It was too little, too late.

Having finished cutting the key, Willi flipped a switch that started a second wheel turning. He pressed the cut edges of the key against the spinning buffer to smooth the rough edges. Then, turning both wheels off, he listened for sounds in the hallway. Everything was quiet. The police had moved on.

Getting up, he stretched and removed his work apron. He decided that Herr Kippenberger would close shop early today. There was a place called Café Lorenz that, he was told, served sausages that were extra spicy, the way he liked them. Maybe he'd give the place a try before crossing the border into East Germany. There would be no lines for Willi to stand in. There was a section of fence along the border where there were no land mines. The Stasi used this section to slip their agents and operatives back and forth across the border. The Stasi took care of their own.

As Willi closed up shop he let out a laugh. *Kippenberger's Keys*. He was proud of himself for that one. For a man who opened doors with a lockpick, the idea of owning a shop that made keys had a nice touch of irony.

Chapter 37

Saturday, March 23, 1963

Willi was hoping it was nothing. It would complicate things with Mady. Yet he couldn't shake the feeling that something wasn't right at Ramah Cabin. And as much as he hoped they weren't trying to pull one over on him, he wasn't about to let them make a fool of him.

With Gael it was jewelry and just about anything money could buy. Willi knew she'd never love him. He didn't care. He liked the way she looked on his arm, the way people would gawk at her—dazzling in a sleek evening gown and diamonds—then look at him and wonder how someone with his looks could get such a beautiful woman. For Gael's part, she loved things more than she loved men, and so, because Willi gave her money, theirs was a mutually beneficial arrangement.

With Mady it was the same in that Willi knew she would never love him. But then, it was different in that Willi would give anything for her to love him. He was realistic enough to know that he had nothing Mady wanted by way of possessions or personality. In order to have her, then, he had to find her price. Unlike Gael, Mady's head wasn't turned by possessions. The only thing Willi saw that she consistently treasured were those retarded people. It was something he never understood about her, but he didn't have to understand. All he had to do was know it and then use it to his advantage.

Blackmail was the only leverage he had over Mady. The day he learned that the retards had been smuggled out of K7 under pretense of death, he knew he'd finally won. He now had what he needed to gain control over Mady Schumacher. Willi rarely felt giddy, but there was no other word to describe the thrill that shot through him at that moment of realization.

That was why he was hoping they weren't stupid enough to try to put one over on him. It would ruin everything. Until now, he pretended he hadn't noticed little things such as people speaking English behind closed doors. Naturally suspicious, he could only conclude they were learning a different language so they could keep things from him. Willi didn't speak English. There were other things as well, things harder for him to ignore. The blind guy mostly. The one who used to meow like a cat.

For starters, there were the Foster Grant sunglasses. Mady had explained that to him. Some James Dean nonsense. Willi let this one go. If the kid wanted to comb his hair every thirty seconds, by itself there was nothing suspicious about that. But a few days after Christmas, Willi spotted the boy navigating down a dark hallway, wearing the dark glasses, his hands out in front of him feeling the wall.

The remarkable thing about this kid up to now was that he didn't act blind. So why was he acting like a blind kid all of a sudden? And then, not long ago, the kid was pouring milk into a glass and it sure looked like he was peering over the tops of his Foster Grants while he was doing it.

Also, what was this thing with him calling everyone "man"?

Back from his West Berlin assignment, Willi sat on a stool at the kitchen counter chewing on a piece of bread. Mady had been chopping canned tomatoes for supper and had excused herself for a moment, leaving Willi alone.

He heard them first. Apparently they didn't know he was in the kitchen. They were laughing and talking to each other in English. When they reached the doorway that led into the kitchen, Elyse pulled up short and hit the blind guy on the arm to shut him up.

Guilt was plastered all over her face.

"Excuse us, Herr Reichmann," she said in German, and the two hurried into the front room.

"Come back here!" Willi shouted.

They didn't.

He heard the front door open, so he went after them. They were hiding something. He was certain of it. Running down the hall in pursuit, Willi heard the front door slam. Several strides and it was open again. Elyse and the blind man were in the garden, approaching Mady and Witzell, who were conferring about something. Witzell was hoeing the ground, preparing it for seed.

Elyse and the man reached them, and Elyse whispered something to Mady.

Mady's eyes grew wide with alarm. She pushed past Elyse to confront Willi.

At that moment, everything fell into place. Willi knew their secret, though he didn't know the purpose behind it. First the deception to get them out of K7, and now another deception to get them out of Ramah Cabin. But to where, and why? They were moving the kids out and replacing them at Ramah Cabin.

"Ah! There you are!" Mady said to Willi. "I need your help in the kitchen." She grabbed Willi's arm and attempted to turn him back toward the house.

Willi stayed planted where he was. "Something's going on here," he said.

Witzell stood between Willi and the couple. He handed Elyse his hoe and said in a voice loud enough for Willi to hear, "Be a dear and take that to the shed for me? Tomcat, you go with her."

"Stay where you are!" Willi barked.

"Willi, please don't badger them," Mady said, making a second attempt to turn him around. "If we don't get supper started soon . . ."

"Tomcat, come here!"

Tomcat started toward Willi, but Elyse stopped him by holding tight to his arm.

"I don't know what's going on around here," Willi said. His anger was growing at the very poor attempt at deception. Did they take him for a fool? The two were probably laughing at his expense when they were talking in the hallway earlier. "I said come here!"

Tomcat shrugged free from Elyse's hold on him. He approached Willi. Witzell intercepted him.

"If he said anything to offend you," Witzell said, "I'm sure he didn't mean to. He's a good man. Respectful."

"They didn't know I was in the kitchen," Willi said. "I caught them speaking in English. And it's not the first time."

"A second language," explained Mady. "Part of their education."

Willi knew lying, and Mady was not a good liar.

"This person is *not* blind," Willi said. "I'm not going to tell you again. Come here."

Witzell looked at Tomcat. He patted him on the shoulder.

Tomcat walked up to Willi and said, "So what's it going to take to convince you that I'm—"

Willi ripped the sunglasses from Tomcat's face, revealing eyes covered by white shields.

"Careful with the shades, man!" Tomcat said.

Konrad's idea to get Viktor over the Berlin Wall had required one essential element.

"We need Tomcat," he said.

Word had been sent to Park. Coordinating with Herr Witzell, plans were made to sneak Tomcat back into East Berlin. Rather than risk an incident similar to the one when they sneaked Tomcat across the border the first time, Witzell finagled a one-day pass for him and a blind boy from K7 to visit a West German ophthalmologist.

Park and Tomcat met them in West Berlin.

According to Witzell, Park was subdued. He felt bad that he still hadn't come up with a plan to get Viktor free. Ironically, they'd considered the very tactic they were using to get Tomcat back in. But for reasons known only to some anonymous East German official, the Communist government approved an emergency medical one-day pass for a blind boy but refused to grant one for a boy with Down's syndrome.

Tomcat reentered East Berlin at roughly the same time Willi assassinated the West German navy captain.

A few weeks later a letter from Park reported that Fletcher Green was glad to be back at UCLA. He was taking his studies more seriously now.

Chapter 38

Monday, April 29, 1963

Josef Schumacher's funeral was mercifully uneventful. Mady wished Elyse could have been there. Sharon Lewis did a good job filling in for her.

Witzell officiated. There was discussion about getting Mady's and Lisette's minister to perform the ceremony, but Witzell insisted on doing it himself. "Who better?" he pleaded more persuasively than was necessary, for it didn't take much to convince everyone. With tears in his eyes he said, "It would mean so much to me."

And so Witzell once again became Reverend Wilhelm Olbricht, slipping into his ministerial role with the ease of donning a favorite old overcoat. He made all the necessary arrangements—casket, gravesite, headstone, as well as the order of service.

On the day of the funeral, standing at the head of the casket, Reverend Olbricht gave a heartfelt eulogy in the dappled shade of a pair of mature oaks. There was a slight breeze with no bite to it. Spring had arrived.

Mady linked herself on each side to Lisette and Sharon. Konrad stood next to Lisette. Though less than half a meter separated them, any gap was too much. More than ever, especially considering the occasion, he desired to touch her, to place an arm around her shoulder and pull her close to himself, or to have her arm linked to his with her head resting against his shoulder.

Standing opposite them, on the other side of the casket, were the doubles, all acting in character, and Viktor. His grief was real. He didn't understand what was happening and, though it seemed cruel at the time, everyone thought it best not to try to explain the plan to him until Tomcat returned to the house later that night.

In the shadow of the towering medieval gray stone church, its windows boarded up, those who knew the deceased shed genuine tears under the watchful gaze of the border guards who patrolled the Wall.

It was Lisette's dream about Pastor Schumacher that gave Konrad the idea of digging a tunnel in the graveyard. Having photographed the old church, it was on his list of possible crossing sites, although his thought had been to use the interior of the church because of its close proximity to the Wall. The church had been ordered closed and its windows boarded up. After several nights of observation, Konrad had crossed it off his list. The border guards used the old edifice themselves for a variety of reasons—as shelter from the wind on cold nights, to sneak a smoke, and occasionally as a place to entertain female companions who visited them while on duty.

Until Lisette's dream he'd never thought about using the graveyard. The guards never ventured there. Trees sheltered many of the graves from the view of the nearest watchtower. One problem was that the door the guards used to enter the church was located on the graveyard side of the building. However, when they used this door their minds were usually on things other than their guard duties.

As Lisette described her dream, it seemed to Konrad that Pastor Schumacher was asking them to let him help take Viktor across the border. His grave would provide the portal to freedom. And so, under the guise of relocating Josef's body from an unmarked grave in the hills north of Berlin to a proper church gravesite, the entrance to the tunnel was dug in plain sight of the border guards. The headstone and the ceremony honored the memory of Mady's husband.

Pastor Josef Schumacher
1913–1944
His light shines still.

But the body inside the casket was that of Tomcat, who was very much still alive.

The entrance to the tunnel had to be built quickly and in such a way for it to look like a normal burial to the border guards who were posted nearby. The crucial piece of construction was already at the site. Konrad's job had been to get it in place. Tomcat would shore it up from below ground.

It was Lisette who had simplified the design of the portal. Konrad drew up a rough sketch of what they needed, which included a frame, three hinges, and a flat sheet of wood strong enough to support several inches of soil. He had it all figured out. Where to purchase the wood. How much everything would cost. How much time it would take him to build the portal—only an estimate since he didn't know where he was going to get the necessary tools. He explained that once he had the tools, the majority of time would be spent constructing the frame. He wanted to use dovetail joints so they wouldn't have to use hammer and nails to put it together at the cemetery.

"So, what you're building is a door," Lisette said.

"Like a door," Konrad clarified. "Only horizontal and without a latch or knob."

"It sounds like a door to me."

"Well, yes. Anyway, we'll dig a lip around the edge of the grave. There will be a few risky moments when we're putting together the frame, but once that's done we can have the turf ready to go. Tomcat will then construct the vertical supports from below to take the weight off the dirt lip. We'll bury with him the wood he will use for the supports."

Lisette looked again at the drawing. "It's a door," she said.

"Like a door." Konrad was becoming agitated.

"Not like a door. It *is* a door."

Konrad sighed, gathering up the plans.

Lisette wouldn't let him go. "It has a frame like a door," she pointed out.

"Yes, it does."

"And hinges."

"Yes, it has hinges."

"And the flat part? The plywood? It opens and closes."

"Yes, it opens and closes."

"It's a door."

Exasperated now, Konrad said, "Fine. Have it your way, it's a door." He turned to leave.

"Then why not just use a door?" Lisette said.

Konrad stared at her.

"I mean, we have plenty of doors here at Ramah Cabin. They're already constructed, the hinges already screwed in place. If we use one of them, there's no need to get tools we don't have, or buy wood, or spend time constructing anything. Why don't we just use a door?"

By evening the tunnel entrance was ready for installation. They used the door to Konrad's bedroom. A blanket was hung in its place for privacy. On the day of the funeral Konrad and Hermann's double donned gravedigger's overalls and dug an ordinary grave with one alteration—the top edge of the grave had a lip.

The door was hidden beneath squares of turf that were normally used to top off a fresh grave. Following the ceremony, Konrad and his helper pretended to fill the grave, tossing some of the dirt around the coffin but none on top of it. The excess dirt was carted off. There was always excess dirt; there was just more than usual at this particular gravesite. When no guards were looking their way, they quickly lifted the door with the turf. It fit precisely into the lip of the grave so that the grass appeared flush.

Everything went as planned, and within hours after the funeral the tunnel entrance was in place. Later that night Tomcat rendezvoused with Witzell, who had been waiting for him a few blocks away, as previously arranged. His report was equally positive. The ventilation they'd devised had given him plenty of air. He had no difficulty shoring up the door. The first test, with himself climbing out, went smoothly. And one thing more—he thought the funeral service was touching.

The actual tunneling began the next night. They dug in shifts. Tomcat worked double shifts. Unlike the others, he needed no light to guide him. He knew every inch of the tunnel in the dark better than the others did using flashlights. Because of this, it was decided a light system—which would add extra time and expense to the project—would not be necessary. During the escape Tomcat would lead them through the tunnel in the dark. The blind leading the sighted. Somehow it seemed fitting that the one who would lead them to freedom be the same one whom the Communists regarded as inferior.

Thursday, May 30, 1963

Not since Hadamar had Konrad felt so alive. It felt good to remove the dirt from beneath his fingernails each night, to have aching muscles, to fall into bed weary from exhaustion and all for a worthy cause. Between the exercise and regular eating, he'd started putting on weight.

He'd had dirty fingernails before. Dirt was synonymous with life in the trenches on the Russian front. And his body had been tested before, during his training as a Hitler Youth and then later as an SS soldier. But the weariness he felt now was different; it came from being involved in a cause worth fighting for, and even dying for.

For the first time he felt like a man.

A godly man. A man worthy to stand with the likes of Josef Schumacher.

Konrad had no fear for himself. He had but a single thought: get Viktor and the others to the side of freedom. After that, nothing else mattered. Let them catch him. Send him back to prison. Execute him. All he prayed was that God would let him be successful in this one thing, and then finally his life would count for something.

Mady didn't take part in any of the digging. Neither did Lisette or Sharon Lewis. Their jobs were to keep on working at the shoe factory, mostly for appearances' sake, so that everything appeared normal. The day the three of them failed to show up for work would be the day alarms started going off. One unexplained absence wouldn't draw much attention, but all three women absent at the same time would not be overlooked. Actually, it was the kind of thing the East German officials looked for. A father missing work the same day his children were absent from school, or a husband and wife both missing from work on the same day. Multiple absences signaled an escape attempt. Another important reason for the women keeping their jobs at the factory: their combined income was needed to support Ramah Cabin until the day of crossing.

This didn't mean they didn't do their share of work at the tunnel. A major problem proved to be disposing of the dirt. They employed a variety of deceptions to accomplish the task.

For instance, baby carriages were used. Usually at twilight the women would push the carriages past the graveyard. A typical evening stroll. An exchange took place—an empty baby carriage for one filled with dirt. The women would then proceed to one of the many places in Berlin that had yet to be rebuilt following the war. Nearly two decades after the end of the war, many blocks in downtown Berlin were still nothing but rubble heaps. Who would notice a little extra dirt?

Another way for them to dump the dirt from the tunnel was by scattering it around freshly dug graves. Cemetery gravediggers came to expect leftover dirt when they returned to fill in a grave following interment.

Yet it was inside the church itself that became the favored place to get rid of the dirt. An annex had been under construction when the church was closed down. The walls had been built, the roof was but a skeletal structure of beams, and the floor was earthen. A perfect hiding place for a load of dirt. By the time the tunnel was finished, Konrad figured they had raised the level of the annex floor by a good four to five inches.

Wednesday, August 7, 1963

According to Konrad's calculations, the tunnel was now long enough. They began digging upward for the surface. Mady orchestrated preparations to leave Ramah Cabin. There wasn't much to take. It wasn't as though they were going on a holiday, or even on a weekend trip to the Western sector. They would have to travel light.

The closer the tunnel came to completion, the more depressed Mady became. She reached beneath her bed and pulled out a stationery box. It was an old box but not dusty. It had been cleaned off a short time ago during their move from Kellerstrasse. At that time she had cleaned it, though she hadn't opened it. Kneeling beside her bed, she rested the box on her legs, gently skimming the lid with the palm of her hand, debating whether or not to open it.

After several moments of going back and forth, Mady lifted the lid. Josef's Bible lay inside. Setting the box aside, she pressed the Bible to her chest. It was the only thing she had left that had belonged to Josef. There were no photographs. What few she took with her during the flight from the first Ramah Cabin were lost when she and Lisette helped the children to cross a stream in the journey back to Berlin. Halfway across, Viktor grew frightened of the rushing water. He began kicking and flailing his arms. It was all Mady could do to hold on to him. She lost her purse in the struggle, along with all the personal items in it, including the pictures of Josef.

In her room, Mady hugged the Bible as if it were Josef himself. She recalled the first time she realized how much she loved him. It was after they were married. After his capture at Hadamar. He'd left her love letters of sorts hidden in the files of sermons he'd preached. Reading through them sitting on the floor of his office, she'd fallen in love with her husband all over again. She remembered how she prayed desperately to God that night—for she thought she'd never see Josef again—for the chance to show him how much she loved him.

In His goodness, God granted her wish. And while Josef returned to her broken in body because of the atrocities the Nazi doctors had inflicted on him, he returned stronger in faith and in his devotion to her. More times than she cared to remember, he shamed her with his devotion. Not that he ever meant to. He would never do that. It was just that when she saw the level of his devotion and compared it to her own, she felt unworthy to be his wife.

It wasn't that he had been perfect. Josef was slow at coming to decisions, but once he did, he then committed himself to a course of action. For him there was no turning back, no quitting. Others may have met adversity with excuses and rationalization, but Josef seemed to feed off it. As a child she never thought she'd meet a man she could admire more than her father. Josef was twice the man her father had been, only she had to nearly lose him before she recognized it.

How she wished he were here now.

With reluctance, Mady set her late husband's Bible aside, on top of the bed where she'd been stacking things, deciding what to take and what to leave behind. The Bible landed next to a stack of newspapers.

Whether God, an angel, or Josef himself had guided her hand, all she knew was that the moment the Bible touched the bed she was struck by its proximity to the newspapers. It was as if the Bible and the newspapers sat in opposite pans of a scale. Only they weren't being weighed. Mady's soul was what hung in the balance.

In one pan, the one with Josef's Bible, was her husband's everlasting love for her, his legacy, everything she wished she could be but wasn't.

Stacked in the other pan were newspapers. Not a random collection of dailies but sections she had saved from the papers ever since the day they began seriously discussing how to get over the Wall.

She had thought it was just one of those oddities of life—when one started thinking about something, the *thing* was then noticed everywhere. Like when she and Lisette began working at the Schönner Shoe factory. Up to that time, she'd paid little attention to the make of a person's shoes. Her only concern was that all the children had them, with Tomcat being the exception of course. But when she began her job manufacturing Schönner shoes, Mady started seeing them everywhere. Now she could spot a Schönner shoe halfway across a department store. So it was with the Wall. Now that preparations were under way to breach it, every time she looked at a newspaper it seemed there was a story about people being captured or killed while trying to get out of East Berlin.

"Only four percent of those attempting to cross the Wall illegally make it." Wasn't that what Herr Witzell said after touring the Wall?

The newspapers were folded in such a way that the stories of failed crossings were on top. One by one, Mady looked at the headlines, some including pictures.

Woman Leaps to Her Death as Fascist Friends
Urge Her to Jump from Four-Story Building

Five Men Shot in a Hail of Bullets,
Attempting to Cross Spree in Stolen Boat

Child Falls to His Death from Rope Strung Across Wall

Escape Thwarted When Man Found Hiding Under Hood of Car,
Battery and Radiator Removed

Man Found Strapped Under Car, Attempting to Escape

Woman Drowns in Spree River, Attempting to Flee

Three Men Shot by Border Guards

Homemade Balloon Crashes at Zehlendorf, Family of Five Dead

Families. Mothers. Fathers. Grocers. Church members. Neighbors. People just like them. Like Lisette. Konrad. Tomcat. Viktor. Ordinary people who tried to cross the Wall. And failed. Now they were dead or in prison. What made Mady think she and the others would succeed where hundreds before them had failed? What made her think she was any different from the 96 percent who tried and never made it across? If they were caught, could she live with herself knowing that she was responsible for Lisette's death or imprisonment? Or Viktor's? What would they do to a retarded man in prison?

Would the next feature story in the newspaper be about a group who attempted to smuggle a retarded man across the border? Would the account of their failure have pictures of their bodies? Of Viktor or Lisette lying lifeless on the ground?

Here it was, set before her in all its ugly truth, confronting her, forcing her to choose—her fears, stacked up in black and white. And Josef's faith, the faith he'd used to overcome his fears. Side by side. Weighing her in the balance.

It was inevitable. She knew she had to make this choice sometime. She could have slipped Josef's Bible back in the stationery box and set it aside. For some reason, she put it on the bed, next to the newspapers.

Which course to take? How much she wanted to be like Josef, to move forward in faith, not looking back but doing what was right for no other reason than because it was right. Trusting God—in life, and in death.

But what if they failed and she lost everything? Hadn't that been Josef's fear too, that his failure would endanger her and their baby daughter, Elyse? And it did endanger them. But it also drew them closer together. What was the alternative? Her father.

Mady sat back on her heels, stunned by the thought.

Her father.

He too had been afraid back then. He chose a different course, all the while wanting the same thing. He gave in. He collaborated. Sold out to protect his family.

To protect his family.

He wasn't afraid for himself. He was afraid for them.

And what happened?

He lost them all. His wife. His daughter. His ministry. And at what price? The love and respect of his daughter.

How different he was now as Herr Witzell. Stronger. More willing to take risks. More like Josef.

More like Josef.

Mady stared at her dead husband's Bible.

She stared at the newspaper accounts, a collection of her fears.

Grabbing the newspapers, she flung them onto a corner pile. A pile of things she would be leaving behind. Leaning forward, her forehead resting on Josef's Bible, she prayed.

She committed herself to being a worthy partner to her husband and his legacy of courage.

She forgave her father. Something she should have done long ago.

Then she stood. The decision was made before God, before Josef. Her fears remained, but her resolve was stronger. No turning back. Ever since returning to Berlin she'd withdrawn from life, hid behind a thick cloak of anonymity, never dared to stand out. And she hated herself for it. She was tired of cowering, tired of cringing. It was time to live again.

She'd begin by going to her father and telling him she loved him, that she was proud of him like she used to be, even more so because of his courage to change, and also because of his patience with her.

When she turned toward the doorway, it was blocked by a presence.

Willi.

"What happened to Konrad's door?" he said with a devious grin. "Someone busting out, or busting . . ."

His eye caught hold of something on the floor. He stepped into the room and stood over a newspaper.

Woman Drowns in Spree River, Attempting to Flee.

A trail of newspapers lay scattered on the floor. Willi's eyes jumped from one to the other.

Escape. Attempting to Flee. Woman Leaps. Stolen Boat. Willi looked up at Mady. She could see it in his eyes.

He knew.

Chapter 39

They surfaced within a meter of Konrad's calculated exit, a good forty meters beyond the Wall. Tomcat broke through the ground like a gopher. He'd surfaced behind a dilapidated wooden fence next to an abandoned brick warehouse. A few scraggly bushes gave them additional cover. Konrad's fear that they might come up under the building itself, hitting the bottom of a cement foundation, proved to be unfounded. An exit door was constructed with an empty metal barrel nailed to the top. When the door swung open, the barrel hit the side of the building at just the right angle to prop it open. Not by design, just a happy coincidence.

With the tunnel complete, Konrad and Tomcat returned to the East German side. Two blocks from the tunnel's entrance, Hermann's double stood atop a building that served as a lookout. He commanded two flashlights—one with red cellophane covering the lens, another with green. No one worked on the tunnel without a lookout.

Equipped with a pair of binoculars, it was his job to keep track of the guards. Any time a guard ventured near the graveyard, he signaled red. Those who were digging had learned to lift the grave door just a crack to check for a red warning light. The lookout would signal green if the coast was clear.

From inside the tunnel, Konrad lifted the lid. A green light flashed. He and Tomcat scurried out of the grave. Lisette was waiting for them with an empty baby carriage in an alley opposite the church.

"We need to do a test run," Konrad said.

There was no objection from Lisette or Tomcat.

"Tonight."

"Tonight?" Lisette said.

"Already there's a sliver of a moon," Konrad said. "If we don't test it tonight, we may have to put off Resurrection Day for a month."

Since spring they'd been referring to the day of their future crossing as Resurrection Day. It was Herr Witzell's idea. In typical preacher fashion, he expounded that it was fitting because on that day they would descend into a grave, die to their old lives in East Berlin, and rise to a new life on the freedom side.

"How long will it take you to do a test run?" Lisette asked.

"Us," Konrad corrected her. "How long will it take *us*. You're going too."

Lisette took a small step back. She'd been in the tunnel before, but not far. Not far enough that she'd ever been on the freedom side of the Wall. While she'd come to a peace of sorts over the idea that she was part of an escape attempt and could at any moment be arrested and sent to prison, the idea of making an escape, in her mind, was still off in the future. And here was Konrad talking about crossing the Wall with the same casual tone he would have used to suggest they walk across Alexanderplatz to a different store.

"What exactly are we going to do?" she asked. She was stalling. Trying to summon a measure of courage.

"Make a tunnel run. Time it. Make sure it's safe."

Lisette looked to Tomcat. He sided with Konrad on this. Just a walk in the park, according to them.

"You're saying we're going to escape to West Berlin tonight?" she said.

"And back again."

"Back again."

Simple as that.

"And if we're caught?"

Konrad shrugged. "Then the others will know it's not safe and we will have saved them from getting caught."

"Are you sure there's enough oxygen in that tunnel?" she said.

"Maybe the two of you need to take a couple of breaths of fresh air."

"No need," Tomcat said. "We're talking crazy."

He was grinning. So it was all a joke.

Konrad looked at his watch. "We have to get going." To Tomcat he asked, "Did you bring the bag?"

They weren't kidding.

Tomcat walked a short distance, felt behind some garbage cans, found what he was looking for, and pulled out a canvas duffle bag.

"What's in that?" Lisette asked.

"Part of the test," Konrad said. "One man. One woman. One piece of luggage."

"And Tomcat?"

"He's the guide. There's no light in the tunnel."

"And we're coming back?"

"You don't think I'd leave the others behind, do you? Come on. It's getting late."

Lisette took a few wobbly steps forward. "If you would have told me at breakfast that tonight I'd pop through a hole into West Berlin . . ."

"What did you think we've been doing all this time?" Konrad said.

"This is different," she said, taking a deep breath. "We're actually going to escape. Tonight. Right now."

"And come back," Konrad added.

"That's the craziest part of all."

Konrad stood at the edge of the alley. He paused a moment to let his military training kick in—an intense focus that set aside anything that wasn't related to the present objective. But it was more than that. It was a slowing of time, an acute awareness of detail, an acceleration of thought and reflex. It had been so long since he'd used these skills, he was almost surprised he was still able to recall them.

He positioned himself to see the lookout. The light glowed red. Konrad held up a hand for the others to wait. When it changed to green, he gave Tomcat a go-ahead pat on the back.

"Tomcat's leading?" Lisette whispered.

"Our advantage," Konrad whispered back. "We'll go on the darkest night of the month. Now shush."

Konrad pulled Lisette forward until she was sandwiched between himself and Tomcat. Keeping less than an arm's-length distance between them at all times, the trio slipped across the cobblestone street, into the grassy graveyard, slaloming between headstones. Tomcat's bare feet guided them quickly and unerringly, as quickly as a sighted person would move in broad daylight. Within a minute and a half, Konrad's bedroom door was lifted and the three of them were crouching inside Josef Schumacher's grave.

It was pitch-dark.

"Put your hand on Tomcat's back," Konrad whispered to Lisette.

She did. He moved forward, paused, and then began the descent.

"Now feel for the ladder."

Lisette reached forward, unable to see her own arm or hand. Her fingers brushed dirt, then a wood rung. She found another rung with her foot. The ladder took them straight down thirteen meters. Tomcat was waiting for them at the bottom.

She grabbed on to his arm and didn't want to let go. "Why can't we use lights?" she said, her heart pounding, and not from the climb down.

"Too risky." Konrad's voice came from above her. He was still descending the ladder. "Call me overly cautious, but even the smallest beam of light coming from inside a grave will draw attention to itself."

"But I can't see anything!" Lisette whispered.

"Just follow Tomcat," said Konrad.

Tomcat hunched down. With Lisette's firm grip on his arm, he pulled her with him. She eventually had to let go.

"How do I follow him? I can't see anything!"

"Listen."

At first all she could hear was the pulse of her own heart in her ears. Then, as she listened harder, she heard it. Humming. Softly. A Frank Sinatra tune.

Lowering herself the rest of the way on all fours, Lisette followed the humming. Her head hit the top of the tunnel. She ducked lower and followed the song. She recognized it. One of Tomcat's favorites. Something having to do with getting under a person's skin.

After a while the monotonous nature of crawling coupled with exertion so that now her heart was beating more from effort than from fear. She could tell when she was falling behind. Occasionally she'd rise up too much and touch the top of the tunnel or wander to one side or the other and be bounced back rudely. Maybe it was best she couldn't see what she was crawling through, she told herself. All of life had been reduced to one task: crawling. Buried in the earth in a grave 130 meters long, there was only one way out, and that was to crawl. She worked her hands and legs mechanically, having no perception of where she was heading or how far they'd gone. Some moments later she also closed her eyes. For some reason, that made the task easier.

"Halfway," Tomcat said.

Behind her, Lisette could hear Konrad's breathing, slightly labored, and behind him the sound of a canvas bag being dragged through the dirt.

Breathing became harder. The air hung heavy and dank. The dirt felt wet beneath her hands, and the wetness seeped through the knees of her pants. Was it her imagination or was the dark getting darker? A worm of panic wriggled in her chest near her throat. She tried to ignore it. She commanded herself not to think but to concentrate solely on putting one hand in front of the other, one leg in front of the other. Keep moving.

She bumped her head again.

The tunnel was getting smaller. Closing in on her.

The worm in her chest spawned another in her belly.

"Konrad?" she said, slowing.

Konrad bumped into her. "Keep crawling!"

"Nearly there," Tomcat whispered.

The tunnel began to ascend. Her breathing became even more difficult. She told herself it was from the exertion; her mind feared they were using up all the air in the tunnel.

Just when Lisette's shoulders and legs started aching to the point she didn't know if she could continue, Tomcat stopped humming again.

"End of the line," he said. "Wait here."

Lisette did as she was told. Reluctantly. She was taking Tomcat's word that they'd reached the end. Their present location looked and smelled and felt like every other inch since they'd first begun descending into this elongated grave. Had they been on a treadmill and never moved an inch, she wouldn't have known it. They were many meters underground, in the dark, struggling to breathe, and she was reaching a point where the worms of anxiety had grown larger than reason's ability to control them.

Then she heard an encouraging sound. The groaning sound that a wooden ladder makes when it bears the burden of weight. The groaning stopped and there followed a moment of silence.

The next thing Lisette saw was a patch of night sky, dotted with stars. Fresh air—wonderful night air—fell upon her. It was the sweetest air she'd ever tasted.

Tomcat's face appeared, covering a portion of the stars. His hands reached out, calling to her. "It's clear," he said in a soft voice.

Without hesitating, Lisette climbed the ladder. Nearing the top, she slowed as the danger of what they were doing reasserted itself. If they were caught now, would they be sent back?

"Keep going," Konrad said from behind her.

Lisette emerged into West Berlin. Moments later, with Konrad on one side and Tomcat on the other, the full realization of where they were hit her. They'd done it! She began to weep.

She looked at Konrad and Tomcat to see if they were feeling what she was feeling. They both stood with hands on hips, chests rising and falling, the way men stand after accomplishing a difficult task. The fact that they'd all just escaped Communist East Berlin didn't seem to faze them.

"Welcome to West Berlin," Konrad said with a broad smile.

Tomcat was grinning like a monkey.

"What?" Lisette said. "I know that look! You two are up to something."

Konrad snatched up the canvas duffle bag at his feet. He handed it to Lisette. "Go in there," he said, pointing to the warehouse. "Just inside, around the corner, and change into this."

Lisette took the bag and looked inside. There was a dress. One of her Sunday dresses. "What's going on?" she said.

"All in good time," said Konrad. "We'll wait for you out here."

Chapter 40

Konrad Reichmann! You devil!"

Lisette stopped dead in her tracks when she saw where he was taking her. They had rounded a street corner and were now on Kurfürstendam. In the dark, the landmark red-and-white stripes of Café Lorenz's awning, ablaze with light, announced carefree times and sumptuous cuisine.

The duffle bag had contained a change of clothes for Konrad too. Following a quick stop in the public washroom of a hotel lobby, the two of them strolled down the busy thoroughfare as though they were longtime residents of West Berlin.

At the café Konrad pulled out Lisette's chair for her. Unlike cafés in East Berlin, the mood here rang festive, the chatter light and airy. No one sat glancing around anxiously to see if anyone was listening in on their conversation. People spoke openly and freely. It was like a dream. One moment they were standing in a gray, depressing alley of Communist East Berlin, the next they were seated at a table in the brightly lit, colorful and romantic Café Lorenz.

"I feel so guilty," Lisette said. "Mady and the others . . ."

"We don't have to tell them," Konrad said.

"And Tomcat?"

"He's sworn to silence."

"No, I mean, we just left him sitting in the dirt beside that warehouse."

"Who do you think gave me the idea?"

"Tomcat? Why, I wouldn't think—"

"Actually it was Elyse's idea. She told Tomcat how special this place has been for you."

Tears edged Lisette's eyes. Happy tears. She reached across the table and placed her hand on top of Konrad's hand. Despite the smudge of dirt he missed on his left temple, he looked handsome, mature, healthy. It had been a long time since he'd looked healthy. However the evening progressed from this point on, Lisette knew it would be memorable. This was Konrad's night, and she was content to let him develop it like he did one of his photographs.

Konrad felt the warmth of her hand on his. Whatever the evening brought, it was worth all the risk for this moment alone.

A waiter appeared beside their table. He handed them menus.

Lisette looked to Konrad.

"Anything you want," he said.

Lisette ordered the plum cake with crumb topping, and Konrad the Sacher torte.

After the waiter left, suddenly they both realized that, while they were in a magical place, it was just the two of them. And, to their dismay, they'd dragged their history through the tunnel with them.

An uneasy silence came between them. Konrad blamed himself. He was staring at Lisette and got caught. Since her return to Ramah Cabin, he'd not allowed himself anything but fleeting glances. He would go to great lengths, sometimes awkward lengths, never to be caught in a room alone with her. He told himself that was what she wanted. He didn't want her to feel uncomfortable, or for her to get the impression that he expected they could ever pick up where they had left off, or that he expected she would ever forgive him for his seven years of silence.

Now he wasn't so sure coming here was a good idea. When Tomcat told him about Café Lorenz, the idea came to him. At the time it sounded like a good idea. But now . . .

He swallowed hard.

What was this power she had over him that she could produce such strong feelings in him? This was a mistake. At Ramah Cabin he was able to keep them in check. Here, now, they were too strong. The feelings were overwhelming him. *She* was overwhelming him.

"Who would have thought?" Lisette said lightheartedly. "Two kids from Pankow, sitting here at Café Lorenz."

"Pankow. Seems like a couple of lifetimes ago."

"Can you see Neff in a place like this?" Lisette laughed.

Konrad forced a smile. "They'd throw him out of the place for putting dessert in people's shoes."

Just when he felt himself to be at his weakest, she hit him with a memory of Neff. It was innocent enough. She didn't mean anything by it. Even so, the wound Konrad suffered over his failure to protect his friend from being killed still lingered. He doubted there would ever be a time when he heard Neff's name and did not feel a stab of guilty pain.

"And Ernst," Lisette said.

She was unaware she'd hurt him. Good.

"Imagine, Ernst married to a Frenchwoman and living in America, building rockets. I still can't believe it. I'll tell you one thing, though. Seeing Ernst again and getting to know that French bombshell of his is probably the greatest attraction of America to me."

"We were an odd group growing up, weren't we?" Konrad said. "Life was so much simpler then. I miss those times."

"Of course you do. Everyone loved you. You were the pride of the Third Reich."

Konrad didn't know what to do with that statement or how to respond. So he said nothing.

"I'm sorry," Lisette said, lowering her head. "That was unkind. Just when you think you've escaped your past, you say something like that and realize how much it still has ahold of you."

"I'd forgotten that those weren't always happy times for you," Konrad said. "As for me, thinking back on it, I can't believe how blind I was. How gullible."

"We were young," Lisette said.

"Pigheaded and foolish."

"We were all deceived."

"Pastor Schumacher wasn't," Konrad said.

"No. No, he wasn't. But he was an exceptional man. Besides, we've paid the price for our sins." She reached across the table again and squeezed his hand. "Paid dearly. You more than anyone know how dearly we've paid."

"Although, I wonder . . . has it been enough?" Konrad said softly.

Lisette retreated to her side of the table. She stared at her hands.

Konrad winced. It had always been like this between them. The moment they started to get close, one of them would say something that would initiate the hostilities again.

"Konrad, do you ever wonder what it would have been like had the Third Reich been victorious? It seemed that was the way things were going, at least at first, didn't it? Nothing could stop our armies."

"The world would be a worse place than it is now," Konrad said.

"You sound so certain."

"The Third Reich was built on a foundation of hatred and destruction. Nothing good or lasting could have come from it. It was doomed from the start."

"Professor Reichmann! I'm impressed," Lisette said.

"Pastor Schumacher taught me that."

The waiter came with their orders.

"It looks so luscious," Lisette said, picking at the whipped cream topping with her fork.

"Too luscious to be spoiled by talk of politics," said Konrad.

Lisette laughed. "Is it possible for two East Germans to have a conversation that doesn't involve politics?"

Konrad's fork was poised midair. He watched Lisette take the first bite. Recently, every time he stole a glance at her, he fell in love with her all over again. Lisette wasn't aware she was being watched.

"I do have something I've been meaning to talk to you about," she said.

Konrad sank his fork into the Sacher torte. "Sounds serious."

Serious enough for Lisette to set aside her utensil, fold her hands in her lap, and take two attempts to speak before finding the words—or the courage—to say what was on her mind.

"Herr Gellert still wants to marry me."

"He'd be crazy not to," Konrad said with a lightness that surprised himself. "Are you considering it?"

"I don't know what to think of it."

"You've obviously gotten under his skin."

Lisette giggled at the obvious Tomcat-Sinatra reference. The moment her laughter faded, an uneasy silence took its place.

She resumed eating, and the only sound at their table for several minutes was the clinking of forks against plates.

"You never told me how the two of you got together in the first place," Konrad said finally.

She gave him a cautious once-over look, perhaps weighing his intentions, then launched into sharing a tale of a lonely man who had buried four wives, all of them older than himself. It was Lisette's sewing ability and punctuality that had attracted him, and her pleasant nature that won him over. She told Konrad that Waldemar—Konrad hated the sound of the name—had been hurt when she informed him she wouldn't be marrying him.

"For a Communist, he really is a sweet man," Lisette insisted.

She told Konrad how Waldemar hid in his office at the shoe factory for weeks following their breakup. Then, like a mouse venturing out into the open, he began walking the floor again, a little farther each day. His first words to her were casual. Cordial. After which he'd scurry back to his office. Over time, however, he began lingering in the vicinity of her work area, like he'd done before, and two days ago he leaned over her sewing machine and, touching her hand, with a humble, pleading voice, asked her to reconsider her decision and marry him.

"Given his past history," Lisette concluded, "I'm surprised he hasn't married another woman already."

Konrad did his best to listen to her story. He hated hearing it, but he loved the storyteller. It gave him a chance to stare at her under pretense of paying attention.

"Of course, now there are so many complications," Lisette said.

That snapped him back to the topic at hand. "Complications? You haven't given him an answer?"

"What do you suggest I say to him? 'Herr Gellert, I'm sorry I can't marry you because at the moment we're—' " she looked around, and even though they were in the Western sector, she leaned closer to Konrad and whispered—" 'in the middle of digging a tunnel under the Berlin Wall?' "

"That's the only reason you have?"

"No, silly. There's my obligation to Mady and to Viktor and the others . . . and Elyse. If I marry Herr Gellert, I'll probably never see Elyse again."

"And then there's the greatest complication of all," Konrad said.

Lisette's eyebrows raised. She wasn't following him.

"You know," Konrad said.

Lisette's gaze fell. She looked guilty, as if he'd guessed her secret. With her fork she pushed crumbs around on her plate. "It's that obvious?"

"To me it is."

"It's temporary," she said. "It'll pass."

"What are you talking about?"

"Going back. The tunnel. You said it was obvious."

"We were talking about reasons why you couldn't marry Herr Gellert."

"That's what I'm talking about!"

"What does the tunnel have to do with that?"

Again Lisette leaned forward. "Keep your voice down!" she said.

"What does the tunnel have to do with your marrying Herr Gellert?" Konrad repeated.

"How can I marry Herr Gellert if I don't go back?" Lisette replied.

"Not go back?" Then it dawned on Konrad. "Oh! You're afraid to go back!"

"You said you knew!" Lisette said, embarrassed that he'd tricked her into revealing her fear.

"You shouldn't," Konrad said.

"Shouldn't what?"

"Shouldn't go back. You're right. Why should you? You're safe here. Tomcat and I can get the others across."

"I'm going back," Lisette said emphatically.

"But you just said you were afraid to go back."

"That's what I said. And I am. But I'm going anyway."

"For what purpose?"

Lisette shook her head. "Not so fast, Herr Reichmann. First, you tell me what you were thinking. You said there was another obvious reason why I shouldn't marry Herr Gellert."

Konrad folded his arms, smiling. "You're just playing cat and mouse."

"What?"

"You know."

"I don't know. Tell me."

Konrad leaned forward. "You really don't know, do you?"

"Konrad!"

"I love you."

Several moments passed before Lisette regained enough of her senses to realize she was staring at him with her mouth open.

Konrad took her hand even though she still held her fork. His voice came out low, choked with emotion. "It's always been you, Lisette. Since we were children. In the church youth group. It's always been you. Though it seems like the whole world has conspired to keep us apart—and we've done a pretty good job of it too—I've always known that God made you for me, and me for you."

She continued to stare at him, not saying anything. She didn't have to.

Without releasing her hand, Konrad pushed back his chair and stood. He went to her. He didn't have to go far. She met him halfway.

There, in the middle of Café Lorenz, they clung to each other. Oblivious that anyone else was around. Or that they had become the center of attention.

Their lips found each other. Her mouth was warm with tears. She thrust her hands in his hair and caressed his face. It was like a hundred dreams Konrad had dreamed while shivering in a dirt trench on the Russian front or while feverish on the hard wooden slats of a bed at the gulag. The back of her dress felt smooth in his hands. Her hair smelled more of tunnel than it did of perfume, but that only made him love her more. Above all was the inconceivable wonder that this was happening at all.

A spattering of applause convinced him it was indeed reality.

Lisette drew back. She'd heard it too. Her face was red with embarrassment, but like him, she didn't want to let go. She was going to have to be the strong one, because now that Konrad had her in his arms, there was no force on earth save her alone that was going to break his embrace.

The unthinkable happened. She stepped back.

Quick glances revealed that everyone's attention was fixed on them—those seated at the café's tables as well as those strolling by. There were a few disapproving glances over the public display of affection, yet mostly there were smiles. Konrad didn't care. Nothing could ever take the sweet memory of this moment from him.

Their waiter appeared with another man beside him. Konrad guessed him to be the manager.

"An anniversary?" the man asked.

"No," Konrad said.

"An engagement, then?"

Konrad looked at Lisette, who was looking at him. "Yes," he said.

Beaming, Lisette replied, "Yes!"

They left Café Lorenz in high spirits but arguing. Emil Lorenz, owner and namesake of one of the brothers who started the café in 1832, insisted on picking up their tab, saying that their display of love contributed to the happy, romantic atmosphere, something that was a hallmark of the establishment. And for the first dozen steps the happy couple remained happy, that is, until Lisette asked Konrad, "Where are you taking me?" Obviously they were not heading back to the tunnel.

"To a hotel," Konrad said.

Lisette didn't take another step. She gave him a scathing look.

Now Konrad was offended. "After all these years, you should know me better than that!" he said. "I'm going to put you up in a hotel until we can join you later."

"But I told you—I'm going back," Lisette said.

"No, you're not."

That started her walking again. In the direction of the tunnel.

"It's too dangerous," said Konrad.

"All the more reason for me to return."

"Can't you see, it's not necessary! Only a fool would go back if he didn't have to."

She turned to him. "So now I'm a fool?"

"I'm only saying that it's foolish for you to return."

She started walking again. "You'll have to knock me unconscious or tie me up to keep me from going back."

Konrad knew that when she got like this there was no dissuading her. Still, he refused to concede defeat.

They were still arguing when they reached Tomcat. Lisette grabbed the canvas bag and disappeared into the warehouse. "I'm changing my clothes," she said.

Tomcat shuffled his feet self-consciously for a moment before leaning toward Konrad and whispering, "Didn't go well, huh?"

"We're engaged," Konrad said.

"Engaged?"

"Yeah."

"Congratulations?"

Their crossing back into East Berlin was as long and silent as it was black. Konrad said nothing. Lisette said nothing. Tomcat didn't hum, Sinatra or anything else.

On reaching the interior of the gravesite, Konrad squeezed into the lead. He lifted the door just a crack. The signal was green. The three escapees popped out of the grave and soon were walking the streets heading back to Ramah Cabin. From his vantage point, their signal man would see they were out and then head back using a different route. If all went as planned, as it had up until now, he would arrive at Ramah Cabin approximately fifteen minutes before the others.

The night was damp and the alleys were dark. The mood on the Eastern side, even without encountering anyone, felt oppressive in a palpable way, taking on the atmosphere of a concentration camp. There was no merriment here, only fear and suspicion. Not until they reached Ramah Cabin could they relax. Until then they avoided contact with others if at all possible. They moved in the shadows and in silence, which seemed fitting given the mood of the travelers. At least two of them.

It wasn't until the cabin came into sight and they climbed the last hundred meters of dirt road that Konrad resolved to take Lisette aside and apologize to her. The night had been too special to leave it like this.

He was about to say something just as Lisette swung open the door. She stopped at the threshold. Although Konrad couldn't see the one speaking, he recognized the voice.

"Don't just stand there. Come join the party!"

It was Willi.

Lisette moved forward, but it was as though her legs had turned into blocks of ice. From behind her, Konrad could see a small portion of her face, just enough for a bit of the old intuition to leap alive inside of him.

Tomcat was next to step over the threshold. It was then that

Konrad saw that things had gone wrong. Terribly wrong. All the current inhabitants of Ramah Cabin were seated in a circle, their legs and hands tied—including Hermann's double, who had preceded them by a matter of minutes—while Willi sat on the arm of the chair where Elyse's double sat. Mady had a black eye and her cheek was swollen with a red welt, the kind a cane would make.

"Come in, come in!" Willi said, sounding like a jovial host. "Konrad, were you born in a barn? Close the door behind you."

"What's going on, Willi?" Konrad said.

"It's fascinating, really." Using the barrel of a pistol to point with, he said, "Did you know that this young woman is not Elyse? Her name's Sharon Lewis and she's a student at UCBL, BCUL, or some such nonsense school in California, USA."

He stroked her cheek with the barrel of the gun.

"The resemblance to our own Elyse is striking, wouldn't you say? What is it the English say? Oh yes, she's a *dead ringer* for the real thing. Now, I ask you, Konrad, what is a lovely American co-ed doing on this side of the Berlin Wall?"

While his tone was playful, his eyes appeared hard and threatening. How much did he know? He knew about the doubles, but did he know about the tunnel? Mady's eye and her swollen cheek—Mady, of all people!—indicated Willi had used force. If pressed, would he use deadly force?

Chapter 41

After tying up Tomcat with the others in the front room, Willi complained of being hungry, so Mady offered to scramble him some eggs and warm up a few leftover biscuits. Pleased with the offer, Willi lovingly stroked her cheek—the unbruised one—with the back of his hand before untying her. Then, with the pistol pressed against her neck, he followed Konrad and Lisette into the kitchen.

Mady pulled a large iron skillet from a cabinet and went about lighting the stove. Willi motioned for Konrad to sit down. Konrad moved to the end of the table, positioning it between himself and Willi. It wasn't much of a plan, but then, Konrad didn't have much to work with. Hopefully Willi would sit opposite him, and then Konrad would wait for something to distract his brother. He'd shove the table, knocking Willi over, and try to get to the gun before Willi could recover.

"Eh, eh, eh." Willi waved the pistol side to side much like a mother would wave an index finger to warn a child. It was as if he'd read Konrad's mind. "Move your chair against the wall," he ordered.

Konrad did as he was told, well out of reach of the table. He sat down.

Lisette stepped to the counter, opened a bread box, and unwrapped two biscuits from a tea towel. Willi had granted her request to assist Mady with making him breakfast. It was doubtful Willi was just being kind to her; he wanted Lisette in the kitchen for some reason. But what was it? The only indication he had given so far was when he said, "Look at us! Just like old times, isn't it? We're all that's left of the old gang."

He was forgetting Ernst, but Konrad didn't bother to remind him.

Mady cracked two eggs in the frying pan.

Settling back in his chair, Willi started to set down the gun but then thought better of it. Konrad was struck by the way he handled the piece. Willi had never been good with guns. Loud noises had always frightened him. That, and his unnatural fear of death, which he associated with guns. As a little boy, whenever their father took out one of his rifles to clean it, fiddle with it, or just admire it, Willi would cover his ears and run from the room screaming. Even as a Hitler Youth, he refused to touch a firearm. Konrad was in the SS when he heard that Willi had been assigned to the infantry. He'd often wondered how his brother would adapt to the army. Apparently he'd adapted well enough, because the man seated at the kitchen table appeared to be quite comfortable with a gun in his hand. Had Konrad tried his table-shoving plan, Willi would have nailed him before he had a chance to set the table in motion.

"So, brother," Willi said, "what's with all the Americans? And where are the real retards?"

"Would you like some sliced tomatoes?" Mady interrupted. "They're in the garden."

Willi looked over his shoulder and gave her his wise-weasel look. "Surely you jest," he said. "And give one of my chickens a chance to fly the coop? Eggs and biscuits will be just fine."

Lisette had placed the biscuits on a baking pan. She opened the oven and slid them in, though the oven wasn't warm yet. After Willi turned back, she and Mady exchanged fearful glances.

"Now then, Konrad," said Willi. "You were explaining the Americans."

"Konrad," Mady said, "will you get a plate for Willi?"

The cabinet that held the plates was located just to the left of Konrad. His eyes met Mady's. Was she trying to tell him something? He stood and reached for the cabinet handle. As he did, out of the corner of his eye, he saw Willi raise the gun as effortlessly as he would a hand.

The gunshot was so loud it rattled the dishes.

Lisette and Mady jumped. Konrad dropped to the floor with a sickening thud. In the front room, one of the girls screamed, then began sobbing.

"Konrad!" Lisette cried, rushing past Willi to Konrad's side.

"He's all right," Willi said. "I could have done worse. *Should* have done worse, if for no other reason than for all the deception that's been going on around here. Which reminds me, Konrad—why is the door to your bedroom missing?"

Konrad lay curled up on the kitchen floor, grabbing at his right leg as blood leaked onto the floorboards. A pool of red formed.

Lisette grabbed a towel from the kitchen counter and wrapped it around the wound.

"Higher," Konrad said, wincing. "Above the wound."

Lisette repositioned the towel, tying it as tightly as she could. "Willi, how could you!" she shouted.

"He didn't ask permission to get up from his chair," Willi said, amused. "Hey, Konrad, remember what Father used to do to us when we got up from the table without asking permission?"

Konrad and Lisette concentrated on stopping the bleeding. Mady stood behind Willi at the stove. Willi's eggs sizzled in the pan.

"He'd backhand us," Willi said, answering his own question. "Then we had to stand at the table, holding our chair out in front of us until he told us we could put it down. If our arms got tired and the chair touched the floor, he'd backhand us again."

The flow of blood from Konrad's wound had all but stopped now, but the pain was intense.

"Know what made me think of that?" Willi said. "I had Father do that routine with a chair after I returned from the front. Only when his arms got tired and the chair touched the floor, instead of hitting him, I killed him."

Konrad looked up at his grinning brother.

Willi laughed. "Thought you'd get a kick out of that." He craned his neck toward Mady. "All these years Konrad thought Gunther Krahl killed Father. It didn't matter that Krahl had no reason to kill him. But Konrad and me? We had plenty of reasons." Turning back to Konrad he said, "You know, I always thought you'd be the one to do it. Guess I just got tired of waiting on you. And now look at you. Afraid to kill. Who would have thought? Someday—if you live long enough, that is—you're going to have to explain that to me. I mean, with all that expert training they gave you, for you to—"

"Your eggs are ready," Mady said. She lifted the iron skillet with both hands.

Willi was just starting to turn his head to respond to Mady when, with a hollow clang, the hot skillet slammed into the back of his head. Scrambled eggs and grease flew everywhere. Willi hit the kitchen floor a second before his gun, which skidded across the floor, stopping only when it came in contact with Lisette's leg. She snatched it up and handed it to Konrad.

Willi lay unconscious, sprawled out on the floor with scrambled eggs on his back and cheek.

"What do we do with him?"

They formed a semicircle around Willi, who was bound and gagged on the couch where, just moments before, they'd been tied up awaiting their fate at his hands. He had just regained consciousness. His eyes jumped wildly from person to person. He wiggled, to test the ropes or to get comfortable, until the large lump on the back of his head touched the back of the sofa. Then he winced and said something that was muffled. His eyes watered. He got no sympathy from those who stood over him rubbing their wrists where the rope had chafed them.

Konrad sat in the chair next to the sofa, his bandaged right leg stretched straight. Tomcat was in a back room comforting Viktor, who had started crying uncontrollably once he was untied.

"We can't just let him go," Sharon Lewis said.

That was followed by a round of murmuring agreement.

"I say we kill him," Hermann's double said. When everyone looked at the one who dared say out loud what many of them were thinking, he added, "What? He was going to kill us!"

Willi's eyes bulged with horror. He began shouting, but all that got past the gag was a pathetic whine.

"There will be no killing in my house," Witzell said.

"Herr Witzell is right," said Konrad. "No killing."

Willi looked at his brother with amused eyes.

"As long as he's alive, we're all in danger!" Hermann's double said.

Konrad sat forward in his chair, a painful maneuver for him. "He's my brother; I'll take care of it." He leveled a no-nonsense gaze at Hermann's double until the younger man backed down. "Nothing's changed," Konrad continued. "Does he know about the tunnel?"

Willi's head cocked to one side.

"He does now," Sharon said.

"It doesn't matter," said Konrad. "The tunnel's finished. And with Willi out of the picture, you doubles are no longer needed. We'll notify Park immediately and start moving you out of Berlin as planned."

Witzell said, "In a way, this worked out for the best. It'll be easier getting all of you out of Berlin now that Willi's under control."

"What do you mean by 'getting all of *you* out'?" Mady asked her father.

With an expression that accompanied difficult news, Witzell said, "We need to talk."

The others followed Mady and her father down the hall, each to their rooms to make preparations to leave, leaving Lisette and Konrad with Willi.

"So what are we going to do with Willi?" Lisette said as she leaned over Konrad to inspect the bandage on his leg.

"For now, keep him tied up. At least until the doubles get out of Germany."

Satisfied with the condition of the bandage, Lisette sat on the floor next to Konrad. She draped an arm casually over his good leg. "And then?" she said, looking at their captive. "If you let him go, you know he'll try to stop us."

Willi shook his head side to side, making a muffled promise that he wouldn't do what Lisette just said he would do.

Paying no attention to him, Konrad said, "We'll take him with us."

"What were you saying out there?" Mady closed the door to her room, giving her and her father some privacy. Once it was latched, she leaned against it, her arms folded.

Much healing had taken place between them in the last few days. Herr Witzell had all but disappeared and in his place emerged Mady's father, the man she'd idolized as a little girl. Only now he appeared kinder and more loving than she ever remembered him being back then.

"I'm not going with you," her father said. "It was never my intention to leave Germany."

"And you waited until now to say something?"

A few days ago, had he told her, Mady might have felt mild disappointment. But now, just when she was beginning to know and love him again . . . She began to weep.

"I lost you once," she said. "It would kill me to lose you again."

Her father smiled and his eyes turned glassy with tears. He held out his arms to her. She needed no further encouragement. She rushed into her father's arms, a place she hadn't been since the day she married Josef Schumacher. His arms closed around her in the most natural of embraces.

"What about Elyse?" she said.

"Tell her that her grandfather loves her very much."

"No. I refuse to leave it like this."

"Mady, I'm old. But more than that, I'm German. I don't belong in America."

"Then we can all live together in West Berlin. Elyse can join us there."

"No, you must move to America. There's no guarantee that, if the Soviets move their tanks into West Berlin, the Americans will stop them. And even if they do, what then? Another war? No, Mady. You've suffered so much in your lifetime. You deserve to live in peace and freedom. Go to America. Marry Colonel Parker. He loves you."

"I'm not going to marry Park!" Mady said.

Feeling helpless, Mady clung to her father. There would be no changing his mind. The man was a stubborn German and would always be a stubborn German.

So they stood there. Neither one of them letting go, neither one wanting this embrace to end.

"You need to give yourself permission to love again," her father said.

He was a bulldog, her father. Not only was he stubborn, but once he got an idea into his head, he wouldn't give up until he got his way.

"I'm not marrying Park," Mady said again.

"He's a good man."

"I'm not marrying Park."

"A lot like Josef, don't you think?"

"I'm not marrying Park."

"Strange, isn't it?" her father said. "When you and Josef first got married, he tried so hard to follow in my footsteps. How things change."

"What do you mean?"

"Ever since Hadamar," he said, "all I've done is to try to follow in *his* footsteps."

Chapter 42

Friday, August 30, 1963

Resurrection Day.

It was the perfect night for it—pitch-black and raining so hard that, had there been thirty-nine more days of rain like this one, they could just as well have built an ark and floated over the Wall. This being Saturday had worked to their advantage too. Lisette, Mady, and Elyse's double, Sharon Lewis, wouldn't be missed at work until Monday morning, long after they were gone. Sharon had become herself again earlier that morning and departed Communist East Germany using her student visa. She was the last of the doubles to leave. Park had flown over from America and was waiting when each of them returned to the West Berlin side.

Herr Witzell's decision not to escape with them solved the problem of their need to find a lookout, though his job was harder tonight than on any previous night. Situated on top of an apartment building with binoculars and two flashlights, one red and one green, his view was obstructed by the rain, with sheet after sheet coming down between him and the graveyard. To make matters worse, raindrops on the binocular lenses worked to distort the images before him. Although the occasional flash of lightning came to his aid, illuminating the cityscape and casting the church, graveyard, guard tower, and surrounding streets and alleys in an eerie whitish blue light, such a thing occurred only for an instant and hardly ever when he needed it. Therefore, the success of the escape effort rested squarely on

Tomcat's shoulders, now more than ever.

The escapees were in position, ready to move into the graveyard once Herr Witzell flashed the green light. They had lined up in an alley with their backs against a brick building, standing under the eaves to keep out of the rain. Viktor was whimpering. He didn't like the dark or the rain. It had taken a concert of pleas just to get him out of the house. Now he sounded like an abandoned puppy dog. Fortunately the sound of the downpour drowned out his crying.

Willi, the unwilling escapee, lay calm and silent. No trouble at all, for he was unconscious. Herr Witzell had administered a strong sedative, compliments of the K7 facility. Willi had been covered and then strapped to a sled with runners. The plan was for Tomcat to pull the sled through the tunnel using a rope. Konrad wanted to do it, but his leg wound prevented him. Walking without crutches was still difficult, crawling even worse. Yet he wasn't about to let them delay the crossing by even a day, let alone another month or two while he healed.

Once they got the green light, Tomcat and Konrad would lead the way, pulling Willi behind them. They would lower Willi into the tunnel, with Lisette and Mady to follow after with Viktor in tow.

Under the heavily dripping eaves, which was almost like standing behind a waterfall, Lisette snuggled under Konrad's arm. Their faces were drawn close together so they could feel the warmth of each other's cheeks.

"This is it," Lisette said. "Tonight West Berlin. Tomorrow we travel to America. I never thought that someday I'd live in America."

"Are you sad to be leaving?" Konrad asked.

"I'd be sad if I was anyplace else but by your side."

Konrad kissed her. Her face being wet, she tasted like rain.

"Green light!" Mady said.

"See you in a few minutes," Lisette whispered, giving Konrad a fierce hug and a peck on the lips.

Tomcat, barefoot as always, pulled the sled with Willi on it into the open. Rainwater drummed against canvas as the sled passed under the waterfall.

Konrad was right behind him. "Lead the way," he said to the blind man, fully confident of the younger man's abilities. Dark. Wet. It didn't matter. Tomcat had practiced in all kinds of weather. Snow proved to be the hardest for him since it piled up and concealed the earth's contours and numbed his feet. Rain, however, didn't seem to faze him.

Three steps into the darkness Viktor let out a wail behind them, loud enough to rouse the dozing border guards. The boy screamed for Tomcat not to leave him. Mady and Lisette covered his mouth with their hands, spoke soothingly to him, assured him, doing everything they could to restrain him, but with each step Tomcat took, Viktor cried all the louder.

Konrad and Tomcat had no choice but to turn back.

Up on the rooftop, the light continued to flash green.

As soon as Tomcat was in arm's reach, Viktor lunged at him, knocking Lisette against the wall of the building and pulling Mady behind him. It took Tomcat a good five minutes to calm Viktor down.

"Don't leave me, T-cat, don't leave me! I'm scared!" Viktor said, his head buried against Tomcat's chest, his hands clutching at Tomcat's arms.

"I won't leave you, Viktor. Be cool, okay? I'm taking you to see Elyse, remember?"

"The *real* Elyse?"

"The real Elyse. But you have to be cool, man. Understand?"

"Cool, man," Viktor repeated.

Only it was beyond Viktor's ability to be cool. A second attempt mirrored the first: Tomcat took but a few steps when Viktor went ballistic. It didn't help that, at that moment, lightning lit the alley with the intensity of a hundred photographers' flashbulbs.

On top of the roof, the signal light shined red.

Witzell wiggled the flashlight with the red lens to give it a sense of urgency. Border guards. Three of them. Had it not been for the lightning, he might have missed them. They were on foot near the front of the church. With one hand holding the flashlight and the other the binoculars, Witzell tracked their movement.

All three carried rifles. All three were hunched over, beaten down by the rain. The lead guard approached the church's front door and rattled it. Locked. They disappeared around the back of the church, reappearing on one side. One of them pulled at the side door. It opened and they entered, the door closing behind them. There were no windows on this side of the church, the side facing the graveyard, only the door.

Witzell waited in the rain, staring at the door through an opening around his collar. He shrugged his shoulders to reposition his overcoat as rain hit the back of his neck. A trickle snaked down his spine. Without lowering the binoculars, Witzell set the red flashlight aside. He reached for the green.

His hand froze, but only for an instant. Driven by desperation, it felt around frantically for the red flashlight.

One of the guards had stepped just outside the door, and a small explosion of light illuminated his face for a second, followed by a tiny orange glow. He'd stepped outside for a smoke.

Witzell found the light. It flashed red. Again he wiggled it for emphasis.

"What'll we do now?" Lisette asked.

"We wait," Konrad said. "The light's red."

But that wasn't what she was asking and he knew it. It was just that, at the moment, he didn't have an answer to her question.

"Tomcat will have to take Viktor," said Mady. "Lisette, you go with them. Konrad and I will pull the sled."

"It's heavy," Konrad said.

"We'll manage."

"What if I helped you with the sled?" Lisette offered.

"Someone needs to help Tomcat with Viktor."

They stood looking at one another. No one had a better plan, and so it was decided. Konrad felt his anger rising, more from helplessness than anything else. The last few months digging the tunnel he'd grown stronger and felt better than he had since the gulag. Now when he was needed most, he was handicapped. All because of Willi.

He checked the skyline. The light was still red.

Witzell groaned when the guard lit another cigarette. He muttered out loud when the first guard finished his cigarette just as a second guard came out and lit up. If there was any consolation in the delay, it was that the rain had started to let up.

He adjusted his position in an unsuccessful attempt to relieve his aching hip joints. He was too old for this sort of thing.

After a while, the side door to the church opened and the second guard stepped back inside. Witzell waited a full minute before changing the light to green.

"All right, here we go," Konrad said.

Mady said, "Viktor, you go with Tomcat. It'll be dark, but it'll be okay."

Viktor nodded, but the nod lacked enthusiasm.

Tomcat had Viktor hang on to his arm with both hands. They started off. Slowly.

From under the eaves, Konrad and Mady watched the trio cross the street and into the graveyard. Just then the rain started up again.

Konrad thought he heard Viktor whimpering.

At that moment the heavens let loose. They could barely see across the street now. Nor could they see the light atop the roof.

The rain came down with such unified force that it felt to Witzell as if a huge wet hand was pressing down on his back. Water cascaded off the rim of his hat. It pooled up around him deeper and deeper so that he had to hold the flashlights under his arm when not in use, otherwise they'd be submerged.

He was blind.

He couldn't see the alley. The church. The graveyard. Nothing of consequence. Could Mady and the others see the light? Possibly, since it projected a beam. The problem was, with his inability to see the graveyard, Witzell didn't know which flashlight to use. He'd been holding the green steady, assuming all remained safe. But was it?

After several anxious moments he switched off the light. Better no light than the wrong one, he figured. Feeling helpless, he stared into the deluge, kneeling in water up to his thighs, soaked to the skin now. His body began to shiver while his mind focused on what was happening below him. They were depending on him.

Witzell prayed for the rain to let up.

What he got was a burst of lightning. The field before him became a snapshot. A horrifying, sickening snapshot. Because what he saw in that instant of light was the side door to the church standing open and a border guard, his rifle strapped conspicuously to his back, emerging from the building.

Witzell fumbled for the red flashlight. In his haste, one of them eluded his grasp. It splashed into the pool of water at his knees.

Let it be the green one that fell! Let it be green!

It was too slippery and dark and wet to try to read the markings on the flashlight in his hands; the quickest way to determine its color was to switch it on, which he did but not before turning the light on himself just in case it was the wrong color. The last thing he wanted to do was to flash green with a guard walking into the cemetery.

Witzell found the switch. He uttered a silent prayer.

A red beam hit his chest.

Splashing, Witzell scrambled to his feet, holding high the red flashlight, waving it frantically from side to side in hopes that his only daughter would see it.

"The light's red!" Mady cried.

"Keep going!" Konrad said.

They had started out when the rain was at its heaviest, unable as they were to see the signal light through the downpour. It was a mutual decision, prompted by their concern for Viktor. They'd told him he would be crawling in a tunnel, even practicing the exercise earlier at Ramah Cabin by making a tunnel of furniture and sheets. What they hadn't told him was that he would be climbing into a grave to get to the tunnel.

Viktor's concept of death and graves and the spooky reputation of graveyards was anybody's guess. Still, the last thing they wanted to do was to get him to thinking about such things before the escape. Tomcat, the one who knew Viktor best, felt confident that he'd be able to show Viktor there was nothing to be afraid of once they got there. Yet, after the incident with Viktor in the alley, Mady wasn't so sure. What if Viktor flew into a rage in the middle of the graveyard?

The decision to start out was made even simpler after Konrad said, "If we can't see anyone, they can't see us. I may not have Tomcat's feet, but I've been through the cemetery dozens of times. Let's go!"

The response he received came by way of a groan. Not from Mady but from the sled under the canvas. Willi was waking up.

Shouldering the sled's rope, Mady put down her head and pressed forward. The sled moved only a few inches. Not until Konrad put his shoulder into the rope did it slide with any momentum. But only haltingly, for every right step sent fire up and down his right leg.

Now, halfway into the cemetery, they were committed.

Lightning flashed, and Konrad noted they were walking off course. They were closer to the church than he thought. He also saw a figure—one that stirred nightmarish memories of gulag guards, those with clubs that rained blows of death—only this man happened to be a border guard and he wasn't far off. In fact, he was just to their right, emerging from the church. In the split second that encompassed the flash, the guard's back was toward them, all the better for Konrad to see the weapon strapped there.

Heinz Garbe closed the door to the church, hitched his coat up around his neck, and turned toward the cemetery. It was his third night on the job. His first at this post, and he was eager to prove himself.

At age thirty-nine he was older than all the other guards who had made up his training class. After ten years in the printing business—a profession his father-in-law had forced him into—he was anxious to be out in the fresh air again. Even on a night like this. By the time he'd completed his military training as a youth, the outcome of the war had been decided, this despite the Third Reich's promise of a secret superweapon that would turn the tide of the war once again in Germany's favor. Most of Heinz's military duty, then, lay in the last stand defense of Berlin. Nine of ten boys in his unit were killed during this time, with Heinz being the only lucky one. The Russians overran his position one night with such force and swiftness that there was little gunfire. The result of that night landed Heinz in a prison camp, where he spent nearly a year.

Like all the other Berliners, once he got out, he did his best to build a life within the Communist regime. He met and fell in love with Heddy, whose father ran a print shop. Before he knew it, Heinz was a printer with a wife and four children. Heinz hated printing. Especially the jobs his father-in-law brought in. The man printed propaganda posters, a lucrative business. *"Communist money spends just as well as anybody else's money,"* his father-in-law was fond of saying.

But Heinz hated being part of the Soviet propaganda juggernaut. Staring at sheet after sheet of the same slogans every day made him sick. And if he opened one more barrel of red ink, he thought he'd go insane.

So he quit and joined the border guard. His father-in-law wasn't speaking to him anymore, his wife either. But Heinz didn't care. He was back outdoors where he belonged. That, more than anything else, was what had attracted him to the job.

Leave it to his superior, a man ten years younger than himself, to choose tonight for a little hazing.

"Go patrol the graveyard," Walther had told him.

Manfred, the third man of their patrol, did a poor job of concealing his laughter. He was a wimpy, bossy sort who needed a gun to appear tough. Heinz took an instant dislike to him.

Heinz knew that there was no graveyard patrol, but he stepped out just the same, wondering what sort of childish prank they'd cooked up for the new guy. It didn't matter. Heinz preferred the pouring rain to the company of Manfred any night.

A zap of lightning blinded him momentarily just as he stepped outside. Heinz blinked several times and saw only white flashes, echoes of the original flash. For a moment he could have sworn he saw two figures nearby. It looked as though they were draped with a chain or something similar, just the kind of thing he might expect from Walther and Manfred. He blinked again and they were gone.

The rain came down heavy, the night cloaked in darkness.

With his shoulders hunched, his rifle still strapped to his back, Heinz Garbe sloshed into the graveyard.

Chapter 43

Mady had spotted the guard at the same time as Konrad. To her credit, she didn't panic. Konrad thought she might, then remembered how Mady and Lisette had led half a dozen children across war-torn Germany. She was experienced at this. Without hesitation, she'd pulled harder on the rope in a new course, away from the guard.

She ran into Tomcat.

No words were needed. Konrad handed Tomcat his rope and then moved to Mady's side to help her. The sled picked up speed, and soon the church and border guard disappeared behind them.

As they approached the grave of Josef Schumacher, they could hear Viktor's voice coming from the ground. He was crying. Konrad winced when he saw a crack of light along the edge of the grave.

"What . . . ?" Konrad began.

"It was the only way to keep him quiet," Tomcat said, knowing an explanation would be required when the others reached the grave. "Knock three times," he added.

Konrad bent over to lift the door, knocked three times. The light went out.

"It's me, Viktor," Tomcat said. "I told you I'd come back."

"Let's make this quick," said Konrad, looking in the direction of the church. His heart lurched because he could actually see it. The rain was letting up again.

A muffled sound came from the sled. Not just moaning but intelligible sounds. Willi was fully awake now.

Konrad spoke into the grave. "Lisette, get Viktor into the tunnel!"

Lisette tried to coax him, but Viktor wouldn't move.

Konrad scanned the graveyard and saw the guard walking along the perimeter of the Wall, walking toward them. "Tomcat," he said.

"But who's going to help you?"

"Now, Tomcat!"

The rain had suddenly stopped. Turning on his heel, the guard peered their direction as he reached for his rifle.

Tomcat jumped into the grave. Somehow he managed to get Viktor out of the way.

"Get in!" Konrad told Mady.

"I'll help you. . . ."

Time had run out, so Konrad pushed Mady into her husband's grave. Her legs folded beneath her when she hit bottom. Lisette helped pull her deeper into the tunnel.

Konrad moved to the side of the sled.

Willi's muffled voice came from beneath the tarp.

"Shut up, Willi," Konrad said.

But Willi began shouting louder.

"I warned you." Though his leg burned so intensely that he almost passed out, Konrad shoved the sled and his brother sideways into the grave. It toppled over the edge. Konrad rolled in after it, landing with a thud on top of his brother. He reached up and pulled shut his bedroom door to close the grave. "Everyone be quiet!" he said.

Konrad didn't know if Willi had been knocked unconscious or if he was afraid of what his brother might do to him if he made another sound, but surprisingly, he remained still. So did Viktor.

Heinz Garbe cautiously entered the cemetery, unsure as to what he saw. It appeared that three people had shoved something into a hole in the ground, then quickly followed after it. But it all happened so fast and before Heinz could get out his flashlight. And now he wasn't certain exactly which grave marked the strange activity.

It was about what he'd expected from Walther and Manfred.

Three corpses climbing out of a grave to claim one of their own and bring it back to the netherworld.

He cocked his head. Was that music coming from underground? Singing? *Funny. Very funny,* he thought. A Sinatra tune, for the old-timer. Amusing.

He'd hoped to identify the grave, to reveal the players in this little drama and then march them back to Walther and Manfred at gunpoint. But again, in the dark he just couldn't tell which grave they had ducked into.

After a while it occurred to Heinz that the longer he looked, the funnier it would be to Walther and Manfred. So he decided to change his tactic.

He switched off his flashlight and continued his patrol.

On the rooftop, the weather cleared just in time for Witzell to see the border guard grabbing for his weapon. If he felt helpless before, this was much worse. His daughter, Konrad and Lisette, Tomcat and Viktor, all were about to get caught, and there was nothing he could do to prevent it from happening. No amount of warning with his flashlight could save them now.

His heart pulsing in his throat, he watched as first Tomcat and then Mady disappeared into the grave. He gritted his teeth so hard as Konrad pushed the sled into the grave that his jaw hurt.

Then he prayed. He prayed as he'd never prayed before while the guard searched the area and, thanks to the Lord, shouldered his rifle and walked away as if nothing had occurred.

Witzell didn't know what the guard was thinking, or what he thought he saw, but he was convinced that at that moment an angel of God had slipped down into the graveyard and covered the man's eyes with heavenly hands to keep him from seeing the escape.

His work done, Witzell took one last look at the grave into which his daughter had disappeared.

"Good-bye, my Mady," he whispered. "I love you. May you find peace and joy in your new life."

As he turned to leave, once again his vision was blurred, only this time not from rain.

"See anything spooky out there?" Manfred asked Heinz when he entered.

Heinz Garbe shook the rain from his coat and joined the two other members of his patrol, who sat with their backs to the wall, a lantern glowing between them. The floor of the empty building was littered with beer bottles and wrappers of all kinds. This room had obviously been a regular unofficial break room for the guards, and for some time.

"Spooky?" Heinz said.

"Yeah, you know. Ghosts and goblins."

"Saw a lot of rain."

Heinz grinned to himself. He wasn't going to give them the satisfaction of knowing that they'd almost tricked him into falling for their idiotic prank. The last thing he would ever admit to these two was that he'd heard a Sinatra tune coming from one of the graves.

Chapter 44

They got Viktor down the ladder, but once at the bottom he clung to Tomcat with both arms, making it impossible for them to continue on. He left them no choice but to risk using a flashlight.

Viktor's eyes were wide with terror, darting this way and that, settling on nothing, frightened of everything—the depth to which they'd climbed, the black hole in front of them, and the close quarters of the dirt walls, along with the many roots sticking out that he thought to be snakes.

With much coaxing, Mady and Lisette pried him off Tomcat long enough for Tomcat to help Konrad lower the sled with Willi on it. From the sounds Willi made beneath the tarp, the sedative had worn off completely. At one point his struggling caused them to nearly drop him half the length of the shaft.

The second Tomcat's feet touched the tunnel floor, Viktor was once again all over him, his arms acting as rubber bands around Tomcat's waist. How were they going to get him through the tunnel? They discussed several possibilities as Tomcat sang quietly to Viktor to calm him. One idea was, for the moment, to have Tomcat and Viktor remain right where they were. The others would go through the tunnel and then find a place where they could get sedatives for Viktor. There was even talk of bringing the sled back and pulling Viktor through like they did Willi. That was when Tomcat had an idea.

"Hey, Viktor," he said. "Remember when we were kids and we walked all that way, all of us?"

"Aaron! Aaron! It's my turn to be Aaron!"

"That's right, Viktor. It's your turn to be Aaron. And Frau Mady is Moses. Remember? She tells you what to say, and you tell the rest of us."

Viktor liked that idea.

"Frau Mady . . ." Tomcat prompted.

Everyone was encouraged with Viktor's willingness to play the game. At least he wasn't screaming, and his grip on Tomcat had loosened somewhat.

"Come to me, Viktor," Mady said, "and I'll whisper in your ear."

Viktor looked around uncertainly. He wanted to play, but he didn't want to let go of Tomcat.

"Come here," Mady said.

Viktor's eyes filled with tears over his dilemma.

"Do you want someone else to be Aaron? Maybe Fräulein Lisette? She hasn't had a turn."

"No, me!" Viktor cried.

With great reluctance he released his grip on Tomcat and inched toward Mady. His arms remained outstretched toward Tomcat as he moved.

Mady whispered to Viktor, "It's time for us to go on a journey."

Viktor repeated her words.

She whispered the next part.

Viktor said, "We will not walk. We will crawl. It will be long. It will be . . ."

"Go ahead. Say it," Mady urged.

Viktor was growing afraid again. "D-dar . . . d-dark."

She whispered more.

"But we will n . . . n-not be a . . . a . . . afraid. For God is with us."

Everyone cheered for Viktor.

"Now," Tomcat said, having retrieved a length of rope they'd used to lower the sled, "do you remember this part, Viktor?"

Viktor's eyes lit up with the memory. Tomcat tied the rope around his own waist, then around Viktor's waist.

"I'll go first, then Viktor, then—"

"No, no, no, no!" Viktor shouted.

"Viktor! Calm down!" Tomcat said.

But Viktor wouldn't calm down. "Frau Mady first! Frau Mady always first!"

He was right. Mady had always led the way before.

Mady called to Viktor. She whispered in his ear again.

Viktor repeated faithfully what she'd said. "This time, Tomcat is the leader until we reach the end of the tunnel."

As long as it was part of the game, Viktor agreed to the new rules. Tomcat first, then Viktor. Mady and Lisette followed them. Konrad came next, pulling his brother on the sled.

Mady raised the question of Konrad's leg, but Konrad brushed it aside, saying, "If he gets to be too much for me, I'll just leave him behind. Someone can come back for him. Someday."

Konrad added that last part for Willi's sake. He got the muffled protest he'd hoped for.

The light was doused, and they set out into the tunnel. As they feared, within seconds Viktor began to whimper and balk. A couple of times Lisette nearly got kicked in the face.

Tomcat began to sing. Frank Sinatra, naturally. He told Viktor he knew a song about how Elyse had gotten under his skin. Viktor liked that song. He crawled while Tomcat sang. After a few verses, Tomcat changed the lyrics to "I've got you under the ground."

Viktor thought that was hilarious.

Tomcat pushed up on the wooden panel that was the exit to the tunnel. He paused and listened.

There was a shuffling of feet.

"Tomcat?"

He recognized the voice. It was Park.

The door lifted off of him.

"Hello, Sharon," Tomcat said.

"How did you know? Oh, my perfume, right?"

Tomcat smiled.

Park helped Viktor out next, who was glad to see Sharon Lewis but was insistent on seeing the real Elyse. Tomcat had promised him.

"I'll take you to see her," Park said to Viktor. "She's in America. I'll take you to her."

Next out of the tunnel came Lisette. Then Mady.

Lisette gave Park a big hug when she saw him. Mady brushed

herself off and offered Park her hand.

No one else emerged from the hole.

"Where's Konrad?" Park asked, staring down into the tunnel.

"He fell behind. Between the bullet wound and the sled . . ."

Park nodded, staring into the hole and listening. He heard nothing.

Thirteen meters below the earth, in pitch darkness, Konrad grappled with his brother.

Midway through the tunnel, somehow Willi managed to work himself free of his restraints. Konrad had told the others to go on without him when it became obvious he was slowing them down. With the tunnel being too narrow for another person to help him, it seemed the logical thing to do. At the time, as far as anyone knew, Willi was still secure. So Konrad had been left to proceed at his own pace.

He would pull until his leg was ablaze with pain and then rest awhile. After one rest period, he began pulling the sled again, and it was startlingly light. Willi was free.

Konrad shouted into the darkness.

All he heard in return was the labored breathing of Willi crawling the opposite direction. Konrad's first thought was to let him go. What could he do to them now? The tunnel would be compromised, but by the time Willi was able to alert anyone, everyone would be on the West Berlin side.

Everyone except Herr Witzell.

Konrad went after his brother. His leg felt like someone had jabbed a hot poker into it and was twisting it with every move.

He could hear Willi's breathing getting closer. Konrad felt a shoe brush his hands. He had to be careful. If Willi realized how close he was, all it would take would be one kick in the face. Konrad would never see it coming.

He timed the tackle by sound. Willi's foot struck him in the cheek, but just by accident. Konrad pulled himself up on Willi's legs. He lowered his head as Willi wormed around and tried to attack him. The two brothers wrestled in the dark, bouncing from one side of the tunnel to the other. Konrad's strength was waning fast. He was already tired from pulling Willi on the sled halfway through the tunnel. The pain in his leg grew worse by the minute. And Willi, out of sheer luck because neither of them could see anything, had managed to land a couple of blows to Konrad's face. Konrad tasted blood.

They'd been staring at the hole in the ground for nearly twenty minutes. It had stopped raining. The ground was soaked, the air thick with a musty smell. Even though they'd emerged from a tunnel, there was a closed-in feeling due to the low, dark ceiling of clouds.

"I'm going back for him," Tomcat said.

"You can't help him," Mady said. "There's not enough room."

"Maybe I can relieve him. Crawl over him, let him go on ahead, and I'll pull the sled the rest of the way."

That made sense.

"All right," Mady said. "But be careful."

Tomcat descended into the tunnel.

Ten seconds later he came back out again, holding the end of a rope. "Somebody take this," he said.

Park grabbed the rope. Tomcat crawled out and took up the rope again with Park.

"Pull," Tomcat said.

There was a bumping sound as whatever they were pulling hit the rungs of the wooden ladder on its way up.

The next thing Tomcat knew, everyone was laughing. "What's so funny?"

"There's Willi, but where's the sled?" Lisette asked.

Mady described what she saw to Tomcat. "He's hog-tied," she said. "You pulled him up by his feet. He's covered in dirt, and from the looks of him, Konrad pulled him most of the way by the seat of his pants."

"No sled?" Tomcat asked.

"Not that I see."

Konrad followed his brother out of the tunnel. He looked like he'd wrestled with the devil himself.

Park's hands were on his hips. He shook his head and laughed. "You did it," he said to all of them. "You really did it! You beat the Wall! Amazing. Now let's get you all to a hotel where you can clean up and get something to eat. You can rest a day or two and then we'll take the last leg of the journey. I promise, this one will be a lot easier. It has cushioned seats and drink service."

Mady approached Park and asked, "What happens to Willi?"

"The West Berlin authorities want to talk to him. A contract killer fitting Willi's description, possibly a Stasi agent, has been slipping across the border regularly to assassinate key officials, most recently a West German navy captain."

"And if Willi's not the assassin?"

"There are several options. We can keep him bottled up for a couple of years."

Mady stared at him for a long time before saying anything. Park let her. Without offense. He'd made promises before. Now it was up to Mady to decide whether or not to believe him.

"Thank you," she said. She placed a dirty hand on his shoulder, stood on tiptoe, and kissed him on the cheek.

Park wasn't expecting affection from her. But he liked it. He liked it a lot.

"You wrestled him and tied him up in the dark?" Tomcat was asking Konrad.

"Don't mess with me in the dark," said Konrad. "I've had years of fiddling around with film canisters in lighttight bags."

Tomcat grinned. "Maybe we should give you some kind of honorary blind person trophy or something."

"From the looks of us," Lisette said, wiping the palms of her hands on Konrad's sleeve, "we should all be awarded trophies as honorary gophers." Her hands were no cleaner, and Konrad's shirt no dirtier, for the effort.

Viktor, who was his normal happy self again, thought being a gopher was a great idea, but then no one was wanting to get him underground again.

"Let's get all of you into clean clothes," Park said, waving his arms. He looked like a tour guide who was engaged in loading passengers onto a bus.

"Not all of us," Mady said.

"What do you mean?"

Mady lowered her head, not making eye contact with anyone. It was obvious she had something to say, and it wasn't easy for her to say it.

"Not all of us are going to the hotel," she said.

She had their attention.

Mady took a deep breath. She placed a hand on Park's arm. "I want to thank you for all you've done for us. I know I haven't shown my appreciation like I should have. If it wasn't for you, we may not have gotten all the children to freedom. You've proven yourself to be a good friend to Josef and me. But I can't go with you."

Stunned, they all looked at one another.

"Mady?" Lisette said.

Mady turned to her closest friend. "I'm going back."

"No," Park said.

Mady turned to Park. "You said it yourself. It's amazing that we're standing here in West Berlin having this discussion. The tunnel is still operational. How can we just walk away from it when so many people are risking their lives to get out of East Germany?"

"Mady, that's admirable," said Park. "It really is. But you have a responsibility to the others."

"Only because Josef made it my responsibility. We didn't know the Hadamar children when Josef rescued them. We didn't know they would grow up to be sweet Viktor, Hermann the Parcheesi champion, Marlene the artist, and strong-willed Annie. Josef rescued them because they were German children. And on the other side of that Wall are more German children and their parents and grandparents who are oppressed and dying, and here we have a tunnel that leads to freedom.

"Park, you understand, don't you?" Mady said. "If there were Americans trapped on the other side of the Wall, wouldn't you be doing the same thing? I'm German. And as long as there are Germans I can help, I've got to help them."

"Not alone, you won't," Konrad said, stepping to Mady's side.

Lisette stood on Mady's other side. She took her friend by the hand. "Wither thou goest, I will go," she said.

Park stared at them with sad but understanding eyes. "What do I tell Elyse? She's expecting me to bring her mother to her."

Mady said, "Tell her that her grandfather Olbricht and her mother love her very much."

Chapter 45

Despite her impassioned reasoning, climbing back into the tunnel turned out to be the hardest thing Mady had ever done in her life. No one made it easy for her.

Park urged them to stay the night, just one night in West Berlin. Lisette liked the idea. She said it would be like the weekend shopping trips they used to make—her, Mady, and Elyse. But it wasn't like that at all. At least not to Mady. While she had faith in the tunnel, it wasn't like hopping aboard a train and going home.

And then there were Tomcat and Sharon Lewis. Seeing the two of them together. Mady had been around Sharon long enough to know she wasn't Elyse. One could put the two side by side and Mady would not be confused. But put Tomcat beside Sharon and there was just something about the pairing that made her heart ache something terrible for Elyse. To know that all she had to do was to say the word and she would be reunited with Elyse was just too much for Mady. If she didn't go back tonight, she knew she'd never go back.

Tomcat wanted to go back with them too. Mady was prepared for this. He was a good man. She forbade him to come with her. It was bad enough that Elyse would be disappointed with her mother's decision; Mady wasn't about to deprive Elyse of Tomcat also.

"But you need a blind man to guide you," Tomcat insisted.

"We'll just have to struggle along without one," Mady said.

Konrad and Lisette came to Mady's aid. They argued that since

Tomcat had taken Viktor this far, it was his responsibility to deliver him to the States, where the Hadamar Six would once again be reunited and Pastor Schumacher's dream made complete.

Tomcat reluctantly agreed, though the actual parting was emotional for him.

Without the thrill of escape to energize them, the crawl back into East Berlin was tedious. The earthy darkness seemed to stretch on forever. At one point Konrad stumbled onto Willi's sled, which he had to then drag the rest of the way to clear the tunnel. At another point, when his arms were aching and he thought he heard Lisette behind him give out a weary moan, Konrad did his impression of Tomcat singing a Sinatra tune. The laugh buoyed them up for a time.

With heavy arms they climbed the ladder, and Konrad lifted his bedroom door just enough to check for guards. It was later than he thought. The dark sky showed the signs of approaching dawn. Pressing Mady and Lisette to exhibit a quickness none of them felt, the three of them were soon crouched once again beside Josef Schumacher's grave.

Only a person who had been in prison for decades would understand what they felt. Only a short time ago, they stood on soil where they were free, where life was respected, where they had rights. Where they stood now they had none of those things. Even to be caught standing where they were at this time of night would mean detention, interrogation, and—if their answers were not satisfactory—prison, possibly even death.

Fear put new energy into their tired legs. They moved quickly, silently, through the alleys and streets of East Berlin, toward Ramah Cabin and home.

"He's gone," Mady said.

As the first shafts of morning sunlight broke through holes in the clouds, the three of them walked from room to empty room.

"Maybe he's at K7," Konrad suggested.

Mady's grief was evident. "He told me he was going to disappear," she said. "That he'd done it once before; he'd do it again."

Lisette appeared from Herr Witzell's bedroom. "He packed clothes. His bureau is empty."

"He's gone," Mady repeated, though she didn't want to believe it. "I was hoping we'd get back before he left."

"Did he give you any indication of where he'd go?" Lisette asked.

Mady picked up a pillow from the couch and mindlessly tossed it onto a chair.

"It's best he left," Konrad said. "With three people not showing up for work at the factory tomorrow morning, the people's police will move quickly."

Lisette agreed. "Herr Gellert won't waste any time reporting it."

"Then neither should we waste time," Mady said.

"Where to?" Konrad said.

He was hoping that, since Mady had evidently given this more thought than the rest of them, she would have some place in mind.

"Wherever the wind blows us," Mady replied.

"How long have you been planning to come back?" Konrad asked her.

"Two minutes before I announced it."

"Oh," Konrad said. "Well . . . two minutes. There you have it. I was afraid maybe it was just a spur of the moment decision."

"I can see my role in this threesome is going to be that of peace-maker," Lisette said.

"Let's clean up, pack a few things, and get out of here," Mady said.

Tuesday, September 3, 1963

With a frown of concern Park hung up the phone.

From the other room came a cacophony of happy sounds: Ernst Ehrenberg's distinctive cackling, the bossy tone of Annie's voice as she shouted to be heard, Viktor's giggle, and Elyse's lilting laughter.

Park stood beside the phone for a good two minutes after hanging up. The news wasn't good. His mind sifted through possible courses of action, including whether or not to spoil the boisterous reunion in the next room. What was it about this group that they would be deprived of even one afternoon of happiness?

He stood in Ernst's home study, a warm room with cherrywood

paneling, thick gray carpet, and a large, orderly desk with a model of a Redstone rocket perched on its corner. The impact of the news was wearing off, and Park's mind started working again. He moved to the doorway and stood there until he caught Ernst's eye. He motioned for him.

Rachelle, who was seated on the far side of the room, watched the festivities. At the moment Hermann was trying to slip an ice cube down Annie's back. Rachelle caught a glimpse of Park out of the corner of her eye. Her expression changed to match his. She was as intuitive as she was beautiful. Park marveled at how a skinny egghead like Ernst could come to be married to such a woman.

"What's up?" Ernst asked.

Park told Ernst to close the door.

"That was Harrison in West Berlin."

"Your contact?"

"Willi's escaped. They believe he slipped back across the border into East Berlin."

The raid on Ramah Cabin came as a Stasi blitzkrieg. Doors were kicked off their hinges. Armed men charged through the rooms, and for every one who entered, there were three behind him sealing the perimeter tight.

To get this kind of manpower, Willi had lied. He told his Stasi contacts that the cabin contained a nest of American spies, even though he knew that all the Americans who had once been there were now gone. He wanted Konrad and Mady arrested, Konrad especially. The fact that he'd been roughed up gave his story just enough credibility to pull it off.

His escape from the West Berlin authorities couldn't have been simpler. After Park handed him over, he was taken to the city jail and placed in a holding cell with a group of drunks and prostitutes. It was supposed to be a temporary deposit, but it was more temporary than intended as it turned out. In the wee hours of Sunday morning, the West German authorities were notified of his location. They said they'd send a man first thing Monday to pick him up.

That weekend the number of occupants in the cell grew to be more than double its legal capacity, consisting mostly of boisterous drunks. The majority of these were American GIs, this being the weekend preceding the U.S. observance of Labor Day. Rather than tie up his Monday court docket with a bunch of smelly hung-over men, a lower-court judge decided to order a general amnesty for all the weekend drunks. The cell doors were opened and there followed a mass exodus.

Willi simply moved with the flow. He wasn't missed until Monday morning when the government officials came for him.

He reentered East Berlin at his usual place, where Stasi agents and their operatives crossed freely, the same place he crossed after killing the West Berlin captain, Alfred Kleiber. And, just as he had then, Willi had murder on his mind. Only this time it was murder that still lay in the future, aimed at his brother, Mady, and Lisette.

The Stasi net that was thrown over Ramah Cabin came up empty. A few Stasi agents would be reprimanded for this, others demoted or possibly dismissed. Willi didn't care. After all, he wasn't Stasi. He'd lose credibility as an operative, but only for a while. Credibility was not his usual currency anyway. He dealt in blackmail to get what he wanted, a currency that was recognized by most everyone.

After the smoke cleared, Willi stood alone in the shambles that had once been Herr Witzell's house. He was furious. His anger was fueled by a strong desire for revenge. He'd found them once. He'd find them again. There was still the tunnel. Willi's escape to East Berlin wasn't exactly headline news. Chances were that Mady and the others hadn't heard of it. A stakeout of the tunnel was in order. Maybe he'd get lucky. But, in truth, he hoped he wouldn't.

Now that Mady and Konrad and Lisette and Witzell had slipped through his fingers, he hoped it would take a while longer to find them. That way he'd have more time to plan their deaths. He envisioned their end as being entertaining. And slow.

Tuesday, September 24, 1963

Konrad knelt down on the roof of the warehouse, binoculars in hand. At his knees lay two flashlights, one with a red-colored lens, the other green. It was a clear night. Dark. No moon. Mady and Lisette awaited his signal in an alley below, and with them waited Herr Lippmann and his five-year-old daughter, Anna. The day the border closed, Herr Lippmann's wife, Else, was on the West Berlin side visiting her mother. Anna hadn't seen her mother for nearly two years.

Herr Lippmann was a kind, gray-haired man who looked too old to have a daughter so young. A washing machine repairman, he vouched for Mady to his landlord, saying he had known her since they were children in Charlottenburg. Mady never knew why he'd stuck his neck out for her. Maybe he saw the desperation in her eyes. But because of his recommendation, the landlord had rented them a flat. After meeting Konrad, Herr Lippmann began taking him along on his service calls, teaching Konrad the washing machine repair business. It was steady work, mostly because on the weekends German men with idle hands tended to take their new washing machines apart to see how they ran. Inevitably, they never ran as well, if at all, after that. And so the repairman was called.

Herr Lippmann and Anna were prime candidates for the tunnel. The three-person rescue team had formed some operating guidelines. They would always discuss the merits and dangers of each rescue before approaching the actual party with their plan. The decision had to be unanimous. For whatever reason, even if just a gut feeling, any one of them could voice a veto. However, when it came to Herr Lippmann and Anna, the vote was not only unanimous but enthusiastic. They wanted to help reunite Herr Lippmann with his wife and Anna with her mother as much as they wanted to reunite the Hadamar Six.

From the rooftop, Konrad surveyed the graveyard. The guards were on schedule. This being the case, the coast would be clear to move to Josef's grave in just a couple of minutes. Konrad smiled. Pastor Schumacher would have liked Herr Lippmann. They were two men cut from the same gentle, low-key cloth.

Konrad inspected the area surrounding the grave. It looked undisturbed, just like it had on Resurrection Day. Only drier. Much drier. *What a night that was,* Konrad thought.

He reached for one of the flashlights.

The guards were circling the church, heading for the side door. Did all the guards know about that side door? It was used so frequently, he wondered if it was printed in a training manual somewhere.

They reached the door and the two guards disappeared inside.

Konrad raised the flashlight. He'd waste no time. This being the first rescue since Resurrection Day, and the first rescue without Tomcat, he wanted to give Mady and Lisette plenty of time to get Herr Lippmann and Anna into the tunnel.

The last of the three guards turned and looked over his shoulder, taking one last glance around before going in. Konrad waited. He studied the guard, his movements, his habits. He wanted to be as familiar with the guards as they were with each other.

Finally the third guard stepped inside the church and closed the door behind him.

Konrad gave the signal.

Chapter 46

Rendezvousing at the flat, Mady, Lisette, and Konrad reviewed the night's rescue attempt.

"You flashed red," Mady said.

Beside her stood a dejected Herr Lippmann and Anna. They had hoped to be in West Berlin by now.

"It was Willi," Konrad replied.

"You're certain?" Lisette said.

"He was dressed like a guard but he moved like Willi, and his left hand was stiff, clawlike. I know my brother. It was Willi."

"Well, that confirms it," Mady said. "We've lost the tunnel."

Lisette placed a comforting hand on Herr Lippmann's hand. "We're so sorry, Herr Lippmann. Anna."

Anna huddled against her father. Her eyes filled with tears; her lower lip trembled. Her father lifted his arm. She buried her face against his side and sobbed.

"We'll get you across, Anna," Konrad promised. "It may take a little longer, but we'll get you across."

After Herr Lippmann and Anna left, Mady retired to the bedroom where she and Lisette slept. Their flat consisted of two rooms—a living area and kitchen, and a bedroom. Konrad slept on the floor in the living area. They could sit on the old saggy green couch, but as for sleeping, a pile of bricks would be more comfortable. She'd excused herself, saying that lovebirds needed time to themselves. But right now, it was she who needed alone time. The disappointment she felt over failing to deliver Herr Lippmann and Anna to West Berlin was devastating, a bruise to her soul. It gave the loss of the tunnel faces and a price. A high price.

Konrad was right. They would reunite Herr Lippmann and Anna with Else. Right there and then, she made a vow they would.

How? She didn't know. But they would. They just would.

Slumping onto the edge of the bed she shared with Lisette, its mattress little better than the couch, she reached for a photograph that was propped against the table lamp on the nightstand.

She smiled as she looked at it. She always smiled when she looked at it. She could be ninety years old and still she'd smile every time she looked at it.

It was a photo of her kids in Cedar Ridge, Alabama. All of them. Standing on free soil. Smiling. Laughing. With Ernst and Rachelle, and Park.

It had been delivered general delivery to a box Park used for his students. Before leaving them in West Berlin, they'd arranged to use it, knowing that Ramah Cabin could be compromised. None of them thought it would be used so quickly, however.

They were surprised and delighted when, less than a week after Resurrection Day, there was a letter delivered to it. With this photo and also a warning.

On the back of the photo, in Park's stiff letters, were written the words, *Package you delivered, returned. Insufficient postage.*

Cryptic. But with all of the children accounted for in the photo, it could only mean that Willi was back in East Berlin.

Mady tried not to blame Park, though it did seem typical of his promises.

Tonight, when Konrad flashed the red signal, she knew their fears had been realized. They'd have to figure out a new way to get people across the border. Until they did, countless people like Herr Lippmann and his daughter would be forced to live in misery, separated from loved ones.

Mady kissed the tip of her finger and with it touched the photographic image of Elyse.

Friday, October 4, 1963

When news reached Cedar Ridge that the graveyard tunnel had been sealed off and that Konrad was digging another tunnel, Tomcat packed his bags and placed a long-distance phone call to Park in California.

"Get me back in," he pleaded. "You've got to get me back in."

As determined as Tomcat was about returning to East Berlin, Elyse was just as determined that he stay with her at Cedar Ridge. She used every weapon in her arsenal to change Tomcat's mind. She tried logic—*"Konrad is both resourceful and capable of digging another tunnel."* Pleading—*"You just got here! You can't go back now!"* Anger—*"You're thinking only of yourself!"* The silent treatment—three days of shunning, followed up with a barrage of questions—*"How are you going to get across? How are you going to live? There's no factory wages to support you, you know. Don't you love me?"* Challenging his sanity—*"You must be crazy!"* And finally she tried emotional blackmail—*"If you return to East Berlin, don't bother to come back!"*

Yet it was a battle Elyse knew she couldn't win. Still, she had to try. She knew she was being selfish. At times she felt guilty about it; other times she didn't care. All she knew was that Tomcat was here. They were safe. Happy. They didn't have to worry about people overhearing them in public here in the States. She couldn't even begin to describe what it was like to live in a place where the climate was devoid of fear and suspicion. And she knew she loved Tomcat and he loved her. But she also knew that Tomcat was a man who loved his family, and if a family member needed him, he'd be there for them. So, in the end, while she hated having to let him go, she loved him for the reasons he was going.

"When do you leave?" she asked.

"Two weeks," Tomcat said.

"So soon?"

"Park made the arrangements."

They walked casually hand-in-hand along a dirt trail that meandered through the woods. It was unusually hot for this time of year. Out of the early evening sun and among the trees, however, it was cool and refreshing. The creek still ran winter cold. A small grassy spot jutted from an outcropping of rock that was shaded by a variety of foliage. This was where they often came to get away from bossy Annie, clingy Viktor, and the ever-boasting Parcheesi king, Hermann.

Elyse settled into their spot. Tomcat sort of flopped beside her. Here they talked. Elyse started out by describing the way the town looked from their elevated view, and the colors of the sunset. Tomcat wiggled his bare toes in the grass and described the odors of the forest. He also got an occasional whiff of hamburgers frying from the Red Ball Truck Stop below on Highway 72.

"You'll come back to me?" Elyse said.

"Unless I find someone prettier."

Tomcat prepared himself for the expected slap on the shoulder. Elyse didn't disappoint him.

"I'm worried," she said.

"Don't be."

"See? That's what worries me the most. That attitude. You make it sound like going back and forth across the border is a casual thing, like there's some kind of revolving door. How many times have you crossed? I'm afraid the law of averages is going to catch up with you."

"I'll come back," Tomcat said. "I promise."

Elyse plucked a blade of grass. She tickled Tomcat's cheek with it. He shooed her hand away. She did it again. He shooed. She did it a third time.

Turning suddenly, Tomcat tackled her, pinned her arms against the grass. She laughed, struggled halfheartedly, and then grew still, looking up at him, at his grinning face set against a darkening sky.

He lowered his face. At the moment their lips touched, Elyse closed her eyes. The sky, the grass, the world—all of it faded. The only thing that existed was his lips pressing against hers. He raised up, kissed her again, then slid his lips to her cheek, then farther down so that his cheek caressed her cheek.

"Marry me," he whispered.

"What?"

She threw him off.

"I'm serious," he said. "Marry me."

His asking her wasn't a surprise. Had they not gotten married someday—that would be a surprise.

"You're going away."

"This way you know I'll come back."

"You make it sound like a deposit."

"More like a promise."

"How about if I just take your word for it?"

"Elyse, I'm serious! Isn't marriage itself a promise, a promise between two people to love each other and spend the rest of their lives together? I want to make that promise to you."

Elyse was sitting up now, staring into the distance, thinking, weighing, evaluating, worrying, but in the end, loving. Loving him for loving her. Loving him for wanting to ease her mind. Loving him for making the promise of a lifetime.

"Yes," she said. "Yes, marriage is a promise. And yes, I'll marry you."

Friday, October 11, 1963

Two wedding ceremonies were held on this date. Elyse Schumacher married Tomcat Scott at Cedar Ridge in Huntsville, Alabama. For Tomcat to enter the United States, he needed a surname, so he used the name Herr Witzell had given him at K7. Marlene and Annie were Elyse's maids of honor. Tomcat had two best men, Hermann and Viktor. Park gave the bride away. The happy couple honeymooned at the best hotel in Huntsville, compliments of Ernst and Rachelle Ehrenberg.

On the same day, Lisette Janssen married Konrad Reichmann in East Berlin in a small church ceremony. The choice of date was not accidental. When word reached East Germany about Elyse and Tomcat's wedding, Konrad took a cue from his blind friend and proposed to Lisette. The date was also Konrad's idea.

"Since we can't be at each other's weddings in person, why not celebrate our weddings in spirit?" he said.

The ministers of the two ceremonies were happy to oblige. Vows were altered accordingly.

"As Elyse Schumacher pledges her love to Tomcat Scott, will you, Lisette Janssen, vow to love, honor, and cherish Konrad Reichmann as long as you both shall live?

"And as Tomcat Scott pledges his love to Elyse Schumacher, will you, Konrad Reichmann, vow to love, honor, and cherish Lisette Janssen as long as you both shall live?"

Mady's wedding present to Konrad and Lisette was to give them the bedroom in the flat while she slept on the floor next to the stove in the kitchen. The happy couple honeymooned for a night.

Digging on the new tunnel resumed the next day.

Chapter 47

Friday, October 25, 1963

The weekly edition of *LIFE* magazine hit the newsstands, an oversized publication with an established reputation for prize-winning photographs and news features that read like short stories, and all for a quarter. This week's headlines:

Scotland Yard Thriller: $7-Million Train Heist:
On the Robbers' Trail

Master Plan for the Negro, March on the Capital

The cover featured a smiling Frank Sinatra and his laughing son, Frank Jr., with teaser copy that read, *New Sinatra Sound—Frank Jr. Takes After Pop*.

Inside, on page 32, was printed a poignant story:

East Berlin Tragedy
Man Dies Just Yards Away From Freedom

The black-and-white photo filled the page. It showed a crumpled figure tangled in barbed wire, lit by the floodlights from an East German guard tower. The camera angle was at ground level. The man's face couldn't be seen. His hair was light in color and tousled. Lying on his side, a shoulder rose up like a mountain. His bare feet appeared to be dirty. A pool of blood formed beside him, fed from an unseen streaming wound.

The story, a single column, overlaid the photo in reverse type.

The crack of a rifle, followed by an eerie silence, brought a tragic end to several moments of high drama in East Berlin last week. Bystanders on both sides of the border looked on in horror as an East Berlin man lifted a five-year-old girl to safety and freedom. His reward? A bullet in the back.

Just minutes before this picture was taken, Tomcat Scott rescued the girl who, in an escape attempt gone wrong, got caught up in the barbed wire. Two unidentified men left her behind when the alarm sounded, abandoning her to avoid their being captured themselves.

According to those who witnessed the incident, Tomcat Scott was not among those trying to escape. Hearing the girl's cries, he emerged from the darkness and, with no regard to his own personal safety, freed her from the barbed wire.

Surrounded by armed guards, now caught in the barbed wire himself, the scene illuminated by spotlights mounted in the guard towers, Herr Scott ignored the shouts of the guards and lifted the girl to the top of the Berlin Wall. Hands from the other side quickly pulled her to safety.

Out of anger, or perhaps frustration, a shot rang out, and Herr Scott collapsed into the barbed wire. He lay there wounded, tangled in the wire for hours. The guards refused to give him medical attention and prevented others from offering him humanitarian aid.

There, just a few feet from freedom, he died. While his efforts were heroic, his heroism isn't the most amazing part of the story.

Tomcat Scott was blind.

Chapter 48

During the next two decades Mady Schumacher's rescue team helped thirty-nine people escape East Berlin. In all, three tunnels had been dug to carry out the escapes. The first one, entering through her husband's grave, became the conduit through which his dream of rescuing the children marked for death at Hadamar was finally realized.

The second tunnel ran under the outskirts of Berlin and had its entrance in an old winery. A large cask served as the portal. Herr Lippmann and his daughter, Anna, were the first to escape successfully through it. Several more successful escapes were made before that tunnel was lost to them when one of the escapees dropped his coat at the threshold. A visitor to the winery became suspicious and informed the police after he saw half of a coat sticking out the side of a wine cask.

This was the tunnel they were digging when Tomcat was shot while rescuing the little girl who got caught in the barbed wire. Her escape attempt had nothing to do with the tunnel or Mady's rescue efforts. The little girl's crossing the border so close to where a tunnel was being dug was merely a coincidence.

The third and most successful tunnel began in the basement of a house on Westerstrasse, which was owned by an older couple who had gone to school with Mady's mother. The tunnel exited on the West Berlin side behind a backyard toilet, not the most pleasant of locations, though the escapees didn't seem to mind. Freedom was still freedom even when at first it didn't smell like a bed of flowers.

A total of twenty-six people escaped through the third tunnel. Had Mady and the Dittmer babies made it across the border, they would have brought the total to thirty.

Mady heard about the Dittmer babies almost by accident. She overheard a friend at church telling another woman a sad story about three boys recently orphaned. The oldest boy was eighteen months old. His twin brothers were nine months younger. The parents had been killed on the autobahn in a head-on collision. With no other relatives to care for the boys, a kindly retired minister had taken them in. His description sounded very much like Mady's father.

Mady knew it probably wasn't him. Reverend Olbricht would be in his eighties at the time. What were the odds? But her heart didn't want to listen to reason. She hadn't seen her father since he disappeared on Resurrection Day, and if there was any chance this Good Samaritan was him, any chance at all . . .

Because of the risks involved in rescue work, Mady, Lisette, and Konrad had established some ground rules. A close call with Herr Lippmann and Anna taught them that it was wise if only one of them had contact with potential escapees. As much as they all had fallen in love with Herr Lippmann and Anna, a slip of the tongue by Anna to a playmate nearly uncovered the entire operation. This contact gave the appearance of being an intermediary. With each new rescue, as contact was considered, they would discuss the needs of the potential escapees. The one most suited to meet those needs became the contact person.

Another ground rule was that the potential escapees were never told about the method of escape until the day of escape. The first time the escapees saw the tunnel, then, was when they entered it. Because this kind of crossing made certain physical demands on a person, some candidates had to be eliminated from consideration. Elderly couples, for example. It broke Mady's heart to do such a thing.

The Dittmer babies were an exception. Mady insisted so. There was a lot of discussion on this one since each of the babies would have to be carried across. However, Mady would not be dissuaded. She said if she had to carry them across one at a time, then that was exactly what she'd do.

So Mady became the contact person for the Dittmer rescue. She made inquiries, located the children, and made the contact. And while she didn't find her father, she did find a kindly old man and three precious little boys. She also found, skulking in the shadows, Willi Reichmann.

Monday, November 13, 1989

The scene at the Wall was chaos. A spontaneous celebration of the downfall of evil. One celebrant, a bright-eyed brunette from New Jersey, compared the event to the famous scene from *The Wizard of Oz*. An impromptu chorus sang:

"Ding Dong! The Wall is down.
Which old Wall? The Wicked Wall!
Ding Dong! The Wicked Wall is down."

Reunions were the theme of this momentous day. Family members—some who lived within sight of each other and yet were separated for decades by the accursed Wall—embraced for the first time in twenty-eight years. For Elyse and Lisette to see each other again without risk of death or imprisonment, without having to crawl through an earthen tunnel, was not only joyous but miraculous. They and all those around them were united by an electric excitement.

Radios blared rock music, interrupted frequently with special news reports on the sudden collapse of the Berlin Wall. By midmorning the flow of East German Trabi cars had slowed somewhat. Earlier that night, in the wee hours when Elyse had first arrived at the Wall with Park, a steady line of these cars poured out of East Germany and into the light of cameras flashing. The cars' occupants grinned and waved through the windshields at the throng that greeted them.

In one place, a long line of newsmen holding microphones were camped out opposite an equally long line of news cameras, connected to news trucks with satellite dishes by black electrical cords. Bathed in white light, the newscasters provided viewing audiences the world over with pictures and personal impressions of the historic moment. Literally, the eyes of the world were on Germany. Cameras panned the scene. Everywhere groups of people embraced, kissed, jumped up and down, drank, talked, sang, and wept.

Standing in the midst of the reunions, Elyse couldn't help but feel her hopes rise against her will. Two weeks previous, her mother was to have emerged from the third tunnel with the Dittmer babies. She never showed up. No one had heard from her.

Now people walked in and out of East Berlin at will, in plain sight of the armed border guards. Had her mother waited two weeks . . . But who knew two weeks ago that such an event would happen? No one knew.

God knew, didn't He? God knew this day would come. Surely He wouldn't let something happen to her just two weeks shy of the end. Not after all the years she'd risked death and imprisonment to help others escape while she could have fled herself. Instead, she went back. Time after time she turned her back on personal safety and risked danger all over again for someone else. God would reward that kind of effort, wouldn't He?

Lisette kept assuring Elyse that Mady was all right, but Elyse knew that was hope talking, not fact. Despite the celebration all around her, her hope seemed to be meeting the same fate as the Wicked Witch of the West. It was melting.

She knew this Wall too well. It was an unforgiving monster. It took her Tomcat from her while he was performing an act of compassion. The only man she ever loved. Her husband, whom she had lived with for only a few days. Was her mother one of the Wall's last victims?

Elyse couldn't celebrate with the others. Anxiety for her mother and a growing concern for Park and Ernst overshadowed the joy of seeing Lisette again. She stared across the border. It had been six hours since East Berlin had swallowed the two men. And while the thought of crossing over into Communist territory paralyzed her legs and restricted normal breathing, she could wait no longer. She had to go in. She had to know.

She took a tentative step toward the border. By far there were more people coming out than going in. That said something, didn't it? She took another step, smaller than the first.

"Are you sure?" Lisette said. "I'll go with you."

"Am I the only person who remembers how quickly things can change?" Elyse said. "The border's open, but there's no guarantee it'll stay that way. Remember how quickly it closed?"

"You stay here, dear," Lisette said. "I'll go in. Wait for me here."

Elyse took hold of Lisette's arm, gripping it with a ferocity that frightened them both.

"Elyse, honey? Tell me what you want me to do."

Elyse took a deep breath. "I have to know," she said.

Without releasing her hold on Lisette, Elyse began making her way toward Checkpoint Charlie. It was slow going as they wove their way through a tide of humanity that moved the opposite direction.

Standing beneath the shingled overhang of the guard post stood American soldiers. From the perplexed expressions on their faces, they weren't sure what to make of the flow of people. In the last forty-eight hours, their post responsibilities had changed dramatically. It wasn't all that long ago when Soviet and American tanks faced off against each other on this very street while the world held its breath.

Elyse and Lisette kept walking. The East German guards came into view. And the barbed wire. Elyse had purposely avoided looking at the barbed wire at the American post. It caught her attention here. Her gaze became tangled up in it so that she couldn't yank her eyes away.

She stopped.

"What's wrong, dear?" Lisette said.

Then she saw what Elyse was staring at.

"Don't look at it," Lisette said.

She tugged gently, urging Elyse forward. Elyse didn't move. Nor could she remove her eyes from the coils of silver spiked wire.

"Elyse, look at me! Look at me!"

Lisette cradled Elyse's jaw and physically turned her head away from the barbed wire.

Elyse began to weep.

"Do you want to go back?" Lisette asked.

"I . . . I can do this."

"Take your time. Just keep looking forward, your eyes on the road. Try not to think about it."

They were moving again. Past the first row of barbed wire. Almost to the border.

Elyse gasped.

She froze.

Lisette looked in the direction of Elyse's gaze, expecting to see more barbed wire. But that wasn't what Elyse was looking at.

"Oh, God. Oh, God . . ." Elyse whimpered.

"Oh dear," Lisette said. "Elyse, honey, I'm so sorry you had to find out this way. I wanted to tell you."

Ten meters in front of them, in the middle of the street, talking to a gang of youth wearing leather jackets, stood Tomcat.

Chapter 49

Tomcat was unaware that they'd spotted him.

Elyse's knees failed her. It was all Lisette could do to keep her from slumping onto the stone street.

"He made us promise we wouldn't tell you," Lisette said.

Elyse stared openmouthed at her husband. Lisette didn't know how much her friend was hearing at the moment, but she explained anyway. She couldn't have stopped now even if she wanted to.

"He was thinking of you. How hard it was for you when you thought him to be dead. It tore him apart, Elyse. And, well, you know the risks, the uncertainties. Who was to say the next time he wouldn't survive? He couldn't bear to put you through it a second time. So until he escaped himself, he made us promise not to tell you."

"How?"

The question came out as little more than a croak.

"The guards thought he was dead. They tossed him into the back of a truck like he was garbage. A short distance out of town, the driver and the other guard stopped for a smoke. While they leaned against the hood of the truck, he slipped away."

Elyse couldn't take her eyes off her husband. The leather coats surrounding him stared openly at his blindness, but they weren't rude to him. Everybody was friends today. Tomcat was asking them questions. They were pointing at the Wall and saying something.

What was he doing here? Tomcat was no good alone in crowds, where everything kept changing.

While Elyse's eyes stayed fixed on Tomcat, Lisette's attention was completely on Elyse.

"Are you all right, dear? Can I get you anything?"

"You can help me to my husband," Elyse said.

As they drew closer, Lisette called to Tomcat. The expression on his face was one of relief. He said something to one of the youths, pointing in the direction of her voice. They turned and looked. Tomcat thanked them and approached Lisette.

"Good, you came back across. I didn't know how I was going to find you. This is a zoo, isn't it? Anyway, Konrad thinks he's found . . . Wait, did you find Elyse and Park?"

"Hello, Tomcat," Elyse said.

Tomcat hung his head and started stammering. "Elyse! Forgive me," he said. "It was shameful, I know, but you have to understand . . . I couldn't bear to—"

Elyse's crushing hug forced all the air from his lungs, making speaking near impossible. It took him a moment to recover. When he did, the hugs and kisses were returned in kind.

From behind a hedge across the street, Konrad studied the apartment complex through binoculars. He would have preferred doing this at night. If someone saw him, how would he explain he wasn't some kind of pervert or stalker? Maybe they'd think he was a Vopo or Stasi. He could only hope.

The shades to the window he was watching were closed. The Dittmer flat. At least it was the address he'd been given.

They'd established ground rules to protect themselves. This was the first time the ground rules worked against them. Mady had been the sole contact with regard to the Dittmer babies. When she didn't show up at the tunnel as scheduled, no one knew where to begin looking for her. Their concern grew when after several days she didn't return to the flat. Even though they didn't keep records of any kind, Lisette and Konrad went through Mady's things, hoping to find some clue as to the location of the Dittmer babies. They came up empty.

Their only recourse was to retrace—as quietly as possible—the line of contacts that put Mady in touch with the Dittmers in the first place. They began at church, only to learn that the woman who had heard about the orphaned boys had taken holiday at Hiddensee, a resort on the Baltic Sea, and would be gone a week.

Just this morning, after Lisette had gone to the Wall to meet Park and Elyse, Konrad came up with an address. He wandered to the flat, noting its location. As anxious as he was to find Mady, his instincts warned him to take things slowly. Hence the surveillance.

The flat was on the third floor. Konrad had hoped to get more information before making contact himself. Anything would help.

Just then, the curtains shook, then opened.

Mady.

She pushed back one side, then the other. Cradled in one arm lay a crying baby. Before Konrad could reveal himself or make any kind of a signal, she turned, said something to someone, and then disappeared.

Konrad started to push through the hedge, then quickly pulled back. Again, instinct overruled the urge to act. Resuming his vigil, he raised the binoculars.

Two hours later, having seen nothing more in the window, Konrad left his spot behind the hedge, rushed forward, and was soon taking the stairs to the third floor. He met no one in the stairwell or hallway.

Before knocking, he listened at the door to the flat. A baby was crying, possibly two. With there presumably being three babies inside, it was a safe guess that at least one of them would be crying no matter what the hour. He knocked softly.

The door opened, just enough for Mady to peek out.

Konrad said nothing. Neither did she, but her eyes said that something was wrong.

Help? Run?

"Open the door, Mady," a familiar voice said.

She took a few steps back while pulling the door open.

In a corner, sitting in a comfortable chair, was Willi, a rifle across his lap. "Just like fishing," he laughed. "Use the right bait, wait long enough, and you'll catch the big fish."

Elyse had never heard the streets of East Berlin sounding so happy. There weren't parades or parties on every street, just the occasional celebration coming from a house or a flat. But for gray, suspicious, depressing East Berlin, that kind of spontaneous joy was as unlikely as a party breaking out at the city morgue.

She felt that same revelry, as her arm was now linked with Tomcat's. She never thought it would be there again, and now that it was, she was never going to let go. She was angry, to be sure, hurt by the conspiracy of silence that had caused her so many nights of heartache and loneliness. Yet she had decided to deal with that later. Right now, joy was paramount. Tomcat was alive. And his report gave her hope that the mystery surrounding her mother would have an equally happy ending.

As foolish as it sounded, Konrad had sent the blind Tomcat to search for Lisette and the others while he followed up a lead on Mady's whereabouts. If all went well, Konrad would meet them back at the flat by early afternoon. If not with Mady herself, then with news of Mady. If he didn't show up, he left the address of the Dittmer flat with Tomcat. Just in case.

Lisette, Elyse, and Tomcat took the S-Bahn back to the flat that served as escape central. When they arrived, they found Park and Ernst standing outside with their hands in their pockets.

As on so many other streets today, a small but happy reunion took place. Lisette invited everyone inside. She served them all bread with cheese spread, and coffee.

It was eleven o'clock.

Willi looked at his watch. He pushed a finger under his eye patch and scratched. Slouched in the overstuffed chair, his crippled hand lay on the armrest, his good one on the rifle. To challenge his ability to swing the rifle into firing position would have been foolhardy.

"Mady, bring me some coffee," he ordered.

She got up from a rocking chair next to one of three baby cribs. Konrad sat on the floor beside her. One of the twins started to cry. Mady stopped on her way to the kitchen to check the baby.

"He needs changing," she said.

"You get my coffee," Willi said to her. "Konrad, you know what to do."

Konrad had done all the diaper changing since he'd stepped inside the flat. Willi got a laugh out of seeing a man with an SS tattoo on his arm change a baby's dirty diaper.

Piecing things together from a combination of Willi's boasts and

Mady's whispers, Konrad learned that from start to finish the Dittmer mission had been a hoax designed to snare them. Willi added a "finally" to one comment, so apparently this wasn't his first attempt. The combination of babies and an old man who fit Reverend Olbricht's description had done the trick. Mady hadn't seen the old man since the day of the planned escape, but she learned he was a reluctant participant. In typical fashion, Willi had used blackmail, something about the old man's son and his position as an accountant. They never learned where Willi obtained three babies.

It was an unforeseen detail that tipped Willi's hand. His original plan had been for Mady to go through with the escape, since she'd refused to divulge any details to the old man. The night of the escape, however, two of the three babies developed fevers. Mady took one look at them and told the old man the escape would need to be postponed. This change of plans upset the old man greatly. He became so distraught that he managed to talk Mady into making the escape as planned.

They bundled up the children and set out for the tunnel when, just a few blocks into the journey, Mady changed her mind, convinced that it wouldn't work and that they were endangering the babies. They were just too sick to travel. She insisted they turn back.

When they returned to the flat, an angry Willi was waiting for them. He didn't know anything about the fevers or Mady's reasons for aborting the mission. All he knew was that they'd turned around unexpectedly. He concluded Mady had seen through the charade.

Had Willi been patient, he would have found the tunnel, Konrad, Lisette, and Tomcat a few days later. But Willi was never known for his patience; he was known for his craftiness. And that was when his plan changed and Mady became the bait.

The new plan worked well enough to snare Konrad, though now Willi wanted them all. This time he wasn't going to let his impatience rob him of landing the blind man and Lisette.

"It's one o'clock," Elyse said. "How much longer are we going to wait?"

The others didn't seem to share her anxiety. If they did, they didn't show it. Her mother had disappeared. Konrad said he'd be back, and wasn't. But more than that, it was this place. The flat with the stained walls and brackish water. The colorless surroundings, both inside the flat and out. Having lived for years now with Park in bright, open California, she'd forgotten how the dingy and oppressive atmosphere of East Berlin could suck the life out of a person. And the fact that her "dead" husband was sitting next to her didn't help any.

Park seemed to notice how uncomfortable she was. "What's the plan?" he said, coming to her aid.

Everyone turned to Tomcat.

"We have an address," he said. "Park, you and I will knock on the door. Ernst, you keep watch outside. You know, just in case."

"What'll I do if something happens?" Ernst asked. "Call the police? I have no weapons."

Tomcat grimaced. He understood fully the aged rocket scientist's dilemma. "Wing it," he said. "That's about all we can do."

"I'm going with you," Elyse said.

Tomcat patted his wife's hand, a little too condescendingly for her taste. "Honey, why don't you and Lisette both stay here."

"Cork it. I'm going," Elyse said.

"Cork it?" Tomcat said. "Cork it?"

Lisette said, "We're all going."

"Did my wife just tell me to cork it?"

"Yes, I told you to cork it," said Elyse. Then, as an afterthought, "And I'm not your wife."

The good feelings over Tomcat's sudden appearance were wearing off. Anger was taking their place. Only now was not the time for the estranged couple to address their problem.

"What do I do if you don't come back out?" Ernst asked.

"California has changed you," Tomcat said to Elyse.

"Being a widow for over two decades has changed me," she said.

"If we don't come out," said Park to Ernst, "send Elyse in after us. She's ready for battle."

She knew Park well enough to know this was his way of trying to lighten the mood and at the same time inform her that now wasn't the time for this discussion. He was right. It wasn't. They were in East Germany, open border or no open border. Her mother was missing. She would just have to put her anger on hold and kill Tomcat later.

"What does 'cork it' mean, anyway?" Tomcat said as they left the flat.

2:15 P.M.

"They've been in there for thirty minutes," Elyse said.

She, Lisette, and Ernst stood across the street from the apartment complex bearing the address Konrad had given Tomcat.

"What should we do?" Ernst said to Lisette.

"Normally I'd go get Konrad."

"What about the police?" Ernst asked.

"No!" Elyse said.

All her life Elyse had feared the Vopos. Even in America it took her years before she could look with trust at a man with a badge. Here, involving the police could very well prove worse than anything that was happening in that apartment.

"I agree with Elyse," Lisette said. "We're on our own."

"Do you have any weapons at the flat?" Ernst asked.

Lisette looked up at him. She'd known Ernst all her life. He was the brainy one. He'd never been much of a warrior. Her first response, which remained unspoken, was, *Ernst Ehrenberg, even if we had one, would you know how to use it?* But because of the situation, and because she hadn't been around Ernst for a long time, she chose a more polite response: "No, no weapons."

"I'm going up," Ernst said.

"We're going up," Elyse said.

"No one's going up," Lisette said.

"Everyone's going up," came a voice from behind them.

Turning, they saw a thin man with long, straight, oily hair. He wore a trench coat. Beneath it was a gun.

Chapter 50

Willi squirmed in his chair. Smiling, he told everyone, "This is the best day *ever*! All I expected was Lisette and the blind guy. Now look what I got! Pretty Elyse, and not some imitation this time. A tall American. And a rocket scientist! I finally got my rocket scientist! Ernst, where were you forty-four years ago when the Soviets were willing to pay thousands of rubles for you?"

"You've grown old, Willi," Ernst said, "and ugly."

"Shut up, rocket boy, or I'll blast you to the moon right now," Willi said.

Konrad sat on his heels against the wall. He'd scooted closer to Willi's chair to make room for the parade of people who had been walking through the front door.

Willi saw him, gave him one of his weasel-like glances of warning, and repositioned the rifle so that it was pointed at Lisette. Konrad got the message. One move from him and Willi would pull the trigger. Willi's accomplice—Willi called him Toad—stood with his back to the front door, pistol in hand.

"What are you going to do with us?" Park asked.

Willi looked genuinely perplexed but in a joyous way, sort of like a boy who didn't know which Christmas present to open first.

"I don't know," he said. "I really don't know. I'm open to suggestions."

No one took him seriously.

"Of course I have plans for this one," he said, giving Mady a wink. "As for big brother, I've plans for him as well. Shot him once and didn't do a very good job of it, as it turns out. So, I guess I have part of a plan. Tell me what you think." He looked at his brother. "Now, I know I'm going to kill him. I've known that since our tussle in the tunnel. And I know I'm going to kill him with Papa's rifle." He patted the rifle on his lap. "I just don't know where. I've been thinking about taking him back to the old homestead in Pankow. Doing it there. What do you think?"

"I like it!" Toad said with a grin.

"Willi, you've always been demented," Ernst said.

With one quick movement that defied his crippled appearance, Willi swung the rifle toward Ernst. He would have pulled the trigger, Konrad was sure of it, had Mady not stepped in front of Ernst.

"Get out of the way, woman!" Willi yelled.

Toad moved nervously toward the door. "Willi! This isn't a good place, you know? All these people around. Let's go to the country, like we planned."

Konrad had seen enough. Maybe because he'd seen it before. Maybe because he relived it night after sleepless night. A crazy man with a weapon. The lives of the people he loved at stake. First it was Gunther Krahl, now his own brother. His nightmare was playing itself out all over again.

Thinking of Krahl, he'd struggled with his conscience. The Third Reich had taught him to kill, while his faith argued against such violence. It was one thing to face a personal threat, yet quite another when a loved one was in danger. For Konrad there was an additional fear. He'd killed before, and it frightened him how easily killing came to him. He feared that if he started killing again, he wouldn't be able to stop himself.

The nightmare of Ramah Cabin was in his hesitation. His moral dilemma had almost cost Tomcat and Lisette their lives. He'd lived with that near-fatal mistake for forty years now. Was he going to repeat it? The room was filled with people he loved.

Would he have to kill to save them? *Could* he kill to save them?

Konrad squirmed.

"Easy there, big brother," Willi said while keeping the rifle pointed at Lisette.

Lisette made eye contact with Konrad. Ever so slightly, she shook her head, warning him not to do anything foolish.

Toad, too, had his eye on Konrad. From across the room, Toad pointed the pistol at him.

For a long moment all movement in the room froze.

Then Willi, sounding very chipper, said, "Toad, you and me got some killin' to do today. We best not delay."

Toad was amused. "Say it, Willi. Say it! Like them American cowboys say it."

Willi grinned and said, "Head 'em up, move 'em out."

Toad laughed.

Willi planted his cane on the hardwood floor and scooted forward in the chair, careful to keep his rifle in position and away from Konrad.

Konrad wasn't focusing on the rifle. Just as Willi reached the point of indecision, between sitting and standing, Konrad kicked out his foot.

Willi's cane clattered across the floor.

Startled, Willi had no choice but to fall back into the chair. He'd been caught off balance. The deadly end of the rifle swung upward toward the ceiling. Konrad had to reach Willi before he gained control of the rifle.

Toad reacted by taking a step forward, his gun aimed at Konrad. But Lisette stepped toward Toad, and the movement distracted him. Just enough.

Konrad went for Willi's rifle. Willi saw him and swung it out of Konrad's reach. Only it was a ruse. Konrad didn't want Willi's gun. He wanted Willi. With the speed he used against Willi in the tunnel, Konrad's other hand grabbed Willi by the front of the shirt. He pulled his brother out of the chair, on top of himself.

Falling, his arms flailing, trying to grab on to something, anything, Willi let go of the rifle, and with a speed that comes from desperation, Konrad snatched up the gun.

Before Toad had time to do anything, Konrad had Willi in his lap with their father's rifle across his throat, choking him. If Toad were to shoot now, he'd likely hit Willi.

Toad grasped Lisette, shoving the barrel of his pistol in her ribs. "Let Willi go!" he shouted.

Konrad increased the pressure against Willi's throat. Willi gagged. "Tell your friend to put his gun down," Konrad said. He released the pressure enough for Willi to talk.

Willi began to giggle.

"Tell Toad to put the weapon down!" Konrad shouted again. He pulled on the rifle until the giggling stopped. Then he let up again.

"T . . . Toad!" Willi gasped. "Put it down."

Wide-eyed, Toad said, "You sure, Willi? If I put it down . . ."

Willi started giggling again.

"Willi?" Toad took an inquiring step forward.

Right into the heel of Park's hand.

Toad reeled backward, slamming into the door. Lisette grabbed the gun from him. Without a weapon, his nose bleeding, probably broken, Toad scrambled for the doorknob and was quickly out the door. No one tried to stop him.

"It's over?" Tomcat asked.

"It's over," Elyse said.

But it wasn't over. Not yet.

Konrad's struggle had just begun.

Konrad slumped with his back against the wall. Willi sat between his legs. Giggling. The two brothers were alone in the room.

"That's a disgusting habit," Konrad said.

"I can't help it," Willi replied. "I giggle in the face of pain or death. I don't know why, I just do."

"You have since we were kids. It's embarrassing."

"Well, I'm sorry I can't be more like the perfect Konrad Reichmann," Willi said.

The others had gone to the flat to gather together some things, then to Café Lorenz on the West Berlin side of the border. They were going to walk across. It was still hard to believe. They were going to walk across in full view of the guards. And they weren't coming back.

There would be questions from immigration officials. They'd answer them. There would be a pile of government forms. They'd fill them out. There would be lines to stand in, waiting rooms to sit in. They'd stand. They'd wait. Whatever was required of them, they'd do until every last one of them was safe and free in America. Ernst had already planned a barbecue at Cedar Ridge for them, even though it was November.

"You're not going to kill me," Willi said.

Konrad had eased up enough on the rifle for his brother to talk, but not enough for him to think Konrad was going to let him get away.

"What makes you think that?"

"You've changed. You couldn't kill Krahl; you won't kill me. What's that all about anyway? You used to get carried away in the Hitler Youth outings pretending to kill the enemy. You were good at it in the SS, otherwise they wouldn't have promoted you like they did. Killing is what you're good at, Konrad."

Konrad pulled on the rifle. Willi choked. Giggled. Konrad let up.

"Remember when we used to wrestle?" Willi said. "Maybe I should rephrase that. Remember when you used to practice your wrestling moves on me?"

Konrad didn't reply.

"What exactly are we doing here?" Willi asked. "We both know you're not going to kill me. You could have killed me twenty-six years ago. Instead, you dragged me all the way through that dirty tunnel, for crying out loud. Why would you do that if you were going to kill me?"

Konrad said nothing.

"You know the sad part of all this?" Willi said.

"What's that?"

"You're going to let me go because it's your nature, and I'm going to come after you again because it's *my* nature."

"Did you really kill Father?"

"See what I mean?" said Willi. "You can't even believe I killed Papa. I did. I made him hold that stupid chair out in front of him until it touched the floor, then I plugged him. I plugged Gael too."

"You killed Gael?"

"Ask Toad. I mean, if you ever see him again."

"Why?"

"I was tired of her. I knew Mady would never give me the time of day as long as I was married."

"Mady would never give you the time of day, period."

"So how long are we going to stay here? I'm hungry."

Konrad didn't answer. He stared across the room at nothing in particular.

"You know I'll come after you," Willi said. "I'm a weed in the garden of life."

"A weed."

"Like that, do you? Actually it was Gael who came up with it. She meant it as an insult, but it's rather insightful, don't you think? You never get rid of weeds. You spray and pull and work, and still they keep coming back. Year after year. Just when you think you've licked 'em, up they pop again. And what good are they? They don't do nothing but ruin people's gardens. Face it, Konrad. Your brother's a human weed."

"In the gulag I held a friend in my lap like this," Konrad said. "Only he was already dead. It was my job to pull the teeth from his mouth with a pair of pliers, the teeth that had gold fillings. He was a good man. A good friend. He saved my life once. I couldn't save his. Just like Neff. I couldn't save his life either."

Willi giggled.

Konrad stared vacantly across the room.

Willi giggled some more. He giggled so loud the neighbors in the next flat could probably hear him.

Café Lorenz was overflowing with revelers when they arrived. Tomcat and Elyse quickly selected chairs and sat huddled behind a menu, involved in an animated discussion.

Park pulled out a chair for Mady and took a seat next to her. He'd dreamed of doing this for her back in 1961, the day the border closed. Mady reached over and put her hand on top of his. Each of them held a baby, as did Ernst, who insisted on holding one. After reuniting with Konrad, they'd turn the babies over to the authorities.

Lisette, like in '61, was distracted. She'd look at the menu for a moment or two, nothing would register, and so she'd find herself scanning the crowd. This time for signs of Konrad.

Ernst was jovial. "Nothing like a little life-and-death tension to give a person an appetite," he quipped. "Following a rocket launch we'd all go out to a restaurant and order two meals each."

"How do you stay so thin?" Mady asked.

Ernst grinned. "A clear conscience and a pure heart."

Lisette pushed back her chair. She got up and left the table without a word.

She and Konrad met on the sidewalk in front of the café. She'd seen him coming.

He walked in a daze, seemingly unaware of his surroundings. He looked pale, sullen. His hands shook.

His wife helped him to the table.

"What happened?" Ernst asked.

They all waited for an answer. Elyse and Tomcat came out from behind the menu and stopped fighting long enough to hear what Konrad had to say.

But Konrad said nothing. He just sat down.

Mady persisted. She wanted to know Willi's fate. Of all people, she said, she had a right to know. Still Konrad gave no reply, and after a while Park was able to get Mady to stop asking.

Years later, Mady asked Lisette if Konrad had ever said anything about what happened between him and Willi that day. Lisette said he never spoke of it but that fresh nightmares began that night and continued throughout the rest of his life.

Epilogue

Tuesday, December 24, 1989

Cedar Ridge.

Heiligabend, Christmas Eve.

Regardless of their situation over the years, Mady had always managed to provide a Christmas tree for the family. Some years it was little more than a pine branch with thin strips of newspaper that she'd painstakingly cut with shears for tinsel. This year, however, Ernst and Rachelle made up for all the lean years. They went all out. In the center of the room stood a glorious twelve-foot fir tree. The ornaments that hung on it were many and varied, including hand-blown glass birds and angels.

In previous years the Ehrenberg family had gone the way of most of America with multicolored lights. Then came the craze of artificial aluminum trees with a rotating color wheel floodlight. But for this occasion the tree had been lighted with paraffin candles clipped to the limbs with metal holders, to match the tree Pastor and Mady Schumacher had in 1939.

The highlight of the tree trimming came when Konrad, Lisette, and Ernst placed four ribbon-mounted coins on the tree—the same coins Pastor Schumacher had given them.

Marlene and Elyse led the group in carols sung in German. *"Leise rieselt der Schnee"* and "O Tannenbaum." Mady and Lisette sat next to each other and watched the fulfillment of Josef Schumacher's dream: the Hadamar Six finally safe. Safe and free.

Marlene had earned a master's degree in graphic arts and worked at a studio in Huntsville. On the weekends she sold her watercolors at the mall.

Annie was married and had two children. She was a good mother and the undisputed head of her household.

Hermann played games all day and got paid for it. He was the manager of the local YMCA.

Viktor defied the odds for a person with Down's syndrome by still being alive. Ernst employed him as a janitor of the Cedar Ridge facility.

When Mady and Lisette weren't crying, they were leaning against each other, whispering, pointing, and laughing.

"I wish your father could see this," Lisette said.

"Me too."

They'd always hoped that Reverend Olbricht, or whatever name he was using now, would surface again, like he'd done before. They were still hoping. Though the odds of him being alive were increasingly thin. If he was still alive, he'd be ninety-one years old.

Outside, a Volkswagen van pulled up. Its arrival was framed by the large picture window.

"Ah! My Christmas present has arrived!" Park said. "Special delivery, from California." Setting a glass of punch aside, he hurried to the door and held it open.

In walked the Hadamar Six doubles. Sharon Lewis and Fletcher Green, wearing Ray-Ban sunglasses, and Connie Hayes and the others. Alexandra Moffett, ophthalmologist and Mady's double, was conspicuously absent. Park didn't offer an explanation, and Mady didn't ask for one.

When the initial uproar of their entry settled down, Mady insisted on taking pictures. Park jumped at the idea, lining everyone up in front of the Christmas tree, all the doubles paired with their Hadamar Six counterparts. Viktor felt left out until Ernst grabbed a broom and stood next to him, announcing loudly that he was Viktor's twin.

What a picture it made. Park surprised Mady a year later by giving her a copy of the photo, enlarged and made into an oil painting. She treasured it all her life. But in years to come, on nights when she was feeling homesick for Germany, it was the little Polaroid she took out of the desk drawer that she wept over.

"So, where are you going, dear?" Lisette asked Mady.

"I've decided to give California a try. That's where Elyse is."

"And Park?"

Mady smiled. She looked down at her hands. "We'll see," she said. "Have you and Konrad made a decision?"

Lisette nodded. "We're going to stay here in Huntsville. You'd think Konrad and Ernst were joined at the hip. And Rachelle is such a dear. You know, she still suffers bouts of depression from the war."

Mady patted Lisette's hand. "You'll be good for her."

In the far corner of the room, Tomcat and Elyse huddled together. Their smiles were infrequent and forced.

"Do you think she'll ever forgive him?" Lisette asked.

Mady shook her head. "I don't know. She's made an entire life without him. They're talking about moving in together. To give it a try. It's a start."

A clinking of spoon against glass quieted the room.

Park stood in front of the fireplace with glass in hand. "A toast," he said.

Everyone reached for their glasses and stood.

"Forty-five years ago," Park said, "the world declared us enemies. As a patriotic American I joined the army to do my duty to defeat the enemy. Who could have foreseen that when I was shipped to Germany, I would find not enemies but family? Largely because of one man. I never had the privilege of meeting him face-to-face. My contact with Josef Schumacher was limited to two-way radio. Yet even in that limited medium, I met a man whom I came to respect and admire. What impressed me most about him was his genuineness. Even through the static I could hear in his voice the love and devotion he had for each of you. And now look at you. What was that man thinking?"

Laughter. Tears. Hugs.

"The only reason we are all standing here today," Park continued, "is because of Josef. With an unwavering faith, he put his stamp on every person in this room. A bold impression of courage in the face of overwhelming odds, of love that never gave up, and of an undying desire to live free and in peace."

Park raised his glass.

"To Pastor Josef Schumacher. Never underestimate the power of a life well lived."

Following the toast, Konrad and Ernst thanked Park for his remarks. Lisette joined them, reaching for her husband's hand. Mady walked past Konrad and Ernst and wrapped her arms around a surprised Park and kissed him.

"You know what this party is missing?" Ernst said.

"My thoughts exactly," Konrad added.

"Lisette," Ernst said, "if I brought in a radio, do you think you could find us a little Christmas music?"

Author's Note

On August 13, 1961, the East German border closed suddenly with troops, barbed wire, and the destruction of roads. Soon after, a wall of concrete blocks rose up with astonishing speed. As East Berliners challenged the wall, some successfully, improvements were made. As a result, the Berlin Wall went through four generations of improvements over two decades. While the escape portrayed in this story takes place during the wall's second generation, elements of the wall described in the narrative include improvements made to later generations. This was done intentionally. My desire to portray the full extent to which the Communist regime went to keep its citizens from escaping overcame my desire to be historically accurate. In similar fashion, I chose to use a copy of *LIFE* magazine that was released two months earlier than indicated. When I saw that Frank Sinatra was on the cover, I thought it was the perfect edition for this story. Its actual date has little relevance to the story.